Death Among Brothers, Book I

A Sumarai Comes of Age

Death Among Brothers
Book I

A Samurai Comes of Age

武士

a novel

Marc Charles

The Ross House Press

Published by
The Ross House Press, an imprint of Canopic Publishing

Canopic Publishing
389 Lincoln Ave.
Woodstock, IL 60098
www.canopicpublishing.com

Book and cover design by Phil Rice

Charles, William Marcus II

A Samurai Comes of Age: Death Among Brothers, Book One / by
Marc Charles

Third Edition

ISBN-13: 978-0-9971695-6-0 (alk. paper)
ISBN-10: 0-9971695-6-7 (alk. paper)

For Sako, who makes it all worthwhile

Contents

Death Among Brothers, Book I

A Sumarai Comes of Age

Preface

In early1969, I stepped off an airplane at Kadena Air Base in Okinawa, a twenty-year old Marine second lieutenant with gold bars on my collar replacing the stripes on my sleeve. With the exception of Canada across the Ambassador Bridge in Detroit, I had never been outside the United States. The first thing to hit me was the smell. It was a combination of hot soy in a skillet, open binjo sewers, and the acrid bite of burning automobile tires as Okinawan protesters snake-danced around torched cars chanting "go home" in pigeon. Everything was different. I felt I'd fallen through a looking glass.

The world was much larger then. Heartland Americans seldom saw Asians. When we did, Hondas and Toyotas did not come to mind. That would follow. In those days, the derogatory characterizations from WWII and Korea were our references.

U.S. Armed Forces bases in Asia were bastions of home town America, designed to give the soldier, sailor, airman, and Marine everything he could find in any-town USA—well, almost everything. What many young men wanted they found outside the compound gates in the "vill," short for village. Cheap beer and female companionship topped a lot of lists. Beyond these baser drives, very few were interested in the history or culture of the country in which they now resided.

But a very small group were curious about the marked differences beyond their own culture and the one that existed just beyond the gate. My discovery of the martial arts changed my world forever. Through books, constant questions to sensei's, and searching the island on an old Honda motorcycle, I learned that the Okinawans had kingdoms and diplomats at the ancient Chinese court in Peking when the Japanese had no cities or cohesive culture and were busy foraging for food on rocky beaches. The Japanese who came to Okinawa much later did so as vanquished people from wars in Japan and commenced to trample the island culture. The islands had been known by their Chinese name of Lieu Chu for centuries, but the new conquerors from the north had trouble with the "L" sound. In the Japanese language the "L" is sounded as an "R," so Lieu Chu became Ryuku, the name the island chain was known by until the late 20th century. At the time, very few knew this. Most didn't care to know.

In 1969 the Okinawan people wanted to be Japanese, not the servants of the American military. They were not the less-human species our culture assumed. If you took the time, they were warm, they were forgiving of our oddities, and they demonstrated martial arts that seem almost magical—vanquishing larger foes by controlling their force. Such was not common knowledge in 1969 outside of Asia. For the next two decades I would spend a lot of time in the orient trying to learn from all.

I have walked the Shwedagon in Rangoon and climbed the Badaling Great Wall in China, breathed the soot-filled air of Shenyang and coughed the red dust of New Delhi. I have been amazed and humbled by Mother Teresa and her oasis of calm among the slums of Calcutta and dodged unmentionable waste on city sidewalks in the metropolis now known as Mubai, then called Bombay. I have watched around the clock cremations at Pashupatinath Temple in Kathmandu, dined with the Gurkha and wandered the streets of Nepal during a beggar's moon. I've watched the beaches of Sri Lanka at their most peaceful and seen the aftermath of civil war in the north. I've dodged lightning strikes in Kuala Lumpur, wandered the back alleyways of Singapore, and bartered for a kris in Jakarta. I have taught self-defense in Dhaka, Bangladesh, and gotten lost in the tenements of Hong Kong and the maze that is Kowloon. I've done time on Yankee and Dixie station in Viet Nam and explored off the beaten path in Kaohsiung, Taichung, and Taipei, Taiwan. I have trained in the jungles of the Philippines and learned to eat bat, owl, and other delicacies from Negritos. I have also ridden Jeepneys, studied Escrima and given karate and kobudo martial demonstrations to Manila police. I have wandered Thailand from Phuket to Bangkok to the Golden Triangle. I have traveled Asia as a Marine on official assignment, sometimes as a traveler, infrequently as a tourist, and often as a student of martial arts trying to accumulate more skill. But Okinawa was the first stop on my Asian odyssey, and Japan captured my heart.

Eventually I would become a Roku-dan (sixth degree black belt) in Okinawan Kenpo Karate and a Roku-dan in Kobudo (the weapons of Okinawa). I would also obtain a Shodan (first degree black belt) standing in Shorinryu Karate, and I studied under some brilliant instructors in Aikido, Aikijujitsu, American Kenpo, and other art forms. I have founded Okinawan Kenpo and Kobudo schools in Virginia and Hawaii, and taught hundreds of Marines on aircraft carrier hanger decks, amphibious well decks, and embassy Marine houses in every clime and place.

I trained in backyards, garages, alleyways, and in some very small dojos as well as some of the grandest. Whether searching for a kris in Jakarta or katana in Kamakura, I tried to cobble out a sense of history in each one of the countries visited while adding to my arsenal as a professional Marine. I have spent much of my adult life studying, working, and living in Asia. For thirty-four years I have been blest to be married to a remarkable university educated Japanese lady who claims I know more about Japanese history than she. She is wrong; I don't. But I have made it a point to learn about the unique warriors of ancient Japan.

Japan's history has been one of strife. Remains found in burial tombs ranging from the fourth century AD are ringed with swords, spears, helmets, shields, bows, arrows, and all manner of martial gear, attesting to the military sophistication and mindset

13

of the people. The culmination of this warrior ethos led to the establishment of a military government in 1185. Yoritomo Minamoto seized control of Japan when his unsophisticated bushi warriors easily defeated the more civilized noble army of the emperor in engagements known as the Genpei Wars.

Yoritomo did not want his tough country warriors to fall victim to the bureaucratic malaise of other conquering armies as they adjusted from conquerors to rulers. He also was a little paranoid—looking over his shoulder and listening for footsteps of the next ambitious warlord from the provinces wielding a sword and a bow in search of glory. Yoritomo moved his army and his paranoia eastward to Kamakura and established the bakufu (government). It was the first centralized government run by a military junta in Japan's history. Some form of this junta, with samurai at the helm, would rule Japan for the next 683 years. In 1868, the last Tokugawa shogun would resign and power shift back to the emperor (Meiji Restoration), ending the rule of the samurai.

The word "samurai" derives from the verb saburau, "to serve." The samurai and their earlier cousins, the more proficient bushi warriors, were unique in the annals of history. Their allegiance to their overlord was fanatical. Their willingness to die and the ritual suicide of seppuku (more commonly termed hara kiri—belly cutting) set them apart. A samurai's life was to be "light as a feather," and he had to be ready to lay it down at a moment's notice.

Another tenant of the samurai that set him apart from other ruling classes of the world was the code of the warrior— Bushido. In the 19th century Nitobe Inazo would write a bestseller called *Bushido, the Soul of Japan.* (President Teddy Roosevelt bought five dozen copies for family and friends.) Bushido teaches that men should behave according to an absolute moral standard, one that transcends logic. What's right is right, and what's wrong is wrong. The difference between good and bad and between right and wrong are givens, not arguments subject to discussion or justification—and a man should know the difference. The Eight Virtues of Bushido were: 1) Rectitude or Justice; 2) Courage; 3) Benevolence or

Mercy; 4) Politeness; 5) Honesty and Sincerity; 6) Honor; 7) Loyalty; and 8) Character and Self Control. Upon these pillars rode the chivalry of the samurai.

The death knell of the samurai was sounded with the ascension to power of Ieyasu Tokugawa and the 265 years of peace he and his progeny presented the country. In 1600 he was victorious at the battle of Sekigahara. Three years later he became the founder of a shogunate in a dynasty that would last 265 years—until 1868. These 265 years of virtual peace reshaped the country.

Once control was established, people could move about. Intra-country trade flourished. Harvests were stabilized, subject only to natural disasters, not the ravages of war. Hunger was still an issue, but not on the grand scale of the preceding 200 years of the Warring States Period.

Ieyasu was a visionary and an intricate planner. But like the law of unintended consequences, many of his edicts eventually proved counterproductive to the government that wrought them. His burdensome taxation of large landowners brought many of them down, releasing a flood of master-less samurai onto the economy. These ronin (wave-men who floated from place to place without allegiance to a master) were warriors in a land of peace. They had no jobs and no way to get them. Many put up their swords and became laborers or artisans. Others became bodyguards for gangsters or outright brigands themselves, abandoning all the precepts of Bushido.

Another unintended consequence was kyodai goroshi, or "relative killing." Ieyasu had been specific in dictating the manner in which his successors would be chosen. They had to come from his line. Whether legitimate or not, any male progeny was to be considered by the chamberlain (the departing shogun's chief of staff), the Tairo (greater counselors) and the Roju (lesser counselors)—a total of about eight men.

Unfortunately, Ieyasu left many progeny. Because many owed their livelihood and power to continued favor of the shogun, they had a vested interest in who might ascend to the shogun position. Some attempted to influence the outcome.

15

Many of the progeny would not live to make the trek to Edo for an audience and evaluation. They would die of mysterious causes, suddenly and without warning, or they would fall victim to "bandits." Of course, none in the government wanted a scandal tied to their actions, so third party assassins were used. Who better to employ for such a task than shonobi no mono ("children of the grass"—ninja)?

The Tokugawa's gift of peace to the land meant the samurai had no wars to fight. The constant honing of martial skills was not required. Bushido gave way to getting ahead in a country where merchants controlled trade and money. The country's hierarchical symmetry was turned on its head. samurai had few skills with which to make money. They did have power, still being at the apex of government. Needless to say, corruption was rampant at every level. As always, the commoner paid the price. Young samurai were either schooled in the art of corruption and influence peddling or they were taught the old ways of Bushido with few means to get ahead or to test their ability. This led many of the dedicated to test their martial skills via musha shugyo (warrior's pilgrimage).

The acolyte would travel the country stopping in dojos (martial schools) trying to perfect his skill with the sword. If he lived, he might become famous. If he died, then he had been true to Bushido. But whether he became famous of not, if he lived and adhered to Bushido he was relegated to the life of a pauper, living off the largess of others. The era of Tokugawa peace had simply made the samurai obsolete.

In the following novel, Hideki, the protagonist, is one of the young descendants from the line of Tokugawa Ieyasu. He and his older brother Naga are summoned to Edo at the announcement that the current shogun is retiring. Hideki is a likeable seventeen year old and a little of a rapscallion prone to ducking his samurai responsibilities for more time in the dojo. The sword is his life and Bushido is his mantra. He dreams of being a great swordsman but has trouble even beating his older brother—until he sees a real master swordsman on his own musha shugyo challenge and defeat the head of Hideki's dojo.

On their trek to Edo for an audience and evaluation, Hideki grows from a daydreaming teenager to a responsible adult, dealing with his first crush on a female, assassins out to extinguish his life, and deceptive and corrupt police and government officials. He is aided in his journey by a deadly master duelist, a young ninja steeped in the old ways of the shinobi, and a princess of a large ninja clan who unknowingly falls in love with her target.

Hideki attracts a loyal following because of his childlike belief in Bushido as cure-all for everything, but he becomes internally conflicted when he learns his code may not provide all the answers. And if his brother does become shogun, Hideki will never be allowed the opportunity to become the swordsman he wants to be.

Writing a novel is the easy part. It is generally a solitary endeavor. Getting the book ready and into publication is not. This is where the real work starts. Superstar authors have a team of high speed, low drag, Teflon coated wordsmiths ready and willing to slice and dice each sentence. I have had to rely on a team of well-educated, well-read and well-meaning people to give me a hand. They all have my heartfelt thanks. Sako Charles for her expertise on all things Japanese and discovering my monotone delivery of each chapter is an instant cure for insomnia. Mary A. Charles had to suffer through a chapter at a time when direction was an elusive goal. Her insights proved most helpful. Michelle Charles read the entire first manuscript and gave invaluable suggestions from a voracious reader's perspective. Ashleigh Charles Palmer gets my thanks for telling me definitions in sentences slow down the action.

Pamela Charles gets many, many thanks for too many things to mention here, not the least of which is putting up with my musings during writer's block and reminding me that readers do not need three paragraphs to describe socks. Who knew? James L. Charles, J.D. gets my thanks for his time and for pointing out minor characters were often more interesting, thereby planting a seed for a sequel. I am thankful to Dr. Raleigh Charles for suggesting I take advantage of Tom

Tyner's expertise and good-naturedness. I am deeply indebted to Tom Tyner of Middle Tennessee State University's English Department for his detailed work in turning my scribbling into English and for introducing me to Phil Rice of Canopic Publishing. Phil Rice, my publisher and partner, turned the English into prose and put up with sophomoric questions.

There are many others that I ought to thank but they are in other countries in obscure dojos teaching the next generation martial arts.

William Marcus Charles II, MBA
Lieutenant Colonel, USMC (Ret.)

Death Among Brothers, Book I

A Sumarai Comes of Age

Chapter 1: The Lesson

Five men on their knees, foreheads wedged into the hot dirt, paid tribute before him. This part never felt comfortable. It did not seem proper for five village headmen, most twice his age, to prostrate themselves to him. Bowing to grandfather Jii was proper. He was the senior Yoshinobu. He had fought beside Ieyasu at Sekigahara. Everyone bowed to Jii. Bowing to his older brother Naga was also proper. Naga acted old, although only three years separated them.

Hideki had never felt comfortable with older people bowing to him. It was not that he lacked self-esteem or confidence. He was samurai. Self-esteem, confidence, and superiority were his birthright. Bowing just did not seem important to Hideki. Balancing the census rolls would be a better use of the five men's time. Then he could get to the afternoon dojo practice without worrying whether Jii would scold him for another job half completed.

The dojo was important. Honing his skills with a katana was important. Becoming the best swordsman in the land was important. Bowing and apologizing for problems was a waste of time. It accomplished nothing. However, he would have to let the drama play out for a few moments. He was committed now, but he tuned out the denials and moanings coming from the bowed men. He instead focused on the noon sun penetrating his brown summer kimono. The rays felt like a shower of fine hot needles from which the thin cotton fabric across his shoulders afforded scant protection.

He was glad he was not required to keep his head shaved like most young samurai men. Leaving the sides long, pulled back into a heavily waxed chonmage and folded forward on the shaved pate was ridiculous in Hideki's mind. Naga did not agree. His older brother wore his hair in the latest Edo style. Hideki thought many things that Naga did were strange. Naga had always been everyone's favorite. He was destined for great things, they would say. Maybe he was, but the great things he was destined for held little interest for Hideki. He lived for Bushido.

Grandfather Jii had never been a slave to fashion. The old man's approach to life was function over form. Hideki smiled as he thought of the tough old warrior who had raised him. If it were not for Jii's Zen philosophy, he would be wearing sunburn on the top of his head instead of a rich mat of thick black hair pulled back into a stiff-tied tail at the crown of his head. As uncomfortable as the sun was across his neck and shoulders, Hideki knew it was twice as hot for the five figures prostrated before him in the oven of the valley floor. Unlike Hideki in his lightweight kimono, they were clad in heavy woven cloth. Peasants did not have summer and winter wear. They just had wear.

He glanced away from the bowing old men and caught sight of the peasants stealing glances in his direction from the rice fields on either side of the road. The farmers were knee deep in the murky water carefully pulling something from between the rice shoots. The Yoshinobu lands yielded 250,000 koku of rice. A koku was enough to feed one person for one year. The peasants' hot and strenuous efforts allowed support for 250,000 people. Both men and women worked side by side. Hideki wondered what kind of bad deeds they had committed in a past life to come back as peasants. Maybe they had done nothing. Maybe the priest at the temple school was wrong. Maybe Hideki was just lucky to be born a samurai. He knew he was fortunate to live in Kii. The valley between the two mountains was verdant and was an ideal place to learn the ways of the warrior. Kii had a proud martial tradition full of battle lore, and he was one of two Yoshinobu princes. For him, life was good.

Hideki leaned on the stone jizo at the side of the road. This one was large. Most religious statues along the roadsides were small, less than knee high. This one offered shade. The omnipresent sun not only penetrated from above, it bounced up from shining surfaces of flooded rice paddies that stretched from the narrow road in the center of the valley to the mountains on either side. Some poor traveler, or maybe one of the village peasants, likely planted a tree to shade the jizo in memory of a loved one lost, or perhaps simply to help speed a prayer skyward.

Like all the jizos he had seen in his eighteen years, this one had the vague outline of a man in Buddhist robes. It was four shaku high, so it came up to his chest. He thought it would support his weight, and he was right. But as soon as he leaned on it, the peasants stopped working. No one complained. They just straightened up, let their tools hang limp in their hands and looked at him with blank stares. He did not feel threatened. They were farmers. He was samurai. They had small tools in their hands. He had a brace of razor sharp swords in his belt. However, their silent stares felt eerie.

"So much for the traveler theory," Hideki thought. "Obviously a village shrine of some sort."

Jii had always taught him to respect the villagers' superstitions. "They have a right to them," Jii would say. "They don't have much else."

Hideki straightened up. The peasants immediately returned to their chores in the dark water.

"Let me whip some respect into their lying backs, Lord," Aoki offered as he brandished the wooden bokken before the five bowed peasants. "This practice sword will drive the lies from their bodies and get this annual census sorted out once and for all," Aoki proclaimed as he waved the weapon. One of the men moaned.

"Better pull him off before this gets out of hand," Hideki thought. He could always count on Aoki to leap in blind and make much out of little. Now he had the five village gonin bowing on the road in broad daylight fearing for their lives.

"If I were not here, they would be hurt," Hideki realized.

"Aoki is strong. He is stronger than me." Nevertheless, as old Jii so often said, "Strong is good; but smart and strong is better." Aoki would continue to have trouble with smart. If Aoki were an example of samurai treatment of rice farmers, it was no wonder there were always rumors of rebellion and uprisings.

Aoki had transferred into Kii from the Yoshinobu Edo mansion a year ago. His transition to country life had not been easy. He was eager to make a name for himself and continually tried to impress old Jii and Nagamasu. He had quit trying to impress Hideki because Hideki didn't want to listen to his bragging about things that mattered little. If Aoki had something interesting to say about swordsmanship or tactics, Hideki would listen, but Hideki had judged Aoki to be mostly muscle and hot air. Besides, Hideki had little interest in his exploits with women or the drinking parties of Edo.

Hideki did envy Aoki's travels. One day he wanted to see the entire country himself. He dreamed of visiting all the famous dojos and learning new martial skills. At the top of that list of dojos would be the famous Yagyu School in Edo. But that would have to wait. He had to fix Aoki's blunder first. He could not have the five village headmen bowing in the hot sun and losing face to the villagers on either side of the road and expect anything good to come of it. It was not the Yoshinobu way.

"Easy, Aoki," said Hideki soothingly. "There is no reason to threaten. I'm sure it was an honest mistake."

Capitalizing on Hideki's tenor, and one to seize any opportunity, Emo, the chief villageman, looked up toward Hideki.

"Yes, Lord, it was a silly mistake. I remember now. Ichi-san has four children, all boys, and they work in the rice fields with their father. I had forgotten the last two."

"You had forgotten the last two so that your rice tax would be lower, you lying cur," Aoki accused.

"Relax, Aoki," Hideki said calmly. "It is the way of the world for peasants to be cunning and deceitful to samurai." At Emo's frown, Hideki quickly added, "And it is likewise in our nature to threaten and bully the poor peasant out of his rightful harvest so we ourselves can be fed."

All eyes moved to Hideki. "Lord, it is bad enough when you say such things to me, but I cannot believe you say it in front of *these*." Aoki pointed with his practice sword as if he were describing animal droppings.

"What would you have me do, Aoki?" Hideki asked. "If we beat the peasants, who will work in the fields to grow the rice that you and I eat? If we take too much, they starve. If they starve this year, we starve next year." He then pointed to the peasants working the fields. "Do you know what they are doing? Do you know anything about rice cultivation?"

"No Lord, such is not a samurai's place," Aoki stated with disgust.

"Life is a delicate balance, Aoki. We must do all we can to keep it in harmony."

Aoki stubbornly pursued the argument. "All I know, Lord, is if it were not for that unbelievable memory and your ability to mimic all you see, these five would have struck two more peasants off the roles of the Yoshinobu clan."

Hideki smiled. Aoki would always try to get the last word.

"Rise gonin," commanded Hideki. All five rose to a kneeling position, but only Emo looked Hideki in the eye.

Hideki spoke first. "It is a game, Emo. You lie to me, and I try to catch you. If I am doing my job correctly, I should catch you. If not, you will get away with moving two more people to your cousin's village where the Matsudaira have 500,000 koku of rice. They eat better over there, and here we have fewer mouths to feed. Is that about the size of it?"

Emo smiled and shook his head. "Your wisdom is beyond your years, young master. Yes, you are correct."

"Well, because I did catch you," Hideki mused. "There should be punishment." Hideki saw a look of fear pass over Emo's face. "What if you bring one boy back and leave the other to fatten on Matsudaira rice until our harvests can support another body?"

The old headman smiled. "It will be as you say, young master."

"Great. There will be no need to mention this incident to

my older brother or to Jii, understand?" Hideki asked, looking at both the headmen and Aoki. All nodded their agreement.

"Okay, we are finished then. Aoki, we still have time to get to the dojo for the afternoon session if we hurry. I'll race you."

Hideki and Aoki raced on foot above the rice patties along the dikes, each being careful not to step on the water-saturated rice shoots. The peasants were used to the familiar image of the young Yoshinobu prince dashing across the estate. They did not expect him to stop and return their bows. To do so would surely be a sign of respect, but they knew him to be in a constant state of motion. They also knew him to be benevolent and respectful most of the time.

All three of the Yoshinobu family treated the farmers well. The two older men were aloof, but the youngest was different. He smiled as he made his way around the huge Yoshinobu estate. His constant grinning usually induced sympathy for what was perceived as slowness of mind. Such thoughts evaporated when Hideki opened his mouth and spoke. He could talk with anyone. He knew many family members by name, asked after their health, and was engaging on most all subjects of farm life. That was a most un-samurai-like characteristic. Therefore the peasants bowed as the two young samurai streaked across the paddy dikes and along the creek that fed them, up the far bank, through the stand of cryptomeria trees, over the grassy knoll and down the backside into the amalgamation of shacks that made up Kii village. Samurai could afford to race around and play. Peasants were not samurai. They only had time to work, eat, sleep, and worry.

Hideki and Aoki, both breathing heavily, slid to a halt in the powdery brown street outside the village dojo. It was the largest of the twenty or so buildings that made up the village and the only one with a tile roof. All the rest of the roofs were thatch. Jii built the dojo so that the samurai retainers of the Yoshinobu and their young men could practice Bushido. The way of the warrior required constant practice and organized schools. When the samurai were not practicing with their wooden swords, the villagers used the building for community festivals and for ceremonies, like weddings and funerals.

From outside, Hideki could hear the "thwack" of stout wooden practice swords striking each other. Both young men shouldered past the late comers and raced to the entrance. There they removed their footwear. Using cloth rags from inside their kimonos, they knocked dust from their feet and ankles, selected their practice bokken hanging on the wall, and took their place in line.

The second-in-command of the dojo took his place at the right side, forward on the floor. With the sempai's command of "Kyosuke," everyone scrambled to find their correct place by rank and came to an erect position of attention. A large man took his position facing the class.

"Rei!" shouted the sempai, and all bowed in unison to the man in front.

The sensei facing the class acknowledged the bows with a slight nod of his head. "Get into position with a partner. We will practice gyowaza," he ordered.

All the students broke into two-man teams and commenced free-form attacks and defenses—the essence of gyowaza.

These drills continued for several minutes as the teacher moved from group to group, correcting stances and strikes by hitting the offending party on the legs with a bamboo stick about the length of a sword.

"I hope he doesn't come to me with that thing," Hideki whispered to Aoki.

"Fat chance he's going to hit the younger brother of the Lord that provides his rice," Aoki proffered. "Most likely he'll hit me as he corrects you."

Hideki smiled. "Maybe I should make some mistakes to see how painful is the correction."

Aoki's nostrils flared and he renewed a strong attack to Hideki's head. "This is the one place I can raise lumps on your head and never get a harsh word for it, Lord." He made the last word sound like a slur.

"Ma te," yelled the sensei. Everyone stopped. "What

do you want?" The question addressed a newcomer at the entrance. The newcomer smiled despite such rudeness.

"Are you the sensei?" he inquired.

"Yes," replied the teacher. "Who are you?"

"I'm looking for a match" was the simple retort.

"I'm teaching here," the sensei replied. "I don't have time for the likes of you."

"I was misinformed," the stranger replied. "I was told you teach Bushido here, the way of the warrior. I would not have troubled you if I'd known you taught sewing."

There was a collective intake of breath as the insult to their masculinity registered.

The sensei was having trouble regulating his breathing. "Very well, you want a match; a match you shall have. Select your weapon," he said, pointing to the wooden practice swords hanging on the walls.

The stranger pulled his kodachi from the thick cloth obi that belted around his waist and placed the two real swords carefully on the floor. He removed his straw sandals, knocked the dust off his feet and padded over to the wall. Hideki was intrigued. The sensei was twice the size of the challenger, and the sensei had just selected a subuto from the wall. This could only mean the sensei intended to maim the challenger as the subuto was longer and much heavier than the bokken. The subuto developed muscles. Its weight alone made it much too dangerous for sparring.

The stranger did not seem concerned. Was this the confidence of mu shin that Jii was always espousing? Was this the warrior state of "no mind"? How could you fight with no mind? Jii and his classical Chinese strategy and Zen puzzles. Maybe one day it would make sense.

The stranger first selected a wooden practice short sword. He placed this wakazashi in his left hand and selected a common hardwood bokken of normal katana length for his right. He moved back to the center of the dojo and faced the sensei.

The angry sensei took a position opposite and did not bother to bow. "What marker should we put over your grave?"

The stranger smiled. "You may call me Takezo, if need be," he said.

"Humph," snorted the sensei. "A peasant's name for a peasant's manners. How fitting."

The sensei then slipped into an aggressive left foot forward stance, the massive sword held high above his head pointing to the heavens.

The stranger remained calm with both feet shoulder-width apart as if he were talking to a friend. His hands drooped beside his legs, the wooden swords pointed at the ground.

The sensei inched closer and closer to the stranger until he was within striking distance. The stranger did not move. The sensei let out a blood-chilling yell and struck with a powerful overhead blow with all of his considerable weight behind it.

Hideki studied the stranger. Never had he seen such calm. He was either very good or he was going to be very dead. Many men had died from blows struck from bokken. The subuto would crush a man's skull. This was going to be messy.

Just before impact, the stranger stepped into the attacking sensei. Hideki could not believe the courage it took to accomplish that one little step forward. All in the dojo, to include the sensei, had expected the stranger to leap back out of the way. Instead, he pivoted into the attacker with the right side of his body while bringing up the short sword in his left hand to his head to ensure deflection of the descending blow. At almost the same time, he brought his right arm up and delivered a massive blow to the forehead of the sensei with the stranger's entire body weight behind it multiplied by the forward motion of the attacking sensei. There was a resounding crack followed by a thump as the stranger's sword hit the sensei's head and the unconscious sensei hit the hardwood floor.

While everyone else watched the inert body of the sensei, Hideki kept his eyes on the stranger. The stranger returned to his real swords, laced up his sandals, placed his swords in his obi at his waist, bowed to the dojo, left his wooden swords on the hardwood floor, and swept the room with alert eyes just long enough to find one pair of eyes fixed on him. Then he exited.

"Did you see that?" asked Aoki.

Hideki closed his mouth to give himself time to answer. "Oh yes," Hideki responded, "two swords, move into the attack, remain calm and bring all your energy into one blow. I saw it." He wondered what old Jii would say. "Two swords ... no samurai fights with two swords. It wasn't Bushido."

Chapter 2: People of the Grass

Yoshi's mother-in-law sat by the fire pit, her legs folded beneath her, stirring the soup in a black kettle. It was almost noontime, but the hut was dark. It was a large hut compared to most mountain shacks. The sides were made of odd-shaped boards and the roof was thatch. The smoke from the fire pit wafted up into the peaked thatch, then escaped out the openings in the side. Despite three candles burning inside, an open door and three small windows with bamboo shades rolled up to let in the noonday sun, visibility remained limited inside the hut.

As his mother-in-law stirred the soup, Yoshi watched her daughter on the bedding at his feet. Both the old woman and he winced every time the young woman moved from side to side, clutching her belly and groaning. The old woman peeked into the boiling brew to determine its readiness, but Yoshi knew that the pain and vomiting would not let the young woman keep any food down. At Chiyo's head, her brother bathed her forehead with a wet cloth in between thrashings.

"What could this be, Yoshi-san?" asked Daichi.

Yoshi shook his head. "I do not know brother; it is as if she has been poisoned."

That got Daichi and the old woman's head up. She rushed to Chiyo's side. She took Chiyo's hand in her own and felt inside the elbow. With the aid of a candle, she went to a spot behind the girl's ear and then to the side of the throat.

"You may be right Yoshi," she said with alarm in her

31

voice. "Her ki is flowing too strongly but she is not hot with fever."

"Can you identify it oba-san?" Yoshi asked, almost pleading.

The gray-haired woman opened one of her daughter's eyes and examined it with the candle flame drawn near. She repeated the process with the other eye, and then checked the girl's fingertips. Next, the old woman moved to the foot of the futon and checked her daughter's toenails before raising the soles of her daughter's feet. She made small indentations in her skin, and studied the marks.

"Wisteria vine, I think," the old woman said with confidence.

"You can help her?" Yoshi questioned.

"I could with enough 'human root,'" the mother stated. "But we have none in the village."

"Where can I find some?" Yoshi asked.

"The Chinese doctor in the castle town below will have some. Ginseng is one of his cure-alls," the old woman said with more than a little scorn in her voice. "But it is very expensive and we have no money."

"It is a poor husband who cannot provide for his family, oba-san," Yoshi declared. "I will find a way."

The mother looked relieved. "Buddha smiled on us the day you asked for Chiyo's hand. With my husband dead, I was worried about Chiyo and Daichi's future. But no more."

Yoshi went to the corner to retrieve his conical straw hat. He also stooped to place a flat throwing knife inside the crown and a five-bladed throwing star into his left sleeve. The five blades were a sign of the Dewa ninja.

"Expecting trouble?" asked Daichi.

"We are people of the grass, Daichi, true shinobi no mono," Yoshi replied. "We always expect trouble. Besides, someone poisoned your sister. I want to know who and why ... before I kill them."

"Are you sure it was poison brother?"

"Daichi, you, your sister and mother are Dewa ninja. How old were you when you learned to detect wisteria poison?"

"About four or five years, I think," responded Daichi.

"Exactly," Yoshi emphasized. "Chiyo knows how to detect it as well as you or me. Someone had to deliberately disguise its odor and taste to fool her. We've only been married for one month, but I have loved your sister since we were children playing in these mountains. I'm going to hurt someone for this." He spoke firmly, not boastfully.

Yoshi started to exit the hut when the village headman's shape filled the opening.

"Yoshi, you are summoned to the meeting hut."

Yoshi kept walking. "Not now."

The headman stopped him with an outstretched arm. Yoshi halted in surprise. This behavior was not polite and was certainly not the Dewa way.

"I'm sorry Yoshi," he began, "but the person requesting your presence is very high placed in the families. In fact, I believe him to be the leader of the Five Families. I have never seen him before, but I have heard of him. I think to ignore his summons would be bad for you and our village. Please go see him before you run whatever errand you are on." Yoshi looked to his wife on the floor. She was resting a little more peacefully now. Then his eyes went to Daichi. Finally, his gaze rested on his mother-in-law. She nodded slightly.

"So then," Yoshi asked, "where is this mystery man?"

"In the meeting hut. I told him you were on the way," the headman stated as he stepped down into the street and disappeared around the corner of a hut.

Yoshi stayed in the hut's darkness. He turned and walked to Daichi. "Brother, this has all the signs of a contract. I want you to do two things for me. First, if I don't return with human root today, promise me you will get it for Chiyo."

Daichi nodded. "Hai."

"Second, in case I can't come back and establish communications, I want you to provide it for me."

"You want shadows, brother?" asked Daichi.

"Yes. I have no way of knowing where or when we may depart, so put a five-man team on me. Use our relatives. We'll make contact in the normal way."

"It will be as you say Yoshi," Daichi said. "You are number two in the village anyway."

"More than anything else, I want Chiyo safe," Yoshi said, looking at his mother-in-law.

"Do not worry son-in-law," the old woman vowed. "She will be safe."

Yoshi looked her in the eye and remembered all the times he had seen her cripple samurai. He believed her.

"Domo," he said as he turned into the light of the street and headed for the meeting hut.

Yoshi stepped down from the hut into the main street of the village. It was little more than a goat track covered in a light green spread of creeping weeds and dandelions. Reddish furrows carved through the greenery. Rapid running water poured down from above when the clouds bumped up against the mountain each afternoon and released their liquid to speed its way down to the creeks in the valley below.

As he stepped down, he closed one eye. The brightness of the mid-day sun compared to the darkness of the hut would rob him of his vision once he entered the meeting hut. Therefore, he used the old ninja trick of closing one eye to keep from totally losing his night vision in the new building.

He tied on his conical straw hat and squatted to lace his zori sandals on his feet. He was dressed like every other male in the village. His top garment was a faded indigo peasant jacket patched at the elbows and shoulders. The billowing sleeves came halfway to his wrists. The garment folded in the front with cloth straps knotted on his left hip and again on his right to keep the jacket about his body. His trousers were made of the same heavy cotton canvas as his jacket and tied at the waist in front. The garment fit loosely on Yoshi's slight frame, with ample leg space ending at half calf. The pants used to be white long ago; now they had a dingy gray appearance thanks to the mud in the creeks below. He paid his appearance little attention. His clothes were not what the Five Families were seeking.

As Yoshi approached the large meeting hut, he scanned the village with his open eye. He strained to detect danger. He registered nothing. He stopped in front of the meeting hut before stepping up onto the entrance. His keen senses still registered no threat. This was unusual. He knew there to be at least one dangerous man inside the hut, yet he could not sense his presence. Something was not right.

Yoshi slid back the wooden door and stepped up and inside the darkened hut. Immediately he moved to the right, kneeling on one knee with his hat off and his right hand on the flat throwing knife.

"Moshi age masu," Yoshi said as he switched eyes.

"Yoshi-san?" the voice in the dark questioned. "What are you reporting?"

"Just my presence," Yoshi responded, straining all of his considerable ninja skills to discern how many others were in the dark hut. His haragai gift of seeing through the darkness was not functioning for some reason.

"I guess you are wondering who I am," the voice said.

Yoshi was quiet. They would get around to telling him everything they wanted him to know.

"I realize it is a little unusual for you to be summoned this way," the old voice said. Yoshi remained quiet. Patience meant reward. That is what his new bride often said. "I have watched your progress over the years. You are your father's son. Despite being young, you are quite adept. You are a veteran of four assignments." The voice was cold despite the praise.

An old man with a shaved head and wearing monk robes and prayer beads stepped from the shadows. "You are a resourceful shinobi no mono, but you respect the old ways." He extended his hands with the index fingers joined at the tips, thumbs overlapping, and the rest of the fingers folded under. His hands moved in a blur, tracing intricate patterns in the air.

Yoshi interlaced his own fingers and traced equally intricate but slightly different signs.

"Excellent," the old man said. "You do not find many who know kuji-kiri these days. It takes a true ninja trained in the old arts to give the correct signs and counter signs of nine symbols cutting. That is why I have sought you out for this assignment."

The old man changed the subject.

"Oksan wa genki desuka?" he asked, inquiring after Yoshi's wife.

"Hai, genki," Yoshi lied, indicating his wife was fine.

"That is not what I hear," the old man continued. "I hear your new young wife is in bed with pain and only the human root medicine can cure her."

"You are well informed, old one," Yoshi replied. Few within the village knew of his wife's sudden illness.

The old man reached into his robes. Yoshi's thumb tightened on the small throwing blade held between the straw hat in his lap and his right thumb.

"This is ginseng, the human root medicine from the Chinese doctor," the old man offered. "It is a down payment on your next contract."

Yoshi's outer expression did not change. Nevertheless, his blood was boiling. Now he knew why his Chiyo was ill.

"Are you sure it will cure her?" is what he asked instead.

"Oh, I think so," the old man stated noncommittally. "It is very expensive medicine."

"I hope so," Yoshi stated. "I would hate to have to abandon an assignment to come back and find some more."

The old man smiled slightly. "Yoshi-san, are you threatening your elders?"

"No threat," Yoshi stated. "Just peeking into the future."

Yoshi bowed his head, reached up and took the packet in his free left hand and placed it inside his outer garment.

"Good," the old man said. "I knew we could trust you."

From behind the old man, a striking woman in white pilgrim garb stepped out of the shadows. She was older than Yoshi, but might have been pretty in different surroundings. Yoshi noticed her place a shuriken into her sleeve. "Probably poisoned tipped," he thought to himself. "I guess I made the right choice."

Now that Yoshi could see her, he could feel her presence—almost. It was not right. Was she a ghost? Instinctively he looked down to her feet. She had feet. Therefore, she was no ghost. Nevertheless, why could he not read her aura with haragai? A ninja should not doubt his prowess. This woman made him uneasy.

"Your mission will be difficult and will involve this," the old man said as he held up a three-leafed hollyhock mon in gold leaf on the side of a tobacco pouch. Everyone knew the symbol.

"You want me to kill the shogun?" Yoshi asked in total disbelief.

"No," scoffed the old man. "He's almost retired anyway. Your target is from the house of the Shinpan."

"You want me to kill someone from the house that provides direct descendants to the Tokugawa? It sounds like you need a crazy man."

The old man continued to talk as if he had not heard Yoshi's complaint. "Your target will be in either his Kii estate or his Edo mansion. His name is Yoshinobu Nagamasa."

Yoshi shook his head. "You want me to kill someone from the Tokugawa family who may ascend to the shogunate at any time. I will be lucky if all that happens to me is death. It is beyond suicide."

The old man frowned. "Such pessimism does not become you, Yoshi."

"And that old bastard Hanzo is said to be running the metsuke for Chamberlain Yagyu. I'd need an army to get past all the security and the spies," Yoshi continued to complain.

"If you start immediately, you will catch him in Kii, where he will only have samurai retainers as security. Besides, you will have support, Yoshi," the old man stated as he nodded to the woman. "This is Sachi. She will supply you with all you require." Every instinct told Yoshi to run, to get as far away as possible from these crazy people, but he knew he had heard too much.

Yoshi bowed slightly to Sachi. She did not blink or return even a nod.

Yoshi knew he "was bought and paid for." If he refused now, he would die along with his sick wife. He was angry. He should have never come into the hut. As usual, his curiosity and willingness to please overcame his caution. Inside he was cursing himself. Outside he was calm.

"I could try and kill them both now," he thought. "No, you don't get high up in the Five Families without some skills. They would be hard to kill. Besides, they probably did not travel here alone." Yoshi strained his haragai but could detect no one else. He had no doubt there were others waiting outside somewhere. If he hesitated in the least, he would be dead. He was in a dilemma. He knew he could not get out of the assignment. His wife of one month would be a widow, if they let her live.

"Do we have paper?" Yoshi sighed.

The old man nodded to his cold assistant. She pulled a single rolled scroll from her robes and extended it to Yoshi. He unrolled the scroll and began reading. It was traditional for Ninja to sign contracts as a way to pass debts and obligations from one generation to the next. Longevity was a ninja's dream.

Yoshi took his small blade, nicked his left little finger, and allowed the blood to drop onto his right. He traced his mark on the bottom of the paper. There, it was sealed.

The old man nodded. Sachi stepped toward Yoshi to pick up the contract and stopped to trace a design lightly on Yoshi's cheek with her fingernail.

"Sweet Yoshi," she murmured. "There is no need to worry. Both you and Chiyo will be well cared for."

Yoshi stared into those cold gray eyes.

"Oh, I'm not worried Sachi-san. If anything happens to Chiyo, I will find you," he stated flatly.

Sachi stopped smiling and stood up angrily.

"We understand each other, peasant. Go say goodbye to your sick wife. We leave within the hour."

"So much for niceties," Yoshi thought. "But, I owe you and the old man for poisoning Chiyo. Ask anyone, I always pay my debts. You may have won this time, but I'm not finished with you."

A good ninja knows when and where to pick his battles. Yoshi did not betray his real feelings. Instead, he bowed to both, stood, turned, and left the hut.

The old man sat on the floor and moved his hand over

his bald head. "And what did you think of our young assassin, Sachi-san?"

Sachi moved behind the old man and remained standing. "He is arrogant and inexperienced and does not know his place."

The old man removed a white towel from inside his jacket and wiped a light coat of sweat off the back of his neck.

"Did he have no qualities that impressed you?" he asked patiently.

"None Oto-san," she stated with conviction.

"So you are questioning my judgment?"

She knew he had laid a trap for her. He had detected she was upset by the meeting and had played with her, using her agitation as the catalyst. "Never, Oto-san," she stated as she knelt and bowed to her father. "You are the boss of the Five Families. It is not my place to question you."

The old man nodded. "Well spoken Sachi-san. So examine yourself. What caused your agitation?"

"I do not know," she responded, thinking about the brief meeting. "I was fine until he made that not-so-veiled threat about hunting me down if anything happened to his wife."

"And why did that bother you, Sachi-san?" he asked quietly. "Surely you have received threats before."

Sachi grabbed her upper arms with both hands and involuntarily shivered. "I do not know Oto-san," she answered truthfully. "It may be that despite his boyish innocence I detect that he could very well make good on that threat."

"Excellent! That is my girl. You are correct. It is because of his incongruous countenance that he is so dangerous," the master confirmed. "You are very familiar with every aspect of the ninja life. I have taught you well. Now think of a young man, in the prime of his life, who embodies the highest skill level in all those disciplines. Now think of the same young man who is also a master of the old ways. A man who is a master of the magic—the dark arts—the ways no longer taught because the skill has been lost over the generations." The old man spun around and continued to talk. "Now imagine that same deadly combination inside the countenance of an innocent. Yoshi can fool anyone. He is a chameleon. He reminds those that pay attention to him of their younger brother or favorite nephew. He does not look dangerous. But if his wife dies, I will not sleep well again."

"Oto-san?" Sachi's eyes opened wider. "Surely you exaggerate Father."

The old man smiled up at his daughter. "No Sachi-san. I do not. Have you heard of haragai?"

"Yes, but I thought it a legend."

"A legend, yes, because its secrets have been lost. Yoshi's father had the gift. He could see through the darkness. I understand he passed the gift on to his son. That is why I need Yoshi for this contract. It is another reason he is so dangerous. Luckily, the ginseng I gave Yoshi contains the antidote for the wisteria poison you placed in her drink. She should be up and around in a day or two. You are going to have to be very careful around him. While I have trained you well, you are not in his league in a one-on-one fight. I am not sure I could defeat him one-on-one myself. So swallow your pride and help him as much as possible. Besides, he will probably not live through this assignment. He is correct. It is suicide."

Sachi shivered. "What an interesting man," she thought.

Chapter 3: The Foxes

"Congratulate your father, children. He will be the next shogun," directed Michi as she spooned rice into her husband's bowl. Yorifusa Juro smiled at his wife's praise and watched her perform the simple task of refilling her sons' rice bowls. He marveled anew. Her movements were economical and so very feminine. He found wonder in her every graceful motion. She was the epitome of womanhood and Juro considered himself a lucky man.

Catching himself in this un-samurai-like pondering, he wondered why she intrigued him so. "She was not beautiful," he mused. In fact, his mother had warned him that she was plain. Maybe if lined up next to the painted geishas of Kyoto, she might seem plain, but she had never looked plain to him. The long rich black hair, porcelain features, intelligent dark eyes, pouting lips and unbelievably soft skin had mesmerized him from the beginning.

Michi was more. She was very devoted to him and their two boys. He found that fact in itself attractive. Juro felt his loins stir as he watched her rocking motion to stand in the tight kimono and shuffle in the pigeon-toed motion the restrictive hem required. She moved to the sliding door and retrieved a new tray left by a kitchen maid on the hardwood floor outside the room.

Married for fifteen years, Juro had never felt the need to seek out companionship outside the confines of their bedroom. During the many times that he was away on Tokugawa duty, he could not wait to get back to her. She was an ardent lover who took as much pleasure as she gave.

"Strange," he thought. "If I strayed I would diminish her stature in some way. I think it would be hard to live with betrayal in her eyes." He watched her kneel down between her sons. He took in the nape of her neck, the familiar roundness of her shoulder, and those inviting hips that centered on her ankles as she sat in the formal style they adopted at every meal. The old soldier's ditty came to mind: "Good wife; better mother; best lover." Yes, he had many things to be thankful for in Michi. He continued to smile at her. Michi caught his gaze and blushed, as if reading his mind.

"Omedito gosaimusu, Chichiue," offered twelve-year-old Masasue as he sipped tea from a lacquer cup.

"Domo Masasue," responded Juro, thanking his youngest son for his offer of congratulations.

Not to be outdone by his younger brother, the fourteen-year-old Masashige chimed in with, "Omedito," as he hoisted a bit of fish to his mouth.

"Thank you both," said Juro as he reached into the lacquered box to pluck a radish on the ends of his ohashi.

"But becoming shogun is not a certain thing. It is much like trying to get this radish to stay on the ends of our eating sticks."

"What do you mean, Father?" asked the younger Masasue. Juro liked his inquisitive mind. He should go far if given the chance.

"There are factions behind the hollyhock crest of the shogun that wield a lot of power, and they may not want me as shogun," Juro explained.

"How can that be, Father? You are by far the best qualified, I'm sure," offered Masasue.

"The current shogun's sons, stupid," the older Masashige said, chastising his younger sibling.

"Do not call your brother stupid, Masashige," Michi corrected.

"Good advice Masashige," Juro said. Then to Masasue, "Your older brother is correct. The current shogun has two sons. The older son was mothered by a concubine, some say.

Whoever the concubine was, if she ever existed, she is long gone. A wet-nurse was provided to fill in for the missing mother. The wet nurse became very powerful, currying favor with all the right men. She influences much in Edo castle. She even has a title. She is called Tsubone, although her real name is Lady O'Fuku."

"What does it mean Father?" asked Masasue.

"It means Wet-Nurse in Waiting," snapped the older brother.

"What is a wet nurse?" asked Masasue as he picked up a rice cake to munch.

"We will save that discussion for another time, boys," said their mother.

Juro smiled at his wife.

"The factions go back as far as your ancestor Tokogawa Ieyasu," started Juro.

"Oh, I know him Father. He was the great one!" exclaimed Masasue.

"He founded our dynasty, you dunce. He was your great grandfather," Masashige sighed as if speaking to an idiot.

"Masashige, I will not tell you again to cease speaking to your brother in such a tone," said Juro. "He is younger than you and less experienced. However, he is your brother. Family honor demands you help him and Bushido demands you protect him. Do I make myself clear?" he asked.

"Yes Father," responded Masashige. However, that did not stop him from glaring at his younger brother.

"So why can't you be shogun?" asked Masasue again.

"Well, I still may, but it is highly unlikely," Juro answered. "You see, Ieyasu fought a great battle," started Juro.

"I know, at Sekigahara," chimed in Masasue.

"Yes, where he defeated the armies of the Toyotomi. The families that were allied with Ieyasu would become known as the Fudai," said Juro, referring to the "inside families."

"And the families that were neutral are called Tozama," Masasue answered. "Everyone knows that."

"Yes, but what you may not know is that the Fudai families are considered more loyal and were given large holdings along the Tokaido Highway leading to Ieyasu's capital here in Edo. The Tozama kept their lands but do not participate in the government. However, the current shogun has taxed them severely and there has been some unrest."

This time it was Masashige who interrupted, "What's all this got to do with picking a shogun?"

"If you will be patient your father will tell you," Michi laughed.

"Okay, at the head of our government is the shogun, not counting the emperor in Kyoto, who doesn't govern. The shogun is the power. Assisting him are one or two personal counselors or chamberlains. Currently there is only one ... the old fox Yagyu Munenori. Beneath the shogun are the Tairo. There are two of them, Sakai Tadekatsu and Sakai Tadakiyo. They advise in grave matters of state. Below them, to help manage the daily affairs is the Roju. There we have four: Itakawa Shiganori, Sakai Tadakiyo, Abe Tadaaki and Naomasu Nagai."

"But father," interrupted Masasue, "Sakai Tadakiyo is in both."

"Good listening skills, Masasue," praised Juro as he patted his younger son's head. "Tadakiyo is an exceptional samurai and serves in both. This helps keep the Tairo aware of what the Roju is doing."

Pointing his ohashi at both boys, Juro said, "Now to continue, the Roju are responsible for keeping the government running. They appoint ministers that are in charge of the temples, finance, judges, police, and city government. In short, they are in charge of everything."

Older brother saw his chance. "So everyone has a vote on who the next shogun will be?"

Masasue looked at his older brother and rolled his eyes in disbelief.

"No Masashige," corrected Juro. "Only the Tairo and Roju vote."

"Can they vote for themselves?" asked Masasue.

"Good question, Masasue," Juro praised again. "No, both the Tairo and Roju are from fudai families. Shoguns come from the shinpan families who are direct descendants of Ieyasu.

That is why we usually do not serve in the Tairo or Roju. We do not manage. We either lead the nation or remain in seclusion … if we're lucky."

"I get it father," said Masashige. "Those in power in the Tairo and Roju want someone as shogun that will leave them in power."

"Extra rice for you, Masashige," Juro praised. "That is correct. So now, you both see why you have to study so hard. If picked as shogun, you have to know the workings of the government from day one. Your decisions as shogun affect many people."

"So who do we have for competition?" asked Masasue.

"From the current shogun's family there are the two sons. The nineteen year old is Iemitsu. He also has a younger seventeen-year-old brother named Tadanaga. Strangely enough, Tadanaga is the favorite of his mother," said Juro. "She pushes as hard for Tadanaga as O'Fuku pushes for the older brother Iemitsu."

Michi looked up in surprise. "How can a mother favor her second son over her firstborn?"

"There could be many reasons, my love. One reason may be the rumor that Iemitsu prefers the company of men over women." Michi gasped in surprise and brought her hand to her mouth to cover her dropped jaw.

"What is the younger brother like, Father?" asked Masasue.

"He is said to be very strange. There are rumors that he is mentally imbalanced. There have been reports that he flies into uncontrollable rages and has killed several servants."

"Is there anyone else we have to worry about, because it sounds like you are the best choice?" the inquisitive Masasue observed.

Juro swallowed and stopped to ponder. "Well, who are the three families of the Shinpan?" he asked, never able to pass up a teaching opportunity.

"Our Yorifusa clan in Mitto province, the Yoshinao family in Owari province, and … and … ," Masashige trailed off.

"And the Yoshinobu in Kii," finished Masasue. "That

would be Uncles Nagamasa and Hideki."

"Correct," said Juro. "I have very smart sons. The current shogun's oldest son is from Owari. They had another heir, a cousin, but he died under mysterious circumstances last month."

Michi shivered and moved to the sliding shoji screen and pulled it back to ensure the guards were on duty in the courtyard. She looked at her two sons and then at her husband. "Kyodai goroshi," she said. "We are supposed to be living in a time of peace, but it is just like in the Warring States Period when we had to worry about brother killing brother. I thought my sons had escaped such madness."

"Mysterious circumstances," inquired Masashige. Then he glanced out the open shoji screen to ensure guards were there as well.

Juro smiled to ease the tension. "Come away from the screen, Michi. We are safe here in our Edo residence. We have our own retainers with us and the city police patrol the streets outside," Juro said with reassurance in his voice, though he also reached behind him and moved his dual swords to within reach.

As Juro turned back to his rice bowl, an arrow whizzed through his left ear, slicing it in half and burying the head of the arrow into the tatami mat in front of Masasue.

Michi screamed and threw back the screen, shouting for help. Juro felt and heard two thumps behind him. Without looking, he reversed the eating sticks in his hand, pivoted on one knee and embedded his ohashi into the eyehole of a fox mask worn by an intruder who had dropped to the tatami floor from the ceiling above. The fox masked intruder screamed loudly, flopped backwards and spasmed in death.

Ignoring his mangled ear and the blood flowing freely down his neck, Juro grabbed his katana from the sword rack and pulled the blade from the sharkskin-covered scabbard just as the second fox-masked intruder raised a short sword high over Masasue's head. Masashige leaped in front of his younger brother, his short sword drawn and pointed at the attacker. Juro had an instance of pride in his oldest son. Juro took advantage of the moment of hesitation Masashige created by eviscerating the fox intruder with one earth to sky strike. Blood and intestine plopped to the tatami. The stink of the offal in the closed room was overpowering.

Michi summoned her courage and took a position in front of her sons with her small tanto drawn from the brocade holder in her obi. Two more foxes dropped to the floor in front of Juro as two crashed into the room through the rice paper shoji separating the inner residence. Michi turned to face the two attackers coming through the wall with the point of her knife. Both foxes struck at once, slashing her throat and shoulder with their swords. Blood spewed high from a severed carotid artery.

"Hahawe," screamed Masasue as he leaped for his mother's fallen body.

"No!" cried Masashige, as he reached to restrain his younger brother. Too late, one of the foxes severed the young boy's head with a horizontal strike as the other lunged for Masashige.

Juro dispatched both of his foxes with a sky to earth strike and a lunge to the throat. He spun back to the center of the room just in time to see Masasue's little head roll on the floor.

"Arrrgh!" he screamed and lunged at Masashige's attacker. His violence drove the fox back a step. Then Juro redirected his strike down the centerline of the first attacker, changing directions in the last minute to go to the right, striking and severing the second fox's sword arm. He brought the sword back to centerline in time to deflect the other attacker's slash. Masashige drove his short sword into this attacker's spleen, as his father slashed his forehead open.

"Well done, Masashige," Juro complimented. He saw the look of appreciation in his oldest son's eyes turn to pain as an arrow pierced his throat from back to front. Masashige tried to speak but blood was pumping out of both wounds and he dropped in a heap onto the tatami.

Juro spun in a mad rage to find three more foxes had dropped down and two had charged bows. Both of his sons were dead or dying and his beloved was gone. Juro's samurai eye judged the distance to the bowmen.

"Too short for yadome-jitsu," he told himself. Deflecting arrows with a sword was not a martial art he had mastered. He charged. The first arrow did deflect off his sword by a lucky turn of the wrist in yadome-jitsu style. The second one caught him deep in the chest and pierced a lung. He willed himself to continue. The war madness was on him. In one stroke, he cleaved the first fox bowman's head from side to side and severed the second's throat. The third fox ran his sword into Juro's torso, breaking ribs as it went inside. Juro could not ignore this tremendous pain and screamed. The enemy was so close he could feel his breath through the ridiculous wooden mask. The fox clutched the handle of his sword that spitted Juro's upper body. Juro tried to raise his sword to strike him but his faithful sword would not answer the call. He could see a new foxes dropping from the rafters. One raised a blade high above his head and in his final moment Juro knew he would not be shogun.

Chapter 4: The Classroom

Old Jii adjusted his fan inside his obi next to his waist as he addressed his grandsons. "The final stages of any discipline is where you forget what you have learned, cleanse your mind, and accomplish whatever you set out to do without being aware of it yourself. You begin by learning and reach a point where learning does not exist. It is the way. It is Bushido."

He glanced at both students to ensure they were writing legibly. Calligraphy and Zen were important to a samurai's education. He smiled to himself. He was proud of these young men and his pride had more than a little to do with the fact that he was their grandfather.

"Hideki, quit dragging your wrist," Jii corrected. "You are Yoshinobu, not one of those peasants from Owari. Straighten your back and straighten your life," he chided.

Jii was hard on Hideki, but for good reason. His youngest grandson was a likeable young rogue with tremendous talent but a tendency not to apply himself unless eating or swordsmanship were involved. As an 18 year old, the eating was understandable. Jii often told him that half of the family's 250,000-koku rice stipend was to feed him. Hideki's second love was the katana, and he would practice sword techniques for hours if Jii would let him. Jii had to admit the youngster was good, but he was never able to break through and become the master swordsman he strived to be. Jii believed that Hideki's flaw was that he lacked confidence in his ability. His older brother Nagamasa did not have Hideki's speed or technique,

yet Hideki could not best him. Nagamasa was confident—
therefore he was victorious. If Jii could give Hideki a little of
Nagamasa's confidence, he would be a natural warrior.

Hideki's ability to see something one time and copy it
amazed Jii. But Hideki refused to take seriously anything that
didn't involve sword play. Getting Hideki to do the smallest
chores required of a samurai often required Jii having him do
it over. It wasn't that Hideki wasn't smart, he just didn't apply
himself to things he thought unimportant. The trivial and the
mundane bored Hideki.

"By the Lord Buddha, Hideki," Jii moaned. "Can't you
keep your lines straight?"

"He's too busy thinking of his next match, Jii-san," Nagamasa teased.

Hideki scowled at his older brother. "Wait until I show
you what I learned today, older brother. It should bring a lump
to that inflated head of yours."

Nagamasa looked up from his calligraphy. "You actually
think you can penetrate my defenses little brother? If so, it
would be the first time."

"He is right, Hideki," Jii said. "You have never bested
your brother."

"I have a feeling today will be different," Hideki stated.

"Nagamasa," Jii praised, "your characters are excellent."
Nagamasa bowed to Jii.

"It is because of your superior instruction, Jii-sama,"
Nagamasa flattered.

"Oh please, Naga," Hideki sighed. "Do you have no
samurai pride?"

"Do not chastise your older brother, Hideki. He is the
head of the Yoshinobu family. Besides, his calligraphy is flawless," said Jii.

"Yes, yes, I know," Hideki said as he concentrated on his
calligraphy. "Naga is perfect in all ways and I am flawed in all
ways."

"Urusai Hideki!" yelled Jii. "You are not defective in any
way. But when you shirk your responsibilities like you did today
with the peasant census, you make even me wonder."

"Not me Hideki," chimed in Naga, smiling. "I find you defective in every way."

Hideki jumped up, spilling his ink stone onto the hardwood floor and overturning the small wooden desk with his calligraphy papers. He raced to the side of the room and pulled a wooden practice sword off the wall. This he threw to Naga. He selected a bokken for his right hand and snatched a smaller wooden wakazashi representing a short sword for his left. Then he moved to the center of the floor.

Naga caught his bokken in the air and pushed his calligraphy desk aside. He placed his wooden sword in his left hand and moved his right into the kimono sleeve, coming out at the chest of his kimono and freeing his right shoulder. He tucked the useless right sleeve into his obi at his waist. Once done, he moved the bokken to a two handed grip, right hand leading, taking up the traditional two-handed right side forward stance with the point of the sword at eye level. He waited for the attack he knew would come.

Hideki took up the relaxed stance he had seen earlier in the dojo. He stood with feet shoulder width apart, hands hanging limply at his sides, the swords in each hand, tips pointing at the floor.

Initially shocked by the rude interruption of his training, Jii watched the two young men. His samurai blood took over. He forgot his calligraphy. Combat overshadowed everything else in a samurai's life. In addition, when these two fought, it was always a good fight.

"I just wish once, for his sake, that Hideki would win," Jii thought.

Hideki would always show such promise and then not follow through. He was good at every martial art taught him. Jii thought that if he would apply himself, he could be a prodigy in all he attempted. However, he would not follow through. It was as if Hideki did not want anyone to know how good he really was. He would show great genius in the beginning only to stop short of mastery. Ever since their parents had died so many years ago and Jii had taken over their teaching, he had sent them to the best schools and best teachers. All the teachers said the same thing. Naga would work hard and develop mastery. Hideki would burn like a bright star and then act as if he were not interested anymore. They all said it was a shame because he had the capability to be their best student. If Hideki were to grow into a man, he would have to learn how to finish things.

"Make it today, Hideki," Jii thought.

Naga inched closer to Hideki, ready to bring his sword up and to the right or left to deflect Hideki's attack. He knew it would come. He knew what it would be. Hideki never varied. It would be a thrust to the chest followed with a strike to the shoulder. He loved his little brother and wanted him to do well. However, Hideki had always been impatient, breaking first with an attack and giving Naga the edge.

"He'll attack soon," Naga said to himself.

When Hideki's expression and stance remained motionless, Naga inched closer. Now he was within striking distance of Hideki.

"Hideki will break," Naga said to himself again. Now sweat was starting to pop out on Naga's forehead.

Jii watched both. "This is a new Hideki," Jii mused to himself. "He is calm." He shifted out of his sazen sitting position to unfold his legs in front. The motion caused Naga to glance in Jii's direction.

"By Amida," Naga cursed. He had let himself be distracted, leaving himself vulnerable.

Jii could not believe his eyes. He had shifted position and made deliberate noise to break Hideki's concentration. Hideki had not broken. Naga had. This was remarkable. "What has happened to our Hideki?" Jii wondered.

Naga whipped his eyes back to Hideki. Hideki had not moved. He looked as calm as ever. Naga slowly raised his sword back and up until his head and right foot were closest to Hideki. "Hideki will take this bait," Naga insisted to himself. "He cannot resist the opening." Hideki did not move. "What is this?" Naga wondered. He could not stand here all day with this nitwit. He had things to do.

"Arrrghh!" screamed Naga as he brought the sword's

arc down towards Hideki's head. "I'll show the little twit," he thought as he put all his weight behind the strike.

Jii gave a sharp intake of breath as he saw the move develop.

"Hideki, you will never learn," Jii thought. Then the world changed.

Hideki moved his right shoulder into his brother's attack as he brought up the short sword in his left hand to the side of his own head to deflect the downward blow. As his momentum moved Naga's sword to the left and downward, Hideki brought the long bokken in the right hand up and smashed it down on the top of Naga's head, cutting his power at the last second.

"Ahhhhh!" yelled Naga as he dropped his sword to the floor and clutched the reddening lump on his shaved pate.

"Omedito gozaimus, Hideki," Jii congratulated. "Omedito indeed. I have never seen a better executed technique."

"You are lucky, Naga," Hideki stated to his pained brother. "You put so much power behind your strike that I almost could not control mine."

"What happened?" Naga asked as he checked his head for blood. "I was an inch from braining you and then I was on my knees. Where did you go?"

"I told you, I saw a very remarkable swordsman today," said Hideki. "But come, we must get some cool water on your head or the lump may be permanent. That would really end your chances for a suitable marriage," laughed Hideki. "I'll show you what I learned later."

Jii watched the two brothers go out. He was happy. He looked down to the wooden swords on the hardwood floor.

"Two swords," he pondered. "Is it Bushido?"

Chapter 5: The Call

Yoshi watched the two brothers walk from the large room into the inner rooms of the mansion, one holding his head. It had been a good match. He had watched it from the rafters of the building across the courtyard where he had hidden half the night and all of this day. He knew there was very little chance of detection. For one thing, it looked like his targets did not employ ninja. On the other hand, if they did, they were better at their tradecraft than he. "Ridiculous," he muttered to himself. Ninja were the first thing any ninja would search out. Nevertheless, he had seen no evidence of any spies.

He put his eye back to his looking glass just in time to see the old man pick up the two wooden bokken and place them back on the wall, then close the sliding doors that opened onto the courtyard. Yoshi collapsed his looking glass and started to replace the thatch in the roof where his glass had protruded. Just as well; he had seen enough.

They were both good swordsmen. However, the younger one had an aura about him that disturbed Yoshi. "What am I feeling?" he asked himself. "Is it goodness?" Yoshi pondered before moving. Sometimes haragai could be a curse. "Yes ... goodness!" Yoshi agreed with himself.

That was as closest he could come to defining it. The younger brother radiated a "goodness" that was strange in a samurai. Would he kill? He was a samurai so he would kill. Yoshi had just watched him almost brain his brother. So maybe it was not goodness after all. Maybe he was feeling that the young man was destined for something else—for greater things.

"Urusai," Yoshi scolded himself. He could not be thinking about a target. He knew the rules of the people of the grass. "I live in shadows. I die in shadows. I do not walk in the light," he repeated from memory.

The light was for normal people. He was ninja. He could only think of his mission and his clan. Nothing else mattered. However, he was coerced into this assignment and that was not the ninja way either. It certainly was not the Dewa ninja way. Poisoning his wife was inexcusable. But neither he nor his family took precedence in an assignment. "That last one is hard," Yoshi thought to himself.

He found he really missed Chiyo. He looked at his hands. He could kill with these hands. "But I can also kill with feet, knees, elbows, and shoulders, and I can make a lethal weapon out of almost anything. I am a well-trained killer," he recited. Then he grinned, remembering the hours of training with his father. "And I am a master of camouflage," he said dutifully under his breath.

Then Yoshi shook his head to clear his thinking. He could not afford to identify with a target by thinking of him as human. He was about to depart from his hiding place when equestrians thundered up to the compound gate. From his vantage point, he could only see the tops of their heads.

"Open the gates in the name of the shogun," the authoritative leader proclaimed.

Yoshi watched as grooms took the horses and the three messengers walked inside the compound. Yoshi was trying to determine if he would take a route over the roofs or under the floorboards to listen to the meeting. Just as he was about to cover the hole in the thatch roof and move to a better vantage point, the room next to the courtyard in which the brothers had fought opened and the doors peeled back. Women and young boys bustled about, wiping down the hardwood floor. Small, round, woven mats dotted the room amidst freestanding paper lanterns. The evening light waned. Yoshi's luck was holding. The same room he had been spying on was to be the meeting room for the messengers from the shogun. He smiled to himself. He remembered his father saying, "Luck is ninety percent preparation." He would not have to move. He got the glass back into place and went through the drill of tightening and relaxing all the muscles in his body to stave off cramping. He slowed his breathing, got his eye behind the glass, and smiled again. The placement of the mats in the large meeting room meant he could see everyone's face.

"I wish Chiyo was here," he thought. Wanting her was certainly about the physical and mental joy she would bring, but more importantly, she could read lips much better than he could. She had tried to teach him, and he had gotten much better, but if they were speaking in that Edo dialect, he would have a hard time keeping up.

The chief messenger took position at the head of the room on the raised place of honor that was approximately four inches off the hardwood. Nagamasa faced him in a seated position on the hardwood. Jii was to Naga's right and slightly behind. Hideki sat to Naga's left and slightly behind. The chief messenger sat cross-legged and his two assistants did the same, slightly behind on his right and left. To Jii's right, with his back to the open courtyard, sat the Yoshinobu counselor. To his left were Yoshinobu clan samurai in descending rank down both the outer and inner walls of the dojo, which was now the ceremony room.

The chief messenger reached into his lightweight outer hoari jacket and pulled out a white paper folded rectangular with a golden hollyhock emblem on the outer cover. "Mina no mono, kike!" he dutifully shouted

The Yoshinobu all bowed to the crest of the Tokugawa shogunate.

The messenger opened the letter and began reading in a loud and authoritative voice: "The Yoshinobu are to journey to their Edo mansion in all haste. They are to take thirty retainers for the trip and sufficient staff to run their Edo residence indefinitely." That was it. He folded the letter back up into the paper outer cover, thrust it back into this garment, and bowed to Nagamasa. The Yoshinobu all bowed again.

The old messenger had streaks of grey throughout

his hair. Nevertheless, he was still lean and hard looking. He turned his sitting position to his left so he was addressing Jii. "I remember your heroics at the left flank at Sekigahara, Yoshino-bu-san," he beamed.

Old Jii smiled at the thought. "And I yours, Fusa," Jii replied.

The old messenger shook his head approvingly. "This house befits a samurai family. Function without the trappings of the merchants you see all over Edo these days," he said. "Would you believe I saw a Christian cross and Portuguese chairs, tables, and dishes in a high ranking samurai's Edo home not more than a week ago?"

Jii rocked back in the expected disbelief. "The old ways are the best ways, Fusa," Jii stated. "We should carry them on in our children."

Fusa nodded appreciatively. Then he turned back to the center of the room. "But your home is almost like a battlefield headquarters. I see no feminine touch here. Do you not give your wife free hand in the home?"

"Hai, Fusa. I lost my wife several years ago to the spring fever, and my nephews have not taken brides yet," Jii offered.

Fusa nodded agreeably. "Yes, it is hard when we outlive our loved ones." Then, abruptly, he looked back at Jii. "I would love to spend the evening drinking and honoring our fallen comrades, but we must depart once the horses are rested."

"Yes, reminiscing is what we old men do best," Jii laughed. "Please follow the page to your rooms and bath. Refreshments await you afterward. We will wake you at first light. We'll catch up another time." Jii bowed.

"Thank you for your hospitality," the chief messenger said, returning the bow. Then they stood up and filed out of the great room in procession behind a young samurai boy.

Once the messengers had left, Hideki spun toward Jii and was about to speak when Jii held up his hand to stop him. Jii turned to the chief counselor on his right. "Please dismiss the men and set the watch."

The chief counselor bowed. "Hai." Then he spun to face the men along both sides of the room. "Mina-san, everyone is dismissed. Section one takes the first watch."

When all the men had bowed and walked backwards facing Nagamasa, bowed again at the entrance and departed, Hideki could not contain himself any longer.

"Finally, Edo at last!" he exclaimed. "It's where I've always wanted to go. I can visit all the famous dojo's and maybe even get a lesson from the Yagyu themselves."

Jii frowned in disappointment, happy now that he had dismissed the retainers so quickly. "It is always 'you' that you think of first. When will you learn that a samurai must serve others first?"

Hideki frowned. "Okay, who should I be thinking about?" he asked.

"He means me, Hideki," replied Nagamasa.

Hideki looked at his brother in surprise. "Why you?"

Naga smiled. "Because, little brother, we are being summoned to Edo and we have to go quickly. That in itself is a huge undertaking. Then, upon arrival, the counselors of the Tairo and the Roju will judge us. They will test us to see if we are worthy. But the real reason Jii wants you thinking of someone other than yourself involves the fact that two shogun heirs and family members have met with premature deaths in the last month. All died at the hands of a band of deadly thieves plaguing Edo that call themselves the Fox Gang. The entire Yorifusa family, including men, women, and children, were wiped out last week, or so said one of the messengers."

Hideki dramatically gripped his sword hilt. "You expect trouble?"

Jii answered for him. "We always expect trouble Hideki. The closer we get to Edo, the more we have to expect trouble from foe and friend alike."

"Let's be very wary," said Naga. "Let's start with doubling the guards and let all know what happened to the Yorifusa. We're a long way from Edo, but we should start being careful from this moment forward."

Jii nodded in agreement. Hideki nodded as well. "It shall be as you say, Naga," Hideki said.

Fifty feet away and one level up, Yoshi silently folded his looking glass again as the sliding doors below were closed into place in the great room across the courtyard.

"Just my luck," thought Yoshi. "Doubling the guard means I'll have to catch them in Edo or along the way. Then Yoshi thought of a way to turn the bad news into something good. He could swing by the village and visit his family in the next few days. There was no way the Yoshinobu could ready themselves for travel in less than three days. The thought brought a smile to the assassin's face.

Yoshi placed the looking glass into one of several pouches sewed inside his outer garment and moved through the rafters on mouse feet. He exited the building via the loosened roofing thatch and moved along the roof to the tree with large limbs overhanging the thatch. After a short climb down and a jump over the mansion walls, he was into the shadows along the dirt road that made up the main thoroughfare of the village. He removed the hood and wrap that covered all of his face except his eyes, then took off his black ninja jacket and reversed it to reveal a drab gray color with the symbols for Abe Courier Service. His small straight ninja sword tied across his back was removed and wrapped in a brown woven mat with the gray side out and tied across his back for the world to recognize as his outdoor sleeping mat. Next, he retrieved a six-foot staff and a large box wrapped in a gray kerchief. The staff went through the kerchief and everything went across his shoulder.

Yoshi paused a moment to get into character. He thought about a courier and his distinctive gait, visualizing the rhythm, playing it over in his mind. Then he started the shuffling lope that was faster than a walk but slower than a run. It was the gait used up and down the Tokaido, the road connecting Kyoto to Edo, by couriers to conserve energy but eat up miles. A short time later, he was at the entryway of his temporary abode. It was a dilapidated shack but home while he needed it. He first checked for any signs left by friendly people of the grass. Seeing none, he then instinctively looked for any obvious disturbance caused by an enemy. Only then did Yoshi approach the broken wooden door. He was about to slide it back when he quickly and silently jumped to the right. His haragai sense had alerted him—someone was in his shack.

Yoshi was about to retreat when he heard a distinctive feminine voice. "Kyotsukete, ne, Yoshi. Why are you so nervous? You are among friends."

Yoshi stepped into the shack, turned around and sat down in the iriguchi to remove his footwear. With his back to the one room shack and his feet at street level, he reached down to untie the straw lowers and cloth uppers that were the distinctive purview of the working class. He then ladled out water from the wooden bucket, poured it into his neck cloth and began washing his legs and feet. Once clean he repeated the process in a pottery bowl for his face and hands. Then he stepped up into the living quarters and faced the female ninja.

"Dostano?" Yoshi asked. "What do you want?"

"Why so irritable, Yoshi?" she replied. "We are on the same team."

"Is that the team that poisoned my wife?"

"She was never in any danger," Sachi said dismissively. "We needed something to get your attention."

"Well, you got my attention and my blood," Yoshi stated, thinking of his fingerprint on the contract. "So I ask again, what do you want?"

Sachi frowned. "I see being nice to you isn't going to work. Okay Yoshi, I want to know what progress you have made."

"I've located the family dwelling and identified the key members. I've determined it is too early to map their movements as they have not made any," he stated as if talking to an infant. "And if you are going to be bothering me with constant reports and second guessing, you can forget the contract."

"You know that isn't possible without making your wife a widow," Sachi reminded. "You've infiltrated the mansion?"

"Of course."

"Any chance of taking the target in the mansion?" she asked.

Yoshi thought before he responded. "None that I've seen that allows for any egress. The compound is a little different than most. There are outbuildings just in from the compound wall that surrounds the main building. Getting from the outbuildings to the main building is the problem, and they have just doubled the guards." Yoshi continued without answering Sachi's raised eyebrows. "Stealth won't do. I'd have to infiltrate and that would take a long time to set up."

Sachi nodded. "So you will have to wait until they leave the compound?"

"Yes," Yoshi replied. "But we may be in luck. I think they are leaving for Edo this week."

"You think?" asked Sachi. "Thinking is not satisfactory."

"Well we are not all as perfect as you. Some of us must think before acting. I was across the compound in an outbuilding trying to read lips. It is not my specialty."

Almost speaking to herself, Sachi murmured, "I told the Oyokata we should not use an amateur for such a mission."

"If you want to call the whole thing off, it is fine with me," Yoshi snapped.

"You know that will not happen. We are not as rigid as our samurai cousins, but to cancel a contract would not reflect well on the head of the Five Families," she firmly stated.

"So that is what he is," said Yoshi. "I thought so, but could not be sure. What are you to him?"

Sachi smiled for the first time. "So, now you are interested in me?"

"Only in a survival sense," Yoshi stated. "Do not flatter yourself."

Sparks danced in her eyes and she instinctively reached into her garment top. Then she relaxed and withdrew her hand. "I was right. You are an unsatisfactory choice in so many ways," she said flatly.

Yoshi poured water into the teapot and hooked the handle on the kagizuru, a chain suspended from an overhead beam positioned above the sand pit in the middle of the room. Then he started a fire with the kindling and charcoal at the edge of the sand.

"Okay, so answer the question. What are you to the head of the Five Families?" Yoshi demanded.

"I am his sempai," she announced proudly.

Yoshi looked up in astonishment. "You mean if the old man dies, the Five Families are to be led by a woman?"

"What of it? I plan and direct most of the operations now," she snapped back.

Yoshi slowed his breathing. She had just admitted she ran the Five Families. Was he supposed to know this? Why is this cold killer almost flirting with me? He had better tread lightly.

"My apologies, naesan," Yoshi said as he bowed slightly. "I'm sure you are very good at what you do or the old man would not have you doing it. Having a woman in such a high position just took me by surprise."

"I am not your older sister," Sachi snapped, then immediately calmed. "So you could work for a woman?" She moved to the fire and placed two teacups on the raised wood border of the pit.

Yoshi nodded. "Of course, I am working for one now, or so it seems."

Sachi took out a small pouch and placed a pinch of tea into one cup and was about to do so for the second cup when Yoshi reached out with amazing speed and snatched it with his hand. Sachi looked up with a blank expression. Yoshi smiled and placed his own tea into the second cup.

Sachi smiled. "Maybe you are not an amateur after all, Yoshi-san."

Yoshi bowed. "If I was really good, I would be boiling and scrubbing the inside of the pot as well."

"No need," Sachi said as she poured the boiling water first into Yoshi's cup and then her own. "We still need you."

Yoshi sipped the tea and smacked his lips. "Oishi desu," he said in appreciation. Then he physically relaxed.

"So tell me, daughter of the Five Families, why you have reservations about me."

Sachi sipped her tea and thought for a moment. "How do I tell you without giving offense and thereby endangering the mission?"

"Why not just tell the truth?" Yoshi suggested.

"Very well," she said. "You are young. Ergo your focus and dedication are called into question."

"It is true that you are older than I," Yoshi agreed.

That comment won him a scowl. "I have been studying since I was six," she stated.

"So has every ninja in all of Japan," Yoshi countered.

"Yes, but I have been studying with the head of the Five Families," Sachi said.

"Well, he may not have been the head of Five Families, but my father was well respected by many, including the head of the Five Families," Yoshi stated. "And he was my mentor before I was six."

Sachi sighed. "Okay, let's say you have made your point. The second character flaw is the gravest anyway," she continued. "You are an idealist and a romantic."

"What is wrong with that?"

"You think too much," Sachi accused. "You most likely married that peasant girl out of some sense of obligation. You protect her family when that brother of hers is almost useless and her mother is nothing more than a witch with a knack for forest goblin brews." Then, without stopping, she asked, "Why didn't you wait for a more suitable match?" Before he could answer, she continued. "You are conflicted. You are an assassin, and by the Oyakata's words, a good one, yet you live your life to please others. I cannot totally trust an assassin who helps others. That is why I find you dangerous to this mission," she triumphantly concluded.

Yoshi sipped the last of this tea. "I see. Then nothing I say will change your mind." He started to put out the fire.

"No argument?" she asked. "No witty rebuttal? Now would be the time to change my mind and to reaffirm your allegiance to the Five Families and myself."

"No, I have made it a habit not to argue with stubborn people," he sighed.

Yoshi put out the fire, retired to the far corner of the dark room, pulled up his gray blanket, and went fast to sleep. He hoped she would not slit his throat.

Chapter 6: Succession

Sachi lifted the basket that was concealing her entire head. The straw area from which she normally peered had most of the weave thinned and was fine for looking forward, but it distorted her peripheral vision. She needed all of her senses now. With her basket hat, white kimono stuffed into a white hakama tied at her knees and below her calves with white kiahan gaiters, white tabi and waraji sandals, and holding a shakuhachi flute, she looked every bit a komuso—a "priest of nothingness." They were famous for visiting the shrines of Edo and few people paid them any attention as they usually asked for alms.

She saw nothing out of place and slowed her pace as she came upon a small noodle shop. Upon entering, she heard the greeting "Irashiai dozo" from the shop woman who was moving from one hard wood table to the next. Once heard, the cook behind the counter echoed the welcome but with a monotone sighing that betrayed the sincerity of the greeting.

Sachi bowed slightly and took off her basket hat. She held it in one hand with three fingers displayed on the outside as she said "Ocha desu ka?"

"Hai," the shop Girl's reply came as she moved behind the counter to bring the requested tea.

Sachi sat down on the wooden bench and placed the shakuhachi on the rough tabletop. She pushed her hair back into place as she scanned the shop's patrons. It was not difficult. There were only three. Judging by the smell emanating from their leather vests, dirty loincloths, and muddy straw sandals, the two stable men had nothing for her. They were too busy loudly slurping noodles from their wooden bowls. The third man was elderly with gray hair and a scar that ran from his chin to above his sightless left eye. He seemed unimportant. Nevertheless, he held his teacup with three fingers showing on his left hand. Sachi made the countersign by placing two of her fingers of her left hand on her face. The old man moved two fingers to his dead eye as if it still bothered him.

Sachi sipped her tea, watching the wide dusty street and the constant procession of town people, beggars, samurai, and ronin that passed in the human parade staged on every street throughout the bustling capital of the Tokugawa shogunate. Even though she had gotten the "all clear" signal from the old ninja watcher, Sachi wanted to see for herself. She knew her craft. Relying on others could get you killed. She savored the full cup of tea and convinced herself that the old spy had been correct. Nothing was out of place. No one was watching the Edo domain of the Five Families that was located directly across from the noodle shop.

Assured of her safety, Sachi placed one copper coin on the table, picked up the long flute, placed her basket hat over her head, exited the noodle shop, and walked directly across the street to the Abe Courier Service shop. She parted the two-piece cloth curtain and stepped onto the welcoming alcove, then she turned around and, removing her sandals, sat facing the street. To her left she noted the straw cloaks hanging on wooden pegs with a simple wooden nameplate above them. There were ten pegs in all. Half were empty.

As Sachi stepped up to the main floor, she called, "Tadaima," thus alerting the household of her return. Immediately a feminine voice responded with "Okaire." It was more than a welcome. It was recognition that Sachi posed no threat to the inhabitants of the large store and could go about their business as usual.

Sachi would have liked to go to her room, get out of her traveling clothes, and have a nice hot bath, but that would have to wait. Hoping that she did not smell too badly, she moved to the central quad that opened onto a square courtyard boasting flowers and a single cherry tree that had lost its bloom several months ago.

Of all her childhood memories, coming here with her father in spring to view the flowers and the cherry blossoms was among her favorites. She sighed. Then she laughed. It ranked right up there with crippling that ronin on her fourteenth birthday when she was at the hot spring in Hakone. The idiot had tried to rape her, but it had been a bad mistake on his part. Any further sexual pleasures he would enjoy would be vicarious.

Now that she thought about it, this Edo headquarters held many good memories. She remembered slipping the sharpened hairpin into the base of the skull of the Yoshiwara pimp and watching him twitch himself to death. She had been sixteen when tasked to infiltrate a high-class brothel on her father's orders. The pimp had been a pig who had gotten rich on the bodies of young women. They lived in squalor while he lived in a big comfortable house. They drank stale water, ate millet, and tried to work off impossible debt while he drank sake and ate sea bream. He had deserved to die.

The ability to kill and steal away was not the real attraction in her life. It was the freedom and empowerment. She could go anywhere and become anyone. She had seen things that no nobleman's wife would see. She had done things that they could never imagine.

True, she would probably never marry nor have kids; her destiny lay in another direction. She ran a network of sixty-five spies and assassins, and she knew more about the country than most diamyos. She certainly knew more about life than their dutiful wives who stayed home keeping the cook fires burning while their self-important husbands drank and whored in town. Samurai wives would seldom travel and most would never leave the confines of their little domains. She, on the other hand, came and went as she pleased. Her training gave her great confidence. Unlike most women of the age, she did not live in fear. She knew from experience that she could fight and win against most samurai, and very few ninja would offer her much of a problem either. She had absolutely nothing to fear from everyone else.

Overall, life was good. Yes, killing that pimp had been enjoyable. Not all missions were. She hated some, but she could not choose her assignments. When she went out, people died. Sometimes she did not like it, but she did it. It was who she was. She had come to terms with it. Either she would inherit the Five Families, like her father wanted, or she would meet her own death. She was ready either way.

Sachi knelt at the closed paper door and uttered, "Moshiage masu," to signify she was reporting. The door slid back from the inside, revealing her father seated cross legged in the company of five men. As Sachi moved onto the tatami flooring inside the room, she knelt and bowed first to her father and then to the five men.

"What news have you, Sachi?" asked her father.

Sachi bowed again. "The preparations are proceeding, but our man could not get to the target in Kii," she reported. The old man raised his eyebrows, but did not ask a question. Sachi proceeded. "He infiltrated the compound and had a plan in place when the target's family was summoned to Edo. He will have to strike along the way or in Edo."

One of the five men glanced at the old man. He received a slight nod in return. The man addressed Sachi. "Hime," but before he could get out the rest of his inquiry, Sachi interrupted him.

"Don't call me that! I am no princess."

The old man bowed and apologized. "Gomen nasai, oyabun. No offense was meant. Isn't waiting until Edo dangerous? The metsuke spies are bound to spot him."

Sachi smiled, but her eyes did not. "Yes, Ichi, it is dangerous. No doubt if we had given your family the task instead of this outsider, you would have executed it by now." Her words revealed the hidden condemnation in Ichi's question.

Another man spoke up. "We all assume you brought in this country cousin for a reason. We know not to second-guess the oyabun of the Five Families. We just wonder if a mission of such importance should have been entrusted to someone outside the families."

Sachi looked to her father.

The old man fixed his gaze on the questioner in the fifth position. "Is that how you feel also Go-san?" Then, addressing the group, "Is that how all of you feel?" The fifth man nodded. The old man repeated the question for the second, third, and fourth positions. They all nodded in agreement that bringing in an outsider was a problem.

"Okay," the old man said calmly. "You are all excused. We will meet again by the regular signal."

Upon their departure, the old man smiled at Sachi. "And what did you think of the Five heads of our ikki today?" he asked.

Sachi frowned. "They are dull men who seem to question everything."

"And do you know why?" her father asked.

"My guess would be they are old and unimaginative men," Sachi stated.

"They are testing you," he said.

Sachi looked surprised. "I have led this ikki for over five years, why are they testing me now?"

"Because we are vulnerable and they sense it," he replied.

Sachi did not answer. Knowing the ways of her father, she opted for silence.

The old man continued. "I am already ten years older than the last head of the Five Families when he died of old age. My days are numbered, and they have made pacts with each other to ensure you do not succeed me."

"The bastards," she cursed. "I will kill them in their sleep."

"Sachi," the old man chided, "when are you going to start using your head instead of your sword?"

Sachi bowed. "Gomen. I am sorry, Father."

"How much support do you think you can count on when I'm gone?" he asked.

"From what you just said, none."

"And why do you think I picked Yoshi for this mission over the Five Families' objections, as well as your own?"

"I assume he has some skill you value, or that you want blame to fall outside the Five Families," she said.

"Correct on both counts, Daughter," he said proudly. "Yoshi is skilled. In fact I would say that Yoshi may be the best around."

"Father, I've watched him. He almost walked into his shack without noticing me inside," she protested.

The old man smiled. "Almost is the difference between living and dying in our world. Call it luck, call it karma, haragai, or witchcraft. He's almost failed in four different assignments, but didn't," the old man stated. "But more importantly, you need a man who is loyal. You see tonight what you are facing with the succession. So tell me how you and Yoshi got along."

"Not so well," she said, making two fists in her lap. "He is the most exasperating country bumpkin I've ever met. He has no respect for our positions; he acts like he knows everything and doesn't need our help; and he still blames us for poisoning his wife."

"He will get over that," the old man mused. "He will know that the poison wasn't lethal as soon as he spends some time at home with his mother-in-law. Her mastery of herbs and potions is impressive." He pulled his long, narrow pipe from his obi at his waist and fished for his netsuke charm that was attached to the tobacco pouch. He placed a pinch in the tiny bowl and ignited it with the candle from the paper lantern at his elbow. "Tell me what you think of him as a person."

Sachi took a deep breath. She knew there were no single questions with her father. Everything was a test. "He must be as skilled as you say, as he got into and out of the Kii mansion quickly and was able to gather good intelligence."

The old man nodded, which was his way of saying, "continue."

"He is skillful at camouflage. I watched him approach his shack from a position he could not see, and his acting as a courier was flawless. I would have sworn he was one of ours."

"And?" the old man prompted.

"And that ability of his to see through walls is a little bit unnerving," she admitted.

"Haragai," the old man stated.

"Yes, haragai," Sachi repeated. "I've never known anyone

who possessed it." Then, looking directly at her father, she asked, "Does anyone in the Five Families possess this ability?"

The old man tapped his pipe into the small brazier to his left. "Not anymore. It is a lost art, I'm afraid."

"So why does he have it?" she asked.

"Who knows?" the old man replied. "I've only known one other and that was Yoshi's father. Some say it is part of the black arts, wrapped up in the ability to cast spells and place people in a trance. I do not know about that. I was taught the black arts and I don't have this ability."

Sachi asked another question. "So haragai is why you chose him for this mission over my objections?"

The old man rekindled his pipe and took a puff. "What were those objections again?"

"You know very well. He is too young and he is loyal to the wrong people. He is weak," she stated.

"Oh yes, now I remember. He chose a childhood friend as a wife and keeps her brother and mother around," he stated with a nod. "Anything else?" he asked.

"Just that you can't tell him anything because he won't listen. Do you know that he went to sleep right in front of me? It was like he was taunting me to put a knife in his ribs," she complained.

"Did you?" he asked.

"No, Father. You know I would not go against your decisions."

"So let me summarize, my daughter. He is skilled, he is loyal, he possesses power we thought lost to the shinobi, and he trusts you enough to turn his back on you because he knows you would not defy me. Is that about it?"

Sachi smiled. She was always amazed at how her father was one-step ahead of everyone else. "I understand Oto-san. In light of the heads of the ikka questionable support of me, you want Yoshi to act as my aniki. As a big brother, he is loyal, thinks of others before himself, and is skillful and respected. His ability in haragai is an added plus. Even the dullards I saw tonight could not find fault with him."

"That's my girl," her father beamed.

71

"Unfortunately, I do not think he has any use for either of us," she said.

"Do not worry; that will change. Did you tell him of my succession plans?"

"Yes, as you instructed, Father," she confirmed.

"What was his response?"

"He laughed—the rat," she said.

The old man smiled. "As I would expect. But the seed is planted. I have a feeling we are going to need Yoshi's talents before long."

Sensing despondence, she asked, "What is it that you fear, Father?"

The old man tapped his tobacco ashes into the dead brazier. "Someone is playing for very high stakes," he replied.

"Of course, Father. We are targeting one of the Tokugawa heirs."

"Who contracted us?" the old man asked.

"The money came from the brother of a Roju member," she said.

"So someone in the Tokugawa government is attempting to control the outcome of the shogun's succession," he said.

"Nothing new in that," she commented. "They do not call it kyodai goroshi for nothing. Fratricide in the government is what keeps us busy."

"True, but why did they come to us?"

"What do you mean Father? The Five Families have existed for one hundred years," she defended.

"True, but we are not the largest. The Iga and Koga shinobi are much larger. Why not go to them for this contract?"

"I assume they want to remain anonymous," she suggested.

"Yes, and what better way to remain anonymous than to eliminate the assassins after the deed?"

Sachi did not have to fake her shock. "You think we are in danger?"

"I am sure of it, Daughter," he stated. "How have the other heirs died?"

"If you believe the street papers and criers, they were

killed by bandits during robberies—bandits called the Fox Gang."

"Bandits, huh?" he sneered. "How is it a bandit gang wanted throughout the country raids at will in some of the best protected houses in the nation? Why have the police no leads? Why have we no information on them? Why have Hittori Hanzo and the metsuke no leads? How can a bunch of dim-witted bandits elude the government and the shinobi on mono?"

Sachi shook her head. "You are correct. That is most disturbing. Do you suspect the police are in league with the gang?"

The old man shook his head in exasperation. "Just when you make me proud, you miss the point."

"Gomen Oto-san," she apologized. "What is the point?"

"Think Daughter! What does having no clues on such a large and obviously talented bunch of killers suggest?"

Sachi sat upright. "They are *ninja*," she blurted.

"That's more like it, Daughter."

"But who?" she questioned.

"Unknown. And that is what worries me. It is neither the Iga nor the Koga, as they both protect the Tokugawa. Hattori Hanzo and the Iga run the metsuke and provide security for the Edo castle, but the Koga are on retainer as well for security. So it must be some family we know little about who is well funded and well informed and working for someone with a lot to gain."

"But Father, someone hired us and you think they will try to eliminate us. If the Fox Gang is ninja, won't the same fate await them?"

"Good point," he praised. "Now you are projecting. However, your logic is more the cause for worry. We are the Five Families, but how many mission-ready ninja are we?"

Without hesitation, she responded. "We are sixty-five strong, but spread over the country."

"Yes," he said. "And how many do you think it would take to wipe out a well-garrisoned mansion like the one wiped out by the Fox Gang?"

Sachi went to work thinking aloud. "Three teams of five

for surveillance. Then send in a team of five for ghost technique to infiltrate and cover the assault. Thirty more needed to carry out the assault and ten to cover the extraction. All in all fifty to sixty ninja."

"Correct," he said. "Even if we had enough time to recall everyone, we would be hard pressed to execute this type of operation, and we are the Five Families. So how do fifty or sixty bandits travel throughout the country without detection?"

"They would either need passes issued by someone high up in the government or they would have to be very good shinobi," she answered.

"I think both," her Father provided.

"So they do not expect to be eliminated for their efforts because ... ," she started.

"Because they expect to be part of the government when their man is shogun," the old man finished for her.

Sachi shivered. "How do we get out of this, Father?"

The old man poked the dead ashes in the brazier with his cold pipe. "I do not know."

The words provided no comfort to the successor of the Five Families.

Chapter 7: Ichijoji Temple

It was getting dark and Hideki was tired. Still, he felt good. Naga and Jii were eating their evening meal safely tucked away in the ryokan. The guard throughout the inn was set. Hideki had inspected it twice, and now the responsibility for the family security rested on the shoulders of the night commander. Hideki was finished. It was still early; maybe he could sneak out and see some of the sights of Kyoto.

Dressed in his ronin garb of gray uwagi uppers with baggy indigo hakama trousers, he could pass for a young ruffian in any of Japan's major cities. He wore straw sandals with ankle high tabi socks and a tenegui head cloth folded and worn as a hachimaki headband instead of a head wrap, completing the attire with a pair of matching high quality old swords stuffed through the obi on his left side.

He intended to explore each of the fifty-three major stops along the Tokaido, the most famous road in Japan. It linked the ancient capital with the new one in Edo, and it was as close as he was ever likely to come to exploring the country. Unfortunately, he knew they would not stop at all fifty-three. He also knew none would compare with Kyoto.

If Naga became shogun, Hideki's life would change. His carefree days were numbered. He would have endless trivial responsibilities and duties and would be under the watchful eyes of the metsuke spies. If Naga did not become shogun, then both of them would be trying to dodge assassination. Therefore, he reasoned, he might as well discover what he could while he could.

He could not believe his luck when Jii had announced they would travel north from Kii to pick up Japan's major highway in Kyoto. Jii said he wanted to see the old capital once more before he died ,and it would be good for Naga and Hideki to see the city where the emperor lived. It was not until later that Jii explained they would not get to speak with the emperor. The emperor was politically perceptive enough not to hold an audience for any potential heir to the Tokugawa. To agree to an audience with the Yoshinobu would be perceived as favoritism, and the emperor owed his livelihood to the largesse of the Tokugawa shogunate.

He had traveled through town and found one martial arts dojo, but their evening session had almost ended. It was just as well. He had seen nothing that he wanted to learn. He turned toward the lights and walked further into town where he found himself in the entertainment quarter. It was brash and raucous. Hideki felt himself grabbed and spun around. A painted woman many years his senior smiled and asked, "Hey samurai, let's go inside for a drink and a good time."

Hideki's mouth must have been open, staring at her one bare breast and half open kimono. He pulled away. "Sorry, I have an errand to run," he gasped

The painted woman looked disappointed.

"Boys, boys, boys; that is all I see. When is a man going to come to town?" she asked no one in particular. Then she looked for someone more pliable.

The scene repeated itself several more times as Hideki slipped through the section. It was not that he was not interested; it was that whenever this type of temptation was facing him, he remembered Jii's admonition: "To sow our seed is easy. But the Christian pox awaits those that frequent the entertainment quarters. And what of your future wife?" Jii set very high standards, Hideki thought. However, he had to admit, although he knew little about the opposite sex, he remembered the warmth Jii and Oba-san shared. Naga had said their parents had possessed it as well, but Hideki was too young to remember his own parents. Still, he had seen the warmth between Jii and his grandmother. As much as she had loved and doted on the two boys, she always had an extra smile and seemed happiest when Jii entered the room. According to Jii, feeling for someone is what made life worth living. Hideki knew her death had hit the old man hard. He had not showed much interest in anything until the shogunate succession came up. Then Hideki had caught a glimpse of the old Jii—giving orders, taking charge, running things.

Hideki kept walking. He stopped, trying to get his bearings. He was not sure where he was. Before him was a large compound with a huge empty lot in front. Around the lot was a waist high rock wall. A large red tori gate signaled the entryway through the wall. When he came abreast of the gateway he saw that the shrine was called Shisendo and that it was dedicated to poets. The temple behind was called Ichijoji. "I care little for poets or temples," Hideki reminded himself, but he was tired and thirsty from walking. A small wooden sign on the gate indicated cool water for weary travelers at the temple well, so he entered.

As he passed into the expansive lot, he heard distressed conversation coming from the porch of the temple. A young girl with peasant clothes was kneeling on hands and knees bowing and pleading. Hideki could not see her face, but her voice sounded young, a teen perhaps. She was under duress.

"Doshin sama, dozo," she pleaded with the police officer. "I have told you all I know. Please believe me."

The objects of her supplication were two men standing on the highest steps just below the temple porch. One was a short, powerful-looking fellow with a round face that looked kind of pinched in, Hideki thought, as though he wanted to sneeze. Sneeze Face was dressed in a summer kimono, but wore it with the hem raised and tucked into his obi, thus revealing white legs and a dirty fundoshi loincloth. When the moon moved from behind a cloud, Hideki saw a long toothpick dangling from his mouth. He was talking around it and tapping his thigh with a jutte. Hideki could never understand the use of such a short and very defensive weapon. The jutte has a short metal truncheon-like center tine of one and one half shaku length with a single upturned tine off the center shaft, supposedly to capture swords. Hideki held the samurai's contempt for such a weapon. Although the weapon was the hallmark of the police, it just looked inferior to a sword in every way.

"Maybe this jutte will take you back to the station and beat some sense into your rather pretty body," Sneeze Face threatened.

"No, please doshin-sama. The abbot will be back shortly. He can vouch for me. I have not left the temple all day," she pleaded.

"Quit your whining. We're liable to take you in and play with you just because it is a slow evening and I'm tired of the prostitutes in the town," the tall one said.

Hideki did not like the tall man's appearance. He was much older than Hideki with a scar on his left cheek. He wore his two swords on the right hip. "I guess he is left handed," Hideki quietly surmised. A left-handed swordsman was not normal. Hideki immediately felt the aversion ingrained in his psyche for anything different.

The tall samurai wore a dirty summer kimono, mud splattered around the hem, with a black haori outer jacket that displayed the man's clan mon, a logo which Hideki did not recognize.

Hideki was agitated by the way the girl was treated, but he could not afford to get into trouble. He could just hear Jii's tirade if he got himself arrested. As he came abreast of the three, he could see the girl plainly. She was young. The two men stopped their harassment of her long enough to turn and stare at the intruder.

"What are you looking at?" the tall one demanded.

For a brief moment, Hideki saw hope on the young girl's face. Then it faded as he responded, "Nothing," and continued to the well and shrine in front of the temple.

"Young hooligan," the tall officer spat as he turned his attention back to the girl.

As he came abreast of the well, a gray-clad courier exited the temple carrying a small, cloth-wrapped bundle and a jo in his left hand. He placed the short staff over his shoulder and started down the steps. He stopped when he saw Hideki, then cast a glance at the two doshin and girl engaged in an intense argument.

Hideki reached for the ladle in the water when a loud shriek from the girl made both he and the courier spin in her direction. Sneeze Face had just touched the girl with his jutte under the left breast. "Dame! Dame!" she screamed, trying to get them to stop.

The courier took a seat on the steps next to the well with his short staff positioned between his feet and passing over his shoulder. He took out a cloth and dusted his leggings. When he spoke, Hideki almost jumped.

"Kage-san, kyotsuke ne, she is quite young."

The two stopped their interrogation of the girl and moved over to investigate this new form of entertainment. "What did you say, vermin?" Sneeze Face asked.

The courier continued to knock dust off his ankles and feet as he responded. "I just asked you to take it easy on the girl as she is very young."

"And who are you to interfere with police business?" the tall officer demanded.

"Just a traveler who thinks the sanctity of this temple is being violated," the courier said, looking up at the two.

Without warning Sneeze Face struck at the courier with his jutte, meaning to split the man's skull. The strike landed instead on the top of the short staff. The courier had moved the jo imperceptibly from its position cradled between his head and shoulder to the point needed to protect his head from the descending blow.

"Outrageous conduct," Hideki said to himself, giving commentary to the cowardly strike by the detective.

As Sneeze Face raised his truncheon a second time to correct his aim, Hideki delivered a concentrated front snap kick to the side of his left knee. There was a loud snap. Sneeze Face collapsed in a scream, holding his knee. The girl grabbed her baskets and ran into the temple and the tall officer moved his left hand to his sword tsuka as he dropped his right foot back in preparation for a draw.

Hideki did not want trouble. He could not afford trouble. He could not afford to die either. All these emotions flooded through his mind. However, the one that trumped them all was Jii's admonition of duty: "There is no wrong too small to right. There is no right too small to defend." Hideki and Naga had heard old Jii's voice teach this from the time they were old enough to learn.

Hideki did not recognize his own voice. "Draw that blade and I'll kill you." He shut everything out. Nothing existed except the pure and certain knowledge that if the left-handed officer started his draw, Hideki would cut him from his right shoulder to his left hip.

No one moved.

Then a voice from the dark of the temple hall said, "He means it policeman. You are finished badgering people tonight. Pick up your baggage and move along. No one here has been impressed."

Hideki did not move. He was staring into the eyes of his opponent.

The unknown speaker moved out of the shadows and onto the porch. Hideki knew his own appearance did not strike fear in the seasoned officer's heart, but this new man was a different matter. He looked strong. His lightweight kimono was thin from use and the katana sheathed in his left hand appeared well-worn in the moonlight. A matching wakazashi short sword protruded from his obi on the left side. His feet were bare and he had a white cloth laid over his right shoulder as if he had planned on a bath. His shoulders were broad and his hair jet black with streaks of gray around the ears. He did not wear the shaved scalp popular in Edo. Instead, he wore a full head of hair tied back in a tall chonmage. His eyes were his most impressive weapon. They were two black coals burning a hole in the tall officer. The unknown speaker looked dangerous.

The officer dropped his hand from his sword and reached down to help his minion up. They proceeded to hobble out to the gate. They almost reached it when the officer turned. "We'll be back," he said.

Hideki breathed again. He wanted to speak but found

he was shaking too much. The courier spoke first.

"Domo arigato samurai-sama," he said, bowing first to Hideki and then to the samurai on the porch.

Hideki finally trusted his voice. "I guess we better leave. He will be back with reinforcements."

The samurai on the porch stepped down beside the courier and sat down to put on his sandals. "I don't think so."

"Why not? We have wounded them and their pride."

"Men like that have no pride," the courier said.

Both samurai looked at him in surprise.

"You are correct courier," the samurai said. "They will have concocted a story by now of their wounding and have moved on to easier prey."

The samurai watched Hideki and said, "You had better get a drink young man. The Ichijoji water is renowned for its coolness."

Hideki dipped the ladle into the water and was about to bring it to his lips when he reversed the handle and presented it to the courier.

"You need this more than I," Hideki said.

The courier looked to the samurai warily as if unsure whether to take it or not. The samurai next to him nodded, indicating it was okay. He gingerly took the ladle and put it to his lips, drinking until the ladle was empty. Before passing it back to Hideki, he took out a cloth and wiped the rim where his lips had touched.

"Domo arigato," he said, then asking, "Why did you give it to me first?".

Hideki took the ladle, dipped it into the pool, brought it toward his lips, and paused. "I did it for two reasons. One, you do look like you have traveled far and therefore needed it more than I did. Secondly, I was honoring your bravery."

"My bravery ... I am not the one who kicked a doshin and threatened to kill a police officer."

Hideki smiled. "No, but you opened your mouth in defense of the girl when I would not. Your actions made me ashamed for not following Bushido."

The sitting samurai smiled. "Amoshiroi. I witness a

courier protect a complete stranger and a sharp-eyed youngster speak of Bushido. How interesting."

Hideki bowed to the older samurai. "Simasen, you probably don't remember me as we were not properly introduced."

"I remember you. You were the only one in the dojo in Kii a couple of weeks ago with sense enough to watch me instead of that idiot instructor I knocked unconscious. That is why I made the comment about you having sharp eyes."

Hideki bowed deeply this time. "Hai, Yoshinobu Hideki desu. Dozo uroshuku onagai shimasu," he announced by way of introduction.

The samurai stood up and returned the bow just as deeply. "Myamoto Musashi, ona gaishimasu," he stated. Then he sat back down. Hideki's mouth must have been open again. "You have heard of me?"

"Yes sensei, who has not? You are famous even in Kii for your many duels. They say you have never been beaten," Hideki managed. "Some say you are Tsukahara Bokuden reincarnated. Some say you are Osensei."

"Osensei?" Musashi snorted. "I am neither Tsukahara sensei nor a sword saint, Yoshinobu-san. I am a traveling ronin on a musha shugyo. I travel the country on my warrior's pilgrimage, trying to perfect myself. And I, like you, try to live by Bushido."

"Musashi-dono. You are living my dream," Hideki proclaimed.

"Call me Takezo, Yoshinobu-san," Musashi said. "Although a samurai, I had humble beginnings and find among friends I prefer my original name."

"Hai," Hideki said. "Please call me Hideki."

"Hideki it is," Musashi said. Then, turning to the courier, he asked, "And what is your name, my courageous courier?"

The courier looked embarrassed. Then he bowed deeply. "I am honored that you speak to me at all. I am just a commoner. I am Yoshi of the Abe Courier Service in Edo. I was delivering a package to the abbot of this temple."

Musashi bowed in return. "A courier perhaps," he stated without emotion. "But I believe you to be more."

Yoshi bowed deeper. "No samurai-san. I am only a courier," he insisted.

Musashi nodded. "As you wish Yoshi, but your skills betray you."

Yoshi raised his eyes to meet Musashi's. "Not many would have noticed," Yoshi complimented.

Musashi brushed off the praise. "To tell the truth, I pay a great deal of attention to men who fight with a jo ever since one defeated me."

Hideki's face showed his surprise. "Takezo, I heard you were undefeated. Is the rumor not so?"

"It is not so, Hideki," Musashi said. "Nor are most of the rumors about me. Twice a young priest and his mother defeated me. The mother was unarmed, but the priest was armed with a jo."

"But how could a short wooden staff defeat a great swordsman like you?" Hideki asked.

Musashi smiled. "How long is your katana, Hideki?"

Hideki responded immediately. "It is two and one half shaku."

Then Musashi turned to the courier. "How long is your jo, Yoshi?"

"Four shaku, samurai-san."

"There is your answer," Musashi said.

"Wait! That doesn't make sense, Takezo," Hideki protested. "If reach were the only answer, then peasants armed with six-foot staffs should defeat a sword every time."

Musashi turned to the courier. "Do you want to tell him?"

Yoshi looked to both men, and then settled his gaze on Hideki. "The rokushaku bo staff is too long. It is six shaku long. It is a good standoff weapon but once a swordsman gets inside it is over for the bo-man. However, the jo's length advantage over a katana does not nullify its advantages. It is short enough to allow reversal of strikes. All the strikes you make with the sword can be duplicated with the jo. In addition, I have the length advantage."

"Well said, master," Musashi praised.

Yoshi looked uncomfortable.

"Domo Yoshi-san," Hideki said. "I think I begin to understand. So I didn't save your life just now and probably landed in hot water with the law for nothing?"

"I wouldn't say for nothing, Hideki-sama. This is the first time in my life a samurai has cared enough to defend me or ask for my advice on anything," Yoshi said.

"You have never talked with a samurai?" Hideki asked.

"Only to be told to get out of the way."

"Well, I don't believe we are that much different, Yoshi," Hideki said.

Yoshi swallowed hard and then continued. "Musashi-sama I understand. He is beyond class distinctions. He lives for his sword. You Hideki-san are obviously high born and privileged. Your speech proves such. Nevertheless, you interfered on behalf of a commoner for justice's sake. Those are not actions expected from samurai. I am intrigued."

"You make too much of it, Yoshi-san. It was you who spoke up first in defense of the girl," Hideki said.

"True, but it was you who shouldered the burden and acted when you thought that I was helpless," countered Yoshi.

"I just cannot believe you have never had a discussion with a samurai," Hideki said.

Musashi intervened. "To address a samurai can end in death for a peasant. Most avoid contact with us. That keeps the peasants alive but ensures the ruling class is seldom in touch with the real world."

"But if you don't talk to samurai, how did you become master of the jo?" Hideki asked.

"You pry too much, Hideki-san," Musashi chided. "Each man has his own secrets. The abbot of this temple is a master of the jo and he was never a samurai nor taught by one. In fact, he was taught by his mother."

"Mother?" Hideki questioned. "I don't believe it. He cannot be much good if taught by a woman."

"Would you rate me as good with this sword?" Musashi asked.

"Of course," Hideki said.

"Then it was the same not so very good jo-man of this temple who defeated me twice," Musashi said.

Hideki looked down at Yoshi, who, smiling, said, "I had not heard that story, but it doesn't surprise me. The abbot is known to be very strong."

"Hideki, your provincial education is showing. That is why you need to take up a musha shugyo of your own. It is how you learn," Musashi said. "There are martial arts all over this country that have no official status or schools. To ensure they live to the next generation they are taught between father and son, mother and daughter, and sometimes mother to son. This knowledge is the priceless heirloom of that family. How do you think the ninja families pass on their skills?"

Hideki nodded. "You are right, Takezo. I misspoke. Jii had just such little known masters come to Kii to teach my brother and myself everything from Naha te to aikijujitsu throwing arts. But none were women!"

"Well, maybe some of them should have been," Musashi said as he slapped his right thigh with his free right hand and laughed.

A young merchant and his wife, bowing to them as they moved to the shrine behind the well, interrupted the three.

"What a night," Hideki said. "I have learned much."

"Yoshinobu is a famous and well-respected name," Musashi said. "On a rainy day many years ago, there was a Yoshinobu who fought with the Tokugawa on the left flank at Sekigahara."

"My grandfather," Hideki said. "He is a wise and good man. He raised my older brother and myself."

"You are lucky, Yoshinobu-san," Musashi said.

"Yes, I know. He brought us up after my parents died. He raised us well," Hideki said with conviction.

Musashi tilted his head slightly. "I was a very young man at Sekigahara and witnessed his bravery from the other side."

The merchant couple's loud clapping interrupted the three again.

"They must be raising the kami asking for a child. This temple has developed a reputation for making a barren wife fertile—if the gods answer when you awaken them with clapping hands," Yoshi said. When the clapping stopped, he continued. "What of you young master, what are your plans?"

"What do you mean?" asked Hideki.

"You are about my age, you are educated, you seem to have a refreshing outlook on protecting the defenseless, and you are headed to Edo. As I have said, I have never talked with a samurai before. What are your hopes and plans for your life, if I may ask?"

"Oh, I see," Hideki said. "I guess my future is being planned for me by others." Then, with an excited tone, he added, "but if it was left up to me, I'd be doing what both of you are doing—traveling the country to make it a better place for everyone."

"Now you sound like that bozu Takuan," Musashi said, remembering the rascal priest with fondness.

Yoshi interrupted Musashi. "Wait Musashi-dono—do all Yoshinobu think this way?"

"Oh yes," Hideki answered. "It is what Jii taught us. Why do samurai have power if not to better society? Being a samurai means serving others. The heart of Bushido is the protection of the weak and defenseless. That goes for war, taxes, or anything else," Hideki said. Then adopting the deep guttural rasp of Jii, Hideki quoted, "There is no wrong too small to right and no right too small to defend."

"Wow," Yoshi said. "They are going to love you and your brother in Edo."

"Why?" Hideki asked.

"Because that way of thinking is counter to what the Tokugawa have been doing in the land for the last ten years," Yoshi explained. "What do you think happens every time the government confiscates a diamyo's lands and dissolves a clan? Even the beggars don't outnumber the ronin in Edo."

The couple clapping again interrupted the three.

"The fertility rumor must have something to do with the poetry," Musashi mused.

"Takezo, do you know this temple?" Hideki asked.

"Yes, the head priest lets me stay when I am in the area,

if there are any rooms. We are great friends now," Musashi
replied. "A musha shugyo doesn't allow for much high living. I
must trust in my wits and the benevolence of others."

"I've heard some ronin take jobs as yojimbo to earn their
way," Hideki offered.

"That is true, but then I'd be using my sword for someone's profit. I would not stain my soul by being a rich merchant's bodyguard."

Hideki looked at Musashi. "You are not joking, are you?"

"No, Hideki, I am not."

"I thought, besides Jii, all the real bushi were dead,"
Hideki said. "In our time of peace I never suspected that I
would meet a man who lives by his sword."

"Yoshi is right. There are too many ronin in the land,"
Musashi said. "Not having a master provides us with a freedom
such as most samurai will never know. But freedom comes
with a price, and the main price is hunger. We must live by our
wits and the largesse of others. Speaking of hunger," Musashi
switched, "have you eaten, Hideki?"

"No, Takezo, I have not eaten."

"Excellent," Musashi said as he stood up and placed his
katana in his obi. "You can treat me and Yoshi to noodles at a
stand just around the corner."

"Gladly," Hideki laughed.

Yoshi rose and placed his jo and bundle over his shoulder. Musashi straightened up as Hideki turned toward the
main gate. Then he froze. Coming through the gate were many
armed men. Hideki counted seven. All carried the two swords
of the samurai.

"It looks like the doshin had friends," Hideki observed.

"I don't think so," Musashi said. "I believe they are here
for me."

"Is this a vendetta?" Hideki asked.

"Not an official one," Musashi answered. "But I knew
people were after me."

"They are dressed like scarecrows, not samurai," Hideki
said.

"The swords look real enough," Musashi said.

87

"Yes," Hideki had to admit. "The swords do look real."

"Yoshi, you and Hideki stay out of this; it is my fight," Musashi said. "Try to protect the couple at the shrine. If this is like the last time there will be no safe ground."

"Hai," Yoshi answered.

"I will not, Takezo. There are rules and procedures to follow in Bushido," Hideki stated assertively.

Musashi started to drift off to the right and away from his new friends. "Only in the history books Hideki," he said.

"Who are you?" Hideki demanded of the scarecrows. "State your names and your purpose."

They just kept coming toward the temple. At about three paces distance they pulled their swords as if on command.

"But there are rules and protocols to follow. This isn't vendetta. This is murder," Hideki protested.

"Hideki, either stay out of this or get your sword out," Musashi commanded as he drew both swords.

Then they all charged Hideki. "Amida Buddha," Hideki screamed as he drew his katana using the fast-draw iai style to deflect two incoming blades and step back a pace. He could not believe this was happening—he had gone from a spectator to fighting for his life in the blink of an eye. On reflex he had drawn and on reflex he was now parrying, striking, deflecting, slashing, pivoting, and chopping at any target that presented itself. He cut ankles, he cut elbows, he cut ears, he cut anything and everything he could get close enough to slice, fighting with all his strength and slipping into that zone he had experienced earlier with the police officer. His initial panic turned to pure focus. All of his training made him move. He did not think; he cut.

The initial onslaught lasted for just a few seconds as Musashi and Yoshi both recovered and came to Hideki's side. With three of them fighting, they faced only four remaining scarecrows as three of their original number lay at Hideki's feet. Then things got worse. Springing up from the hip-high wall surrounding the temple, tan-clad men with fox masks poured into the lot. There were many of them. The four remaining scarecrows saw their reinforcements and were motivated to attack anew. They moved forward with the first wave of the foxes.

Musashi had both swords out. Hideki did not want to waste the time to retrieve his short sword. He was too busy blocking, slashing, parrying, thrusting, and trying to stay away from the foxes' shorter and straighter swords. They had very little wasted motion and fought better than the scarecrows.

Hideki became his sword. He reacted to everything around him. He started to feel more pressure on his left as he realized Yoshi was no longer there. Using peripheral vision, he saw Yoshi pinned to the ground by a long sword from one of the scarecrows. Hideki did not have time to see if the sword penetrated flesh or cloth. He did see that one of the foxes was standing over his new friend with a raised sword aiming for a final blow.

Hideki shifted his katana to his left hand. He drew his wakazashi short sword with his right and spun and threw it with all his might at the back of the fox standing over Yoshi. He did not have time to see it he hit his mark because two foxes were trying to disembowel him. He barely got his katana sword back into both hands and parried when Musashi's katana sliced off the arm of one attacker and Hideki charged head-long into the second fox to negate his distance. He could feel the fox's breath but could not see his face, only the lacquered fox face inches from his own. Hideki held the fox's blade down with his right arm and pulled his scabbard from his obi with his left hand, raised it up and smashed it into the fox mask. Both the scabbard and the mask splintered and broke. As the fox stepped back, Hideki executed a high sweeping horizontal strike and sliced his neck with the tip of this katana. The fox dropped to the ground, twitching and gurgling.

Hideki stole a quick glance toward Yoshi. There was no fox at Yoshi's feet with Hideki's short sword sticking out of this back, but Yoshi was busy pulling a short sword out of a scarecrow's stomach as he relieved him of his long sword. Then Yoshi was moving back to Hideki's side armed with two swords. One more wave came and the three stood their ground, killing those in their immediate front and helping to kill those in front of their neighbor. Yoshi handled the swords with an unusual style. Hideki noticed he trapped the opponent's blade with the two swords and then counterattacked to the body all in one motion.

The momentum of the attack eased. Musashi jumped in front of Hideki and slashed into the darkness. Two arrows dropped at Yoshi's feet. "Move behind the well!" Musashi yelled.

They all retreated to the stone well and ducked down. Hideki looked behind them and saw the young couple cowering by the shrine, vulnerable to the arrows. He bent low and ran to them, motioning to cover behind the well, but they did not move. He physically grabbed the woman by the kimono lapel and dragged her behind him to the well. Her husband followed.

Hideki turned to Yoshi. "Yoshi-san, when we go back up, you stay here and ensure these two are protected," he commanded.

"Hai," Yoshi answered.

The arrows were a mixed blessing. As long as they flew in their direction, the foxes could not mount another attack. Therefore, the arrows stopped. Hideki stuck his head above the well and saw another attack was about to be launched.

"Amida Buddha," Hideki muttered. "These people must really hate you, Takezo."

Musashi looked at Hideki and smiled. "It is amazing who you count as friend and foe in this life." Hideki did not have time to think about that remark as the foxes were coming.

Hideki and Musashi assumed their positions in front of the well and met the onslaught head on. The fighting was fierce. Hideki was aware of Musashi hitting the enemy with shoulder blows, head butts, knees—striking them in the face, stabbing them in the mask, hitting them in the throat with the butt of this sword. Both men used everything in their arsenal.

Hideki had never felt like this before. The blood lust was upon him. He was cutting legs, ankles, arms, throats, and ears—anything he could reach. He was a mad man and felt neither fatigue nor fear. He did feel the burn of two cuts on his left forearm, but they were not bleeding much.

"Amida Buddha," Hideki yelled. A fox had broken through his defense and was poised to thrust a straight sword into his ribs. Hideki saw it all in slow motion but could not stop the attack. Musashi was to his right and could not see the danger. He was going to die in a temple yard.

The fox mask exploded as a throwing star broke open the mask and buried itself into a forehead. The fox dropped in a death spasm, a shuriken embedded in his forehead.

There was a bright explosion in front of Hideki and white smoke everywhere.

Musashi waved Hideki back and out of the smoke. The fox men had broken off the attack. When the smoke cleared, only the original seven scarecrows remained on the ground. The foxes had carried off their dead and wounded.

Hideki finally dropped his sword hand but found he had no saya. He had destroyed it on a fox mask. He looked back at the couple. "Anyone hurt?" he asked.

Yoshi looked down at the young couple. They were too afraid to answer.

"No one hurt here," Yoshi said.

Musashi reached into the dirt at his feet and retrieved the wash towel dropped earlier. He inverted his katana so the cutting edge was skyward and ran the towel from the tsuba at the handle all the way to the kissaki at the tip, wiping the blood from his weapon. Hideki had never had to do this before, but he reached into his jacket top and extracted writing paper copying Musashi's ritual.

Hideki was shaking now. He wanted to talk about what had just happened but seemed to be a few seconds responding to anything. "Strange," he said. "A moment ago I was reacting to everything going on about me. Now I can't seem to coordinate my movements."

"Sit down, Hideki-san. Your weakness will pass. It is always the same the first few times," Musashi counseled.

"Here, drink," Yoshi said, offering the full ladle.

Hideki drank and drank. He found he could not get enough. When finished he stopped shaking and felt only numbness.

"You did well Hideki-san," Yoshi said. "I would not have believed this was your first fight."

Musashi slapped him on the shoulder. "You are a true warrior now, Hideki. All has changed. From this night on you will measure everything by the constant of death—yours and others," Musashi said, adding, "I thank you for helping."

Yoshi looked at Musashi. "Musashi-sama, you do realize that entire attack was not aimed at you?"

Musashi ladled a drink and gave it to Yoshi. "Yes, Yoshi, that became evident when they all went directly after our young friend here. It seems we all have some secrets."

"I'm sure I don't know to what you refer, Musashi-sama," Yoshi said after emptying the ladle.

"I'm referring to a shuriken that came out of nowhere to save our young warrior a few minutes ago."

Yoshi filled the ladle and passed it back to Musashi. "It seemed like the right thing to do at the time. I am just curious about a young samurai heading with his family to Edo for what I assume is the sankin kotai system of the alternate attendance which the Tokugawa shogunate demands. That is rather commonplace. What is unusual is to find a highborn samurai, steeped in classics and martial arts, who thinks of someone other than himself. I am very curious to see how long it takes for the Tokugawa powers to want him dead."

"Judging from tonight, not very long," Musashi said. "It is time to enlighten us Hideki-san. We are touched by your courage and willingness to stand up to great odds. But if we are to fight beside you again, I think it is time to tell us who you are."

"I have told you, Takezo. I am Yoshinobu Hideki. I am on my way to Edo on the Tokaido with my family."

"You must be someone of great importance for thirty men to attempt to kill you in front of a temple," Musashi said.

Hideki glanced at Yoshi. He was quiet and looking on with interest. "I am just who I told you. I am nothing. But my brother is on his way to Edo to be interviewed to be the next shogun."

There was a loud clatter as Musashi dropped his sword.

Hideki stooped to pick up Musashi's sword. He had to do it with his left hand as his right still clutched his sword. He held the retrieved sword out to Musashi.

"I know I have no right to ask, but would both of you like to travel to Edo with my family as my guests?"

Musashi was still speechless as he took back his sword.

"I will go with you Hideki-sama. I am tired of sleeping in the open," Yoshi said.

Hideki bowed to Musashi. "Onagaishemasu," he begged. "I would not stain your soul by offering you a yojimbo position, but I think Jii and Naga would love to meet you both. Of course all your travel expenses would be paid."

Musashi finally opened his mouth. "Hai," he said and bowed. "I will travel with you as far as Edo. My sword is yours."

Chapter 8: The Visitors

Jii's eyes flashed his displeasure. "Urusai, Hideki! I have heard enough. If you weren't wandering around the town unescorted we would not be facing this problem."

"That may not be true Jii-san," Naga interjected. "Let us hear from everyone before we decide who we can trust."

"Very well. Bring them in," Jii mumbled as he waved to the samurai page near the sliding wood and paper door.

They had been traveling for four days. Musashi and Yoshi travelled together with the baggage wagons as Hideki wanted time and distance between them and Kyoto before he told Naga and Jii what had happened. He also wanted time for his cuts to heal. It was easy enough to stay away from them during the day, but at night when they expected him at the evening meal he had to devise an excuse lest Naga notice the bandages beneath his yukata summer kimono.

Musashi and Yoshi did not complain. As Yoshi put it, "I've eaten better in the last four days than I have in the previous four months." Musashi had to agree. Even traveling with the porters in the rear meant rice, daikon, and tea at least twice a day and sometimes three. There was sake in the evenings, but neither Musashi nor Yoshi drank more than two small cups a night as neither warrior wanted to dull his senses or his skills in case he had to protect their new young friend.

Tonight the royal entourage had stopped in Miya, the forty-first station on the Tokaido. They had come fifty-nine ri in four days. Jii had been happy with their progress but not happy

95

with the security. Several times he had been gruff with Hideki over the guards being lax or for not watching alertly enough. The closer they got to Edo, the gruffer he became. After the relaxing boat ride across the head of Ise Bay, Hideki had decided that it was as good a time as any to give them the news about the assassination attempt in Kyoto. Jii had decided to opt for the sea journey instead of the overland trek, thinking there would be less chance of ambush on the boats than on the road, and he had been correct. The cruise had been uneventful.

Jii had been angry with Hideki for withholding such important information, then he had become angrier when Hideki had told him that two men had saved him and that he had offered them positions in the train. "Bukka!" Jii had yelled. "You know about kyodai goroshi and yet you place untried warriors in our midst?"

Now, after the storm of Jii's anger had passed, Naga asked, "Are they to be trusted Brother?"

"I do not know, Naga," Hideki said truthfully. "I only know that I trust them and if they hadn't helped me in Kyoto, I would not be here."

That softened Jii's anger. "Good men are hard to find Hideki. Good friends even harder."

A page moved back the door and motioned two men into the large room. Musashi bowed from his kneeling position before entering and bowed again from his knees once inside the tatami floor. He was dressed in a new kimono supplied at Hideki's command. It was brown with a Yoshinobu mon of a plum blossom on the lapels. It was the nicest kimono that Musashi had ever worn.

The second man entered and looked confused. He wore the same brown kimono, but where Musashi filled his out, Yoshi seemed to swim in his. The sleeves were too big and the hem dragged the floor. It gave him a comical appearance. He bowed too much. He was looking to Musashi for etiquette cues.

"Come in gentlemen," Jii said. "Welcome to our temporary quarters."

Both bowed again.

"First of all, I want to thank you both for helping my

grandson in Kyoto. My family is very dear to me. And I must say, if Hideki is to be believed, and he has always been a truthful boy, then you two were heroic."

"We three," Musashi said. "Your grandson reminded me of a warrior I saw in the rain on the left flank of Sekigahara."

Jii laughed. "Ah yes, Musashi-san, I've heard you were there."

"I was on the losing side that day, Yoshinobu-sama," Musashi bowed.

"No matter Musashi-san," Jii said. "The important thing is that you were on the winning side in Kyoto."

"Musashi-san," Naga said, "we are pleased that you decided to travel with us. Your skill with a sword is renowned even in Kii."

"I can think of no better place for it than in defense of the government," Musashi said.

"Well said, Musashi-san," Jii said. "And what of our friend here in the large robe?"

Musashi looked to this right at Yoshi. Yoshi then realized that he was the center of conversation and bowed.

"Yoshi desu ... a courier for Abe Courier Services, Lord" Yoshi said.

The room was fifteen tatami by fifteen tatami. It was a large square. Naga and Jii set at the head of the room facing Musashi and Yoshi. One page was at the entrance of the sliding doors. Along the walls, three armed samurai sat with sheathed katanas in their hands. Hideki sat between Musashi and Naga, a little outside the circle. Jii was opposite Yoshi. Both Naga and Jii had their katanas within reach and a wakazashi thrust into their obi.

"Raise your head, Yoshi," Jii said. "I want to get a good look at the man who saved a temple girl from rogue police."

Yoshi raised his head and looked at Jii. Then his gaze ran to Naga and lingered there.

"Where are you from Yoshi?"

"From a small village in Shiga prefecture, Lord."

"And what brought you to Edo?"

Yoshi looked confused for a minute. "Hunger, Lord."

"Well you look very young to be traveling all the way from Shiga to Edo by yourself, Yoshi," Jii observed.

"My uncle got me the job, Lord," Yoshi said, bowing.

As soon as Yoshi's head went down, Jii grabbed his wakazashi with his right hand in a lighting fast draw and sent the short sword flying at the back of Yoshi's exposed neck. With his head still down, Yoshi rolled to his right, bringing his eyes up, keeping them focused on this new enemy. When he was right side up in a kneeling position, he drew a shuriken throwing star and stared at Naga's forehead. The armed guards reacted to Jii's actions, unsheathed their swords, and moved toward Yoshi.

"Matte," Jii yelled. Everyone froze. "Well, why didn't you use those stars, ninja?" Jii asked.

Yoshi put them back into his sleeve and sat down.

Jii turned to Musashi. "Did you know he was ninja?"

"I suspected as much," Musashi answered.

"So why would you let a ninja into the presence of the next shogun?" Jii asked.

Musashi looked Jii in the eye. "First of all, it's not certain that he is going to be the next shogun. Second, and most important, I watched Yoshi's skill first hand. I watched him save Hideki's life with a shuriken. He could have killed Hideki or Naga anytime in the last four days. Of course, if I'd seen any indication of such, I would have killed him."

Yoshi looked at him. "That's my defense?"

"Sure," Musashi said. "But I think the truth is a little more complicated."

"Keep talking. You've got me boiling in oil now," Yoshi muttered under his breath.

"I think you are an unusual ninja. You are very skilled," Musashi said, nodding to the short sword sticking in the tatami. "Knowing when something is about to happen is pretty spooky, even for a ninja. There is no way you could have known that attack was coming unless you have attained a high level of awareness."

"Mu shin," Jii prompted.

"It might be the bushi no mind, Yoshinobu-sama, but I

suspect something else. I watched him deflect a surprise jutte strike with the end of a jo and not look up once."

Jii nodded in agreement. "You are thinking haragai?"

"Yes, I believe our friend here is a master ninja from one of the old schools," Musashi said.

"Thanks a lot, Sword Saint. Now you have me being skinned alive before boiling in oil," Yoshi muttered.

"But what is every bit as extraordinary as Yoshi's awareness is his sense of justice," Musashi declared. Everyone looked puzzled. "He could have killed Hideki anytime he wanted. I believe him to be so skilled that he could kill Naga and Hideki now and be out of this room before he is wounded."

"Who is your target Yoshi?" Jii asked.

Yoshi looked Jii in the eye. "My target was Naga-sama."

The guards stepped toward Yoshi.

"Matte," Jii said. "Why isn't he dead?"

"Because I wanted to meet the man and the brother who think 'there is no wrong too small to right and no right too small to defend,'" he said, mimicking Jii's voice.

"So what did you decide?" Jii asked.

"That there might be hope for the country."

"Can I assume my grandsons are safe from you?" Jii asked.

"They are safe with me," Yoshi said.

"Will your bosses know you have betrayed them?"

"They will know eventually," Yoshi said. "Initially, they will be amazed at my skill in becoming a part of your entourage. But as we get closer it will become apparent that my allegiance is to Hideki."

"Just to Hideki?" Jii asked.

"Well, I have fought beside Hideki. I know what he believes and that he will die for his beliefs. Pardon me for saying so, but so far all I know about you is that you speak fine words and throw a wakazashi short sword very well."

"Well put, master ninja," Jii said as he stood up and walked over to the spot where Yoshi initially sat and pulled his short sword from the tatami flooring. He sheathed his sword and called for the page to bring refreshments. Jii sat in front of

Yoshi and poured him sake. "But isn't changing sides frowned upon in the ninja clans?"

"Very much so, Lord," Yoshi said.

"Won't this have repercussions for your family in Shiga?" Jii asked.

"Yes. That is why I've alerted them to move back into the mountains."

Jii continued to press. "How was this accomplished? You have been with us for four days."

Yoshi was warming to the task of being the center of attention among important men. "No ninja undertakes a mission without support and backup," he explained. "I have left two messages that no one would discover except the man assigned to follow me and carry out my commands."

"What kind of messages?" Jii asked.

"What do you think if you find five stones piled up on the side of the Tokaido, Lord?"

"That some traveler has constructed his own jizo to honor a departed soul."

"In our clan, the five stones mean there is a message waiting at the next drop site," said Yoshi.

"How do they know what the next drop site is to be?" Jii questioned.

"Prearranged, Lord; five stones means a drop at the next jizo on the same side of the road. Six stones would have meant the opposite side."

Jii looked over his shoulder to Naga. "Amazing what we don't know, isn't it?"

"Truly, Jii, it is. Yoshi, what if someone happens onto the drop site before your pick-up man?" Naga asked.

"Nothing will happen. The message is on a prayer paper and in code. No one will break it," Yoshi said confidently.

Jii turned back to Yoshi. "How many ninja in that clan of yours?"

"We are a pretty small clan, Lord. No more than twenty men."

"Do you know who you were working for? Do you know who is trying to kill Naga?" Jii asked sternly.

"I believe them to be a large ninja group known as the Five Families."

"And this Five Families, how large are they?" asked Jii.

"No one but the head of the Five Families would know that, Lord," Yoshi replied. "But they are known to be large."

"What will happen when they find you have not killed Naga?" Jii asked.

"They will send others to do the job, Lord," he said. "But first they will kill me."

Jii stroked his face and looked into Yoshi's eyes. "We don't use ninja and therefore know little about them."

Yoshi nodded. "You need to get knowledgeable quickly."

"Why?" Jii asked. "Because the Five Families are still out there?"

"That, and because those fox-masked attackers in Kyoto were no bandits. They were shinobi no mono," Yoshi said.

Jii looked at Naga and then to Hideki. He scooted on his knees over to Musashi and poured him a drink. "What is your judgment on all this, Musashi-san?"

"I agree with Yoshi. They were ninja."

"Then we are at a disadvantage," Jii said, then he addressed Yoshi. "I propose that you come to work for the Yoshinobu family."

"But won't we have the Metsuke ninja when we get to Edo?" Naga asked.

"Only if you are selected as shogun," Jii reminded. "Otherwise it may be the Metsuke coming after us."

Jii turned back to Yoshi and bowed. "Onegaishi masu."

Yoshi bowed lower. "Please, Lord, do not bow to me. I am only a common person. I can pledge you my sword but I will have to talk to the village headman about the others. He may not want to go against the Five Families."

"Well, we'll just have to settle for your sword now. What do we need to do first?" Jii asked. "Should you check the entourage to see if we've been infiltrated?"

Yoshi smiled a little sheepishly. "Pardon, Jii-sama, but I already have. No actions have alerted me."

Jii turned to Hideki. "It seems your impetuousness has

paid off for the family. We have trained retainers who would give their lives for us, but they know nothing about the way of shadows. Now we have our own shadow warrior," Jii beamed. Then he turned back to Yoshi.

"Yoshi-san, you have complete access to our family at any time. I put our safety in your hands."

Yoshi bowed deeply. "I will do my best, Lord."

"Musashi–dono, may we count on your sword as well?" Jii queried.

Musashi bowed his head. "You have my word, Yoshino-bu-sama, but only until I can find my replacement."

"Musashi–san, our family will need a fencing master. This could be a change in lifestyle for you," Jii pointed out.

"I pledge you and your family my sword, Yoshinobu-sa-ma, but my life has been dedicated to perfecting my art. I am graying now and have had a lifetime of battles." Then, glancing at Hideki, Musashi added, "I find great comfort in knowing the next generation may be steeped in the traditions of old." Returning his eyes to Jii, he continued. "But you need younger blood that will grow with the new regime. I will give you my sword and my knowledge as far as Edo. Then I must return to my musha shugyo so that I can complete my pilgrimage. I have a lot of knowledge that I want to give. I am thinking of writing a book and will need solitude to finish it. Besides, once in Edo, you will have the Yagyu as your fencing master, and their blades to protect you."

Jii shook his head. "I wish I could trust to that, but they may be part of the problem. At first when I heard of Hideki's lapse of wisdom in Kyoto, I was angry. Then he told me of you fighting beside one another and I began to believe you were sent from the gods. As you well know, there is no bond thicker than combat. I may love my relatives, but I will put down my pipe and pick up my sword for a brother-in-arms un-til my dying day. If Hideki had such friends, then when we get to a town filled with established allegiances at least we would have a cadre we could trust."

Musashi nodded in concurrence. "However, if Naga becomes the next shogun, the Yagyu will still be the hereditary

Tokugawa fencing masters and my presence could cause problems. There are men stalking me."

"If you are under the Yoshinobu name, you are beyond provincial law," Jii asserted.

"True, but how would it look for Naga during the interview with the Tairo and Roju if I was on your staff? They could question his judgment for having a ronin with over sixty deaths on his head."

Jii turned to Naga. "What do you say to that charge?"

"I'd say all Musashi's opponents died with a weapon in their hand, with malice in their hearts, and—most importantly—facing him," Naga replied.

"And I'd say if they doubted any of Naga's words, they can pick up a sword and face me," Hideki chimed in.

Jii nodded. "Bravado is good in the young, but we must face political facts. What Musashi says is correct; his presence could cause us harm. However, I believe his absence, especially for this trip to Edo, would cause us more harm. Therefore, I take you up on your offer to join us to Edo. Once there, you can make up your mind whether to stay or go."

Jii came to his feet, walked back to Naga's side, and kneeled again. Then in his gruff voice, "Musashi-dono, I promote you to the rank of counselor in the Yoshinobu family with a stipend of 400 koku. You are to advise us on tactics and weaponry and be our fencing master. Yoshi-san, I contract with you to be our eyes and ears and to provide us intelligence that you deem beneficial to the Yoshinobu family. Your contract is worth 300 koku." Then, looking at his two grandsons, Jii asked, "Does everyone agree?"

Naga grunted his approval.

Hideki bowed deeply to Musashi and Yoshi.

Musashi turned his head to Yoshi, "See ninja master, no boiling oil for you today. But screw up once in your new position and I'll start cutting wood for the fire."

Yoshi knew Musashi was not kidding.

The next day the entourage passed through Narumi, the forty-first station on the Tokaido, after a three-ri journey of approximately six miles. The town was small but the wide streets had open markets on both sides of the compacted dirt road. They were famous in the region for the tie-dyed fabrics that were suitable for making yukata, the kimono worn in the summer and after a bath. Many of the women in the latter part of the entourage left the procession and started haggling with the merchants. There was plenty of room for their purchases in the horse-drawn wagons in the rear.

The procession made good time as neither the Yoshinobu men nor the retainer's women rode in kogas. The koga was a palanquin conveyance held by two men on their shoulders. Jii, Naga, and Hideki rode horses but kept them at a walk to keep from pulling ahead. Musashi now had a horse and rode beside Jii or Naga. Hideki was on horseback as well but moved up and down the procession to ensure it stayed together and that there were no security breaches. Jii seemed to relax a little with Musashi and Yoshi in attendance. Yoshi started each morning scouting ahead of the procession, then snaked back to the tail end—always alert, always watching everything.

In the midafternoon they passed through Chiryu, the fortieth station. Because Jii wanted to make it to Okazaki by nightfall, the procession did not stop for a noon meal, but pressed on. It was thirteen ri or thirty-two miles from their last stop to Okazaki. This was a punishing march and all were tired by the time they made the entry onto the longest bridge in the country, the bridge over the Yahagi River.

Hideki stood his horse at the entrance of the bridge and marveled. Musashi pulled up beside him.

"I did not know such things existed," Hideki said.

"It is the longest bridge in the country, I am told," Musashi advised.

From where Hideki sat on his horse, he could see the wooden structure arching over the waterway. The bridge floated on trestles driven into the marshes and on into the riverbed itself. At its highest, it stood two rokoshaku bo lengths off the water. It was six men wide with railings on each side approximately hip high. The entire cortege could continue its orderly march onto and across the bridge without reducing into single file.

"Look, Musashi-sama," Hideki pointed. "It is the castle of the great man himself." On the far side of the river stood the castle town of the founder of the Tokugawa shogunate, Tokugawa Ieyasu.

"What I am looking at are the mountains on the other side. I hope we get to rest here a while. Coming thirteen or fourteen ri in a day is hard traveling for the women," Musashi said.

Hideki's face almost frowned as he pondered. "I believe Jii wants to push on tomorrow and spend a day resting in Akasaka."

"Wise choice for the bachelors," Musashi observed, "but I do not know what the wives will say."

"You have been this way before?" Hideki asked.

"Yes. Akasaka is famous for its entertainment quarters. They are said to have the friendliest girls on the Tokaido."

"Musashi, you should be ashamed. We are on an important mission. We cannot be deterred with foolish dalliance," Hideki said with a hint of disdain in his voice.

"Who is talking, you or Jii?" Musashi mused. "You may do as you please, prince of the Yoshinobu, but I intend to let some pretty young thing pamper me in Akasaka."

"Is it really that nice?" Hideki asked a little sheepishly.

"You mean to tell me you have never slept with a woman, Hideki?"

"It is not of importance. A true samurai must focus on the martial arts," Hideki said in defense.

"True, Hideki, but if you don't use your sword, it gets dull."

Hideki spurred his tired horse toward the end of the entourage. Musashi smiled after him. "Jii has neglected some of his training."

When all had arrived and quartered in the inns, they were surprised to find they had official visitors. This threw the tired retainers into a whirlwind of activity as the household made rapid preparations lest Naga lose face. They scrambled for two hours to set the stage for the meeting in the grand room of the largest inn.

Hideki did not have to worry about strange faces causing a security problem as all other travelers were turned away
the day before by the advance team. Yoshi was busy checking
on all of the inn's employees. Finally, after the Yoshinobu had
bathed and changed into their finery, the Yoshinobu samurai retainers bathed and ate in shifts. Then security was set
throughout the inn.

In the grand room, Nagamasa sat on folded legs on the
raised portion of the twenty-six tatami room. Because of the
close proximity of the river to the west and the sea to the
south, there was a very pleasant breeze blowing through the
inn, and Jii had allowed the sliding walls to the grand room to
be opened in order to allow the air to circulate.

Nagamasa was dressed in the two-part kamishino over
a light blue kimono of the finest silk. From the waist up he
wore the sleeveless kata ginu with wide exaggerated shoulders.
On the lapels of the kata ginu the Tokugawa holly hock mon
signified the shogun's family. He wore lightweight hakama of
dark purple. Despite the breeze, Naga fanned himself with a
collapsible bamboo and paper fan. Behind Naga and against
the wall were his kodachi in vertical stands—a samurai always
had his two swords within easy reach.

To Naga's right and on the lower main tatami floor sat
Jii. He faced into the great hall in the same direction as Naga.
To Naga's left and on the same level as Jii sat Hideki. Outside
the grand room was the courtyard of the inn. The grand room
opened onto a wooden walkway that was approximately two
feet off the dirt and surrounded the courtyard. In the courtyard, a single spago-palm shaded several large rocks. A small
stream meandered through the courtyard and filled a kakei
bamboo fountain that supplied a single shishi-odoshi. The
water flowed into the bamboo fountain, which in turn fed the
open end of the deer chaser that pivoted in the center. Once
the deer chaser filled, the tube would rotate downward, giving
a resounding "clack" as it struck stone. The water would empty
out and gravity would move it back into place for filling again.
While the noise would continue every so often, humans found
it peaceful and Zen-like in its simplicity. The deer did not find

it so soothing. The greenery of the garden was thereby maintained.

Musashi sat among six retainers on the left against the side of the room facing inward on the main floor. All were in fine kimonos with wakazashi in their cloth obi belts and katanas in sayas beside them on the tatami. Yoshi moved into the room and whispered into Hideki's ear. Hideki nodded and motioned Yoshi to Jii and Naga. Yoshi repeated the message to both and then moved silently to Musashi, saying in a low voice, "There are more Ninja in and around and under this inn than I knew existed."

Musashi's eyes darted to Jii, who acknowledged the information but indicated no action. Musashi nodded to Yoshi, and then watched him disappear through the sliding paper door. He next turned and passed the information to the retainer on his right. By the time the news reached the last man in line, all had their hands on their katanas.

A page at the door received his signal from Jii and announced in a loud, high-pitched voice, "Yagyu Munenori, first counselor to the shogun."

Yagyu Munenori walked onto the tatami and up to the center of the room, faced Nagamasa, and knelt. All the Yoshinobu retainers bowed as he entered. Jii, Naga, and Hideki did not. Behind Yagyu came two people. Both were dressed as high-ranking samurai. All wore mons showing black hats with ties. One of the samurai looked very ferocious. He wore the kamishino like Naga, but his clothes were entirely black. His eyes and ears were everywhere.

The second samurai looked alarming as well, but for a different reason. Hideki had never seen a woman dressed as a man before, and he had never seen one as pretty. He swallowed hard. Who was she? Would he meet her again? Would she notice him? Many things raced through his mind at once. He had to fight to focus on the activities at hand.

Yagyu Munenori bowed, touching his forehead to the tatami. Behind him, his two escorts did the same.

"Yagyu no tajima, desu. Dozo yoroshiku onigaishimasu," Yagyu uttered in a deep and authoritative voice.

Naga did not respond.

"Matte, matte, Yagyu-sama," Jii replied. "We are servants of the Tokugawa just as you. There is no need to stand on formality."

Yagyu and his escort remained bowed. "No, Yoshinobu-dono. I am a servant of the Tokugawa. You are the Tokugawa," he declared.

Jii smiled appreciatively. "Dijobu, Yagyu-sama. May our contribution to the Tokugawa family someday mirror yours."

"Domo arigato, Yoshinobu-sama," Yagyu said. "You honor me and my family." Only then did they all three raise their heads. Yagyu stared directly into Naga's eyes, then moved to Jii and finally to Hideki.

Jii grunted in appreciation of Yagyu's good manners before asking, "How may we assist the counselor to the shogun?"

"I came to pay my respects to the potential next shogun," Yagyu replied. Hideki smiled despite the protocol that Jii had tried to drill into him all evening. Naga remained stoic, staring into nothingness above Yagyu's gray head.

Jii acknowledged the homage. "You are always welcome in any Yoshinobu dwelling, high counselor. Shall we dispense with the rest of the pleasantries and call for refreshments?"

Yagyu bowed again. "Thank you."

Jii clapped his hands and the walls moved back as the inn's maids brought in lacquered trays with sake and bowls of vegetables, first to Nagamasa, Jii, and Hideki, then to Yagyu's party and finally to Musashi and the retainers along the wall.

Hideki reached for his sake cup but Jii's searing stare froze him in place. Jii picked up his small ceramic sake bottle, set aside his tray, and glided on his knees to Yagyu. "Allow me, High Counselor," he said as he poured sake into Yagyu's shallow outstretched cup.

"Domo, Yoshinobu-sama," Yagyu said as he held the cup up in Nagamasa's direction with a slight bow.

Naga nodded as Yagyu and his two escorts drank.

Jii turned to the black-clad samurai. "And who do we have here, Yagyu-sama?"

Yagyu nodded at the man on his right. "Let me introduce

the leader of the Metsuke, Hittori Hanzo."

Hittori Hanzo bowed to Jii and uttered, "Dozo yoroshi-ku." Cranking his head to the left, he nodded at the female in male samurai clothing. "This enchanting creature is Hanzo's youngest daughter, Yuki."

"Dojo yoroshiku, onagaishimasu," she stated in a pleasant high-pitched voice.

Jii bowed to each in return. "We are honored by your presence Hanzo-sama. I knew your grandfather."

"Umm," Hanzo grunted in reply.

"But I'm a little confused by your daughter's presence," Jii, continued. "Is it acceptable to have women sit in such meetings?"

Yuki went about eating as if she were not the center of conversation.

"I believe it is imperative, Yoshinobu-sama. And her presence is the reason I have traveled hard for so many days," Yagyu said.

Jii poured a drink for Hanzo. "This is getting very interesting. Please continue."

"When I heard you had been summoned to bring only thirty retainers, I knew something was amiss. The barbarous practice of junshi by seppuku is bad enough," Yagyu explained, referring to the act of following a lord in death, "but we have to stamp out kyodai goroshi before we lose all our finest Tokugawa heirs. You've heard that the Yorifusa family was completely eradicated by the Fox Gang?"

"Yes," Jii responded. "The messengers that brought our summons told us."

"Well, that gang is giving me nightmares," Yagyu said. "I'm supposed to be protecting the Tokugawa so we can make this transition from constant war to continual peace, and a gang of cut throats seems to roam at will—and I know nothing of them."

"They seem to be in many places at once," Jii said, pouring Yuki some sake.

Yagyu continued. "Calling the Yoshinobu to Edo on such short notice with only thirty retainers smelled of treachery to me. So we have been riding for over a week to intercept you as early as possible."

Jii bowed to them. "Go kudo sama deshita."

"Iie, no need to thank us for our hard work. Yorifusa Juro could have been a great shogun. Nevertheless, assassins cut down his entire family. We must stop this kind of politics or we'll be back in the Warring States period again," Yagyu stated.

"Assassins?" Jii inquired. "I was told they were bandits."

"Since when does a gang of bandits overpower an entire household of samurai?" Yagyu replied. "And how can they strike in Mito, then in Edo, and the Metsuke not know about it?"

Jii looked at Hanzo. "That is a very good question Hanzo-sama. Indeed, how can that be?"

"Because they are not bandits, Yoshinobu-sama," Hanzo replied.

"Well, they are not ghosts, surely," Jii prompted.

"We believe they are ninja," Yagyu said.

"How many attacked the Yorifusa?" Jii asked.

"We believe between thirty and sixty," Yagyu answered.

Jii shook his head. "That is a lot of ninja. How can they exist and no one know?"

Yagyu turned to Hanzo. "We are not sure. I have spies all over the country. I know of all the ninja families. This one has eluded us ... but we will find them."

"Could this be the work of the Five Families?" Jii asked innocently.

All three sets of eyes turned to stare at Jii. "Yoshinobu-sama, what do you know of the Five Families?" asked Yagyu. "I heard you do not use ninja."

"I don't know much, I'm afraid. We are country samurai from Kii, so we do not get much information about the rest of the country beyond occasional rumors."

"I am aware of the Five Families," Hanzo said. "I have allowed them to operate, as their targets usually don't concern the government. But if they are involved I will tend to them."

"Anyway, Yoshinobu-sama, I rode hard to get here with

sixty additional retainers and to ask that Yuki here be made personal bodyguard to Nagasama," Yagyu said.

Jii's jaw dropped almost as far as Hideki's did.

Hideki could stand the silence no longer. "I am responsible for Naga's security. Why does he need a personal bodyguard?" he demanded.

Yagyu turned his attention to Hideki. "I am sure you are doing an excellent job in protecting your brother, Hideki-sama, but Yuki is trained in many weapons and I believe she could match swords with any man in this audience. Is that not so, Yuki?"

Yuki placed her bowl down and started looking at each of the Yoshinobu and then at each of the retainers. She stopped when she got to Musashi. "All but him, Yagyu-sama," Yuki said. "I believe he is formidable."

All eyes went to Musashi. Yagyu stared at him intensely. "Yes, I see what you mean, Yuki." Then addressing Musashi he asked. "And may I know your name, sir?"

Musashi remained quiet. Jii spoke up. "Yagyu-sama, may I present a counselor to the Yoshinobu, Myamoto Musashi."

All three of the visitor's heads whipped from Jii back to Musashi. "I have heard much of you Musashi-sama. It is a pleasure to finally meet you," Yagyu began. "I understand you use two swords."

Musashi looked to Jii, who nodded.

"I do use two swords on occasion. And it is my pleasure to meet the head of Yagyu Shinkage-ryu," Musashi said as he returned the bow. "Your fencing style is renowned throughout the land."

"What do you call your system, Musashi-sama?" asked Yagyu.

"I do not have a system, Yagyu-sama. I am beginning to see one in my head, but have not written it yet. I am toying with calling it 'Ni-ten Ichi Ryu'."

"Ni-ten Ichi Ryu?" Yagyu questioned.

"Yes, all my training has led me to believe that in wielding two swords, it is most important that you be of one mind," Musashi explained. "Therefore ... 'Two Swords, One Mind'."

"I see, Musashi-sama. Thank you," Yagyu said. "And what do you think of Nagamasa having a personal body guard?"

Musashi looked to Jii again. He nodded his approval. "I think you had better ask Nagamasa, since it's his body she will be guarding."

Everyone turned to look up at Naga. "If you think it will help, you can bring your maid," Naga stated. There was a pregnant pause as everyone was shocked into silence. Hanzo gripped his hakama in fists as he tried to hold his temper. Yuki stared straight into Naga's unconcerned eyes. Hideki wanted to say something and ease the sting of his brother's words in comparing the lovely Yuki to a common house cleaner. Musashi was ice.

Finally, Jii found his voice. "I believe what my grandson meant to say, is that he will welcome your help," he stammered.

Yagyu stared directly at Naga. The older brother seemed to be preoccupied with finishing his tea and very unconcerned about the impact of his remarks.

Yagyu bowed only slightly in Naga's direction when he announced, "The Yoshinobu are summoned to a meeting with the Tairo and Roju in two weeks' time."

Jii nodded. He was expecting this. Yagyu watched Naga's reaction. There was none. He was inspecting his teacup. Hideki wanted to reach over and slap his brother. He was shocked that Naga would demean the guests—especially Yuki—in such a manner, Hideki wondered.

"Will anyone else be in attendance, Yagyu-sama?" asked Jii.

Yagyu's answer was a little louder than it needed to be. "Yes, I will be there representing the shogun. He has retired from active political life and leaves such courtly matters to me."

Again, there was no response from Naga.

"Anyone else?" asked Jii.

"You are as sharp as my spies report, Yoshinobu-sama. Yes, there will be two women present," Yagyu advised.

"Pardon my old head, Yagyu-sama. I've just gotten used to a female samurai in man's clothes. Now you are telling me that women sit in at the highest levels of government?"

Yagyu looked to Hanzo. Hanzo nodded and asked, "How much do you know about the succession, Yoshinobu-sama?"

"I'm afraid I am very backward. Would you care to enlighten us all, Hanzo-sama?" Jii asked.

"I do so with pleasure," Hanzo replied. "Our current shogun, Hidetada, is retiring. Nevertheless, he may live for another ten years, or so he hopes. The original shogun, Ieyasu, did this when Hidetada came to power. This allows the new shogun to take the reins, but to have a former shogun available close by. There are now four potential successors from the Shinpan, the direct descendants of Tokugawa Ieyasu. Takechiyo is Hidetada's eldest son, now called Iemitsu. There is a second son, Kunimatsu, now called Tadanaga. Then there are the Yoshinobu," nodding in Naga's direction and then to Hideki's. "By Ieyasu's edict, all stand before the Tairo and Roju and a successor chosen. Hidetada must remain aloof to the succession as per Ieyasu's original instructions.

"What is creating friction," Hanzo continued, "is the fact that Hidetada is married to a strong woman, Oeyo from the Oda family. She keeps Hidetada's life in turmoil. I think part of retiring is to be away from her. She is in favor of her second son Tadanaga being the next shogun, probably being against her first son due to his preference of boys over women. She has been currying favor with the Tairo and Roju, and thus attempting to align votes in favor of Tadanaga. As a counter, O-Fuku, Iemitsu's wet nurse, has been doing the same thing for Iemitsu. She is a fearsome force in the palace. She knows everyone and many have fallen under her spell, and she has made promises and threats. She was once a favorite of the original shogun, Ieyasu. Given the court title of Tsubone, she alone has managed to keep Iemitsu's name in play. There is a circus balancing act going on in Edo castle and it will all come to a conclusion soon with the picking of the next shogun."

Hanzo paused for effect, then, pointing at Naga, resumed. "While an unlikely selection, many are speculating that outsiders like the Yoshinobu, who are not tainted by palace politics, may have a good chance to be chosen. Some of the

Tairo and Roju may see Nagamasa's selection as a way out of the snake pit. But it would depend on how he presents himself to the government and at this meeting in two weeks."

Yagyu addressed Naga directly for the first time. "How does the tono-sama feel about his chances of being picked?"

Jii started to speak, "Nagasama feels ..." He did not get any further.

Naga snapped, "Urasai, Jii-sama. I am capable of speaking for myself and the high counselor is no fool. All the fancy speech and court protocols will not impress him!"

Hideki gripped the handle of his wakazashi. This was an unexpected turn of events. Naga was talking down to the shogun's high counselor. "If swords come out I will go for Hanzo first," he thought as he played events in his mind, "and hope that Musashi gets Yagyu."

All three of the guests tensed as Naga rose up, pushed his tray aside and stepped in front of Yagyu. He looked at all three and then sat down. He bowed to Hanzo first. "I ask your forgiveness for my rude remark to your daughter Hanzo-sama. It was impolite and should not have been said." Then turning to Yuki he bowed again. "I apologize to you, Yuki-sama, for the remark, but I had to see what you were made of. If you were the fragile flower that your appearance portrays—had you left in a huff after having been insulted by a country diamyo—then I would have had no more need of you. You are made of sterner stuff, and I would greatly appreciate your assistance in any capacity that you deem appropriate." Turning to Yagyu, Naga bowed deeply. "Yagyu-sama, Dozo oshiette kudasai. Please teach me. I am a country diamyo not worthy of consideration for the lofty position of shogun. However, if that burden befalls me, I will discharge the duties of the office to the best of my abilities unto death. I am not seeking this position, but if it happens, I will need your unselfish guidance and support, just as you have given for the last two Tokugawa." Naga did not raise his head.

Yagyu stared at the top of Naga's head for a long moment. Then he slapped his thigh. "By the Buddha, we have a dragon at last." He turned to Jii. "I am impressed. Most would want to know how to win the position. He talks of service, and a moment ago, he was insulting me to see how we would react. He is well-schooled in the way of the sword," Yagyu said as he bowed to Jii, acknowledging the real mentor. Then he spun back to the bowed head of Naga. "Raise your head Nagamasa, and do not bow it again to me. It is I who serve you," he stated as he bowed lower than Naga.

Jii beamed. "Domo arigato, sensei."

Naga raised his head and grabbed a sake bottle and held it out to pour Yagyu a drink. Yagyu accepted with the shallow bowl in two outstretched hands and drank. Naga repeated the gesture for both Hanzo and Yuki.

"Let's get to work," Naga said. "How will the meeting take place?"

Yagyu nodded in agreement. "The place of honor in the ohiroma of the grand room will be vacant. When in attendance, the shogun sits on the raised portion. However, the current shogun's wife Oeyo will probably be on the main floor to the right, facing you. I believe O-Fuku will be on the main floor just off the place of honor on the left. They will act as if neither exists. Along the left side, to the right of Tairo, will be the Roju in order of rank. I will be between the women facing you." Yagyu paused to ensure all three Yoshinobu understood.

"Once you and Hideki and Yoshinobu-sama"—nodding toward Jii— "enter, you bow. I will introduce you individually. Nagamasa will be first, then Hideki, and then Yoshinobu-sama. Once finished, and while still bowed, each of you will repeat your name and rank. I will then ask you to raise your heads. Please look at me first, then Oeyo, then O-Fuku, then the Tairo, then the Roju. Look into each person's eyes, and then come back to me. I will welcome you to Edo castle and ask all gathered if they have any questions for you. Then the fireworks will begin."

"What sort of questions should I expect?" Naga asked.

"Anything and everything," Yagyu replied. "They will start innocently enough, but will turn ugly quickly. I fully expect that Oeyo and O-Fuku will align together just long enough to try and harm you."

"If I may, my Lord," Yuki bowed, "you have called your-self a country diamyo. Your ability to lead the nation based on limited experience with a 100,000-koku fiefdom will surely be on everyone's tongue. This is the biggest hurdle you will meet."

"Now I'm impressed," Jii said. "Yuki is correct. It is our vulnerable area."

"I'm sure they will all try to trip me. I will just have to try and be prepared, to answer truthfully and with respect," Naga asserted.

"That is about all you can do, Nagamasa," Yagyu af-firmed. "But the vested interests will attempt to bait you, humiliate you, and anger you." Shaking his head in disgust, he added, "We've come a long way since the Warring States era and the days of Sekigahara." Then he turned to Jii. "We fought to end the wars so the people could have peace. Well, we have a semblance of peace, but we have not yet transitioned suc-cessfully into a peaceful government. The top is factionalized. Everyone tries to get ahead and be on the right team. Below it is no better. In Edo, the police are worthless extortionists and the magistrates are to blame. They line their pockets, and the common people have to rely on local ruffians to settle disputes and keep the police at bay. We did not fight for this, and as old as I am, I will not rest until we have fixed it."

Naga looked Yagyu in the eye. "If I am picked, what should I concentrate on first?"

"Good question, Nagamasa. The problems of govern-ment are many. We have too many ronin roaming the cities, getting into mischief. I foresee big problems. In the country, the farmers are as stable as the weather and earthquakes allow. Their problem is being able to eat the rice they grow. We have a merchant class in the cities now that have become very power-ful."

"How powerful are they?" asked Hideki.

Yagyu had to turn to address Hideki. "Very powerful ... they bribe the daimyos to sell the rice to them. They are so wealthy that some can hoard the rice in warehouses and create a false scarcity, driving up prices in the market. When they finally release some rice into the market, they double or triple their profits. But the poor of Edo suffer because they can't afford the new higher prices."

"Scandalous," Jii said. "Why do you let them get away with it?"

"Hoarding is against the law, Yoshinobu-sama, but the police are bribed to turn a blind eye. If someone is caught and brought to trial, the magistrate is bribed," Yagyu explained.

Hideki thought for a moment. "So the power is in the money."

"Yes, that is correct. However, do not underestimate the merchant's power. Most of the large merchants have a small standing army of ruffians with two or three ronin yojimbo bodyguards on staff for sword work. They can be quite violent."

Naga rubbed his chin. "This would require a serious change. It is not something that can be corrected gradually."

Yagyu smiled. "Absolutely!" he proclaimed. "Those are my thoughts exactly." Then he calmed. "But where to start is the real quandary."

"Yagyu-sama, this is a basic question of right and wrong and of having the wrong men in positions of authority. I think we need to start with information," said Naga.

"Information, what kind of information?"

"We must start on each end of the snake and work to the middle. You and I will work on the head with some sweeping changes if I am shogun. However, we must also make changes in the tail. We must start with the officials closest to the peasants. Who in the government are closest to the peasants?"

Yagyu turned to Hanzo, who bowed slightly. "Well you know how it works in the country. The daimyo send retainers to inspect the farmers and town officials. In Edo the officials closest to the commoners are the juttes."

"Who and what are the juttes?" asked Naga.

"A jutte is a single tined weapon that is the badge of office for the local police that work with the samurai detectives who report to the magistrates. Because most of the police are commoners with no martial training, the jutte is given them to defend themselves against swords."

"Against swords? Do not be ridiculous!" Jii snorted.

Yagyu shook his head in the negative. "No, Yoshino-bu-sama, juttes can be a very effective weapon against the average samurai these days, and it is an intimidating weapon against the populace at large."

"I suppose so," Jii sighed. "Hideki here had a run in with just such a person in Kyoto."

Everyone looked at Hideki. He swallowed hard. "What?"

"Tell us of your run in?" requested Hanzo.

"It wasn't much. Two police, that I now believe to be a jutte and a police officer, were accosting a young temple girl and I had the fortune of watching a jo master deflect a jutte strike with the blunt end of his jo without looking." offered Hideki.

Yuki and Hanzo exchanged glances. "That is a remarkable story Hideki-sama. Such a person would come in handy on our trip," Hanzo stated.

"I don't know about our trip, but he sure came in handy a few minutes later when thirty fox-masked bandits tried to kill me."

"What?" asked Yagyu. "Where was this? When was this?" he asked, looking nervously at Hanzo.

"Kyoto at Ichijoji temple, four nights ago," Hideki said.

"Thirty bandits, Hideki-sama? You must be very skilled," Yuki teased with a slight bend in her head.

Hideki got red and shook his head in the negative. "No Yuki-san. Between the jo master and Musashi-sensei, I had little to do."

"Do not believe him Lady Yuki," Musashi stated. "Hideki is very skilled, and initially all thirty descended on him alone."

Yuki tilted her head at Hideki. "Maybe there are two swords I would not want to cross in the Yoshinobu," she said. Hideki's face continued to glow red.

"This is worse than I thought," asserted Yagyu. "If they are raiding in Kyoto, our barriers have failed to detect them. Hideki-sama, can you verify that the foxes are ninja?"

"I cannot, as I do not know their ways. However, Musashi-sensei says they were, and we have a more expert witness who says the same thing," Hideki stated.

"Musashi-san, do you concur?" asked Yagyu.

"Yes. I have fought ninja before as well as the yamabushi mountain monks who were the forerunners of ninja. The foxes were ninja."

"May we speak to the expert that fought them?" Yuki asked. "If he was able to identify them by their weapons or tactics, we might have a better place to start in tracking and eliminating them."

"Beauty and brains, too," Naga mused. He turned to Hideki. "What say you brother? He is your friend."

"I think this is too much light for Yoshi," Hideki replied.

"Nonsense," Jii said. Then, pointing to the page, he motioned for Yoshi, who nervously moved to the center of the room next to Yuki and bowed to Naga. "Yoshi, desu," Yoshi said.

Yuki turned to him and gave an elaborate finger-weave pattern. Yoshi watched, trying to remember the counter pattern, which he then traced.

Hanzo took over the questioning. "Who are your people?"

"We are known as the Dewa from Shiga province, Lord," Yoshi said.

"I thought you were all gone. I knew a master ninja from there as well as a witch," Hanzo said.

"The master was my father and the witch is my mother-in-law," Yoshi said.

"He meant no offense," Yuki injected.

"I know," Yoshi stated.

Hanzo turned to Yagyu. "He is ninja alright and taught by the best," Hanzo proclaimed as Hideki beamed proudly.

"Yoshi-san, were the fox masks you fought a few days ago ninja?" Yuki asked.

"Yes, madam. They were ninja."

"Yoshi-san," Hanzo started. "Could you tell where they were from by their weapons or their tactics?"

"I could not. It was dark and they did not speak. But there were two things that I found unusual ... "

"Go on," Yuki encouraged.

"They were very good in some things and very bad in others. For example, I still do not know how they communicated with each other. I saw no hand signal queuing, and they made no noise, yet they changed formation and attack direction in unison. That was good. However, they used a mixed arsenal. They attacked with swords, used arrows, and then used smoke bombs to cover their retreat."

"Sounds about right," Hanzo said.

"Yes, but when was the last time you saw a ninja group not place their bowmen on the ends or high up to keep from hitting their own men? When they attacked us, they had to break off the attack to allow the bowmen to fire. It was like watching ancient tactics."

"Interesting," Hanzo managed. "You said two things."

"Their technique with the sword was very dated. They used long slashing motions. This gave us time to use entering techniques and cut. Again, it was like watching my grandfather fight," Yoshi said.

"What are your thoughts?" Yagyu asked Hanzo.

"I am thinking a dormant group, recently resurrected, using old tactics," Hanzo surmised.

"Why now?" asked Yagyu.

"Because they have a deal with someone to replace the Metsuke," Yoshi said.

Yuki looked at her father and then at Yagyu. She saw the end of life as she knew it. "He's right."

Chapter 9: The Takaido

The rest of the trip differed greatly. As Hideki expected, Jii had everyone leave the next morning and push on to Fujikawa and then into Akasaka. As traveling went, it was an easy day—just 3.6 ri to Fujikawa and another half a ri into Akasaka. Everyone was tired, the Yoshinobu from Jii's constant push to Edo and the Yagyu from their bone-jarring push from Edo. All were glad for a rest.

The first evening meal in Akasaka was much livelier than usual as Hideki, Jii, and Naga joined Musashi, Yoshi, Hanzo, Yuki, and Yagyu. In the morning Hanzo would depart accompanied by ten Metsuke to run down the new information provided by Yoshi on Fox Gang tactics. Yagyu would remain with the Yoshinobu, using the time to coach Naga and Jii on life in Edo. Jii was well-pleased with this decision. He felt ill-prepared to help Naga in this important area, readily admitting to little skill in the daily etiquette and protocols of castle life. Musashi proposed that Yuki take over security for Naga, freeing Hideki in the evenings to learn more swordsmanship. He then volunteered Yoshi to help round out Hideki's education.

"What can I teach him, Sword Saint, that he doesn't already know?" Yoshi asked.

Musashi turned to Hideki between bites of delicious sea bream. "Do you know how to pick a lock Hideki?"

"No."

"Do you know how to blow in a door using gunpowder?"

"No." Hideki was feeling embarrassed in front of Yuki.

"Do you know how to run and leave tracks that few can follow?"

"No."

"Do you know how to see in the dark?"

"No."

Then Musashi turned to Yoshi. "That should keep you busy until Edo, Shadow Man."

Yuki laughed at Yoshi's discomfort at being Hideki's teacher. Soon all were laughing.

"I should have stayed an assassin," Yoshi groaned. "It was easier."

After the evening meal, Hideki noticed many of the Yoshinobu men pairing up with the comfort girls of the inn. He saw Musashi accompanying a young girl back to the room he shared with Yoshi.

"Sorry, Yoshi," Musashi called over his shoulder. "You can sleep with the horses. I got a better offer."

Everyone had bathed and eaten, and the inn's meager entertainment had been completed when Hideki noticed that the only ones sleeping alone tonight were himself, Jii, Naga, and Yuki. It appeared everyone else had found companionship.

Twice Hideki had to fend off invitations. Girls liked his youthful looks, but he had declined. He was curious, but could wait. Remembering Jii's admonitions on the subject, he thought such an important union had to be more than a minor financial transaction.

From then on, the days ran together. Hideki was still in charge of security for the entire entourage, so his eyes were everywhere. One of the unusual things he noticed was Yuki asking questions of the strangest people along the Tokaido. If the entourage passed other travelers, they would move off the road and bow to the Tokugawa banner, remaining bowed until the last of the baggage porters passed. Yuki would move her horse over to a bowed wood carrier with a huge load on his back and ask him questions. When she would see a bowing female pilgrim in white, she would approach her as well. Hideki assumed she was gathering information from locals about the environs. When he mentioned it to Yoshi, he learned differently.

"Metsuke" is all Yoshi said.

"They can't all be spies," Hideki said in disbelief.

"Yes they can. And they are." Yoshi confirmed.

"How do you get a ninja to walk like that last wood carrier?" Yoshi asked.

"You give him to a wood carrier while he is still a boy. He spends a couple of years learning the wood carrier life, picking the right trees, cutting the wood, carrying it to market for the real wood carrier and after a couple of years, the ninja boy is now a wood carrier and can blend in anywhere as such. The boy's father or uncle retrieves him after the prearranged time and he goes back to his real family to learn more of the ninja trade," Yoshi explained. "It is not magic, Hideki. I have known ninja who are the best potters, the best roofers, the best carpenters in the country."

Hideki just shook his head. "Unbelievable," is all he could manage. "So I suppose you spent time as a courier?"

"Among other things," Yoshi said.

"Life is a lot more complicated than I imagined," Hideki mused.

"Then you are learning," Yoshi grinned.

Yagyu rode with Jii and Naga in the middle of the column. They were always talking and laughing. Yuki rode up and down the column and always had a smile for Hideki. When he saw her, his heart raced. When she smiled at him, he could not help but blush. He did not want to. He wanted to be self-assured like Musashi and just nod in her direction when she came by. However, try as he might, he would always feel his face redden.

In the evenings, before bathing and the last meal, Musashi would train Hideki in the way of the sword. Musashi was a difficult taskmaster, and it was not long before Hideki had bruises all over his arms and shoulders from the master's bokken. But he did not mind. He was learning at a completely new level. It was different learning from a master. A master could show you the technique and the bunkai behind it. Understanding the rationale behind a technique made all the difference in learning. He was learning things he could get nowhere else.

Therefore, he ignored the bruises and stayed with the teachings. He did complain about one thing, but only to Yoshi.

"Why is it that when Musashi instructs me, he talks in riddles?" Hideki asked. "He is not like that at any other time."

Yoshi smiled. "I believe the Sword Saint is trying out his concepts on you to see if anyone else will understand."

"You know, you're going to tease him one time too many times with that Sword Saint title and find your head separated from the rest of your body," Hideki warned.

"I think I am the only one who can get away with it," Yoshi laughed.

"Whenever he is demonstrating a movement, he is economy of motion. I get it right away. But when he starts explaining why, he starts talking about rhythms, and greater circles, and spheres and gibberish that I don't understand," Hideki explained.

"Put up with it," Yoshi advised. "I think you will find no finer instructor for pure combat usefulness."

"Yes, no doubt. But what do all the fancy concepts mean?"

"I think our Sword Saint will write his concepts down someday. Right now he's taking what he knows in his head and trying them out on you, one chapter at a time. Now pay attention," Yoshi said, changing the subject. "See how the gunpowder laid out on this flat rock reacts when I ignite it with the flame from this candle?"

"Looks like a mini festival with sparks and smoke," Hideki said.

"Now look what happens when we take the same amount, bind it in paper, and ignite it with this fuse," Yoshi said while running for the cover of a large tree. "You might want to join me here."

A loud and powerful explosion sent Hideki flying backwards.

"Can you hear me Hideki?" Yoshi yelled at the prostrate form of his friend.

"Only barely," Hideki managed.

"Do you have all your body parts?" Yoshi asked.

Hideki managed to come to a sitting position and check his limbs. "Yes, I think so."

"Good, then that was a successful training exercise in the use of gunpowder," Yoshi said to his pupil. "Any questions?"

The days went like that. Hideki was in heaven. He learned all the things Musashi said he should know and much more. Occasionally, Hideki's sword bearer, Aoki, would ask to accompany him to Musashi's practice sessions. One day, Hideki relented and let him come. Before Musashi arrived, Aoki tossed Hideki a bokken and challenged him. It was obvious to Hideki that Aoki thought they would have a match just like the old days where his boyish enthusiasm and larger muscles would get the better of Hideki. He waited for Hideki to set up, and then charged with a slashing shomen attack from overhead. Hideki could not believe what he was seeing. A month ago, such an attack by a larger opponent would have terrified him. Now he felt disdain. He waited until the full force of the attack was committed, slapped the wooden sword slightly to a new downward trajectory, and then, keeping his sword high, caught Aoki under the chin along the cutting edge of the wooden blade, lifting him off his feet to come crashing down on his back with the breath knocked out of him. As Aoki was sucking in air, Musashi arrived.

"Been showing off, have we?" Musashi asked.

"Not really sensei. More like getting even."

While Aoki was trying to fill his lungs, unsuccessfully, he was turning a bright blue. Musashi reached down, grabbed Aoki's obi, and pulled him slightly off the ground. This created a small vacuum in his lungs and air flooded in. When he had lost his blue color, he attempted to stand but was a little wobbly.

"He got lucky," Aoki said to Musashi.

"No, he could do that to you ten times out of ten. You see, he has outgrown your level of swordsmanship, and if you'd used live blades, you would be without a head now."

Aoki started to respond with his normal pompous manner, but something about Musashi's cold eyes stopped him. "How do I get better?" he asked, respectfully.

"Now that is a good question and an indication that maybe you are trainable. Find yourself a good sensei and dedicate your life to the way of the sword."

"Will you train me?" he asked.

"No," Musashi stated firmly.

Aoki knew it was better to leave than to pursue this line of questioning. He left.

"Don't tell me that was a friend of yours," Musashi said.

"I don't think he was ever a friend, but we used to train in the dojo together with me getting the lumps," Hideki confided.

"He's a bully. It is written all over him, and that bull-like charge is child's play to overcome," Musashi said.

"You saw that much sensei?" Hideki asked.

"Yes."

"You were right that night in Kyoto. Killing with your blade changes a person forever. You look at everything differently. I felt contempt for Aoki when he attacked me with such an obviously inferior technique," Hideki said. "I am no longer the young boy in the dojo that Aoki remembers."

"No you are not. Moreover, with your superior knowledge comes responsibility. You must learn not to put yourself in situations that could lead to your need to fight," Musashi chided.

"Yes, I see that now. For a moment, I wanted to see what it would be like to travel back to a more innocent time. Do not think too harshly of Aoki. He's a young man trying to prove himself, but he doesn't have the advantage of having good friends like you and Yoshi to teach him," Hideki said.

"Hideki, why do you think you have Yoshi and me as friends?" Musashi asked.

"Well, my brother may be shogun?"

"Bukka! Yoshi is staying away from his young wife and has broken a sacred vow to help you. I have temporarily given up my life's journey. We did this gladly because we see in you the future of the country and we want you to have the best possible chance to walk your path," Musashi said.

"Does that mean you will take it easy on me this lesson?" Hideki asked.

"Never."

Aoki never asked to come back to the training. It was just as well. Hideki did not like sharing his new friends with anyone. Not every eighteen year old trained with a professional duelist and an expert assassin.

Yoshida, Maisaka, Fukuroi, and Kanaya were the next four overnights. Seven more and they would arrive in Edo. While in Kanaya, Hideki noticed a subtle shift in security and a great many other things.

Kanaya lies nestled in a crevice of one of those foothills. It's a wide, sandy flat protected by a broad river. Just beyond the flat is a jumble of foothills. The entire flat area was once a riverbed; now the river flows through the center of the flat and offers a panoramic view of the mountains beyond. The river is deceptively deep. Standing on the bank, the water seems shallow enough to wade across. Porters lined both sides of the river. All ages of men squatted along the riverbed, stripped to their fundoshi, awaiting customers to help across for a price. The porters knew where to step. The pilgrim did not. There were deep holes beyond a man's head scattered throughout the riverbed. To walk in the wrong place could bring death, especially if you could not swim.

Like everything in Japan, this enterprise was organized. No one would quote a price until the headman was located. Hideki found him and negotiated a price. It took a while, but the Yoshinobu entourage got across safely. By the time they reached the village of Kanaya most of their wet clothes had dried.

Yuki had developed a routine of which Hideki approved. She would personally supervise the cooks of the inn housing Naga and then accompany the meals to Naga's room. The dishes were placed before everyone. However, on Naga's tray were extra empty dishes. Then the girl who carried Naga's food would dish out a small amount into one of the empty dishes and eat it. If there were no dire consequences, she departed. Then Yuki would take a small bite out of each dish going to Naga to ensure the bowls themselves were not poisoned, after which she would present it to Naga and he and everyone else would eat.

Yoshi, Musashi, Jii, and he would take this evening meal with Naga, but at Kanaya, Hideki noticed that Yuki and her guards started to control access to Naga. After the evening meal, Hideki would make his rounds, check on Jii to see that he was comfortable and then do the same for Naga. In Kanaya, he checked on Jii, bid him goodnight, and moved to Naga's wing. He got there just in time to see Yuki enter his room. This was a late hour for her to be calling on Naga, but Hideki thought it was probably to discuss some security measure for the next day. Therefore, Hideki knelt down to wait. He waited almost an hour before he convinced himself that she was not coming out.

Hideki felt heartbroken. He had thought she liked him and that she was the one for him. Nevertheless, she had chosen his older brother. Well, what should he have expected? Naga may be the next shogun. What was he going to be? Who knew? But it made him jealous and a little angry. For the first time on the journey, Hideki had a hard time sleeping.

The next day, Hideki was too busy getting the entourage moving to pay Naga too much attention, but he noticed Naga to be in a very pleasant mood. They came to Shimada, the twenty-fourth station on the Tokaido. The Oi River was waded using porters as the previous day. Before noon, they were in Fuji-jeda where Hideki oversaw the exchange of porters and horses. Fuji-jeda was the place where Hideki talked to the station officials to get the porterage fares recorded. Then the fearsome climb to Okabe was upon them. Here the Tokaido shrunk to the width of two men. Mountains rose up on both sides, covered in dense forest and thick ivy vines. Along the right side, a torrent of rushing water sought the valley below. Only a stone retaining wall prevented the plunging creek from eroding the Tokaido into nothingness.

By evening, they had attained the high ground and found the little village of Mariko. After getting everyone into the inns, the horses unpacked and stabled, and the security set, Hideki moved to confer with Jii and Naga about the next day's start. He moved to the room assigned to his brother and found Yuki kneeling outside arranging a tray with cups of tea.

"Simasen," Hideki said as he started by.

Yuki rose quickly and placed a hand on Hideki's chest. "Gomen nasai, Hideki. Naga-sama is not to be disturbed. Why don't you come back later?" Her smile was radiant.

Hideki could not believe his ears. "Until you are my sister-in-law, and I doubt seriously that such will ever be the case, no one but Jii and Naga tell me where to go," Hideki snapped as he grabbed his sword handle.

Yuki stared into his eyes. "You would draw on me, Hideki?" she asked.

"If you do not want to have to display those well touted martial skills of yours against my weak blade, ninja, you will step aside," Hideki said.

Yuki stepped back and bowed. "Gomen nasai, Hideki." Then she turned and walked away.

Hideki announced himself at the door. Naga's voice granted him access.

Hideki slid the door back and stepped in. He closed the door with a little too much force, walked up to Jii and Naga and sat down.

"Brother, you smell like horses," Naga complained.

"Yes," echoed Jii. "Why have you not bathed and changed?"

"Because I am the only one doing any real work around here," Hideki snapped.

Jii's tone changed. "What is wrong Hideki? We were just discussing the change in you from the wild boy to a responsible man on this journey."

Hideki felt ashamed. "Gomen nasai," he said. "I just didn't expect to find my path barred from my own family by your personal bodyguard," Hideki said, glaring at Naga.

"That is my fault," Naga said. "I told Yuki to keep people away for awhile. I wanted to discuss what I have learned with Jii and I did not want to have Yagyu interrupt with his constant coaching. I didn't think she would try to keep you from us," Naga said.

"I guess I will have to apologize to her," Hideki said.

"I do not think that will be necessary," Jii advised.

"No, it is necessary," Hideki said. "I threatened her with my sword if she did not step aside."

"That was a little harsh, don't you think?" asked Naga.

"Yes, it was. But I had seen her taking control of you and I guess I felt a little left out," Hideki admitted.

"Boys, you will both get older and have your own families, but never let anything or anyone come between you," Jii advised.

Both brothers nodded in agreement.

The next day, things were back to normal except that Yuki made an effort to stay away from Hideki. He was going to apologize but got busy with getting the entourage started and missed his chance.

By mid-morning, they had arrived at Fuchu, the twentieth station on the Tokaido. Here they had to cross another river. This river was the Abe. As they crossed, they could see more mountains in the background. Fuchu was the boyhood home and retirement dwelling of Ieyasu, the founder the Tokugawa shogunate.

By noon, they arrived at Ejiri at the mouth of the Okitsu River. From here, Hideki could look down to Suruga Bay and see the ships and junks that populated the seaport of Okitsu below.

By mid-afternoon, they arrived at Okitsu. This was an overnight stop. By now, Hideki went unconsciously through the motions of ensuring that all housing, bathing, feeding, and security were tightly set. As exciting as the trip had been, he was looking forward to a destination.

The next morning it was a steep climb to Yui, the seventeenth station on the Tokaido. From here, Hideki got his first glimpse of Fuji-san. Equally inspiring was the look down to see the Tokaido winding its way along the head of Suruga Bay.

Kanabara came next. It was another small mountain village. Then it was down the mountain and on to an area where the Tokaido appeared to float above waterlogged rice paddies on either side. Just past the flooded paddies, they emerged into the sleepy little village of Yoshiwara for an overnight stay .

The next morning it was off again. They walked into

Hana. Here the entire entourage stopped for a spectacular view
of Mt. Fuji. Hideki watched for a moment, and then moved up
and down the column getting it started again. Yoshi had said
they would be entering a dangerous stretch at Namazu where
the trees and forests came right down to the Tokaido. Bandits operated in the area and had a reputation of robbing and
killing travelers, so Hideki wanted to get through the area while
it was still daylight.

Once at Namazu, Hideki saw his worries had been for
nothing. Yoshi had neglected to mention there was a river
on the east separating the Tokaido from the trees. Unless the
bandits were mounted cavalry, they could cause little damage
before he could deploy his forces to protect the column.

As he was studying the terrain, Hideki noticed a peasant
bowing in the grass beside the roadway. On his back was a
large Tengu mask. His jacket was decorated with a strange bird
that Hideki did not recognize. Musashi pulled up beside Hideki
and noticed his gaze.

"The mask is the mark of a pilgrim to the Shinto shrine
of Kompira on Shikoku Island," he said.

"Good," Hideki said. "The only things we haven't had on
this trip are goblins."

"Yuki-san seems a little reserved around us these days,"
Musashi noted. "Has anything happened?"

"Do you mean in addition to me threatening to cut her
open if she ever tried to keep me from my brother again?"

Musashi laughed. "So you've noticed her possessiveness,
have you?"

"I'll say!"

"It is natural. When a woman starts sleeping with a man,
she starts to think she is his wife," Musashi said.

"You know about that too, sensei?" Hideki asked. "Your
old eyes don't miss much."

"It is the way of the sword, young student," Musashi
mocked. "Did she break your heart?"

"Just cracked it a little," Hideki acknowledged.

"Women—they are creatures of the greatest pleasure
and the most exquisite pain."

"I guess I must apologize."

"If you feel like you should, then do," said Musashi.

"Which of your crazy books is that from?"

"None, it's just common sense. She is afraid she has offended you and she cares for Naga. Don't think of it as losing a brother. Think of it as gaining a sister."

"You don't really think they'd marry, do you?" Hideki asked with concern.

"Why not? She's from a highborn samurai family with ninja training. Yagyu is trying desperately to bind himself to the new shogun and Naga is his best bet. I would not put it past the old fox to have devised this plan many months ago," Musashi surmised.

"Amida Buddha," Hideki said. "When do you know if someone is really on your side?"

"It is very hard to tell where power and money is involved. Nevertheless, I think Yuki and Naga care for each other. That is all that should concern us. But to answer your question young Bushi, it is a pretty good indication someone is on your side when they join you in battle against overwhelming odds," Musashi said.

"Yeah, that is what Jii said."

"Pretty smart man, your grandfather."

"I guess we'd better get started. I've heard the climb to Hakone is difficult," Hideki said.

"Whatever you've heard, it is worse."

By mid-afternoon, they had arrived at Mishima, the thirteenth station on the Tokaido. Then the climb to Hakone started in earnest. It was almost straight up. There was no room on the sides of the road, so Hideki lost track of the column as he lost sight of the stragglers. Several times he caught sight of Lake Hakone on the left and Mt. Fuji ahead in the distance. He thought both might be a spectacular sight if he had not been gasping for air. He knew he would be up most of the night accounting for everyone and all the gear on the pack animals. Then, finally, he was at the top.

Hideki ensured the lodgings were ready and then moved to check on the stables. It was late, the sun was long down, and Hideki was still at the entrance of the village checking off arrivals.

"So Prince of the Yoshinobu, you don't eat anymore?" Yoshi asked. He appeared so suddenly that Hideki jumped.

"How do you do that?" Hideki managed.

"Magic. You nobles would not understand," Yoshi said as he presented Hideki with onigiri and a bamboo water flask.

Hideki bowed as he bit into the first rice ball. "This is enough magic for me."

"How many are missing?" Yoshi asked.

"Three women, two wagons and one pack horse," Hideki managed between gulps of the water.

"You worried about bandits?"

"Aren't you?" Hideki asked.

"No!"

"Why not?" asked Hideki.

"Because I arranged for Yuki to send a squad of her ninja at the tail end of the column and not come in until all arrived safely," Yoshi said.

"Why didn't I think of that?" Hideki asked no one in particular.

"Because you are a noble and have little ninja training. You are not supposed to be smart," Yoshi offered.

"Well, I guess it's a good thing I have smart friends, isn't it?" Hideki asked.

"Now you are learning."

"Wait a minute, Yuki agreed to help me?"

"Readily. She said it would give you more time to threaten women with your sword."

"I really must apologize to her for that," Hideki said as he finished the last rice ball. "How long were you going to leave me out here worrying?"

"Musashi said it was about time to bring you in. and Yuki said you had suffered enough," Yoshi said.

"No fool like a young fool, eh?"

"Well, we were all young once," Yoshi said.

"What are you talking about? You are my age."

"Yes, but I am ninja. We are wise beyond our years,"

Yoshi said smugly. "So are you going to your bath and bed?"

Hideki shook his head. "No. This is my responsibility. I'll stay until it is done."

"Good, I'll stay with you."

"You are a true friend, Yoshi," Hideki said.

"Well, there is that also; however, I bet Naga-sama that you would stay. He bet you would not. I like taking money from the next shogun."

"Amida Buddha," was all Hideki could manage.

The next morning, before breakfast, Hideki called a meeting in Naga's room.

"This better be important, Hideki," Naga said. "I'm hungry."

"It is important to me," Hideki replied.

Once Jii sat, Hideki glanced around the small room, mentally checking off each face. Yuki looked sleepy. Yoshi looked expectant. Musashi looked bored.

"All the people I care about are gathered here. I wanted to take this opportunity to apologize publicly to Hanzo Yuki for my actions a couple of nights ago," Hideki began. Then he turned so that he was talking directly at Yuki. She did not look sleepy any longer. Her attention was riveted on Hideki.

"My only excuse for threatening to draw my sword against you Yuki was jealousy. You enchanted me with your beauty from the first, but I was too young to know what to do. Then I noticed you moving to Naga and I reacted badly. I also felt I was moving farther from the only family I have ever known. So I threatened you. I am sorry. It is only natural that you and Naga would be attracted to each other. In addition, I have seen the change you have brought to Naga. You make him happy. For that, I thank you. From this day forward, my sword will never threaten you again. From this day forward it shall only act in your defense. I swear it." With this, Hideki bowed low to Yuki.

Yuki's eyes started to water.

"Great speech Hideki. How long have you been practicing that?" Naga asked.

"Damare Naga," Yuki snapped. "Have you no feelings?"

Naga looked shocked at her outburst.

Yuki turned her attention back to the bowing Hideki.

"Good and noble Hideki, you are the embodiment of Bushido. You protect the weak; you are loyal to the last and someday you will make a woman's heart sing with your love. I would hope that you always remain pure. You have no need to apologize to me." Then she bowed lower than Hideki.

"Okay, now can we eat?" Naga asked.

"One thing first, Lord," Yoshi said.

"Yes?" Naga asked.

"You owe me one ryo."

"Insolence," announced Jii.

"No, Jii, the ninja is correct," Naga stated as he reached into his pouch inside his kimono. He took out a single gold coin and threw it to Yoshi. Yoshi caught the coin and immediately bit into it to establish its authenticity. Once satisfied he nodded to Naga.

Musashi glanced at Hideki and leaned into Yoshi's ear. "He rings true every time, doesn't he?"

"Yes, you can be proud of your child, papa-san," Yoshi teased.

Musashi took a swipe at Yoshi's head with his folding fan, but Yoshi easily dodged it.

"Come on, Sword Saint. We'll be late for morning meal," Yoshi taunted.

Chapter 10: The Noodle Shop

Jii called to Yoshi. Yoshi dropped his maps and reported to the old man.

"Have you seen Hideki?" Jii asked.

"Not since the evening guard postings," Yoshi said.

"Is he with Musashi?"

"No, Lord; Musashi went into town to get his sword polished," Yoshi lied. He had no idea where Musashi has gone. However, he did know his friend had left before the guard was set.

"We just have a few days left before we appear at the castle. Hideki needs to be here to practice," Jii said.

"He is probably exploring the area, Lord. He is in charge of security and must get a feel for our surroundings," Yoshi tried.

Jii was persistent. "Yoshi, I would hate to have anything happen now. Hideki showed such great maturity on the journey to Edo. I would hate to think he is reverting to his old foolishness of exploring new dojos."

"I doubt it, Lord. Musashi is going to be hard to beat as an instructor," Yoshi said with confidence.

"Yes, I know. Nevertheless, Musashi will be departing soon and Hideki may feel he has to find a new mentor. Anyway, I want you to find him and keep him out of trouble. We can't have any scandals attached to the Yoshinobu name just before going to the castle."

"Yes, Lord," Yoshi said as he bowed. "Where the hell am

I going to find the young screw up?" The last he did not say aloud.

Hideki walked and walked. He was in a little inner turmoil and found it impossible to stay within the mansion walls. He saw Naga less and less, and Musashi was due to leave soon. Any time he was around Jii, there were more protocols and rules to learn. Therefore, after the guard was set, he changed into his ronin garb and went for a walk into Edo.

Edo was huge. That was fine. He did not know where he was going. He just wandered, trying to keep his bearings as best he could. He was hungry and sure that he would miss the evening meal even if he were to turn around and go back.

The section of Edo that he was passing through now was very poor. The homes he was passing were of less quality than any he had known in Kii. Heartless Hovels is what Yoshi called them. They really were not houses. They were nothing more than boards thrown together to form four walls with at least two of the walls forming the wall for a neighbor. The roofs were made of boards and tree limbs and thatch and anything else that could be carried up and laid atop. They appeared to find cohesion via rocks and any manner of flotsam propped against them or thrown on top. As he passed, he could see into the homes. Light emanated from single candles. They all had floors of dirt. Yoshi was right, there was very little heart in these homes. The inhabitants were poor.

Walking down the dirt street, he could almost touch the front doors on either side. They were that close together. From the sounds and sights, he figured there was no keeping of secrets from neighbors. The flimsy walls filtered no sounds. He knew what was happening in each house by sound alone. In one, a mother praised a young child for getting her own bedding ready. In another, a wife complained to her man that the rent was due and she had no money for food. In yet another, the wife was squatting in the street crying. In more than one abode, Hideki heard the sounds of fighting.

But it was the smells that assaulted Hideki's senses the most. The place smelled of sweat, dirt, human waste, curry, wet laundry, and thousands of charcoal fires. It all combined to disorient and foster a sense of hopelessness. Yoshi was right!

Hideki wished he could help in some way. But how? The tenements were vast. How could he hope to help? How could anyone? It seemed beyond the powers of even the government. In the end, he just crossed his arms and walked faster.

Hideki was very hungry now. He passed several street vendors with noodle carts. He was tempted to stop but was not sure how it all worked. Was the vendor really washing the bowls after each customer? Did you eat standing up? Hideki saw no benches like those in front of the noodle houses along the Tokaido. He kept walking.

There was a subtle change in scenery. The Heartless Hovels gave way to larger shops. The street became wider. He noticed the same types of signs that advertised the entertainment quarters in Kyoto. He also noticed several small shops open for evening meals. They were not grand. Most were open to the street, but at least they had wooden benches on which to sit and eat. The choices advertised on the cloth signs indicated either udon or osoba. Hideki, preferring the thinner noodles, opted for osoba.

Hideki picked a noodle shop that looked no larger than a row house but had four walls and an entrance off the street. He scanned the interior before proceeding into the business as he ducked beneath the split-cloth sign that announced "Ichiban Noodles." It had a dirt floor and contained wooden tables with plank seats on either side. There were a total of four of them—two on the right and two on the left, separated by a main aisle that led to the back of the room where an old man stirred several black pots over an earthen kamado stove. In the middle was a short bar with bowls and cups stacked neatly. To the right was a small wooden table with flour spread on it, which Hideki assumed was where the cook kneaded and cut his noodles before moving them to the boiling pots.

Hideki glanced overhead. There were rough-hewn rafters about eight shaku off the dirt floor. He pulled his katana and saya from his obi as he entered and was greeted with "Irashiai dozo." This was from a small girl in a drab gray kimono and a white but stained apron with wooden geta on her feet. While the greeting was standard, the enthusiasm was not. Hideki could not help but look at her as she bowed, then went scurrying to get him some tea.

He moved past the first row of tables where two kago carriers were seated slurping noodles. Their palanquin was outside on the street. The table on the left was empty, but so was the last table on the right by the noodle table. On the second table on the left sat a beautiful young woman clad in a colorful kimono with her back to the old cook. She was boldly staring at Hideki. He gave her a slight nod and took the same seat at the table on the right. Now he could see who entered the establishment.

The shop girl brought Hideki a cup of tea and a big smile. Her smile was infectious. Hideki returned it. She was not pretty, but she radiated energy.

"So, young miss, what is good tonight?" Hideki asked.

"Oh, samurai-sama, everything is good. We have the best noodles anywhere," she said proudly.

"Then I will try the osoba," he said.

"Hia" was her reply.

"Hia" came the acknowledgement of the order from the old cook.

Hideki leaned his katana against the bench next to his left leg. He then picked up his tea. He was looking forward to his noodles and hoping he could find his way home through the maze of houses. After he took a sip, he glanced over at the woman on his right. He found her looking at him. "If I'm ever to have romance, I hope it is with someone as lovely as she," he thought to himself.

Her kimono was gaudy. It was a bright blue with red flowers. Her obi was large and trimmed with gold thread in the back. Her jet-black hair, piled on top of her head and held with several long turtle shell hair picks and one large ivory comb, contrasted with her pale, oval face. A folded straw hat was beside her on the bench and a small jo-like walking stick was leaning on her seating bench much like Hideki's katana leaned on his.

Hideki glanced at her face again. She caught him studying

her and smiled. Hideki could feel the warmth starting in his face again and hated himself for it. The young woman saw him blush and laughed. It was not a great guffaw, but a delightful sound like a wind chime moving. Hideki liked the sound of it, even though she was laughing at him.

He whipped his head away and back to his tea, trying to look stern. He felt her rise. "Say something, stupid," he chided himself. "Don't let her get away." What could he say? He did not know.

Hideki jumped when she moved in front of him on the other side of his table and spoke. "Gomen nasai, samurai-sama," she said in a silky voice. "It has been a very long time since I've seen a young man who is still able to blush. I find it rather charming."

Hideki smiled. "I'm trying to overcome it," he said, "but have not managed to do so yet."

"Would you mind if I joined you?" she asked.

"Dozo," Hideki bowed as he invited her to sit with his right hand.

The shop girl went to retrieve a bowl of noodles from the old man for the woman in the blue kimono, but the old man nodded to the woman's new position. Then the shop girl understood and went to wipe down the vacated table. The old man would keep the woman's noodles warm as he prepared the samurai's. Then the shop girl could deliver them together.

"What is your name, samurai-sama?" the woman in blue asked.

Hideki almost blurted out his real name. "Takezo desu," he said.

"I am Myo," the woman in blue said. "I did not mean to cause you discomfort."

Hideki shook his head in the negative. "No discomfort. I have only been in the presence of one other woman as attractive as you, and she chose my older brother."

"How sad, Takezo. Did she break your heart?" she asked.

"Bruised it a bit," Hideki confided.

"Well, older brothers have better opportunities. Maybe she was just being sensible," Myo offered.

"Probably," Hideki said. "But I would like to think that they fell in love with each other."

Myo put her hand to her mouth in mock surprise. "A romantic as well?"

"You are still making fun of me," Hideki accused.

Her smile made it hard to take offense. "Maybe I am, a little, Takezo."

The shop girl brought a steaming bowl of noodles for Myo. Then she did the same for Hideki. Myo and Hideki picked up their ohashi in their right hands and plunged them into the steaming bowl of noodles. In unison they uttered the universal "Itadakemasu" and started slurping noodles by moving the long white noodles from the broth into their mouths using the eating sticks.

"The girl was right. The noodles are good," Hideki thought. He almost forgot his embarrassment in the presence of the beauty across from him … almost.

Loud sounds coming from the street interrupted Hideki's culinary delight. The commotion got louder and then took the shape of three samurai staggering into the little shop.

The drunken samurai were wearing Tosa mon. Hideki recognized them as lesser vassals to the Tokugawa. The mon of the small pine cone was found in abundance on the far-off island of Shikoku, the Tosa domain. Although they swaggered to impress, Hideki knew the Tosa to be Tozama, or "outside Lords." Tozama were the daimyo who had sided with Hideyoshi's Toyotomi heirs against Tokugawa Ieyasu as the latter was trying to unify the current shogunate. The daimyo Lords who had sided with Tokugawa Ieyasu were called Fudai or "inside Lords." These were called the Go-sanke. There were only three of them: Owari, Kii, and Mito. Hideki and the Yoshinobu were from Kii. He learned all this at the hand of Jii who drilled heraldry of all the daimyo into his and Naga's head by the time they were six. It was one of the many lessons drilled into the brothers' heads by Jii's bokken. Hideki massaged the top of his head in reflex at the thought of all those lumps.

Their disheveled looks, dirty kimonos, and stained hakama matched their boisterous entrance. Hideki winced when one grabbed the young girl who shuffled over on wooden getas and sang out "Itashai mase" as she bowed.

The one with a juvenile hairstyle, bushy eyebrows and a four-shaku sword tied across his back grabbed her wrist and pulled her toward the first empty table on the left. The girl shrieked. She looked in desperation at the two kago carriers. They would provide no help. To challenge samurai was to court death. She spun quickly, broke the grip on her wrist and ran back toward the old man, the tips of her wooden getas digging into the soft dirt floor. She stopped at Hideki's table and looked at both he and Myo for help.

"She doesn't know what to do," Hideki said to himself. She was all of fifteen, he estimated, and obviously the product of the burgeoning vendor class. She would have been steeped in their saying that the "customer is king." But she was not ready for the roughness of the samurai who had stopped in for a late-night bowl of noodles after a night of drinking and carousing. She was fearful of their status. She was a commoner and they were samurai. They could easily kill her or her boss and claim she had insulted them. She twisted her towel back and forth in her hands desperately searching for a solution.

Hideki had many things to learn about Edo. It was a city full of mysteries. The street life in this entertainment district was complex. He was not at ease with it yet. He felt like a visitor to a foreign land.

The old restaurant owner wiped his hands on his apron and mumbled, "Dijobi, Hana. Buka samurai. They treat us like dirt and think we have no pride." The young girl, Hana, smiled nervously and took refuge behind the wooden bar. The owner, realizing that Hideki had overheard him calling samurai "stupid," bowed slightly in Hideki's direction and forced a large smile onto his face as he took off his apron. He started bowing as soon as he put his body in motion toward the unkempt samurai.

"A good man," Hideki thought. He returned the bow with a nod. The nod was much lower than was his custom. Then he smiled at the frightened girl and moved his attention back to slurping noodles. "He's also a good cook," he thought.

There was nothing like osoba late at night.

Hideki watched the old man shuffle over to the samurai. With his kimono hitched into his obi to allow freer movement of his legs, he was bowing as he approached them. He had a shaved pate with a short chomagai tied in the back of his head. The top portion of his kimono was tied up under his armpits and over the opposite shoulder by a long cord to keep the sleeves from getting in the way as he worked. Around his head, he wore a white hachimake to absorb any sweat and keep it out of the food. Worn under the chomagai and knotted in the front just above the eyebrows, the old man's headband marked him as an Edo vendor.

He shuffled just short of the samurai's table. "Gomen nasai, minasan, how may I be of service?" he asked.

"Go back to cooking old man," the one with the long sword on his back sneered. "Send the girl back. We're not finished with her."

The old man bowed again. "Gomen nasai, I'm sorry, gentlemen. We only serve noodles here. If you want a pleasure house, the Yoshiwara is full of them. What kind of noodles would you like?" His bow was lower and his smile broader with the last question.

Long sword was not having any of it. He came to his feet, pushing the old man out of the way, making a beeline straight for the frightened girl. "By the blessed Buddha, you'll serve me whatever I want," he crowed as he reached across the bar, grabbing Hana by the apron.

The girl shrieked and spun, loosening Long Sword's grip. She dashed around the bar, but had no place to go except next to Hideki. She stopped and cowered where the wall, Hideki's bench, and his katana all met. Long Sword swore again and moved swiftly toward the girl. He was about to reach around Hideki's back when Hideki repositioned his katana and saya with his left hand so that it was in the samurai's path. The samurai stopped cold. The motion had been unmistakable. To bump into a samurai's sword was unpardonable.

Long Sword eyed Hideki as if seeing him for the first time. He was not impressed. "What do we have here? You are

too little and much too young to want to incur my anger, fool."
Then, pointing to the mon on his kimono sleeve, he asked,
"Do you know what this means?"

Hideki set his bowl down slowly and turned to glance at
the mon. "That you are street actors playing at being samurai?"

Long Sword's glare cut Myo's laugh short. He puffed out
his chest as he pointed at the mon. "We are Tosa retainers,
mongrel ronin. Masterless dogs like you mean nothing to us,"
he bragged as he drew his long sword half a shaku from its
saya over his right shoulder.

The short draw was to frighten Hideki. It did not work.
Hideki returned to his bowl and slurped more noodles. The
room was deadly quiet except for the noise of the ronin eating.
The two koga bearers edged toward the door. They wanted no
part of four samurai fighting in such a close place. It was not
healthy to stay. Myo was all eyes, watching Long Sword's anger
and Hideki's calm.

The other two Tosa retainers made a big show of pushing their bench over as they stood up and pulled their swords
far enough to allow the blades to show. "Don't let this insolent
cur insult our clan, Mondo. Teach him a lesson." The other two
moved to the back of the room and took up positions behind
Mondo.

Hideki slurped, smacked, and eventually let out a little
burp. The samurai's anger reached new heights. "Are we to be
insulted by this bumpkin? He's too stupid to be frightened,"
the short ugly one said. Their eyes went over Hideki's swords.
Both were undistinguished in plain black sayas. The tsubas
between the handle and the blade were equally nondescript.
Hideki's clothes offered no clues of danger either. It was the
standard garb of the masterless ronin. Mondo surveyed Hideki
carefully and concluded he must have recently lost his master,
accounting for his arrogance.

Hideki was calm on the outside and calm on the inside.
He had sized up these ruffians as Musashi had taught. Since
the Tokugawa peace, they were a common enough sight in
Edo. They stood their tour of duty at their diamyo's Edo
residence and with little else to relieve their boredom, sought

the sake and pleasure houses of the Yoshiwara district at night. The Edo vendors who made their living from them often fell victim to their violent outbursts.

Hideki could hear Hana whimper next to him. "The reason I thought you were actors is that no real samurai, schooled in Bushido, would terrify a young girl and her old father in such a manner," Hideki said.

Hideki knew he had space for his katana in the small room. Musashi had taught him well. "Always take advantage of your terrain." He also knew that Mondo could not. The rafters in the roof were too low for his long sword. Hideki spun around on the bench to face Mondo, both hands on his bowl of noodles.

Mondo, seeing that Hideki's hands were on the bowl, saw his chance. Hideki almost smiled. He could hear Musashi in his head. "In everything there is rhythm. First you must learn to attune yourself to your opponent, and then learn to disconcert him." Both hands on the bowl had been the bait and the establishment of rhythm. Now for the disconcert part.

Mondo's draw was traditional sky to earth, meant to sever Hideki from collarbone to opposite hip. Such a cut took tremendous power. It never happened. Hideki threw the bowl and its remaining contents at the two behind Mondo while grabbing his saya and katana at the tsuba with his right hand, lunging upward, letting his legs thrust him off the bench. Hideki jammed the end of his katana handle into the unguarded throat of Mondo. Mondo never got his sword out of his saya. Instead, he fell to the ground trying to get air through his crushed windpipe.

The two remaining samurai separated themselves from the bowl, noodles, and drew their swords. Hideki pushed his saya down into his obi and very deliberately drew the live blade, holding it in his right hand, tip upward, cutting edge down for all to see. Then, with a slight rotation, he reversed the cutting edge upward toward himself and away from the two ruffians. The motion was deliberate and meant to infuriate by implying their skill was so inferior to his that he would not insult his sword with their blood. Furious, they both lunged at Hideki at once.

Hideki rotated his blade down and to the right, deflecting the attack. Then he reversed the motion in a blazing movement as he shuffled left and pivoted on his forward foot, putting his entire body weight behind a strike to the short and ugly samurai's right elbow. The crack was audible as the samurai screamed in pain and fell to the dirt floor, dropping his sword to clutch his destroyed arm.

The last ruffian had to move to the left of his writhing friends in order to gain room to maneuver. Hideki was not allowing it. If he let him move, the girl would be in harm's way. Hideki dropped his sword to the left and shuffled to his right to cut the ruffian off.

The last samurai allowed his surprise to show in the form of a slight sneer. Hideki's head was exposed. The ruffian lunged with his point straight at Hideki's head. Hideki lunged at the same time, just to the right of the attacker's sword point and at the same time raised his sword and struck down, dropping all his weight and the back of his sword onto the man's exposed lead knee. He dropped to join his friends on the dirt floor, screaming in pain and clutching his ruined leg.

Hideki nodded toward Hana. Her shy smile was his reward. Her father moved to his side and bowed. "Domo arigato gozimus, samurai-san."

"Do itashi maste," Hideki replied as he returned his sword into the saya. "Bad manners are not to be tolerated."

Hideki looked down at Myo and found her smiling at him. "Nicely done Takezo. You believe in chivalry as well."

"I believe in Bushido. My sword is to protect the weak," Hideki said, starting to blush again.

"I wonder," Myo said.

"Samurai-san," the old man urged as he looked about the shop. "You should go before the police arrive."

"Why?" asked Hideki. "I have done nothing wrong."

"He is right, Takezo," Myo said. "We should leave before the police arrive. Here in Edo if you have money, you have justice."

"Are you both actually suggesting that I run for defending a young girl from three drunken samurai?" he asked.

"Boy, you are chivalrous and brave and very skilled with your sword, but you are dumb when it comes to how things work in Edo. You do not know how the system works here. Did you see those two kago bearers depart?" Myo asked.

"Yes. They fled to keep from getting hurt," Hideki stated.

"Wrong! They went straight to the police and reported a fight brewing here. The police will pay them for such information. You will be arrested because you are a ronin, and the rest of us will be lucky if we are not arrested also. We go before the magistrate, and he will find all the poor people guilty. We will be sentenced to one or two years of hard labor in one of the mines owned by a high-placed diamyo. The daimyo pays the magistrate for getting cheap labor, the magistrate pays the police, and the police pay the informants. The only people who get nothing are the poor. There is no justice in Edo for the poor!" Myo said. "Now let's get out of here."

"Too late for that," a loud voice called from the entrance. Hideki turned to see two officer detectives and two juttes blocking their escape.

The two officer detectives were uniformed in the kamishino, complete with mon on their sleeves and armed with the kodachi swords on their left hip and a jutte in their hands. The police were clothed in kimonos tucked into their obis, leggings that covered their shins, tabi, and straw sandals. However, their clothing left their thighs exposed from the knees to crotch region.

"You are going to jail," the older officer announced, pointing his jutte in Hideki's direction. "If you give us any trouble, we'll arrest the old man, the girl and this harlot."

Fear played across the old man's face. He protectively grasped Hana's shoulders. "Sumimasen Kagisan. She is all I have. My business would die if either of us had to go to jail."

"It's up to Uchi Benke here," pointing at Hideki. "If he comes quietly, we'll let the rest of you go. But if he tries any of that fancy sword play that laid these patrons in the dirt, then you all go to jail."

Hideki stared at the man. What insolence. Uchi Benke indeed; it was a reference to Musashibo Benke, a giant Yamabushi who defeated every samurai he came across and had the reputation for wrecking taverns, restaurants, and anywhere he fought. He fought a lot as he was on his way to collecting 1000 swords from his defeated foes when his path crossed the young, effeminate, and extremely quick samurai, Yoshimune. Yoshimune defeated Benke, and Benke swore his allegiance to Yoshimune. In the ensuing years, Yoshimune and Benke would win battle after battle in the period known as the Genpai wars.

"Kagi-san, I am confident in my skills. I believe you four cannot subdue me before I kill each of you," Hideki stated.

The two juttes physically drew back at the threat.

The older officer looked at the three on the ground. "That may be Benke, but reinforcements are arriving. Even if you do get out of here alive, the reinforcements will arrest everyone else, and killing a policeman is a death sentence for them."

Hideki looked at Hana, her father, and Myo. "Daijobi, kagi-san, the old man, his daughter and this lovely young woman will not have to go to jail. I will let you arrest me, Amoshiroi," Hideki said. "This may be interesting and enlightening."

"So this is what Musashi did on his musha shugyo," Hideki thought. "He travelled around the country honing his skills, living by his wits, constantly learning. Well, maybe this is a start of my pilgrimage." Then Hideki had to smile. Jii would be beside himself if he knew one of his "boys" had been arrested this close to the castle meeting. Nevertheless, they had to release him as soon as they knew the facts, surely. He really did not want to cause Jii or Naga embarrassment.

"I am innocent of any wrongdoing," Hideki said to himself. "I have protected the weak and upheld the honor of all samurai. I must be on the path of the Way. This is what I was born to do. This is what Bushido is all about. I feel truly alive. Meantime, I can learn more about the Edo justice that everyone complains about. This could help Jii and Brother in their great undertaking."

Hideki clutched both swords and pulled them from his obi, presenting them to the nearest officer. Then he glanced at Myo. "I sincerely hope we meet again."

Myo returned the smile. "Oh, you can count on it."

Chapter 11: Jail

Hideki was amused. First, the detectives added him to their roster of criminals in the outer office of the magistrate's building. Without his kodachi, he felt naked. He didn't feel dressed without the swords. When asked for his name, he thought of giving his real one and then watching the confusion. But, he could not do that to Jii. Having a Yoshinobu in the Hatchobori police blotter might kill him. So taking the events of the night one step further, he invented the name Benki Takezo. He would see the magistrate in the morning. Then two doshin escorted him further inside the building. Finally, two different rokushakubo-equipped doshin shoved Hideki along the dim corridors toward the cells with their six-foot staffs.

The floors were made of highly polished wood, the result of years of attention by the inmates on hands and knees. Unlike most structures, the hall was very narrow. The passageway was only a-man-and-one-half wide. Hideki's trained martial eye understood. One guard could hold off many rioting criminals until help arrived. No paper walls here. Everything was made of massive wood.

The two guards led Hideki to the furthest rooms inside the building. They stopped outside a huge cell with thick wooden bars. At a quick glance, Hideki estimated it contained approximately forty men. The smell was quite repugnant. Unwashed bodies, open waste jars, and fear combined for a noxious aroma that was almost overpowering.

Adjacent to the large cell was a smaller cell with a lone

inmate. "He is doing less well than I," Hideki said to himself. The inhabitant of the smaller cell hung from a beam in the center of the room. His feet hovered above the wooden floor a good two shaku. He was naked except for the fundoshi around his loins. Welts covered his body. Any skin not covered in welts showed bruises and open cuts. His chomagai had come untied and his long black hair hung down around his shoulders, giving him a wild and desperate look. He did not have the shaved pate. Instead, he had a full head of hair like Hideki. The muscles apparent in his beaten body attested to his power and maturity.

Despite his tormented body, Hideki noticed the man's face. He had only one good eye. A jagged scar ran from the eyebrow to the top of his cheek through an opaque and non-seeing eye. The good eye watched everything. The good eye was staring at Hideki. Hideki flinched. He had never felt hate in a stare before. A little shiver ran down his spine.

"If the guards are attempting to break this one's spirit," Hideki thought, "they'll be at it a long time." Just at that moment a brown clad doshin stepped into view in the small cell and brought a long bamboo rod down squarely on the one-eyed man's back. There was a loud crack. There was no noise from the one- eyed man.

One of Hideki's guards removed the lock from the large cell's door while the second guard stood behind Hideki with his bo against Hideki's back. Once the door was swung open, the guard behind Hideki shoved hard with his bo. Nothing happened. He shoved again. Nothing happened. Hideki expected the violent shove and centered his ki. It was a childish display, but he felt better for it. No need to let low-class doshin think he was a pushover.

When he felt his point made, Hideki strolled leisurely through the opened cell door onto a large, dirty, wooden floor with approximately forty of the toughest looking ruffians he had ever seen. They glared at him with open contempt. His slight stature and handsome, boyish looks marked him as their victim. The hackles on the back of Hideki's neck went up. Here was danger. How should he handle it? Was he good enough? He forced himself to breathe slowly and deeply.

A very large and rough-looking man with a scar down his right cheek moved confidently to Hideki's side, grabbed the back of his kimono at the neck and dropped down to the ground, bringing Hideki to his knees. "Oi, Oi, bukayaro! Kneel when you are in the presence of the Oyabun! Have you no manners?" He demanded.

A wake broke in the unwashed bodies as they moved back to reveal an even larger and more sinister-looking bandit enthroned on a stack of tatami mats. "Mystery solved on the missing flooring," thought Hideki. He had the same unkempt look as the rest of the denizens of the cell. His hands were busy inside his thick kimono scratching on the right and then the left. "Sumotori," Hideki thought. His immense size and fat face made his very slanted eyes almost disappear in his skull. "He looks like a human pig."

"Sumimasen," Hideki managed in an almost controlled voice. "I am new to these surroundings and do not know the customs."

"Ha, Ha," scoffed the large man with his hand on Hideki's collar. "He talks funny." The rest of Hideki's cellmates joined in on the laughter.

The pig on the tatami was not laughing. "Bring him here," he commanded.

The large man jerked Hideki to his feet and pushed him in the direction of the pig. Hideki came to a stumbling stop before the former sumo wrestler. Bowing his head slightly, he muttered, "Oyabun, sumimasen."

The pig looked confused and then uttered. "What is your name, where do you come from, and why are you here?"

"My name is Takezo. I am a recent ronin and I am to see the magistrate tomorrow due to a misunderstanding over a girl in a noodle shop around the corner and some ruffians who didn't know how to behave," Hideki replied.

"What clan were you?" the Pig asked.

"My old clan is of no importance," Hideki said and ducked forward as he shot out his left leg backwards, striking scar face in the stomach. Scar face was off balance from attempting to cuff Hideki on the back of the head for his last comment to the Oyabun. The big man's forward momentum combined with the powerful ushido geri from Hideki's back kick knocked the wind out of his large lung area. Hideki turned into him and using mai tobi geri jumped on one leg to get elevated height and struck directly on the scar under the large man's right eye with the ball of his right foot. Scar Face's head snapped back with the power of the kick and went down like a dropped pot. He fell to a heap on the dirt floor and did not move.

There was a stunned silence for a moment. Then an angry murmur erupted as the rest of the criminals started to press in on Hideki. Hideki dropped his hands to his side and assumed a hangetsu dachi. The half-moon stance was supposed to provide the best all-around defense.

"Mate, mate!" yelled the pig man. "No one in this room is a match for this man, except maybe me. Have you no eyes. He did not see Sempai's attack. He felt it. We have an accomplished martial artist in our midst."

The crowd stopped closing in and gave Hideki some room. Hideki turned to face the pig. "Domo arigato, Oyabun. I am in your debt."

"Your speech is that of nobility, samurai. Your clothes cannot disguise your prowess and skill. Are you here to spy on us?"

"No Oyabun, only to learn," Hideki said.

"What have you come to learn? What can the Gumsumgumi teach you?" the Oyabun asked.

"Gumsumgumi, I should have known," Hideki thought to himself. This was one of the more renowned gangs in recent years around Edo. Their members were masterless samurai, out of work laborers and vagrants of all sorts. They ran gambling halls, prostitutes, money lending, and protection rackets all over the new Tokugawa capital. The Yagyu were watching them, but their activities remained secret. They were tough to infiltrate. Their trademark was elaborate tattoos over the shoulder and back called irizumi. The tattoos ran halfway down their arms. Rumor provided they sported the tattoos to identify themselves as outside the law and outcast from society. Given the Japanese dislike of anything out of the ordinary, Hideki could see why the government loathed them. However, Hideki had heard Yagyu explain one night on the Tokaido that the irizumi was to hide the circular armbands tattooed on convicts to identify them as criminals and allow the magistrate to identify how many times they had been in prison. Three circular tattoos were usually the maximum a magistrate would allow before ordering execution. Either way, they were outside of society's norm, and Hideki could understand why they were so paranoid about outsiders.

"Everything Oyabun," Hideki said. "I've lived most of my life in the country. Therefore, the ways of Edo are new to me. I want to learn what every citizen of Edo knows."

"I am Nichi, leader of the Gumsumgumi, the protector of the weak and the righter of wrongs. These are my children," he said waving a meaty hand to include all in the cell.

Hideki followed the motion of his hand, marveling at the collection of human flotsam and jetsam. "Yes, I can see the resemblance."

The Oyabun looked shocked. Then a smile played across his fat face. His eyes almost disappeared. "Do you mock me, ronin?" Nichi asked.

"No, Nichi-sama, I have much to learn. If indeed you are the protector of the weak and the righter of wrongs, I would like to learn more of your ways. It sounds much like Bushido."

"We have our own code, ronin. While we may have borrowed some from the samurai, we pledge allegiance to the group, not a liege Lord. Come, sit—yours is the first intelligent conversation I've had in the month we've been locked up by the shogun's corrupt force known as the police," Nichi said.

Hideki took a position on the dirt floor and looked up at his new mentor. "The government sends many spies in here to learn of the Gumsumgumi and to assassinate me, ronin. We will see if you are one of them or not. Tell me of your life in the country. If you make a mistake, I will know, as my brothers here come from all occupations. Country living is well known to many of them," Nichi challenged.

"Hai," Hideki started to speak. Then he noticed two of the crowd closest to the Oyabun reaching into their kimonos as they angled away, slowly moving in to hear Hideki's story. Hideki jumped to his feet, ran the two steps toward the Oyabun, and dived into the mountain of flesh, toppling him off the other side. He landed on the dirt floor with a sickening thud with Hideki on top of him.

The Oyabun was shaking his head to clear the stars. The attacker on the right appeared first with a wicked looking tanto protruding from his right hand. He lunged the knife at Hideki's throat.

Hideki did not have time to stand. He barely had time to untangle himself from the Oyabun and get to his knees. As the knife was inches from his throat, Hideki shifted his upper body to the left. The point narrowly missed its mark. Hideki clamped his right hand on the extended wrist and pivoted on his knees. An upward kumeda palm heel strike inward to the outside of the attacker's exposed elbow was sufficient.

There was a distinct crack followed by a loud scream as Hideki continued the motion by pulling the wrist down and removing the tanto from the ruined arm. Now Hideki was facing the Oyabun and saw the second attacker come around the other side of the stacked mats, his tanto held waist high.

He was moving fast and straight for the Oyabun's heart. Hideki was too far away to deflect the attack. He twirled the tanto in his right hand so he now held the blade and threw it as hard as he could at the attacker. As soon as he let the knife fly, he knew his aim was off. He was trying for the center of the assassin's chest. Instead, the blade buried itself in the assassin's left eye. He screamed and fell to the floor and twitched as he tried to stop the pain in his head just before his heels drummed a staccato on the dirt floor. Then he was silent.

Around the tatami came Scar Face on the run. He stopped behind Hideki and looked at his Oyabun and the two assassins. Seeing that one was alive and nursing a badly broken arm, he reached down and grabbed the live assassin around the neck and spun his hands fiercely. There was a slight cracking sound as the enemy's neck snapped like a dry twig.

Hideki was amazed. He had never seen such strength in a man's hands before. Just as amazing, both of those powerful hands were now reaching for his head.

"Dame, dame, Goro," the Oyabun managed. "The ronin saved my life."

The scar-faced Goro stopped in his tracks when he heard his master's voice. The Oyabun managed to roll over on his massive stomach and started to stand. Goro pushed Hideki forcefully out of his way so he could help his boss up.

Once the Oyabun gained his balance, he brushed the dirty straw from his hair and bowed to Hideki. "Thank you for my life, ronin. Now you know why Goro was so suspicious. This is the third time this week. I fear the bakfuku is wearying of the Gumsumgumi," Nichi said. "My days are numbered with the government."

Hideki was shocked at such a statement. "Oyabun, surely the government didn't send those assassins. They are the law."

The Oyabun looked at Hideki in disbelief. "You must be from a very far off clan, samurai-san. The entire bakfuku, starting with that idiot shogun and his keepers, the Yagyu, right down to the guards of this jail are corrupt. Their only goal seems to be to make the average citizen's life as miserable as possible. If they are not taxing you, they are hanging you or cutting your head off. From roaming samurai preying on the citizens to wholesale larceny by the daimyos, nothing is too despicable or corrupt for the government to try."

Hideki shook his head in disbelief. "Bushido would not allow this to happen. Ieyasus himself said, that the highest form of Bushido was good government," Hideki protested.

The Oyabun stared at Hideki for a long few moments. "Samurai-san, the Gumsumgumi exists because the bakufu government is corrupt and won't take care of the people. Who are the little people going to turn to when it is their own government oppressing them? We exist because no one else cares," Nichi proclaimed.

Placing a meaty hand on Hideki's shoulder, Nichi said, "You need our protection more than most. At least the lowest of the Edoko, the children of Edo, knows the seasons of life in this town. You, on the other hand, seem to be more naïve than anyone I have ever encountered. Your mind seems as quick as your hands and feet, but your level of comprehension of politics is appalling. No wonder you wound up in jail. No spy would come to us with such a contrived level of ignorance as yours. You are truly a sheep among wolves," the large man said. Then nodding as if convincing himself, "We will protect you and teach you the ways of Edo, ronin. However, you must earn your keep like everyone else. Just as soon as my yojimbo shakes off the effects of your flying kick, he shall be your sempai. You will need a mentor if you are to learn our ways. I will take you on as an apprentice yojimbo. Do you accept the job?"

"Hai, Oyabun. I shall try to be a good bodyguard. However, I do so with the reservation that I may have to depart unexpectedly. But I promise to return," Hideki said.

The fat man laughed. "I'm doing you no favors, ronin. You will earn your keep. If the Yagyu spies are not after my head, then it is the money-hungry Daimyos and their samurai enforcers or the no-good thieves' guild at the river. We'll talk about your comings and goings later." He shook his large head in disgust. "No one has any honor anymore. It is the one thing I miss about the Basho."

"So," Hideki thought. "I was correct. Nichi is a sumotori. Now how did a sumo wrestler from the grand tournaments become the head of the Gumsumgumi?"

Hideki bowed his head in the direction of Goro. "Onegaishimasu, sempai. Oshiette kudasai."

The word "sempai" confused Goro. So did Hideki asking him to teach him. His face showed his lack of understanding.

Nichi nodded. "That's right, Goro. The ronin has joined us. I am making him an apprentice bodyguard. You are going to be his sempai. He says he has come to learn. So teach him and be his big brother," Nichi commanded.

"Hai, Oyabun," Goro bowed. "Wakaremasu," muttered Goro. However, he did not understand at all. All he knew was this ronin had bested him in front of everyone and then saved his boss's life. He did not have any idea how any of it happened. Now he was supposed to teach this young upstart. Goro would just have to find some way to make the ronin pay for his insolence.

Chapter 12: Jail Break

"While I thank you for saving my life, ronin," the Oyabun stated as he surveyed the two dead assassins, "you have made matters somewhat worse."

Hideki smiled. "What could be worse than being opened like a ripe persimmon?" he asked.

"Many things, ronin," the Oyabun muttered. "How about having all the bones in your legs crushed under heavy rocks? Or, I could wind up like our friend there," Nichi said as he pointed to the one-eyed ronin dangling from the center beam in the adjoining cell. "They'll hoist him up higher tomorrow and bring a cauldron of oil in which to boil him."

Hideki winced thinking of the barbarity of such an idea. "What could he have done to warrant such action?" he wondered aloud.

Nichi looked at Hideki as if he had just fallen to earth from the heavens. "That is the point I've been trying to make with you ronin. We do not have to do anything. We just have to be poor, or unemployed, or exist outside the law like the Gumsumgumi. They don't need an excuse."

Hideki glanced at the one-eyed ronin dangling from the center beam in the next cell. "What a waste of superb samurai spirit." Hideki looked the Oyabun in the eyes, "This must be stopped."

Now the Oyabun was smiling. "Those are my sentiments exactly. That is why we exist. It is also the reason we are in here."

"Unpardonable," said Hideki. "Wait a moment; are you

saying that assassins have attempted this before and you've handled it differently than I did?" asked Hideki.

"Usually less permanently," sighed the Oyabun. "They are often spotted, and we break a bone or two or leave them black and blue lying next to the cell door for the guards to find and remove."

"Except for the assassination, it sounds like a game," Hideki ventured.

"Yes, ronin, like a game. Except in this game your skill has upped the stakes. Now we will all be treated as murderers," sighed Nichi.

Hideki knew what that meant. Death by crucifixion was probably the cruelest death. Such was not the way for a samurai to end his days, begging for water and praying for a compassionate guard to pierce his heart with a yari. "So what do we do, Oyabun?" he asked.

"Quiet, let me think," the Oyabun replied.

Then the pig man started giving orders in the manner Hideki understood. "Goro, pull the bodies around behind the tatami mats." Then, looking up into the rafters, "The guards probably already know what has happened, but maybe we had Buddha smiling on us."

Hideki followed his gaze upward. "You mean they spy on you constantly?" he asked.

"Ronin, you truly have a lot to learn. Of course, they spy on us constantly. We are criminals in their eyes. We have no rights. We are denied even that most precious right, the right of privacy. Our every move is watched by the guards above and the spies in our midst," he said pointing to the rafters and the dead bodies behind the mats.

Rubbing his meaty hand over his bald head, the rotund boss of the Gumsumgumi thought aloud, "If the guards saw you dispatch the assassins, they'll be here in a moment to separate us for immediate interrogation. That means death. They'll cripple us first, to get our confessions so it all looks good in front of that corrupt magistrate and then they'll crucify us." The Oyabun looked around the edge of the tatami mats toward the cell door. "That means when they come for us, we'll have to make an escape. We have no choice. If we stay here, we all die," he said as if making up his mind, adding, "Well ronin, are you up for a little adventure?"

"I guess I have no choice, Oyabun," Hideki replied.

"Smart thinking; you are correct. You have no choice, unless you count death a choice," the Oyabun said. Then turning to his second in command, "Goro, we will give them an hour. If they have not come within the hour, you will have to create a disturbance that will get the guards to respond to restore order. Do you understand?"

"Hai, Oyabun," Goro responded. However, he did not understand. He hated it when the boss gave him that sort of order. Now he had to figure out what to do on his own. He was not good at that. It was so much easier when the boss told him exactly what to do. If the Oyabun had said, "Start a fire," then he would know exactly what to do. If he had said, "Start a riot," then again, Goro would know exactly what to do. However, to "Create a disturbance," by the Buddha, what did he mean by that? Should it be a fire or a fight?

The Oyabun saw Goro trying to sort out his assignment. "He'll eventually settle on a path," Nichi said to Hideki. "We'll overpower the guards as soon as they come inside the cell. Your martial skills will come in handy, ronin."

"Where will we go once outside?" asked Hideki. "The streets of Edo are a maze."

"Never mind our destination, ronin," the Oyabun warned. "If you do not know, you cannot betray us. Just follow me and stay close once we leave the magistrate's compound."

"Goro, how would you like to be ainagi to the ronin here?"

Goro's stupid stare told the Oyabun more explanation was required. "The ronin, Goro; he has joined us now. No place will be safe for him. Only we have the network to hide him. He'll need an older brother to show him the ropes." Then turning back to Hideki, "Ototo dijobi?"

"Hai, Oyabun," Hideki said with a low bow at the waist. "I will be honored to be Goro's little brother." Turning to Goro, Hideki bowed again, "Ainigi, oshiette kudasai," Goro's confused look was still on his face. "He's asking you to be his big brother in the Gumsumgumi, Goro," the Oyabun said. "So take good care of him and let your past differences be in the past."

"Hai, Oyabun," Goro eagerly replied, but he still shot Hideki a disapproving glance. Whatever thoughts Goro was thinking took second place to the sound of many guards running toward their cell. They were armed with short wooden cudgels—wicked-looking weapons with spikes driven through them in various directions. The sea of men moved back from the door of the cell and away from the carnage that was sure to come.

Nichi, the Oyabun, snapped an order at Goro: "Hand out the tatami to our toughest fighters and place them closest to the cell door." Goro grabbed two underlings and started the movement of mats to the front of the cell.

A large doshin with a jutte strutted to the cell door. "Oi, big boss of the carrion eaters; your time has come. You are to confess your dirty deeds to this jutte, here." As he said this, he bounced the end of his jutte on his shoulder. "You can come easy or hard; it makes no difference to me."

Hideki believed the doshin. He looked capable of great cruelty. Police interrogation rooms were no fun. He snatched a quick glance at the hanging ronin in the adjacent cell. It did not matter whether large stones crushed you slowly or bamboo clubs flayed your flesh; either way you were doomed. If you survived and did not confess, you were innocent and allowed to leave, usually as a cripple. If you confessed to stop the pain, you were guilty and sent to island prison or executed. Hideki did not see either in his future.

Nichi's response was direct. "You don't have enough men, you thief of honest men's wages."

The doshin pointed in the direction of the oyabun and issued an order. The gate opened and the cudgel-swinging guards entered the cell. They ran into a line of large men using tatami matting to neutralize the spiked weapons.

Hideki saw the larger picture at once. "The general who understands his enemy's weakness and his own strengths will prevail," Hideki said under his breath, reciting Sun Tzu's *Art of War.* "Thanks, Jii," Hideki said. Hideki's job was to get to the jutte-wielding doshin before he realized their objective was escape. He had to get to him before he retreated and locked the cell door again.

A guard rushed at Hideki, aiming an overhead blow with a spiked cudgel meant to impale itself in Hideki's skull. Hideki moved into and on the outside of the cudgel, laying his right hand on top of the plunging arm. Hideki continued the attacker's momentum downward and increased it by using his own force to spin the man 180 degrees from where he came. The attacker crashed into the line of guards, creating a hole into which Hideki darted. Only one more guard to get past and he would be at his target.

The last man was left handed. He aimed a blow to the right side of Hideki's head. Hideki saw the blow coming but was in gyaku hanmi and out of position. His feet were opposite the guard's right foot forward position. This put Hideki at a disadvantage. He was too far away in this position to use the preferred counter of moving inside the blow. Instead, Hideki executed an outside block with his right arm, catching the guard's wrist on the inside, driving it off target. Hideki turned his blocking hand over and captured the attackers left wrist, redirecting it downward below his knees and then upward in a great circle to Hideki's left front as he stepped in the same direction.

The club hand of the attacker ended up neutralized in this position as Hideki's step brought the attacker off balance and reaching upward toward nothing. A quick exchange of hands and Hideki's right elbow was free to drive back into the attacker's exposed ribs. A loud crunch and the attacker went down screaming in a heap. Hideki's eyes came up, searching for the jutte-carrying doshin. Hideki knew he had to get between the doshin and the open door. The doshin noticed Hideki. His confident countenance changed to panic. He turned, stooped down, and fled through the low cell door and closed it behind him. Hideki leaped to the door and pushed on it just as he heard the lock snap into place.

The jutte's face went from fear to smiles. "Didn't end the way you expected?" he taunted. Then he rose and surveyed his guards. They were under tatami mats and immobilized. "Oi, Nichi," the jutte called. "I've got to go find a very large cross for you."

Hideki shoulder's hunched over. "Amida Buddha," he swore.

Nichi came up next to Hideki. "I guess that's it. We all die tomorrow."

They stared after the swaggering doshin as he passed the guards' day room and continued toward the long, narrow corridor leading to the front of the building. He was laughing and tapping his shoulder with the jutte as he strutted across the wooden floor.

Hideki let out a loud sigh, and the jutte let out a loud scream as he vaulted toward the rafters. As the doshin went up, a gray-clad figure came down on the other end of the rope. Nichi and Hideki looked at each other in surprise. The jutte was screaming and calling to guards for help. There was no one to hear. The rest of the guard watch was in the front of the compound at the other end of the long, narrow corridor. They could not hear anything that happened in the center of the building.

The gray-clad figure stared up at his handy work as he tied off his end of the rope on a cell door. He stood and walked backwards toward Hideki's cell to ensure his captive could not get down. Hideki could read the writing on his back: Abe Courier Service. "Yoshi," Hideki cried. "I've never been so happy to see anyone."

Yoshi turned to smile at his friend. Then he surveyed the scene of the wounded men in the cell and the guards immobilized with tatami mats and Gumsumgumi sitting on them. "I don't wonder. By the way, the Old Grey One sends his love and requests your presence tomorrow morning."

"Only two things wrong with that, Yoshi. First, I'm locked up, and second, I don't know where I am."

Yoshi looked puzzled. "You are in jail."

"I know that much," Hideki said. "But once you quit

looking stupid and get me out, I have no idea how to get to the Old Grey One. Edo is a maze."

Yoshi knelt down to examine the lock.

"Can he open it, Takezo?" Nichi asked.

Yoshi's head snapped up in surprise at the name.

"If anyone can," Hideki replied.

Yoshi took out two metal strips from the folds in his jacket and went to work on the lock. "You would have a little difficulty with this one, Takezo," he said, stressing the new name. "It is of Chinese design."

Nichi's impatience was showing. "But can you open it?"

"I believe so," Yoshi said as the lock clicked and opened in his hand. "It is a good thing I spent two years building them."

Yoshi opened the door expecting Hideki to exit. Hideki stepped back and pointed to the door. "After you Oyabun."

Again, Yoshi let surprise play on his face as he rose and ran to the guards' day room.

Nichi had great difficulty in getting through the narrow space but emerged only slightly ruffled. Yoshi returned holding many lengths of rope and Hideki's swords. Nichi understood immediately. He called for Goro to tie up the guards under the tatami and to get the Gumsumgumi ready to move out.

"Domo, Yoshi," Hideki said, bowing. "Now I feel like a man again."

Nichi looked from Hideki to Yoshi. "And how does an out-of-work ronin happen to have a servant handy with a rope and a lock pick?"

"Well," Hideki started, "Yoshi is sort of our family ..."

He did not get the rest out as Yoshi chimed in, "Courier ... I am his family's courier. I actually work for his grandfather."

Nichi looked Hideki in the eyes. "Right, and I am the next shogun. Yoshi here is a ninja if ever I saw one. But he is the first one that has not tried to kill me. I will find the underlying truth of this later. Come ronin, you can help me plan the next leg of our escape."

Hideki had moved over to the adjoining cell where the

one-eye ronin dangled. Nichi came up beside him.

"We do not have time to do charity work, ronin. We must escape now before the alert is sounded," Nichi said. Hideki ignored him and stepped into the cell. He drew his wakazashi and looked up into the good eye. There was no pleading there. His expression was stone, resigned to his fate.

Hideki stepped around behind him. "Prepare yourself," Hideki said. There was an almost imperceptible nod from the one-eyed man. Hideki pressed his blade to the rope and it split immediately. The ronin landed with a thud and fell over on his side. His arms still bound behind his back. Hideki cut him free and set him upright.

Yoshi arrived at his side with a bucket and ladle of water and put the ladle to the one-eyed man's lips. He reached up tentatively at first, then with urgency, and gulped down the water. Yoshi refilled it and he drank again.

"Can you walk?" Hideki asked. His question caused a slight nod.

Hideki and Yoshi lifted him up into a standing position, each taking an arm. He was a large man, a head taller than either Hideki or Yoshi. Once balanced, Yoshi asked Hideki to watch him as he let Hideki take the weight and ran toward the guard's day room. When he returned, he had a guard's kimono. They covered the large man's nakedness and he seemed to recover some confidence and a little strength.

They started toward the day room and the long corridor when the one-eyed man stopped and pointed with his chin at the day room. Hideki understood. The one-eyed man wanted his own clothes and swords. He pointed to an open cubicle. When they emerged, the one-eyed man wore an all-black kamishino. Everything about him was black. His kimono was black. His hakama was black. Even his sword's tsuka and saya were black.

Hideki surveyed the one-eyed ronin. His gaze was drawn to the dead eye with its angry red scar a little above and a little below the socket. He went back into the day room again and emerged with a tsuba and saego from someone's swords.

Hideki cut the cord and tied one end of each length to

the opposing end of the Tsuba. Then he moved the sword guard toward the dead eye. The one-eyed man pulled back instinctively, but relaxed when he understood Hideki's intent.

Hideki placed the Tsuba over the dead eye and tied it in place behind the man's head. With the last section of the cord, Hideki tied back the man's hair so it looked less wild and intimidating. When he was finished, he stepped back to admire his handy work.

"Now you won't be so easy for the police to spot," Hideki proclaimed. He knew he had made the right decision. This man's samurai spirit was strong. He would not bend and he would not break. "Such a man is worth saving," Hideki thought. The man in black reminded him of Musashi.

Yoshi looked at Hideki. "No wrong too small to right and no right too small to defend?"

Hideki shrugged. "I guess." It was all Hideki could think to say by way of explanation.

The one-eyed man bowed his head. "Namae non desu-ka?"

Hideki bowed, saying, "Benkei Takezo," giving his name of the evening.

Yoshi rolled his eyes skyward at the ridiculous name.

"Honto desuka?" the man's raspy voice asked, denoting his non-belief.

"Well, it will have to do for now," Hideki replied. "And what shall we call you? Don't tell me Kuro?" Hideki asked, referencing the black clothes.

The man tried to smile. It was too painful. "You may call me Jubei," he growled.

Yoshi's head snapped toward Jubei.

"Benkei Takezo, from this moment on, I am your man," Jubei rasped.

Hideki felt the warmth creep into his cheeks. "Dame, I am no one's better. Moreover, you owe me nothing. I am sure you would have done the same for me."

Jubei shook his head slightly. "That is the point, Benkei Takezo, I would not have. You defend the weak when it is not in your best interest. You shame me with your Bushido."

167

"Well, we can talk about it when you are well. You are overly grateful now. When you are better, you will see that I've done nothing so great."

"You are the one who doesn't understand. I have been on a musha shugyo for some time to better my skill and myself. Tonight you have shown me a great lesson, and you do not even see it yourself. I will follow you now not out of giri, but to see how you turn out."

"You saw it immediately, didn't you?" asked Yoshi.

"Hai," Jubei replied.

Nichi came up to Hideki. "Okay, we rush them," he said as he pointed to the narrow corridor.

"Simasen, Oyabun," Hideki pardoned himself. "That may be counterproductive. I suggest we use a little strategy."

With Goro beside Nichi there was very little space in the corridor.

"I will listen because you saved my life tonight and because your family courier got us out of that cell. Speak your plan."

"Have the guards strip. Put your best men in their clothes. We can come out laughing and congratulating ourselves on showing those Gumsumgumi a thing or two. When they least suspect it, we overpower the officers in front and bring them back to a cell. We can then split up and go our ways to rejoin at your direction. If we are lucky, they won't know about the escape until much later."

The Oyabun pondered the plan. "I like it. It might work." He turned to Goro and gave the necessary instructions. The Gumsumgumi emerged from the large cell a few moments later in guard clothing and carrying juttes. They moved single file down the narrow corridor. Goro and Nichi followed. Hideki, Yoshi, and Jubei brought up the rear.

It was slow going having to half carry the one-eyed ronin. Hideki noticed that by the time they reached the entrance, no real police officers remained standing. They all were tied and gagged. The entire Hatchobori belonged to the Gumsumgumi.

Nichi came up to Hideki. "Good plan, ronin. You take

your friends and go with Goro. He'll get you to our home."

Hideki started to protest about Jubei needing a doctor. Nichi cut him off. "It will all be arranged. I have a very good doctor on call. Do not worry about him. You can go see this "Old Grey One" in the morning after you've bathed, rid yourself of jail-house fleas, and had some decent food and a change of clothes so you'll be hard to recognize."

"Hai, Oyabun," Hideki said.

"Well, I'm surprised. That is the first command you've obeyed tonight," Nichi said.

Hideki bowed. "Gomen, Oyabun."

Nichi smiled. "If I thought you meant it, I might be impressed. You are one strange person, ronin."

Hideki nodded as they split up and departed. The fact that Nichi was the last one to leave the compound was not lost on Hideki.

When they were several streets distant and the one-eyed man was able to hit a rhythm in his walk, carrying him became easier as the exertion lessened.

Yoshi asked Hideki, "How do you manage to constantly have one foot in the binjo and the other in cherry blossoms?"

Hideki kept looking straight ahead.

"It's a gift," he said.

Chapter 13: New Beginnings

Luckily, they did not have to drag Jubei too far. When Ieyasu Tokugawa set up his capital in Edo, it was mostly swamp and marsh. He lowered an entire mountain so that his castle would be the highest point for miles. He used the earth to fill in the marshes and bogs surrounding the bay, then he set about trying to bring water to the town.

When he first arrived, there were three wells. With only a few hundred town folk, three wells were more than enough. However, with Ieyasu's winning at Sekigahara in 1600 and the declaration of shogun in 1603, getting water to the burgeoning town became a priority. A series of wells with canals and rechanneling of rivers followed. The result was, if you were an Edoko and wanted to transport something heavy, you had two choices. The first was to fight the foot traffic and meandering roads through the capital. The second was to find one of the town's people who made their living on takase-bune, the barges and small boats that populated the waterways. The grid layout of the rivers and canals was much easier to travel, especially if one wished to remain unobserved.

"Seems you've made an enemy of the big dumb one," Yoshi said. "He hasn't slowed down to help us once."

"I'm afraid so," Hideki said as he adjusted his grip on Jubei's arm. "I knocked him unconscious in the cell."

Yoshi smiled. "I would have paid good money to see that."

In between ragged breathing, Jubei interjected, "It

was quite a sight, even with one good eye."

"Save your strength Jubei," Hideki chided. "We don't know how much further we have to walk."

Goro stopped up ahead and yelled at someone, though he was too far away for any of the three to hear.

"Well, at least he's not yelling at us," Yoshi mused.

"Fune," Jubei said, indicating a boat.

"If you keep talking, Jubei–san, we're going to let you walk on your own," Yoshi warned.

Nevertheless, Jubei was correct. When the trio caught up to Goro, he had two shallow-draft barges ready. One was for him and one for the three of them. Goro gave the owners of the barges their instruction, and off they went.

Jubei curled up in the bow on some canvas and went to sleep. "Best medicine for him," Yoshi whispered.

"Do you have any idea where we are?" Hideki asked.

"These little canals all flow into the Kanda canal, so I would guess that Nichi's hideout is in Nihonbashi or Kajibashi right on the main canal. It would be easy for the Gumsumgumi to hide amongst the warehouses and shops, and he'd have easy access by road and a back door on the water," Yoshi surmised.

"Makes sense," Hideki said as he scratched inside his kimono, first on one side and then the other.

"Pick up some friends in the cell?" Yoshi asked.

Hideki was not listening. He was wondering how he was going to get back to the Yoshinobu estate in Kanda.

"You've picked up fleas, Hideki. You need a hot bath," Yoshi said.

"I need a lot of things, Yoshi," Hideki sighed. "I need to know what I'm going to do at the castle. I cannot help Naga. My presence will only cause him grief. I need to know how people that I believe to be honorable like the Gumsumgumi turn out to be thieves, whoremongers, and gamblers. I need to know why the police are so corrupt and why the magistrate condones it. I need to know why everything is so upside down from the way I was taught it should be."

"All good questions, young master. But the best question has to do with what you are going to do to change it."

Hideki shook his head in frustration. "What can I do? I am only one man and not very experienced, as you may have noticed."

"I noticed the same thing Musashi and Jubei did. I noticed a young, idealistic samurai who has the courage of his teachings, right on his side, a love of Bushido, and maybe a chance to influence the government," Yoshi said firmly.

"Is that why you are still with me and not with your young wife?" Hideki asked.

"Musashi has been talking again, I see," Yoshi said.

"He says you are a newlywed and a man of some responsibility in your village. He also said you were a man to be trusted," Hideki repeated.

"Kind words from the Sword Saint."

"Don't you miss her?" Hideki asked.

"Certainly. Once you are married, you become a team. You don't feel right without her," Yoshi said as he momentarily stared into the distance as if his wife were visible on the horizon.

"So why are you still here?" Hideki asked.

"Because if she were here, she'd tell me to do what I'm doing. Anyone can kill for money. How often do you get a chance to make history?" Yoshi asked.

"Is that what we're doing, making history?"

"Well so far all you're doing is making people angry and leaving a trail of broken bones. But with Jii's guidance, your brother's character, and your code of honor, the timing is right for some interesting things to happen," Yoshi speculated.

"What kind of things? Do you think they will actually appoint Naga shogun?"

"How would I know? I am a country assassin. But the primary heir to the shogunate is a known homosexual whose main support is from a conniving cutthroat wet nurse and whose mother is supporting the second son, a known lunatic, even Naga looks good," Yoshi laughed, adding, "He certainly looked good to Hanzo's daughter Yuki." "Ouch," Hideki said. They both looked to the bow of the boat as Jubei rose to a sitting position.

"Did you say Yuki?" he asked.

"Yes, Jubei, Hanzo Yuki; she and Hideki's older brother Naga are in love," Yoshi replied.

"I see," Jubei said and went back to sleep.

"What was that all about?" Hideki asked.

"You really don't know who you rescued, do you?" Yoshi asked.

"Jubei? He's a ronin."

"That may be true, but he is also the heir to the Yagyu family. He is the celebrated sword instructor to the shogun and one-time director of the metsuke. He is Yagyu Jubei, who has been missing for the past year," Yoshi said. "Everybody thought he was dead."

Hideki just stared at Yoshi. "Which foot is that, the binjo or the cherry blossom?"

"Too soon to tell, young prince, but it will surely win you points with papa Yagyu," Yoshi speculated. "I'm not sure about Naga, though, as Jubei and Yuki were supposed to be engaged."

The boats pulled into a small dock in an area with long buildings lining each side of the wide canal. It was a short walk to a side street with two-and three-story buildings on each side of the narrow street. These were not heartless hovels. These were substantial buildings with many rooms and many businesses on the street level. There were craft shops for gold, silver, and tin. There were restaurants. There were umbrella makers. There were more signs for businesses than Hideki had ever seen in one spot. "Kajibashi," Yoshi uttered.

Goro led them to a building that took up a whole city block. In the center was an upscale hotel with an ornate wooden front carved like a temple. Two large cloth banners announced "The Traveler's Rest." There were greeters who met the four inside the building reception area. Here they washed their feet and hands and drank tea to refresh themselves. Goro gave orders and everyone went scrambling to obey. Then Goro disappeared into the bowels of the building. The banto-sama of the hotel came over and made introductions. Two large men accompanied him.

"I am Sasuke. I am the manager of the hotel. You are to

be our guests. I have rooms awaiting you and a doctor is on the way for your friend. These men will assist him to his room. His room is one the doctor is well aware of as we use it as an infirmary. We have a bath in the back of the hotel. Please make yourself comfortable in your rooms and then proceed to the bath at your discretion. Our Oyabun will arrive shortly and he expects a large banquet. You are to be the guests of honor. You will find clean clothes in your rooms. Please follow me."

The two large men picked up Jubei as if he were a feather and laid him gently on a futon. One produced water to drink. A young woman came in and moved everyone out so she could bathe Jubei before the doctor arrived.

Hideki and Yoshi followed Sasuke to their rooms. "I don't want to intrude on the Oyabun's bath. When should we head to the ofudo?" Hideki asked.

"Oh, the Oyabun will take a bath in the other wing of the hotel as will most of his men. The bath out back is for real guests. You will most likely not be disturbed. Please enjoy your stay," Sasuke said.

"You go ahead Hideki," Yoshi said. "I have some errands to run before I retire, and I don't think I'm expected at the banquet."

"Have it your way Yoshi, but you are expected by me," Hideki said.

"Thank you, but a good ninja knows when to duck back into the shadows."

"Well, that is the second time you've saved my life. Thank you," Hideki said.

"No need, Lord," Yoshi said.

Hideki peered into his well-appointed room and turned to bid Yoshi goodnight, only there was no one there. "Like talking to a ghost," Hideki said to himself.

Hideki needed a bath. The fleas were eating him alive. It was late and most guests were in their rooms asleep. Hideki wandered back to the main lobby and then down the corridor to the rear. He actually had to leave by the hotel's back entrance and enter a small compound to get to the ofudo.

Once he stepped into the compound, a clerk sitting at a

small desk to the right bowed to him. In front of the clerk was a small box with coins of many denominations. Hideki did not have any money on him. The police at Hatchibori confiscated all he had. However, the clerk bowed low and handed Hideki a large wooden bowl, a small towel, a sponge, and a small, polished stick with an edge.

Hideki bowed and moved to the washing area. There he stripped, placed his swords within easy reach and began to scoop up water from the pool in the center of the room. He doused himself several times and proceeded to abrade his skin with the sponge. After several more dousings, he ran the edge of the polished stick over his body. Then placing his thoroughly wet clothes in a box he took up his swords and towel and continued down wooden stairs to a roofed pavilion.

The roof was red cedar and supported by massive wooden poles set in a rock wall that surrounded a large onsen, or outside bath. The heat of the water created mist as it met the cooler night air. There were no buildings behind the onsen as the property sloped away toward a large canal. Hideki had the bath to himself. "Heaven," he thought.

He entered the water slowly as the heat burned his skin and he could barely stand the temperature. He kept stepping down further and further into the hot water. He placed the small towel between his legs hoping for some escape from the scalding water, careful to keep the swords in his right hand above the surface. Exposing himself to this liquid furnace was challenging.

He stepped further down, slowly letting the heat eat into his body. As he adjusted to it, he took in the surroundings. A few paper lanterns hung above the water around the rock wall. It illuminated an area of about two shaku around the lantern. He could not see much, just the dull outline of the wall and the lights of the city in the distance. An occasional firefly blinked on the edges of the wall. When he was waist deep, Hideki moved to the side of the onsen and found a rock bench below the waterline. He placed his swords on top of the rock wall within easy reach and he sat down slowly. The heat soaked his body and melted his cares. It felt good. He felt perspiration develop on his scalp. Forgetting where the small towel had been moments before, he used it to wipe his brow. He was almost asleep when interrupted by a feminine voice. "Gomen samurai-san, may I share your bath?"

Hideki snapped awake. He looked at the entrance of the small onsen and saw the outline of a naked female body about to step into the water. "I suppose so. It is not my onsen."

As she moved gracefully into the water, Hideki noticed two things. First, she did not have to adjust to the heat as he had done. She just walked into it as if it were not hot. Secondly, she used the small square towel to cover her breasts and private parts. Everything but her face was in view. It was very disturbing. For the first time, he was glad of the heat from the onsen and the darkness. No one could see him blush.

She moved to a seat on the opposite side of the pool from Hideki. She sighed as the heat penetrated her body. Hideki felt like he should say something, but he did not know what to say, so he kept quiet.

"I'm sorry to disturb your bath, samurai-san," she said out of the darkness.

"You are not disturbing me," Hideki said. "But how did you know I am a samurai?" Hideki asked.

"The swords are a dead giveaway," she said sweetly.

"You must have eyes like a cat to see the swords in this darkness."

"I see sufficiently well, samurai-san. For instance, I can see that you are young and athletic and do not cut your hair in the style of Edo samurai," she said.

On reflex, Hideki shrank down further into the hot water. "What else can she see?" he wondered.

"What is your name, young miss?" Hideki asked.

"No names samurai-san. We are two strangers passing in the night, sharing a bath. We will probably never meet again. So we can talk and be honest with each other," she responded.

"Honest? I am not sure I understand. I try to be honest in all my conversations and all my dealings. What do you mean?" he asked.

"Oh, I mean we can ask each other questions and not

have to worry about the answers. We can speak of trivial and unimportant things and not worry about offense. We can just be honest about things because we are strangers and the results of our conversation will have no lasting consequences," she explained.

Her voice, the outline of her body, and the fact that the only thing that was separating him from her soft naked skin was about six shaku of hot water and a very thin towel all combined to arouse a heat that had nothing to do with the onsen. Embarrassed, Hideki took the towel off his head and placed it back to its original position.

"What family do you serve, samurai-sama?" she asked.

"We are an unimportant clan that serves the Matsudaira," Hideki replied, trying not to sound coy.

"A very influential family, samurai-sama."

"They are, but we are so far down the family tree that very little of the money and power reaches us," Hideki lied, hating that the Yoshinobu existence in Edo required deception in so many levels. But it could not be helped. Tomorrow the Yoshinobu would be meeting at the shogun's castle. He could not cause Naga and Jii anymore embarrassment.

"So when you are not bathing, what do you like to do, samurai-san?" she asked.

"I like to practice martial arts."

"I bet you are very good," she said.

Hideki laughed. "Oh, I used to think I would someday be very strong. But I've found a new teacher who has shown me that being strong and being good are two entirely different things," Hideki said.

"Sounds like a good and wise sensei."

"He is very wise and a good friend, but he is leaving soon, so I shall have to find a new teacher," Hideki said.

"How sad for you samurai-san, And are you new to Edo or have you been here a long time?" she asked.

"I am new."

"How do you like it?" she asked.

"It is so big that it is hard to understand the rhythm. Each street seems to be different."

"Now we get to the area that a woman would want to know. This is where the honesty of strangers comes in. What kind of women do you like?" she asked with a slight purr.

"I don't know. I have not been with many."

"Not been with many? You are young and athletic; have you sustained injuries that might keep you from performing?" she asked.

"Young miss, that is not the type of question you should be asking a naked stranger who shares your bath," Hideki said.

"It is exactly the kind of question I should be asking a naked stranger sharing my bath because we will probably never see each other again. That is what I mean when I say we can be honest. We can talk freely and not have to worry about what we say."

Hideki could see a certain logic in her reasoning, but he was not going to betray his family just because she had a pretty shape. He would keep the conversation light.

"I am able to perform," Hideki said, more softly than he intended.

"Then you must still be a virgin," the woman said. "When you said you had not been with many women, you meant to say you had not been with any."

Hideki was exasperated. He wanted to correct her, but that would require a direct lie. Therefore, he remained quiet.

"Oh, I did not mean to embarrass you samurai-san. There will be plenty of time for women. You are still young yet," she said. "But from what you know now, what kind of a woman do you think you'd like?"

"I haven't given it much thought. I have only been around my grandmother, a few house maids, and two truly beautiful women," Hideki said.

"Please tell me about the two beautiful women," she enthused. "This is rare entertainment for me."

"Now you are laughing at me," Hideki complained.

"Never, samurai-san; I am enjoying the moment with a dashing young warrior, one who happens to be close to me and very naked," she teased.

Hideki readjusted his towel. It was not much camouflage.

"Well, the first truly beautiful woman I've ever been around wore men's clothes," Hideki began.

"Oh, no," she said. "You don't mean to tell me she liked women and not men. I've heard there were such creatures."

"No! Amida Buddha, No!" Hideki protested.

"Good, she said. Then this story will be more exciting. Please continue, samurai-san," she said.

Hideki was more exasperated than ever. He did not know whether to go over and wring her neck for proposing Naga's future wife was a sexual deviant or get up and walk out. The condition of his towel and its enlarged contents precluded the latter. Therefore, he did neither.

"She was a beautiful samurai woman very adept in the martial arts. When I first saw her I could not breathe, she was so pretty. Nevertheless, I was too inexperienced. Despite my trying to get her attention, she was attracted to my older brother," Hideki said.

"Curses on him."

"No, heaven forbid. They love each other. It just wasn't meant to be for me," Hideki said. "I was having a short daydream. Then I woke up."

"So you forgive your brother and the girl?" she asked.

"There was nothing to forgive. Besides, I threatened her with my sword one day, so I am sure she had no reason to desire me. But I believe she and my brother were in love before that regrettable incident."

The woman clapped her hands together in glee. "Oh, samurai-san. This tale has all the trappings of a Noh play; please continue."

"That's it. I will be around her as her brother-in-law and probably bounce her babies on my knee like any good uncle. And I will love her like a sister."

"You are too good. Tell me about the second."

"I know less about her," Hideki began. "I only saw her once and we didn't exchange more than ten words."

"But you love her?"

"I don't know. I know she intrigues me. I know I want to see her again. However, we may be from two different worlds.

I don't know who she is or who she likes or anything but her name."

"So what was her name, samurai-san," she asked in a small voice.

"Myo," replied Hideki.

"And what attracted you to her?" she asked.

Hideki closed his eyes and tried to remember the first time he saw her. "I think it was her openness. I walked into a noodle shop last night. She stared directly into my eyes. She was unafraid and confident. She was also very beautiful. I made up my mind in that very moment that if I ever become involved with a woman, I would want someone like her. No, that is a lie. I wanted her!" Hideki said.

"Oh, samurai-san, that is so romantic. Will you find her again?" she asked.

"Not the way my luck has been running. I'll probably never see her again," he said. "Besides I'm not sure she'd want to see me again anyway."

"Why do you say that?"

"Because a trio of drunken samurai came in and were rude to a young girl, and I ended it with my sword," he said stoically.

"Oh, samurai-san, you don't mean to say you killed them in front of your new love?" she asked.

"No, I didn't use a live blade. I just broke them up a little. Anyway, the police came and I was jailed. So I'm sure she doesn't have the best feelings for me."

"You sell her too short, samurai-san. She was probably impressed with your martial skill and your protection of the girl."

"It was nothing so noble. I interceded because I must. Bushido demands defense of the weak," Hideki said without guile.

"Well samurai-san, it was nice talking to a stranger and listening to your story. My recommendation is not to give up on Myo. She may turn up sooner than you think. Do you mind if I leave first? I have some work to do."

Hideki bowed slightly. "No, I do not mind at all. Meeting

you was most entertaining as well," he said.

She rose from the water and blended with the shadows. Try as he might Hideki could not make out her face. However, he saw everything else. As she rose out of the water and into the night air, the towel had disappeared. The warmth of her body gave off a slight mist as it mixed with the cooler air. Then she turned and moved to the other side of the onsen, stepped out, and was gone.

Hideki ducked his head under water for the next several moments. He tried to think about the census back in Kii, Musashi's treatise on the five spheres of kenjitsu, and Yoshi's combinations of gunpowder in proportion to the damage required. He tried to think of anything that would take his mind off the beautiful creature he had just seen and heard. He tried to think of anything that would stop the throbbing in his loins.

When Hideki returned to his room, there were clean and dry clothes laid out for him. He dressed quickly, belted the obi around his waist and thrust his kodachi swords into place, then moved to the lobby.

Sasuke led him to the opposite wing of the hotel and into a grand room of fifty tatami or more and cedar posts, a high ornate wooden ceiling, and large paintings of sumo hanging on the walls. The wall on one end was made of sliding doors of rice paper and lightwood and opened onto a peaceful garden scene. Throughout the room there were lanterns with candles burning. The abundance of light was not unusual, but the fact that the shades were silk instead of the normal paper variety surprised him. Silk was expensive.

Placed on the floor in a horseshoe shape were lacquer ware trays with short legs. In between the trays were lacquer ware bowls, presumably filled with rice. On the trays were small portions of vegetables, gyoza, nori, and slices of fish. Many of the Gumsumgumi were already filing in and finding seats. They looked and smelled much better after a bath and clean clothes. Some nodded to Hideki; others addressed him as "Yojimbo" and bowed slightly as they went by. Sasuke directed Hideki to the head of the horseshoe and indicated a seat to the left of the seat of honor.

"Dozo," Sasuke said, bowing slightly and indicating Hideki's seat.

Hideki pulled his katana from his obi with his left hand and kneeled down in the Japanese sitting fashion behind his tray. Instantly a young maid appeared and offered to pour Hideki sake. Hideki declined and asked for ocha instead. The girl gracefully stood and departed. When she returned and poured Hideki a cup of tea, only a few seats remained empty. The one on Hideki's left was an exception. Then Goro strode in without acknowledging Hideki's bow and took a seat two places to Hideki's right. At last, Nichi waddled in and took a seat on Hideki's right, at the top of the horseshoe. Hideki bowed a greeting to the Oyabun, as did all gathered.

"Eat and drink up my children. After a month in the Hatchobori jail, I felt we deserved a banquet," Nichi said, evoking cheers and clapping from the appreciative diners. Then reaching for his full sake cup, he raised it and presented a toast. "To my sempai, Goro, who kept me alive the entire time."

Goro raised his cup and beamed. He was getting his due. All joined in with congratulations, "Omedato gozaimus, Goro!"

When the cups were full again, Nichi hoisted his cup. "To our new yojimbo," Nichi toasted. "He saved me twice tonight. He protected me once from assassins and a second time from the guards. Domo Yojimbo," Nichi said as he downed the liquid. Hideki bowed and drained his teacup.

"Now eat up and put the unpleasantness of the last month from your mind," Nichi said. They did.

Hideki returned his cup to his tray and noticed the adjoining tray was now occupied.

"Myo–san," Hideki grinned. "What are you doing here?"

"I am happy to see you as well, Takezo," Myo said, bowing.

"I was afraid I would not find you again," Hideki said.

"Why were you afraid of that?" she asked.

"Well, I know so little about you. I didn't know where to start looking."

"If you are to be around the Gumsumgumi, we will find

each other. Nichi and I do business together from time to time. He lets me keep a room in the hotel and I am a regular in his gambling hall," she admitted.

"You are a gambler?"

"I earn my own money, and occasionally, I like to increase it the easy way," Myo said. "Besides, knowing gamblers and how they do business helps my own business."

"Which is what?" Hideki asked.

"I own a courier service. Well, my father owns it, but it is mine. I run it from top to bottom. In Nichi's world, knowledge is power. My couriers crisscross the country, and I am in a position to see that he gets the latest gossip. He pays well for it," Myo said.

Hideki sighed. "I am relieved. I was afraid you were going to tell me you made your living as a gambler."

"Would it be so bad if I did?"

"Yes. Gambling is part of mizu shobei. It is part of the water world and unstable. It is contrary to harmony, or so my grandfather says. But since coming to Edo, I've found a great many things contrary to my teachings," he explained.

She looked Hideki in the eye. "Well, it is no matter. I do not make my living as a gambler." She poured Hideki more tea. "Tell me of your family. Where do you come from? What are your prospects? Will you be with the Gumsumgumi long?" They talked and talked, and Hideki was not aware of anything else going on around him. She was talking to him as if she were interested in what he had to say. It made him feel worthy, and more importantly, desired. She could have any man in the place, and she chose him. He was dreaming again.

"I see you two are getting along," Nichi said.

They both bowed to the leader. "Hai, Oyabun," Hideki said. "Myo is delightful."

"Is she indoctrinating you on the ways of the Gumsumgumi?" Nichi asked.

"No, Nichi-san," she replied. "I thought it best that he experienced that himself."

"You are probably right, Myo. But he is departing in the morning and I do not know when he will have that experience.

Why don't you tell him about the Gumsumgumi," he suggested.

Myo placed delicate fingers beside her jawline. "Where to begin?" she said to herself.

"Begin anywhere you wish, Myo-san. I love to hear your voice," Hideki said.

"Gumsumgumi is almost a mini government. In the country, you have gonin who are responsible for the village. They provide guidance and ensure that everyday life is in balance so that all live in harmony," Myo began.

"Yes, I am very familiar with village life," Hideki said.

"The lord of the castle is responsible for the same thing throughout his domain. The same is true for the daimyo. The shogun is in charge of the government and he is responsible for the daimyo. Here in the city, there are guilds banded together to protect the interests of the tradesmen. But the townspeople have nothing."

"They have the police and the government," Hideki protested.

"You have seen how that works, firsthand."

"It is not supposed to be corrupt," Hideki said.

"It is not supposed to be, Takezo. But it is," she said. "So the Gumsumgumi has grown up as the shadow government to protect the interests of the townspeople."

"But they are involved in dealings like prostitution, loan sharking, gambling, and protection schemes that hurt the people and undermine the local government," Hideki stated.

"It is true, the Gumsumgumi deal in all those things. Nevertheless, it is a lot like the government. If the man at the top of the government is corrupt or allows corruption to exist, those below him will be corrupt. It is the same with the shadow government. Nichi does not allow corruption. The prostitutes in the government-condoned and sponsored yoshiwara are sexual slaves. They lose their earning power in a couple of years. Once older or sick, the street becomes their home. There is no profit in feeding a non-earning prostitute. Once on the street, they die early. They are killed, either by a customer or disease or starvation. With the Gumsumgumi, a prostitute has meals to eat, free medical care, and gets to decide who her customers are. The group protects her. When she decides to retire, she does so and moves onto other jobs in the restaurant, hotel, onsen, etc. Which is the better for her?" Myo asked.

"What about loans with exorbitant interest rates?" asked Hideki.

"Well, a borrower would receive the same rates or higher if he went to the merchants, and if they couldn't pay, the merchants would go to the magistrate who would seize all the man's property to help pay the balance, leaving the man homeless and without any means to make a living for his family. When the Gumsumgumi have a delinquent debt, they step in and help the man get back on his feet so they will continue to have money paid on the debt. Which system is better?" Myo posed.

"You've already given me your views on gambling, so defend the protection schemes, if you can," Hideki said.

"That's easy to explain. The merchants in the Gumsumgumi territory pay the group protection money. It is never more than they can pay and never enough to hurt the business. For the money, the Gumsumgumi mark the business with their mon or emblem. Everyone knows not to trouble the owner or incur the wrath of the Gumsumgumi. If the Gumsumgumi mark was not on the business, every out-of-work ronin and highwayman in the city would be trying to beat the police to the business to charge unreasonable protection money. It is a price of doing business in Edo, and it is much better to pay the Gumsumgumi for an actual benefit than any of the others for no benefit at all, and that includes the police."

Hideki laughed. "Okay, I surrender. Your point is that the government or the group is only as honest and ethical as the leadership."

"Excellent, Takezo. I will make an Edoko out of you yet," she teased.

"Let's get back to a more pleasant subject, Myo," Hideki recommended. "Let's talk about you."

"I'm flattered Takezo, but you already know everything about me," she said.

"I know almost nothing," Hideki complained. "Why does

such a beautiful woman not have a husband or fiancée?"

"There could be many reasons. But the truth for me is choice," she said.

"Choice?" Hideki asked.

"Yes, I may find a husband or I may not. I may settle for a lover and not a husband. I may never have children. That is okay with me as well. I have been raised by my father to be independent. Our family business requires I go where I am needed. I find I enjoy this freedom. If I find the right man, I will give my heart. However, I will never give myself. I belong to no one and refuse to be defined by another person."

Hideki had a hard time hiding his surprise. "You are just like Edo herself. Here everything I have been taught to be true, isn't. Good is bad, bad is good and you come along and say 'to the lowest level of hell' with convention and travel your own path." Then remembering something, he added, "My teacher says each must find their own path and have the courage to walk it. I think my teacher would approve of you."

Myo smiled. "I am glad, Takezo."

Sometime later, Nichi and then Goro rose and bid the banquet guests goodnight. He stopped between Hideki and Myo. "It is too late for you to be walking home tonight, Myo. Stay here in your room. I'll have someone walk you back to your father's in the morning."

"Hai, Oyabun. I was thinking the same thing," she said. Everyone bowed to each other, and the large men departed.

"Takezo, it has been wonderful getting to know you, but I must retire now as I have many things to do tomorrow," she said.

Hideki bowed as well. "I understand. I wish this evening could go on longer, but I suppose we both have obligations." He started to rise. She waved him back down.

"No need," she said. "I can manage. You finish your drink. We will talk again soon." She rose as only a Japanese woman in a kimono can. It was a type of uncoiling motion from kneeling to a re-positioning of her toes underneath her body followed by rotation upward and forward until she was standing. It was graceful, almost to the point of being sensual.

She bowed and departed with a swish of silk upon silk as she performed the toed-in walk needed to navigate in a lengthy kimono. Then she was gone.

"By the Buddha, that woman makes me ache all over," Hideki thought. Then he rose, bowed to the remaining celebrants, and returned to his room. In the center of his spacious room, a summer futon lay on the floor along with a summer kimono. He disrobed and placed his kodachi on the horizontal, two-tiered sword stand and blew out the candle in the lantern. He lay on the futon and pulled the silk sheet up to cover himself, resting his head on the wooden makura that supported his neck. He found himself very tired. He went to sleep thinking of Myo.

Sometime later, the sound of the fusama door being slid quietly back awakened Hideki. He reached into the darkness and grasped his wakazashi and removed the saya with his left hand.

"Do you plan to kill me samurai-san?" a feminine voice asked.

Hideki shoved the blade back into the saya and replaced it on the stand. The woman knelt beside Hideki and placed her fingers on Hideki's lips. "No names, samurai-san. It will be just like the bath earlier. Then standing up she disrobed. Next, she pulled the covers back and lay down next to Hideki. "You do not have to do anything samurai-san. And have no fear, you could have no better teacher," she whispered.

Hideki had meant to protest until her smooth body touched his. Then his body had a mind of its own. With great difficulty, he separated himself from her embrace. "My heart belongs to another," he said softly.

"I know," she said in between soft kisses to his neck and chest. "You told me in the bath."

"Then how can you come to me like this," Hideki managed.

"Because it is your first time and you need a new teacher," she laughed. "Call me Myo if you wish, Takezo. It will make no difference."

"Myo, is this really you? Was it you in the bath as well?"

he asked, the excitement causing his voice to sound higher than usual.

She smiled in the darkness. "Oh yes, samurai-san. It was me. You do not think I would let you go after telling a perfect stranger in the bath that you wanted me, did you? You cannot escape from me, my gallant warrior, now that I know the truth. I've waited my entire life for a man who is strong enough to protect the weak yet honest enough to win my heart."

Myo rained kisses all over Hideki. However, each time he felt like bursting, she would do something that would bring him back from the brink and then start all over again. He thought he would go mad with desire. Several times he reached for her and several times she moved his hands away as if instructing a child. Nevertheless, when she crawled up and impaled herself on him and he felt her breasts on his chest and her sweet breath on his face, he entered a world that he had never known but would never forget.

Chapter 14: The Castle

The cock had crowed when Yoshi entered the Gumsumgumi hotel and started down the corridor to Hideki's room. Something was not right. Haragai. He darted into an empty room and waited to see from which direction the danger would appear. He did not have long to wait. Out of Hideki's room stepped a very beautiful young woman dressed in a loud kimono. The kimono did not bother Yoshi. The woman did.

She was humming contentedly to herself as she walked and semi-consciously fussed with her hair. She was obviously happy. Yoshi waited until she had turned the corner and slipped out into the hall, then he raced to Hideki's room. He threw back the shoji door and found Hideki snoring. Yoshi sank to the floor. "Buddha be praised," he said softly. It was enough to wake Hideki.

"Yoshi, what are you doing here?" Hideki asked.

"I came to get you to your grandfather. Today is the day the Yoshinobu go to the castle." Hideki sat up quickly. "What time are we to be there?" he asked.

"You have plenty of time. Do not worry. It is after the noon meal."

Hideki lay back down. "Oh Yoshi, I spent the most wonderful night with the most wonderful woman."

"Does she know who you are?" Yoshi asked.

"No, she thinks I'm Takezo," Hideki said.

"You walk a fine line between cherry blossoms and the binjo, Prince of the Yoshinobu."

"What do you mean?" asked Hideki.

191

"I mean if you do not get dressed and get to the Yoshinobu mansion, you will not be standing in cherry blossoms, you will be back in the binjo," Yoshi said as he grabbed Hideki's kimono off the tatami floor. "I heard that you are supposed to ride to the castle in kago, and I do not think the Gray One is going to like it. So we better get a move on."

Yoshi had him back at the Yoshinobu compound in much less time than it took Hideki to get lost the previous night. "I am going to have to remember those canals," Hideki said to Yoshi. "That is really the way to travel in this town."

"You will be sampling the wrong way to travel very soon. Those kago will make you sick if you are not used to them," Yoshi said.

Hideki bathed and changed into his best clothes. Once all preparations had been made, Jii gathered his grandsons, Musashi, Yoshi, and Yuki.

"Naga has suggested and I concur," began Jii, "that Musashi will be in audience with us."

"Excellent," replied Hideki.

"I still think you are foolish to want me there," Musashi injected.

"We have all discussed it Musashi-sama," Yuki said. "Naga is making a statement by your presence."

"What statement? That it is normal to be friends with a duelist?" Musashi mused.

"No, Musashi-san," Naga answered. "That your character will be the model for my undertakings going forward."

"Well said," agreed Yoshi.

"We have all worked hard for this day," said Jii. "I want to thank you all for your efforts. No matter how this day comes out, it has been a great undertaking."

One of the maids bowed her way into the room and whispered something to Yuki. She nodded and the maid departed.

"The kago are here. There are five, one for each of the Yoshinobu and Musashi-sama. The fifth is for the kamishinos and other formal wear for the castle. You must change into much of the clothing upon entering the castle," Yuki said. "The naga-bakama is hard to walk in. The legs are so long that you must slide along the floor on them. Please experiment moving in them before you go in for the audience. Falling over would not be proper," she warned.

"Thank you, Yuki," Jii said and bowed. "And one last thing," he added, addressing Hideki, "whatever happens, you keep quiet."

Hideki bowed. "Hai. But what if they ask me something?"

"Just keep quiet and let me or Naga answer," Jii said emphatically.

As they were about to enter the kago, Yoshi called after Hideki. "Remember the cherry blossoms, Hideki-san."

Musashi turned to Hideki. "What is he carrying on about?"

Hideki shrugged his shoulders. "You know ninja, always talking in riddles."

Although the trip to the castle took longer than it should have because the household retainers preceding and following the kago had to contend with crowd control at several busy intersections, they eventually arrived at Edo castle. The plan was to have the kago transport them onto the castle grounds, but Jii changed the plans. He scrambled out of his kago as soon as it stopped.

"I'm not riding another step in that accursed conveyance," he swore. "My back is killing me." Grabbing the guard commander, Jii barked his command. "We will walk back. Make the necessary arrangements."

The commander bowed his understanding. Then he had the Yoshinobu protection detail line up on both sides of the entrance into the castle. There was a weapons ban inside the castle grounds. Only the castle guards went armed.

The Yoshinobu were relieved of their swords inside the compound. They moved through the outer rock wall of the castle and inside the wooden structure of the keep itself. They shed their sandals upon entering before being led to a changing room.

Once inside, they donned the kamishino, the sleeveless

vest with wide-winged shoulders that was the traditional garb
in the castle for men. Then the extra long-legged naga-bakama was fitted over the pant-like hakama. Remembering Yuki's
admonishment, each tried walking on the tatami. It required
placing both hands inside the slits on the side and grasping the
inside of the front of the garment while pulling it upward to
create enough room to allow a sliding motion forward. It took
Naga the longest to master the movement.

Then the moment arrived, and they were ushered into
the ohiroma, or grand room. Hideki could not immediately appreciate the fine space. His eyes were down as the Yoshinobu
shuffled into position. Jii entered first and moved all the way to
the right. Naga followed and moved to the center. Hideki followed and took up the position to Naga's left. Musashi entered
and moved behind the Yoshinobu. When Musashi was in position, they formed a diamond shape with Naga in the fore. They
all bowed and then moved to a kneeling position and bowed
again. Their heads remained bowed as an attendant introduced
the Yoshinobu by name. As each name was read aloud, the
owner repeated his name and rank to the assemblage. Then
Yagyu Munenori asked them to raise their heads.

Hideki's first thought was that he had never been in a
room so large. Then he realized he was looking into the eyes
of an older woman of slight build with the most piercing
black eyes he had ever seen. He thought she must be looking
into his soul. It made him nervous. Nevertheless, he fought
his panic and forced himself to remain calm, as Musashi had
taught. He was also aware of another woman looking at all the
Yoshinobu, though she seemed much less threatening. She was
actually smiling. Wearing a simple and elegant silk kimono, she
was in much more appropriate attire. Because she sat beside
Yagyu, he knew this must be Oeyo, the wife of the current
shogun, Hidetada. Therefore, the shrew staring holes through
him must be O-Fuku, also called Tsubone, the wet nurse for
the shogun's eldest, Iemitsu. Hideki looked to his right and
saw two elderly men who he assumed must be the Tairo, or senior counselors. To his left he saw four middle-aged men who
he likewise assumed to be the Roju, or junior counselors.

Yagyu was welcoming the Yoshinobu to Edo Castle, but Hideki's eyes strayed back to O-Fuku. She was still staring at him, or so it seemed. He let his eyes move over her to take in every detail. She was small but wiry. She wore a **jūnihitoe**, or twelve-layered robe, and sat by herself to Hideki's left front. Something about the design of the birds on her outer train nagged at Hideki. He had seen it somewhere, but could not remember where. It was a swallow of some kind with red markings. There was graying in her hair, but her aging beauty could not be denied.

Yagyu had just asked the Tairo to start the questioning.

"Yoshinobu-sama," asked Sakai Tadekatsu, "what do you see as the greatest problem before the Tokugawa?"

"We think the greatest problem immediately facing the Tokugawa is choosing the best of the Tokugawa line to lead the country in this potentially perilous time of establishing a centralized government over the country," Jii said.

"Yes, yes, that is extremely important, but assuming a Yoshinobu became the next shogun, what then is the most pressing matter to address. And I'd like to hear from Nagamasa please," Sakai Tadekatsu firmly requested..

Naga smiled. "Certainly, Sakai-dono. My first priority would be to find out who the Fox Gang is connected to in this building and to shut them down."

There was an immediate intaking of breath and murmuring among the Roju and Tairo. "You don't mean to insinuate that someone in this castle is involved with that band of bandits, do you Yoshinobu-sama?" Sakai Tadekatsu asked.

"Yes, Sakai-sama, I do. And by the way, they are not a band of bandits. I believe them to be ninja operating at the direction of someone not only in this castle but in this room."

The murmuring increased in volume. "Outrageous," yelled O-Fuku. "Shame on you, a country daimyo coming in here and accusing this body!"

"A country daimyo I may be, madam. But I am a Tokugawa by birth. The last time I checked the heraldry of the Tokugawa, there was no wet-nurse among the titles," replied Naga.

That was met by an embarrassed silence by the men, but

by joyous applause by Oeyo. "Well spoken, Nagamasa. You are obviously a man of impeccable upbringing and culture despite living in the country. Some people give themselves airs and titles and forget their low birth," she said without looking at O-Fuku. "But do you really believe there is a conspiracy within this room?"

"Most assuredly, madam," Naga said. "This Fox Gang strikes at will all over Japan, evades the government's best efforts to detect them, and seems to focus on the houses of the Tokugawa for assassination disguised as robbery. We have had occasion to tangle with them ourselves and are assured they are ninja and not bandits."

"But how can that be?" Oeyo asked Yagyu.

Naga continued his accusation. "Someone in this room is giving them their targets and masking their movements with special passes. This is nothing more than a form of kyodai goroshi. We have been targets. All the other Tokugawa families with legitimate heirs are dead. Someone supporting either Iemitsu or Tadanaga is the culprit."

"Are you accusing me?" Oeyo asked.

"No madam, I am not accusing you. I said someone in this room. I don't know who yet, but if I were shogun it would be my first priority."

Naga's statement triggered more murmuring, but this time there was concurrence in the low-toned conversations. Hideki noticed that Yagyu had lost control of the questioning, and anyone who wanted was asking a question when the volume of discussion allowed it.

"I want to know the name of the fourth man in your country retinue," O-Fuku said, pointing at Musashi.

Jii bowed slightly. "Let me introduce the Yoshinobu's fencing master and chief strategist, Myamoto Musashi."

Musashi bowed and said, "Dozo yoroshuku."

This announcement brought louder murmuring as both Roju and Tairo moved heads to get a better look at Musashi.

"How dare you bring his killer into our midst!" challenged O-Fuku.

"Madam, every male in here with the exception of me

196

has killed. Even my little brother here has killed when beset upon by thirty Fox Gang members in Kyoto. That is what bushi warriors do. Have you forgotten what bushi do or did you never know?" Naga chastised.

This brought polite laughter from all who still thought of themselves as warriors and a smile from Yagyu.

"This man has killed sixty people I am told. Is this the kind of person the Yoshinobu use as counselors?" O-Fuku persisted.

Naga took in a slow breath before responding. "Yes Madam, it is. Musashi-sama is the essence of Bushido. His sword is his soul. He puts his life on the line every day in an attempt to perfect himself. I see no greater guide to live by than his example."

The men were nodding in approval. Naga had swayed them. He had accomplished the best outcome possible. Instead of being on the defensive, he had attacked and won.

Nevertheless, O-Fuku would not let what she perceived as a weak spot go unchallenged. "I want to hear this murderer defend himself. What do you have to say for taking over sixty lives? Isn't it true one was a 14-year-old boy?" she demanded.

Musashi remained quiet. No one spoke. O-Fuku took strength from the silence. "See, I told you. He says nothing because his actions are indefensible."

There was another long silence. Hideki could take it no more. "He is silent because he is waiting for an intelligent question."

Jii spun and glared at Hideki, but Hideki did not care. His friend and sensei was under attack.

"Speak boy," O-Fuku encouraged. "How do you condone killing a child?"

"I do not, but I do not accept that such a thing happened," he said. "All my years I've spent learning the way of the warrior. From the time I could remember, my grandfather here has taught me the meaning of being a bushi. We are samurai, he would say. We serve before everything else. There is no wrong too small to right and no right to small to defend. I thought I knew what Jii-sama meant. But I did not. I did not

197

until I met Musashi-sama. His life is Bushido. He does not play at being a warrior. He is a warrior. He perfects his skill not to empower himself. He perfects himself to purify himself as the Zen priests teach. He has taught me great skills and taught me that with those skills comes the responsibility not to use them. Musashi avoids situations that may lead to fighting. He is the most peaceful man I know."

Hideki noticed the Roju were nodding in agreement with his defense of his friend. His impassioned speech was pure and undeniable. But O-Fuku had one last salvo to shoot. "I suggest we give the Yoshinobu a test to see if they are indeed the warriors they claim to be or just the country daimyo they appear to be," she said emphatically.

Yagyu turned to her. "And what are you suggesting?"

"I suggest we make him South Magistrate and give him a month to catch the Fox Gang, if he can. If he does, then he's proven to me that he has the right to compete before this body."

The politically perceptive men in the room recognized a win/win situation for them. If Naga captured the Fox Gang, it would take them off the hot seat. The commoners were already clamoring for protection. Moreover, if Naga was correct and one of the people in this room was behind the Fox killings, a solution had better present itself before the whole body toppled. The Yoshinobu seemed the best men for the job. They had no castle history and therefore no ties to castle intrigue and politics. They were no-nonsense warriors. Anyone who could hold Myamoto Musashi's loyalty had to have great character and purpose. If Nagamasa accepted the job and failed, then the decision would be down to two, Iemitsu and his younger brother Tadanaga, and the Yoshinobu allegation would be forgotten.

"I assume that both Iemitsu and Tadanaga have to compete in this same game?" Jii asked.

"Tadanaga is just a boy," Oeyo stated.

"As is Iemitsu," O-Fuku protested.

"Yet, you want them as shogun. Isn't this request a little one-sided?" Jii asked.

There was silence. Then the unexpected happened.

"You are correct as always, Jii-sama. But in this case I wish to accept the challenge." Nagamausu moved his head to take in the entire gathering as he spoke. "My grandfather brought me up to serve the Tokugawa. If I can best serve by helping rid the country of this Fox Gang, then I will."

Yagyu looked to the Tairo and saw their acceptance. Then he looked to the Roju and received their approval. "So be it," Yagyu said. "We will move to make you the new south magistrate, Nagamasa. I will have papers in your hand tomorrow. If there are no more questions for the Yoshinobu, thank you for coming," he said and bowed to Nagamasa.

The Yoshinobu bowed, rose, and backed out of the room several steps before turning and filing out.

Once in the changing room Musashi bowed to Hideki. "I thank you for your kind words, and I hope I have not caused your family trouble."

"I'm afraid I'm the only one in trouble," Hideki said, looking toward his grandfather.

"You are not in trouble," Naga said. "Jii and I knew this would come up when we asked Musashi to accompany us. We also knew you could not keep your mouth shut. We had a rebuttal prepared but figured your passion would sound better."

Hideki looked at his brother in disbelief and then at his grandfather. Both were smiling back.

"You never disappoint, Hideki," Jii said as he reached for his sandals.

"Cherry blossoms," Hideki mumbled.

"What's that?" Musashi asked.

"Nothing, Musashi-sama. Just trying to figure out a way to catch the Fox Gang," he said out loud, "And wondering when and if I'll see Myo again," to himself.

Chapter 15: Inspection

The Yoshinobu kneeled in the large room of their Edo mansion awaiting Hideki's arrival. Yuki was in her customary seat beside her lover, Naga. Jii was to Naga's right. Yoshi was to the right of Jii and Musashi to Yoshi's right. The morning meal was completed. When Hideki entered, he had a large, one-eyed samurai with him, dressed in black.

Both Hideki and the samurai bowed upon entering the room, and both took up the more formal sitting position with legs folded under them. They bowed again.

"I'm sorry for asking for this meeting so early in the morning," Hideki began, "and on such short notice. But I've been giving a great deal of thought to Naga's new assignment as south magistrate."

"I'm glad someone has," Naga sighed, which drew an exasperated sigh from Yuki.

"I know you and Jii have probably thought all this out and come up with your own strategy, but I've become a little familiar with the South District's boundaries over the last few days and have drawn some plans that I hope you find useful," Hideki said.

"Before you continue," Jii said in a rather gruff voice, "don't you think you'd better introduce your guest?"

Hideki stopped and looked at his guest in black as if he were seeing him for the first time. Then his face started to redden. "I'm sorry, Grandfather. It is just that we have spent so much time together in the past few days that I forgot you don't know him." Then turning to Jii, he nodded. "Grandfather, Naga-sama, Yuki-sama, and Musashi-sensei, please let me introduce a friend, Yagyu Jubei."

Jubei bowed to the tatami. "Dozo Yuroshiku, onagaishimasu."

Naga opened his mouth, but did not know what to say.

"Raise your head, Jubei," Jii said. "You are very welcome in this home." Then looking at Hideki and shaking his head, added, "I do not know how you came to be friends with my grandson, but I am glad he seems to be able to attract such talented people," glancing at Yoshi and Musashi as he spoke.

Naga finally found his tongue. "You are very welcome here, and anywhere there is Yoshinobu land."

"Thank you. I am humbled by your graciousness," Jubei said.

"Welcome back, Jubei," Yuki said. "I had not heard that you had returned."

Jubei bowed slightly to Yuki. "It is good to see you again, Yuki-san. Is your father well?"

"He is well. You, however, seem to be much thinner than a year ago when you disappeared, and judging by the bruises on your face, you have experienced some rough treatment."

"Yes, I got myself into much trouble here in Edo upon my return. If it had not been for Hideki and Yoshi, I would now be dead," Jubei acknowledged.

Jii stared from Yoshi to Hideki. "More adventures we have not heard about?"

"Jubei exaggerates, Jii-san," Hideki offered.

Yuki interrupted whatever Hideki was going to say next. "As Jubei's betrothed, I will defend him. You may call Yagyu Jubei many things; and I would like to do so for his clandestine disappearing act last year, but one thing everyone knows about Jubei, he does not exaggerate."

"Jubei, your betrothed still seems to feel the need to defend you against my brother's unthinking tongue. Hideki often speaks before thinking. He meant no offense by it," Naga said.

Jubei smiled. "No offense was taken Naga-sama. Not only did Hideki save my life, he has spent the last few days with me, drawing up this plan with the help of Yoshi. In essence, he has given me a purpose in life. I feel renewed. If I can be of assistance to the Yoshinobu, my sword is yours."

"I for one take great solace in that sword," Musashi said. "Our current situation has reminded me of Sekigahara all over again."

"Do you envision a pitched battle?" Hideki asked.

"He's talking about being hopelessly outnumbered, little brother," Naga said.

Jii laughed and slapped his thigh. "By the Buddha, I am proud that my grandsons marshal such friends to their side. I'm starting to feel young again."

"There is just one more thing that I need to take care of," Jubei said, bowing to Yuki. "I hereby publicly renounce any previous arrangements with Hanzo Yuki."

Yuki blushed and smiled up at Naga. There was a look of relief on Naga's face.

"It only takes one eye to see that you have found happiness, Yuki-san. Omedato gozaimus."

Yuki bowed to Jubei. "Thank you Jubei for your announcement. However, there is no reason for congratulations. I am just Naga-sama's yojimbo."

Jii smiled. "Only if Naga is denser than I believe him to be."

Everyone laughed while Naga fidgeted. Hideki saved his brother by continuing. "Naga, you might think as south magistrate you would have a southern area of the city to preside over. That is not the case. There is a north magistrate. You and he preside over all of Edo, but at different times. Each of you has a tour of duty of one month. Your tour started yesterday."

"Tell me something I don't know, little brother," Naga said.

"Very well, what you may not know is that no matter how corrupt you think things are now, the corruption is, in fact, much worse," Hideki warned.

"How so?" asked Jii.

"Well," Hideki started, "the system is flawed. The current laws and organization encourage corruption."

"I'd like a few more specifics, Hideki, and less rhetoric," Jii stated.

"As you wish, Grandfather," Hideki said. "Naga, you are one of two magistrates. As the machi-bugyo sho, you are responsible for policing and judging. However, you can police and judge only the chonin or commoners of Edo. They call themselves Edoko, thinking themselves children of the city. They consist of three of the four classes of citizens: the farmers, the artisans, and the merchants. The fourth class is the samurai, and you have no authority over them. Their own lords accomplish policing and judging of samurai. You also have only peripheral impact on the farmers, as their lands are on the outskirts of Edo and are rarely encountered by the magistrate.

"Therefore, in essence you judge and police the artisans and the merchants. Two more classes of people inhabit Edo, and they do not fall into any of the specific categories Hideyoshi established," Hideki explained, referring to the man who united Japan before Tokugawa Ieyasu. "The two classes are masterless samurai, known as ronin, and the farmers who flee the countryside to become laborers in the city. The laborers might fall under the merchant class. Merchants hire them. The city is teeming with both ronin and laborers."

"I am impressed, little brother. How did you come by such information?" Naga asked.

"I ask a lot of questions, and I have several good teachers right here in this room," replied Hideki.

"Please continue, Hideki," Naga encouraged.

"Despite serving one month on and one month off, each day you report to the Roju in the castle, even on your month off. This is done to familiarize you with happenings on your month off so you will not be surprised when your month on begins.

"Both magistrates work out of the same building, the Hatchobori. It is a large compound consisting of administrative offices, a police barracks, and a rather large jail. To the Edoko, you are their police, judge, and mayor. You have a komono as assistant from the mid-level samurai yoriki class. Beside the two assistants, one for the south magistrate and one for the north, there are forty-eight other yoriki assigned to Edo. They manage the daily operations of the Hatchobori. They do not have time off, so they actually supervise all activities in their geographical locations. They are the ones upon whom you must rely.

"Each yoriki has several machi-kata-doshin from the lowest-ranked samurai working as detectives. Each has a specific patrol section of the yoriki's area of responsibility. They are called doshin and make about 30 hyo a year—barely enough to keep themselves alive, let alone feed a family. However, they have to employ several commoners who act as laborers. The labors also carry a jutte as their badge of office, and are given the title shitappiki. The doshin and the shitappiki make actual arrests. The Doshin cannot pay the shitappiki from the pitiful amount he is paid by the government. Most, therefore, have business pursuits on the side despite a shogunate prohibition against such. To circumvent this prohibition, they use their wives to run chaya teahouses or taverns or other not-so-savory pursuits in order to make ends meet. They also accept gifts from rich merchants and wealthy Edoko. You can see the direction I am heading. Corruption is almost mandated by the Tokugawa system."

"Thank you for that uplifting report, little brother. What in Buddha's name are we going to be able to do about it?" Naga demanded.

"Not so fast, big brother. You have not heard the worst yet."

"What could be worse than a corrupt government?"

"The vigilantism the corruption spawns," Hideki said.

"Do I want to hear any more?" Naga asked.

"I believe you should," Yoshi injected.

Naga exchanged glances with everyone in the room. "Okay, Hideki, tell me the worst."

"Another way the doshin make money is by arresting Edoko and ronin for minor infractions. Bribes get them off. If they do not have the bribe money, they land in jail. Jail in Edo can be a death sentence in itself. However, if the accused survives the torture at the hands of the roya-minawari, the lowest ranked doshin who act as prison guards, and their rather violent fellow prisoners, then they are off to see the magistrate.

"The magistrate finds them guilty, no matter the evidence, and awards them a fine they cannot pay. In lieu of paying the fine, they receive hard labor sentences in the copper mines of Sado Island or the gold mines owned by one of the Tokugawa diamyo who pays the magistrate a pittance for the labor. Some of the money gets distributed down to the doshin and the system perpetuates itself. It is common knowledge among the Edoko that Tokugawa's capital city has the best justice money can buy."

"Maybe I should not have accepted this assignment so quickly," Naga mused.

"You attacked the O-Fuku in our meeting. It was a brilliant tactic as it kept the Roju and Tairo off balance. However, O-Fuku countered with the magistrate assignment. That was brilliant on her part. She knows the experience will destroy your reputation. You will be dragged through the mud by your association with the crooked system whether you capture the Fox Gang or not," Hideki warned.

"Very perceptive of you, Hideki," Jii said.

"I had a lot of help with this," Hideki said. "The real losers are the two classes of people you are supposed to police and judge: the artisans and the merchants. You can throw the other two catchall classes in with them as well, the ronin and the laborers. To protect themselves, a small industry has grown up."

"You are referring to the gumis," Yuki said.

"You win the prize, intelligent lady," Hideki said. "The gumis, or 'machi-yokko' as they call themselves, are gangs that control vast areas of the city. They provide protection for a fee. They protect the Edoko from the police and anyone else dumb enough to defy them. No doshin or his komono would enter a business with a gumis' sign on the wall and demand a bribe. To do so might mean the end of the man's life."

"Don't tell me you are condoning these thugs?" Jii asked with a raised eyebrow.

"No, Jii-san," Hideki replied. "However, they exist because they provide a needed service abandoned by the government. They exist to protect the common people from the government."

"Protection is one thing; but what about the prostitution, the gambling, the usury, and strong-arm tactics? Surely you do not condone this?" Naga asked.

"I condone nothing. Nevertheless, as was recently pointed out to me, prostitutes for the gumis can refuse clients. They are also under the protection of the gumi. No one would dare harm them. When they become too old to work, they can move into other lines of work for the gumi. None of these things are enjoyed by their sisters boarded up in the government run Yoshiwara district."

"It sure sounds like you are defending them," Jii said.

"Just giving you information Grandfather so that I can follow it up with some suggestions."

"Well, don't paint these thugs as heroes, Hideki," Jii warned.

"Such is not my intention, but it is funny you should mention that. They are already receiving hero status by the Edoko. There are even plays about them. They seem to live by a code that is not too much different from Bushido.

"Their organization is along the line of a traditional family with a ko-bun to oya-bun parent relationship," he explained, referring to bond between a stepchild and parent. "All the foster children of the gumi owe allegiance to the oyabun. Their code is termed jingi, which emphasizes justice and duty. Their loyalty is to the group and the leader. The gumis seem to embrace the jingi based on the character of the oyabun.

"For example, the largest and most dangerous gumi in Edo is the Gumsumgumi. A former sumotori named Nichi leads them. His wakagasira is Goro," Hideki emphasized, identifying Nichi's first lieutenant. "Goro is also a former sumotori. They seem to embrace a protective nature toward the Chonin or Edoko where their main rivals the Yamakai-gumi do not. There are six other gumis of lesser strength in Edo who rule their territories with varying degrees of benevolence, depending on their leader."

"Hideki, how do you know all this?" Yuki asked. "My

Father has been trying to get this type of information on the Gumsumgumi for over a year without success."

"I guess he didn't ask the right people, Yuki-san."

"He runs the metsuke, Hideki. He has many more resources than you," Yuki asserted.

"I think it helps if you saved the Gumsumgumi Oyabun's life twice in one night," Yoshi offered.

Now all heads were staring at Hideki. "It is true," Jubei confirmed. "I was there."

"That does not really matter," Hideki said.

"Oh yes it does," Jii said. "Who did you save him from?"

No one answered, so Jubei spoke up. "I was in the Hatchobori jail and beaten within an inch of my life. Hideki was in the cell beside me with about forty Gumsumgumi. He saved Nichi from two assassins inside the cell. Later, when their attempt to kill Nichi became more overt, the guards rushed the cell, swinging spiked clubs to kill everyone. Hideki managed to escape with the aid of a very talented ninja," Jubei said. Now all eyes moved to Yoshi.

Yoshi looked at Jii and shrugged. "You told me to find him and get him back. In order to do so, I participated in a jail break."

"I cannot believe what I'm hearing," Jii said. "Do you mean to say that our Yoshinobu name is on record as being in jail?"

"No, Grandfather. Do not be ridiculous. I used Musashi's name," Hideki said.

"What?" asked Musashi.

"Don't worry sensei, I used your peasant name."

"You go too far Hideki," Musashi said.

"Sorry, but it was all I could think of at the time."

"Hideki, your ability to gather skilled men to your banner is exceeded only by your ability to gather great information. You mentioned a plan?" Naga asked.

"Yes, I believe it is imperative that you conduct a surprise inspection of the Hatchobori today," Hideki replied.

"To what purpose?" asked Naga.

Before Naga could answer, Yuki cut in. "He wants the

people to see that you are not dragging your feet. There is great fear in the city over the Fox Gang running free. He also wants you to take the offensive with the Yoriki in case they have some plan to bring about your demise early."

Jubei looked at Hideki. "I told you she was better at this than I."

Hideki shook his head in admiration. "You were correct Jubei. Naga, your lovely Yojimbo is ahead of me. The status quo is everyone's friend except yours. Everyone knows you have one month. Then you either are gone to the castle or back to Kii. All they have to do is wait you out. The police have no interest in supporting you. You have to change that. You have to shake up their status quo and give them more reason to help us find the Fox Gang than to sit on their hands."

"I like it," Jii said. "We're thinking like a family now."

"Okay, Hideki. You have convinced us. What is our first move?" Naga asked.

"Here is what I suggest ... " he began.

Hideki pointed out the noodle shop. "This is the place."

"It doesn't look like much," his companion said.

"I have it on good authority that they make the best noodles in Edo," Hideki persisted.

"On whose authority?" the unimpressed companion asked.

"Come, I'll introduce you," Hideki said.

They both parted the cloth banner that hung vertically from the doorway announcing "Ichiban Noodles." They were met with an immediate "Irashiai dozo" from a young lady with a plain, faded kimono covered by a white apron with several stains on the front. Her hair was pinned up on her head, and she wore no makeup.

"You don't sound all that happy to see me, Hana," Hideki said.

The young girl's head popped up from scrubbing the bench. She cocked her head to one side trying to decide if she knew the young samurai who called her by name. Her glance went between Hideki and his companion dressed in black. The one in black frightened her. He had only one eye that seemed to take in everything. His presence seemed to fill the room like some dark cloud. She knew she would remember had she met him previously. He looked fierce. There was something vaguely familiar about the young one though.

She smiled and asked, "Simasen samurai-sama, have we met?" she asked.

"Not formally, Hana-san. We met a few weeks ago when some very unruly tosa samurai decided you were on the menu."

Hana studied his face and then recognition dawned. Her eyes got big and she squealed with glee, "Eeeyaa, samurai-sama," she said, repeatedly bowing deeply. "Thank you for saving me and my grandfather. We searched for you at the Hatchobori but a friend said you had escaped. We were afraid to pursue finding you then." She looked anxiously at the door. "Are you being pursued? Do you need a place to hide?"

"No, Hana, we are not being pursued. However, thank you for the offer. I am happy that you and your grandfather are fine. Where is he?" Hideki asked.

"He will be right back. He went to get more flour for the noodles."

"Did that yoriki come back and cause you any trouble?" he asked.

"Oh no, samurai-sama; he never came back."

The small door at the back of the shop opened and Hana's grandfather entered holding a small, wooden bucket piled high with a light brown substance.

"Grandfather, come and see," Hana said. "It is the samurai who saved us by going to jail."

Recognition dawned on the old man's face and he began bowing low. "Domo arigato gozaimasu samurai-sama. I pray the consequences were not too dire for you."

"Not too dire, grandfather," Hideki said. "But enough of that depressing story, I brought along a friend to taste the best noodles in Edo. He does not believe me. Hana, you did tell me this was the best noodle house in Edo, did you not?"

The smiling young girl tried to put on a serious face. "Honto, samurai-sama, we have the best noodles in Edo. Ask anyone, anywhere. Ichiban is the best!" she said and then went back to smiling.

"That's good enough for me. We'll take two bowls please," Hideki ordered. Then he took up his seat next to the noodle-cutting table. It allowed him to view the main entrance.

"Hai," the old man shouted as he turned to the cutting table to start a fresh batch of noodles. Hana's geta cut into the dirt floor as she raced to the stove to tend the fire. "I'll take care of that Hana," her grandfather called. "You provide out honored guests with ocha."

"Hai, ogisan," Hana replied as she moved off, the wooden geta shoes crunching into the earthen floor.

While they were sipping their tea, two very young doshin came in and took a seat at the first bench on the left. They wore gray, simple-patterned kimonos with the bottom edge pulled up and tucked into their obi, complemented by blue tabi and black haori outer garments. Jubei snorted his displeasure at their sight.

Hideki was not sure if it was from his dislike of all police or their dress. Most samurai looked down on doshin. Most considered them very low ranked due in part to their daily contact with the chosin, or townspeople, of Edo. Their investigations required handling and investigating the dead. Doshin positions went from father to son. No one worked his way up to doshin. Their adoption of the style of dress without hakama was called kinagashi style and was considered inappropriate by most wellborn samurai.

The compulsory "Irashiai dozo" from Hana greeted the two. Surprisingly, Hana abandoned her duties, rushed to their bench, and began chatting with them.

"I'd say you have been forsaken for guests more her age, hero," Jubei observed.

"That is as it should be," Hideki said without emotion.

Hana's grandfather brought Hideki and Jubei more tea. "Gomen nasai samurai-samas, those two come in every day and flirt with Hana."

"She seems interested," Jubei noted.

"Oh she is interested," the grandfather confirmed.

"You approve of them?" Hideki asked.

"They are good boys and just a little older than Hana. They are honest and hardworking. They are newly assigned to the Hatchobori and have not learned bad habits."

"What do you mean?" Hideki asked.

"Well, I probably shouldn't be talking about it, but since you risked everything for us, I'll tell you. The Hatchobori doshin extort money from the shopkeepers throughout Edo," he said. "We either pay or go to jail."

"Why don't you pay the Gumsumgumi?" Hideki asked.

"Because those devils charge more."

"Do those two extort as well?" Hideki asked.

"No, in fact they have shamed a few other doshin away," the grandfather replied. "It must be the young one's infatuation with Hana that protects us."

"Are his intentions honorable?" Hideki asked.

Jubei rolled his eyes skyward.

"I'm sure they are. They are both nice boys. But I have to discourage it," the old man said.

"Why, if they are honest?" Hideki asked.

The old man looked shocked. "How could I hold my head high as an Edoko if my daughter was married to a samurai?" he asked. Then he smiled to soften the insult and went back to his stove.

Hideki looked at Jubei. "Was he kidding?"

"If I had to guess, I'd say he was more serious than kidding."

"But why? If Hana marries a samurai his station in life would be raised as well," Hideki said.

"Hideki, life in Edo is a little different than in the provinces. You have been in Edo for a few weeks now. Have you not noticed the almost defiant nature of many of the citizens? This is not Kyoto or Osaka. Edo is a new city and still very wild. The people who are pouring into Edo are used to a hard life somewhere else. They want the freedom and opportunity a big city gives. Most are very self-sufficient and somewhat prideful." Jubei looked at the old man at the stove. "I'd say he was more serious than kidding."

Hana returned to her grandfather's side, then shuffled over to Hideki's bench and placed two large bowls in front of Hideki and Jubei. "Please enjoy our noodles samurai-sama," she beamed.

Even Jubei reacted to her exuberance. He tried to smile back. Hideki noticed it looked like it hurt. Hideki grabbed his watabashi and with a slight stir of the contents began to slurp noodles. Jubei was more cautious. He sniffed the contents and stirred it slightly with his watabashi, trying to identify all the contents before bringing anything to his mouth. Once he managed a taste, he exclaimed, "These really are good."

"I told you so!" Hideki said.

The two doshin received their bowls and began eating. Soon one of the doshin stopped and reached into this kimono sleeve and brought out a folded paper. He unfolded it and showed it to his companion. Then both looked toward Hideki and Jubei. They put down their watabashi and rose. They came over to Hideki's bench behind Jubei and pulled their jutte.

"You are under arrest," the young one said. "Turn over your weapons and come to the Hatchobori with us."

Jubei ignored him. He repeated his command louder this time.

Hana shuffled over behind Hideki. "No Kimbei-chan, these are our friends. This one saved us from jail and worse," she pleaded.

"Quiet Hana. We have our duty to perform," he ordered.

"Who do you think we are?" asked Hideki between slurps.

"He is the one-eyed devil that escaped last week," the older one said, holding up the sketch of a brigand with an eye patch.

"Not a very good likeness," Hideki commented. "The only resemblance is the eye patch. What's he supposed to have done?"

"We don't know," the young one answered. "Our duty is to bring him to the Yoriki. The lieutenant supervisor will decide what is to be done with you."

"What if he does not want to go?" Hideki asked.

The two doshin looked at each other. "Then it is our duty to force him," the older one said.

"What are you names?" Hideki asked.

"Who are you to ask our names? This jutte is all the authority we need," the younger one said.

"Actually, you are mistaken. That jutte provides authority over the chosin, the commoners of Edo. You have no authority over samurai. That is the purview of the ometsuke and hatomoto," Hideki corrected.

The young one was not so sure of himself now. "We have jurisdiction over ronin, and you two wear no mon," he challenged.

"Again, you are incorrect," Hideki said. "Your yoriki and the last magistrate assumed that authority to make money, selling innocent ronin to mine owners," Hideki said.

"That is not our concern. He looks like the fugitive and we must arrest him," the younger one said again.

"The real reason I wanted to know your names is I hate to see men killed for no reason. If you persist, either my friend or I will kill you. I'd like to know the names of men I kill," Hideki said. "Paying a priest for a sutra is the least we should do and for that we need your names."

"The young one is Kimbei-chan. His friend is Gorbei-chan," Hana volunteered using the familiar child's ending for their names.

Both doshin looked horrified that the two samurai should hear them addressed in such an informal manner.

The young one bowed his head slightly, "I am Shimada Kimbei, dozo yoroshuku," he said.

The older one followed suit. "I am Katayama Gorobei, yoroshuku."

Hideki stopped eating and bowed his head slightly, "I am Yoshinobu Hideki, cousin to the shogun, brother to the new south magistrate and student of Myamoto Musashi. This fine, one-eyed gentleman is Yagyu Jubei, son of the chamberlain to the shogun, master of the Yagyu Shinkage-ryu fencing style, and we both are on official business for the shogunate."

The two doshin dropped their juttes to their sides. Hana

stood open-mouthed and her grandfather dropped a bowl of noodles on the dirt floor.

"Gorobei and Kimbei-chan," Hideki said, adding a little salt to their wounds by using the childish endings to their names, "you have a dilemma. You can either persist in doing your duty … or you can live." Then, looking at Jubei, "You are a master at the katana and have been the fencing master to the shogun. You've seen me practice. How would you categorize my fencing skills?"

Jubei looked at the two behind him. "Formidable," he said.

"There you have it. He is the fencing master to the shogun, and I am formidable. Therefore, you can persist in doing your duty and die, or you can return to your bench, finish your noodles, and when we are done, we will accompany you to the Hatchobori, as we happen to have business there. You may even tell the yoriki that you arrested us. But we will not be surrendering our swords."

Hana's grandfather stepped forward. "Please do as he says Kenbei. Do it for Hana's sake. This samurai is very good with a sword. I watched him defeat four samurai in this very shop."

"That's it. Do it for Hana's sake. She would not want to see any death in her famous noodle shop," Hideki said.

Glad for a way out without losing face, they both turned without a word and went back to eating their noodles.

After a few minutes of noodle consumption Jubei spoke. "I do admire your restraint."

"We promised Jii and Naga that we would act as envoys. I'm just trying to keep my promise," Hideki said.

"Your patience is impressive. I take it your forbearance was learned from Musashi?" Jubei asked.

"Probably. He is always talking about the responsibility swordsmen have not to fight."

"He sounds like my father: 'The best victory is the fight not fought.' Maybe I should have listened more," Jubei mused. "You know, I would have never considered Musashi a sensei."

"Why do you say that?"

"From what I had heard, he is all brute force. Anger and fighting spirit accompany every report I've heard of his fights."

"I don't know about that. There is no doubt he is strong. But he has been a very good teacher in many different ways." It was hard for Hideki to explain how he felt about Musashi. His sensei had taken him to another level in his swordsmanship and in his quest for being a good samurai. He wondered if Jubei was a little jealous.

"The youngsters have finished their noodles and await us," observed Jubei.

They rose from the benches and Hideki placed coins on the tabletop.

"Oh no, samurai-sama; the noodles are free to you," the grandfather said.

"No old man. Noodles of such quality deserve payment," Hideki said, then bowed. "Domo."

As he and Jubei started for the door, the young doshin pulled juttes from their belts. Hideki eyed them sternly. "That won't be necessary, gentlemen; but if you'd walk behind us we'll lead the way."

The young police officers looked at each other and quickly returned the juttes to their belts.

"You talk to them as if they are children, yet you are very close to their age," Jubei commented.

Hideki smiled. "It has a lot to do with Musashi. I feel older than both of their ages combined."

"From a standpoint of experience and training, you probably are twice their ages. I wished I'd had the opportunity to train with Musashi."

"I'm sure it can be arranged, if the sensei sticks around. But you surprise me. I would have thought the fencing master to the shogun would be confident in the dominance of his own style," Hideki said.

"Oh, I am confident in Shinkage-ryu style. However, Musashi the man, as well as his two-sword style, intrigues me. Anyone who has fought almost seventy duels and lived to talk about them must have some interesting things to share," Jubei mused.

Hideki stopped at the entrance to the Hatchobori. Two

sergeants armed with rokushakubo staffs guarded it. They extended their staffs at arm's length across the threshold, creating an "X" and blocking Hideki's entrance.

"What is your business here?" one asked.

"They are with us. We have arrested them," Kimbei said.

"Then why are they armed?" the other sergeant asked.

"If you want to disarm them, go ahead. The tall one is the fencing master to the shogun," Gorobei said smugly.

The "X" barrier formed by the staffs disappeared. Hideki moved into the entrance. Like most Japanese buildings, the main opening was on ground level where footwear was removed. Hideki removed his and stepped up onto the main floor in his tabi while removing his saya and katana from his obi, dangling loosely in his left hand by his side. Jubei did likewise.

The floor was very large and covered in hard wood polished to a high sheen by countless prisoners. In the center was a square sand pit with a stove in the center for keeping the area warm in winter and heating tea year round. One side of the room was made of three large sliding shoji screens with paper panes that let in the light from the ubiquitous garden and courtyard that such buildings surrounded. The far wall was made of the same wood as the floor with various signs adorning it. One indicated the various watch teams and their areas of operations and the yoriki in charge.

At the base of the far wall were several low-lying desks where the doshin could sit on folded legs and write reports. Next to the desks were plain cabinets used to store various police items. Probably full of torinawa or arresting ropes, Hideki suspected. Once a suspect was overpowered with the jutte or close-quarter grappling, he had to be restrained for interrogation. The Edo doshin developed rapid means to tie suspects often while they were still struggling. This required skill and practice. This skill was termed hojo-jutsu and raised to an art form. There were ties reserved for farmers, ties for merchants, ties for artisans, and special ties for women so that knots did not crush breasts.

On top of the cabinets were three portable lanterns with

collapsible paper globes and a metal insert on the bottom to support the candle. The globe attached to a long, willowy, flexible handle which was connected to the top of the globe for patrols at night. Next to the desk sat two square lamps with paper panes on tri-pod stands for use near the desks after dark. Above the desk was a map of Edo divided into sectors for the yoriki's area of responsibility. Off to the right was a hallway. Hideki knew where that went. It shot back to the jail and police barracks. He had taken this route in his escape several weeks ago.

Coming up the hallway were three men Hideki recognized. The yoriki paused when he entered the main room and looked from Hideki to Jubei, then at his two doshin.

"What do we have here?" he asked.

"Kumogiri-sama," Gorobei said. "The one-eyed samurai looked like the paper alert you posted, so we brought him in for questioning."

"And well you should, Gorobei, for he is indeed the escapee from a few weeks ago. And if I'm not mistaken, the other is the one who engineered the mass escape," he said.

With those words, the two doshin that trailed Kumogiri fanned out on either side of their boss and drew their juttes. Hideki recognized the doshin on the left as Jubei's inquisitor. The doshin on the right was the leader of the attempted assassination of the Gumsumgumi the night Hideki escaped.

"But why are they still armed?" Kumogiri asked.

Gorobei was hesitant to answer. "Sir, they looked dangerous; there was just we two, and they claimed they weren't ronin," he managed.

"Nonsense; do you see any mon? They wear no identification of a clan. They are ronin."

Jubei stepped up and to Hideki's left.

"You men surrender your weapons. You are under arrest. If you don't do so peacefully it will go hard on you," Kumogiri demanded.

"I believed you the last time you recited those words and it almost cost me my life," Jubei said. "I will not do so again."

"You cannot think to defy us; we are the law." Kumogiri

nodded to the green-clad doshin on his right, sending him down the hallway to bring reinforcements.

"You are not the government," Jubei corrected. "You are dogs preying on the carcasses of better men. You use your office to intimidate and harass the townspeople to enrich yourselves. You are vermin."

The doshin in brown who had tortured Jubei took a step forward and raised his jutte to crack Jubei's skull. The iron weapon was on its downward path when Jubei stepped back with his left foot and at the same time drew his sword with a lightning earth-to-sky draw, severing the doshin's right hand at the wrist. The severed hand, still clutching the jutte, hit the hardwood floor at the same time the doshin's knees did as he went down grasping his bloody stump, frantically trying to stop the pumping geyser of blood. The whites of his eyes got large and he started to scream. Even in the large room, the screams were deafening. Jubei flicked his sword to the right and down to release any blood and returned it to the saya in his left hand. The doshin's screams subsided into sobs and whimpers.

Jubei looked at Kumogiri. "I guess that hand won't be used to beat innocent men anymore."

Kumogiri was in shock. He prided himself on his fencing ability. He considered himself quite accomplished. However, he had not seen the one-eyed swordsman draw his weapon. One moment the one-eyed swordsman was about to get his skull cracked and in the next, the doshin had no hand. Kumogiri was not used to being threatened. He was used to doing the threatening. Nevertheless, one look at that one good eye and Kumogiri knew he was moments away from his own death.

The pounding of feet coming up the hallway reassured Kumogiri. Now numbers were on his side. His confidence grew as he tried to force his fear down. The entire off-duty squad of police officers fanned out on either side of their yoriki. Juttes were in everyone's hands. They were looking upon the wounded doshin and, wanting revenge, raised their juttes over their heads. Kumogiri managed to smile to himself. Police everywhere rallied when one of their own was injured. He would have these two ronin killed slowly before the night was over.

Hideki spoke to Jubei. "I'm so glad we approached this mission with professionalism and have not let our personal feelings get in the way."

"Sorry, the sight of him made me angry. When he struck, I reacted with reflex."

"Yes, well, try to keep your temper in check while we conduct official business," Then, turning to the yoriki, he asked, "What is your name?"

"I am Kumogiri Denjiro, yoriki of the south magistrate and these are my policemen." He did not bow.

Hideki bowed just his head. "I am Yoshinobu Hideki, cousin to the shogun and younger brother to the new south magistrate."

The juttes that were so threatening a moment ago drooped with Hideki's introduction. Many of the police officers looked to their yoriki for guidance.

Hideki moved his head in Jubei's direction. "My friend here is Yagyu Jubei, son of the chamberlain to the shogun, head of the Shinkage-ryu fencing school, former fencing master to the Tokugawa."

At Jubei's introduction, the police officers physically shrunk back.

"Nonsense," Kumogiri said. "Anyone can claim to be of high birth. Where is your proof?" he demanded.

"I thought you were going to take some convincing," Hideki said. He reached into his kimono, removed a large folded paper, and held it aloft for all to see.

"Do you recognize this? On your knees! On your knees before the emblem of the shogun's representative!" Hideki commanded loudly.

There were sharp intakes of breath and the clanging of juttes striking the hardwood as knees and hands and foreheads touched the floor. The large golden emblem on the outside of the folded paper was the mon of the Tokugawa family. It was the golden hollyhock. No one would dare use it falsely. Even Kumogiri was on his knees bowing deeply.

Using the same loud voice, Hideki commanded, "Two of you, get this fool to a bed and send for a doctor. If he lives, he can use his good hand to empty the honey buckets."

The one-handed doshin exited with cloth rags tied to his stump to stem the flow of blood. Hideki stepped closer to the group, careful not to step in the small lake of the doshin's blood.

"Kumogiri Denjiro, I will leave this document with you. You can waste time comparing the signature with the written directive you received yesterday alerting you to my brother's posting as magistrate. Jubei-sama and I have just eaten our noon meal. Therefore, we are in the hour of the horse," identifying the time period between 11:00 a.m. and 1:00 p.m. "My brother and his advisors will arrive in the hour of the monkey," referring now to the time period between 3:00 p.m. and 5:00 p.m., "for an inspection of the Hatchobori.

"I have given my brother my report on your villainous ways, but he will have to make up his own mind. I would advise all the traitorous thieves and bullies among you to turn in your juttes and go back to your other lines of work. My brother does not take bribes and will not be flattered. Either you are an honest police officer or you can leave today without reprisal. But if you stay and continue to be crooked, you will be punished severely," Hideki concluded.

Jubei stepped around to Hideki's left toward the prostrate Kumogiri. "You do not know how badly I want to kill you and string your intestines along the street. You can thank Buddha and the Yoshinobu for your life. But if I see you on the street, I will have your head on a stick in front of this building." His warning completed, Jubei turned and strode to the entrance.

"That concludes our business," Hideki said and dropped the official decree in the pool of blood at his feet.

At the entrance, he sat down to strap on his sandals. Hideki looked up at Jubei, who had already donned his footwear. "Jubei-sama, I am not used to being the voice of reason and restraint. With you along I have to assume new roles."

"I am sorry Hideki. Every time I think of the humiliation and injury I suffered at their hands, I want to kill them all," Jubei growled.

"I understand that, Jubei. Believe me I do. It offends your

samurai pride. Nevertheless, we have to think of Nagamasa. We are working toward a higher goal here."

Jubei smiled. "You are my junior in years, but my senior in maturity. Maybe I need to study under Musashi."

"Like I said, that could be arranged. Now let's go find Naga."

Chapter 16: Saving the Five Families

"Jii-sama, sumimasin," Yoshi apologized.

The old man almost jumped from his low desk where he had been reading. "Yoshi! You startled me. I will never understand how you just seem to materialize," Jii said in exasperation.

"Sorry to disturb you Lord, but I need a few minutes of your time."

Jii placed the scroll he had been reading on the low desk before him. "You are a valued counselor to the family. Of course, I have time for you. Sit down."

Yoshi moved onto the tatami in his tabi from the hardwood entrance, took up a position opposite the old man, and sat cross-legged in the spot designated. "I have a favor to ask."

"What is it? Do you need more money?" Jii asked.

"What? No, no, I've got plenty of money."

"What then? Do you want to bring your young wife and family to Edo?" Jii guessed.

"Oh no, Jii-sama; they are already here."

"Oh? Why have I not met them? Why don't you move them into the compound. There is plenty of room."

"Thank you, Lord; we can talk about them later. What I want to discuss has to do with your grandsons and the contract on their lives," Yoshi said.

"Okay," Jii said, repositioning from the folded-legs position to the informal cross-legged posture of Yoshi. "Now you've got my attention."

"Lord, I have a plan to cancel the assassination contract on Hideki and Naga."

Jii arched an eyebrow. "Really? I thought Ninjas didn't cancel contracts?"

"Normally you are correct. But these are not normal times," Yoshi said.

"What would make them cancel the contract?"

"We would have to give them something more valuable than Hideki and Naga," Yoshi said.

"I don't have anything more valuable than my grandsons," the old man said firmly.

"They may think you do if we broach the subject carefully."

"Do they suspect you've switched sides?" Jii asked.

"I am sure they do."

Jii's gaze was focused and intent. "What makes you think so?"

"I've been here too long and no one has died," Yoshi said. "Besides, I have been summoned to two meetings with the Five Families which I have ignored. They will suspect me for sure."

"You've been summoned again, haven't you?"

"Yes."

"And this time you plan to go?" Jii asked.

"Yes."

"You know they'll kill you?" Jii asked matter-of-factly.

"Most likely they will try, but only if I don't go prepared with a good plan and something valuable to trade," Yoshi said.

"What do you plan to trade?" Jii asked.

"You."

Jii covered his initial surprise. Then he looked Yoshi in the eyes. "Maybe I'd better hear this plan."

Yoshi walked bent over. On his back were tree branches broken into short lengths and placed in a large wicker basket. The basket rode on his back. One thumb tucked into one of the rope shoulder harnesses kept the basket in place and the other gripped a gnarled walking stick. His dress was that of a peasant. He wore straw sandals without tabi. His legs and feet were dirty. On his lower torso he wore the knee-length monpe or cloth pants. There were holes in the knees and tears on the bottom. A hippari, or short jacket stopping at the waist and ending at the elbows, covered his upper torso. It too had seen better days.

A dirty cloth of indistinguishable color covered his head. The cloth started just above his eyebrows and ended tied behind his head with a flap over the knot. It covered most of his hair. He had carefully placed lines on his face with charcoal and rouge to create the illusion of age. His fingers looked crooked with rheumatism, and the backs of his hands sported carefully-crafted liver spots, a trick of the rouge and charcoal combination.

He walked as if the weight of the world was on his old back. His gait barely kept up with the flow of people. He stopped every so often to try to contend with the heavy load. No one paid him any attention. He was just another wood carrier returning to his humble shack somewhere on the edge of town with the remnants of what Edo housewives had not purchased.

He would probably stop at the Zojoji Temple to pray for a lighter load and more buyers tomorrow. At least, that is what everyone who saw him would think. Yoshi hoped no one would think of him at all. He was invisible in the evening throng of people who were focused on home and an evening meal.

Yoshi slowly and methodically passed through the large three-storied red gates with their red-tiled roofs marking the entrance to the temple grounds. The triple pathways were huge with enough width to allow three horses abreast to enter into any of the three double gates. Once through the gates, a very wide stone pathway wound its way through several acres of trees and buildings.

On either side of the pathway, meticulously attended dirt areas with large evergreen trees encased the grounds. Each one had its own rail fence. Yoshi slowly moved past the large, cast-iron temple bell that hung vertically from its own pavilion of stout cedar poles. Buddhist prayers written on paper strips festooned the wood. The evening breeze made them dance and send the prayers to the Buddha. Passing the bell, he noticed a young woman pouring water from a wooden ladle over a stone jizo statue of the Buddha, incanting a blessing for a loved one.

Yoshi had to force his mind to be patient. This walk to the temple was taking a very long time. He had to remain invisible if he was going to survey the area without detection.

Next, he passed row after row of stone and wooden jizos about two shaku in height, just a little over knee high. Flowers and cloth hats adorned many. Each one reminded someone of a loved one lost.

Finally, he could see his destination. The Ankokuden was a two-storied, wooden building with the pagoda double roof sloping down from its peak and then slightly upward again. On the end of the spine of the roof, he could just make out the golden temple dogs in the fading light. He took his time climbing the steps, resting every fourth and then seventh step.

Once inside, he took care squatting down and letting the large basket come to rest on the floor in the reception area, then extricated his shoulders from the load. He removed his sandals and moved into the main temple room. The main area was small by temple standards, made smaller by the spate of beautifully carved furniture and gold flowers that gilded the statue of the Buddha on the far wall. Many candles and lamps reflected off the ornate, wooden shrine encasing the Buddha, making it appear dark. Hence, the townspeople called it the Black Buddha. Ieyasu, the founder of the Tokugawa shogunate, had made it his family temple. As Edo grew, so grew the items donated. Now it looked more like a warehouse than a shrine.

However, Yoshi was interested in neither the architecture nor the furniture except when it provided him good cover and concealment. He moved to the first room off the main hall on the right in the bent and limping gait of an old man. He placed his hand on the sliding door and stopped to listen. He slid the door back and entered, closing the door behind him. He moved to the center of the room where a small fire pit presented itself. He sat down cross-legged and waited. Reaching into his jacket, he extracted a pipe and tobacco and lit it from a small lantern resting on the sand. Two bowls later, his haragai alerted him to his visitors.

"Welcome, head of the Five Families and Sachi," he said to no one.

Both Sachi and her father dropped lightly to the floor.

"So, you had the courage to show yourself, traitor," Sachi challenged.

"I have betrayed no one."

"Then why are the Yoshinobu not dead?" she demanded.

"Because it would not be in your best interest to do so," Yoshi explained.

"You do not know your place. Such decisions are not yours to make," she said.

She was dressed like her father in white pilgrim's garb. Neither wore hats. Both carried long staffs, but the usual rings at the top were missing.

"I would think you would thank me for not executing the Yoshinobu."

"Why would you think that?" she asked.

"Because your destinies are linked," Yoshi said.

"What are you babbling about, traitor?"

"I merely state what you have already discovered," Yoshi replied, shaking burnt ashes into the pit. The motion drew the pair's eyes to the pipe while his other hand drew two throwing darts from the hem of his pants. "If you assassinate the Yoshinobu, you are next."

Both looked but did not speak. "I thought so," Yoshi said. "You have seen it yourselves. If you had not, you would not be the head of the Five Families."

"You have broken a contract. You know the penalty. You cannot think we will let you walk out of here. Even you are not that arrogant," she said, not concealing her disgust.

"Oh, you may be foolish enough to try," Yoshi said.

"What?" Sachi laughed. "You are not so deranged as to believe you can survive combat with my father and me? Besides, one whistle and there will be ten family members here."

Yoshi looked into the old man's eyes. "Were he in his

prime, no, probably not. Now? Yes! I can defeat you both."

"What arrogance. I've waited a long time for this you country bumpkin. You never should have been selected," she said before placing her fingers to her mouth and whistling a shrill blast.

Nothing happened. No one came. She whistled again. Still nothing happened.

"Save your breath daughter," the old man said. "I believe Yoshi has disabled our reserves."

Sachi's eyes grew wide with anger. "Have you killed all ten?"

"You count poorly Sachi. There were twelve. But to answer your question, no, they are not dead. Not if my instructions were followed."

She turned sideways to Yoshi and flashed a fierce gaze. "So what is it to be, traitor, a fight to the death?"

"By the Buddha, no!" Yoshi said. "And please do not turn back and throw that shuriken in your left hand."

"Be still girl," the old man said. "We are probably surrounded now; we have no reserves and you are trying to bait a very skilled killer. Let's hear what he has to say and then judge what kind of a man he is."

"Thank you," Yoshi said. "I am here to offer a solution to both our problems."

"What kind of a problem do we have?" asked Sachi, pacing around the room behind her father as she scanned the room, searching for any advantage.

"Come sit beside your father, Sachi. I did not come to harm either of you."

Sachi made no move to obey. "Sit daughter," the old man ordered, and she did.

"You were hired to kill the Yoshinobu by someone in Edo castle." Yoshi spoke in calm and deliberate tones. He did not expect an answer and was not disappointed. "It was either a member of the Roju or Tairo. The Fox Gang roams the country with impunity, killing Tokugawa heirs and making the crime look like a robbery and murder. Nevertheless, the Fox Gang is ninja; believe me, I know. I have fought with them."

"Is there a point to this story?" Sachi demanded.

"The Fox Gang is being run by the same person or persons who hired you to kill the Yoshinobu. The Yoshinobu are Shinpan. They are Tokugawa. No matter who becomes the next shogun, this can only end in one way for the Five Families. If the Fox Gang is successful and their candidate takes over, the Fox Gang will become the new Ometsuke government spies. The Iga and Koga ninja will have one last mission. That is to find you and eradicate the Five Families. Whoever engineered this kyodai goroshi will want no loose ends.

"The second scenario is that the Yoshinobu survive. Then you are exposed as contracting to kill a Tokugawa. Hittori Hanzo will then send the Iga and Koga ninja to eliminate you as a threat to the government. Either way you die."

At the mention of Hittori Hanzo, Sachi's eyes got large. "Hittori Hanzo knows about us?" she asked.

"Of course he does. If the hunt for the Fox Gang was not consuming all his time, you would be dead already."

"How do you know this?" Sachi asked.

"He told me so," Yoshi said.

"Hittori Hanzo actually talks to you?"

"Yes, we have spoken several times," Yoshi said.

"I think you boast too much. You are just a little man who has gotten a position in the Yoshinobu household, and now you think yourself grand."

Yoshi looked directly at her. "How can the sempai of the Five Families be so stupid?"

Sachi started to reply when her father's sharp stare cut her off. The old man turned back to Yoshi, "Why do you think she is my sempai?"

Sachi's look of contempt and anger turned to fear. She shook her head from side to side pleading for Yoshi not to betray her. She was not supposed to have revealed herself to him the night they shared his shack. Yoshi shook his head. Her pride would get her killed one day.

"It's pretty obvious. You send me on the biggest contract the Five Families have ever undertaken and Sachi is my babysitter. Who else would she be but your sempai?"

The old man nodded. Behind him, Sachi rolled her eyes skyward. Yoshi could not tell if she was thanking the gods or him. It did not matter.

"My daughter is right. You do a lot of speculating and boasting for someone of such low birth. How is it that you have the ear of the Yoshinobu?"

"I am a counselor to the Yoshinobu," Yoshi stated simply.

Sachi laughed. "You tell that lie with a straight face."

The old man studied Yoshi's continence. He was looking for some indication of a ruse. He found none. "So what has the counselor of the Yoshinobu come to propose?"

"That you cancel the contract," Yoshi said.

"Are you crazy?" Sachi asked. "We cannot cancel a contract. Then we would be like you, and no one would ever hire us again."

"One might," Yoshi said.

"Who?" she asked.

"The Yoshinobu," her father answered for Yoshi. "Just what do you propose?"

"The Yoshinobu are no longer country diamyo. They are here to stay. The grandfather and Nagamasa have already matched wits with the bakufu government and won. They are too dangerous to the power brokers to let them go back to Kii. Whether Naga becomes shogun or not is unknown and immaterial to your situation. He is the best man for the job. Castle politics being what they are, who knows what will happen. But even if he does not become shogun, he is currently the south magistrate and may remain so."

Sachi maintained strict eye contact as he spoke. "Nice story, Yoshi, but what does it have to do with us?"

"The Yoshinobu have no experience with shinobi no mono. They do not have ninja and know nothing about them," Yoshi began.

"And now they will need an intelligence network they can rely upon," the old man finished for him.

"Exactly," Yoshi said. "Whether to help stay on top of criminal activity as the magistrate or to keep abreast of the bakufu happenings across the country, they will need information that is reliable from the only nationwide network not committed to anyone."

"So, you show your true colors Yoshi," Sachi accused. "You want to lead the Five Families."

"You listen, but you do not hear," Yoshi said. "I have no desire to lead the Five Families. That is your job. Mine is advice."

"Yes, but you do recognize that any information we gather would flow through you to the Yoshinobu. It would be like we were working for you," the old man interjected.

"I would initially be the contact, yes. But it would not last long."

"Why not?"

"Two reasons. The first is that the Yoshinobu are smart. They will want to draw you out of the darkness and into their light. While they trust my judgment, and will continue to seek it, I hope, they will want to be as close as possible to the intelligence source. You will have a lot of meetings to attend," Yoshi said, smiling.

"What is the second?" the old man asked.

"I believe if you work for the Yoshinobu there will be a close personal bond between them and your daughter."

"What is he talking about daughter?"

Sachi looked perplexed. "I don't know Father. I have never met the Yoshinobu. Yoshi appears to be talking big again."

"Are you really that dumb?" Yoshi asked.

That made her father chuckle. "Sometimes she is. Sachi, we will not be killed by the government if we side with the Yoshinobu and find and help eliminate the Fox Gang. And we will have perpetual stipends by serving one of the great houses."

"Samurai are always treacherous; you have said so yourself," Sachi protested.

"I agree Sachi. But I believe the Yoshinobu to be different," Yoshi said.

"But you say they know nothing of the shinobi no mono. Our ways will irritate and frustrate them," she said.

"That is true. They do things that are very strange at times, but I have adjusted. Besides, Hanzo Yuki will soon marry Nagamasa and Yagyu Jubei is now supporting the second son, Hideki. I am no longer the only ninja on the payroll."

The old man took in a deep breath. "I suppose I must accept right away or we don't walk out."

"No, you are free to leave at any time. But I would like to bring in some people that may help you make up your mind."

"I guess we have little choice."

Yoshi stood and moved to the door, sliding it open and nodding to someone in the temple's main room. Then he slid the door completely open, retreated to a far corner of the little room, and kneeled. Through the door, Jii entered in all his finery. He was wearing the kamishino. It consisted of a fine, white silk inner kimono, a grey silk outer kimono, indigo eight-pleated hakama from the waist down, and the kata ginu black silk vest with its exaggerated shoulders tied in the front at the waist. The Yoshinobu mon of a single cherry blossom in white adorned both lapels of the kata ginu. Nagamasa, Hanzo Yuki, Hideki, Musashi, and Yagyu Jubei followed him. Jii sat across from the old man. The rest spread out behind him and knelt. They were all armed.

Jii bowed slightly. "Yoshinobu Masashige desu. Dozo yoroshuku," he greeted.

"Sandayu Momochi," the leader of the Five Families said, returning the bow.

"Sandayu Sachi," Sachi said, bowing behind her father.

Jii went around introducing each member of his entourage. The old man's and Sachi's eyes studied each face. Each bowed an introduction. Just after Yuki had uttered her greeting and Hideki was to be next, Sachi blurted out, "Takezo?"

Musashi, beside Hideki, answered, "Yes?"

Sachi looked at Musashi in confusion. "Not you, him," she said pointing to Hideki.

Musashi sighed. "Doubtless you've met him while he was using my old name. He has a habit of trying to ruin my sterling reputation by borrowing my name."

Hideki bowed. "Yoshinobu Hideki, desu," he said. When he

raised his eyes and sought her eyes, she was staring daggers into his soul. Then she would not make eye contact with him again.

Musashi and then Jubei introduced themselves. Yoshi moved in behind Hideki and whispered. "Benjo, neh?"

Hideki turned his head to one side and whispered back, "You dung beetle."

"Wait a little longer. Dung beetles bring cherry blossoms," Yoshi whispered.

"Yoshi came to me with a very interesting proposition," Jii began.

"Lord, before we begin our discussions, as a father I must ask my daughter if she knows your grandson," the ninja leader said.

Sachi bowed her head before her father. "I did not know he was a Yoshinobu, Father. He introduced himself as Benke Takezo, a ronin."

Naga, Yuki, and Jubei could not control their laughter. A stare from Jii stopped them cold.

"And do you still have feelings for this samurai?" the father asked his daughter.

"I did when he was a ronin and interceded to protect a fifteen-year-old girl and her old grandfather and myself from four drunken samurai in a noodle shop," Sachi said. "But how can I, when I know he lied to me and is a samurai of high birth?"

Jii turned to Hideki. "Hideki, do you know this woman?"

"Hai," Hideki said. "Her name was Myo, and she ran a courier service for her father here in Edo."

"And do you still have feelings for her?" Jii asked.

Hideki looked down at the tatami. All eyes were on him. "I guess the best answer would be the one she gave. How could I when she lied to me? But the truth is I have feelings for her and probably always will."

Hideki looked up at Sachi and this time she was looking directly at him. The daggers were gone.

Jii turned back to the old man. "I apologize for my grandson. I cannot believe a samurai would take advantage of a townswoman in this way. I shall discipline him later. What is the world coming to? No one is staying in their class."

The old ninja nodded. "It is all upside down now. The young do not honor the old ways."

On this common ground, they began to speak in earnest to each other. The old ninja was impressed with the lack of guile he detected in the old samurai. Deception and double speak were the old ninja's trade. He found no such devices in the samurai's discussion. He seemed straightforward. Nevertheless, he had not lived this long in his profession by trusting others. However, he had to admit, he was beginning to see what had attracted Yoshi to their banner.

Yuki looked at Sachi and caught her stealing glances at Hideki. Hideki was engaged in the same endeavor. Naga bent over and teasingly whispered in her ear, "I can attest to the fact that ninja women make good lovers."

"I am samurai, just trained as ninja and don't you forget it," she whispered back.

"The best of both worlds," Naga said.

Yuki smiled at him. It was his reward for being chivalrous.

"I suppose if we were to refuse the offer that my daughter and I would be killed," the old ninja said to Jii.

"No, Yoshi made it plain that your safe release was a condition of this meeting," Jii said.

The old ninja looked at Yoshi behind Hideki. "And do you always take the advice of an upstart ninja?"

Jii followed his gaze to Yoshi. "I am not a good judge of ninja. I am a good judge of men. I will always take the advice of good men."

The old ninja nodded. "He is a surprising young man. He respects the old ways but sees the changes ahead."

"I find him irreplaceable. To find an honest man who is both smart and visionary is an extraordinary combination. I do not know what I would do without him," Jii proclaimed.

"I suppose he will act as liaison between our families if I accept this offer?"

"I would have thought so until you discovered the relationship between your daughter and Hideki," Jii said.

The old ninja sighed. "Yes, troubling but strangely reassuring at the same time."

"Yes, isn't it?" Jii seconded.

"Let's you and I hammer out the details of this alliance and let the young folk walk the temple grounds," the old man said, reaching for his pipe.

Jii pulled out his pipe and offered the tobacco pouch from his obi to his new partner. "Good idea."

As Nagamasa stepped through the large wooden doors of the Zojoji out into the darkness of the porch and steps down beyond, he paused for Yuki to catch up. "Not exactly the woman I'd have chosen for my little brother."

"She is a little different," Yuki said. "But I can tell she likes him."

"How, she seemed to ignore him?"

"That's how," Yuki said.

Naga's commander of the guard presented himself and bowed to Naga awaiting instruction. "Commander, keep the guards in place. See that they are alert and have water," Yuki directed. "We may be here for some time."

The commander bowed to Yuki and then glanced at Naga. Naga nodded slightly and the commander departed to see to the orders.

"You've grown very good at ordering my guards around," he said. "They take orders from you as if you were part of the family."

Yuki bowed slightly to Naga. "Sorry, Lord; it is my job as your yojimbo."

"Come, let's go down to the bell. I have a question for you."

Hideki wandered out onto the porch in time to see Naga and Yuki reach the bottom of the steps headed down the pathway. His first concern was for their safety. Then he saw several of the Yoshinobu guard move to surround them from several paces away. He smiled. Yuki's ninja would also be somewhere where they could respond. He need not worry. He felt someone at his back and turned to find Myo standing behind him. She looked annoyed. He started toward her as she turned and moved to the waist-high, wooden rail of the porch.

"Is it safe to talk to you?" he asked with a nervous laugh.

"Who is asking? Is it Takezo or the great Lord of the Yoshinobu?"

"They are one and the same," he said.

She turned and stared directly into his eyes. "You should be ashamed of yourself. I fell in love with a dashing young ronin who tries to protect young girls, old men, and unescorted women. Now I learn it was all a sham."

"Very interesting accusation coming from Myo, the girl who runs a courier service for her sick father ... no wait—it's Sachi who runs an assassination network for her powerful ninja father."

She continued to look into his eyes. He had the same innocent but strong face, the same slight, wiry build she had enjoyed so much. Nevertheless, his dress with the kamishino with its expensive kimono, hakama, and kataginu was now like a bridge between them.

"Oh Takezo, what are we to do?"

"Well, first of all, I hope you don't kill me. Beyond that, I do not know. I do not want to lose you."

"So your appearance in my life was a circumstance of the great lord slumming?" she asked.

"No, ever since I was little I have always explored new places on my own. New things and new people intrigue me. The night I met you I had had a hard day and was searching for a dojo for a workout. But I became lost and hungry. I passed up several noodle shops before I went into Hana's place. Maybe it was destiny that you were inside."

"You lied to me," she said, with a slight pout.

"Looking back on it, if I'd used my real name what would you have done?"

She thought about it for a minute. "I see your point. I would have been honor bound to kill you."

"I was going to tell you the morning after we slept together, but you left in a hurry."

"Yes, I had errands to run. I've been visiting Nichi's every day to see if you'd returned."

"Really?"

"Yes, really; so what are we going to do now?"

"It is my hope that your father will support the Yoshino-bu and we can continue."

"Won't your grandfather object?" she asked.

"He might if he knew. What of your father?"

"Oh, he'd kill me if he knew."

"So we keep it from them," Hideki said.

"Sounds good to me," she said.

Chapter 17: The Bird Woman

The woman made whistling sounds to the caged bird. Her outer robes were of the same brown and white as the bird's feathers. Even the outer garment's weave reflected the bright red marks of the bird's wings. Her calls to the bird were quite good, good enough that on the third attempt the bird answered with the same distinct call. The only satisfaction the woman allowed herself was a slight smile.

The bird was the only physical reminder of her humble beginnings which she willingly retained. The birds had been abundant when she was a girl. She remembered running free in bare feet through the forest and listening to their distinctive whistle. It was far from the prettiest of the birds found in the forest, but the Izu thrush was numerous on the island where she grew up, and the farmers revered it. Her people had believed its presence during childbirth would portend a special future for the baby, and her mother had kept one in a cage in the kitchen portion of the old, thatch-roofed house where she grew up. Her little village was able to communicate using codes created from its whistles and chirps, which was a handy talent in their line of work.

Now the Izu thrush was harder and harder to find. Invaders and predators overtook them, like the people who revered them. If she were successful, that would change.

"My lady, how long must I wait? I have pressing business," the seated samurai said.

The woman turned toward him in a wide motion using her hands to steer the outer robe in the right direction, allowing the many layers to move in a circular pattern and fall into position around her. The movement revealed an ample amount of ankle. She held her head to one side. In her youth, she had landed a shogun with that practiced move. She was too old for it now and her figure was no longer an hourglass, but she was happy that she could still do it, even if it no longer achieved the original effect.

She had been a young girl when the promising young warrior Inaba Masanari had taken her as wife, and she had borne him several children. Her fortunes changed when the great Tokugawa Ieyasu picked her as a wet nurse for his grandson, Takechiyo. Some speculate that the reason she received this plum position was due to the old warlord's roving eye and appreciation for a shapely female. Others theorized it as payment to her husband for convincing Kobayakawa Hideaki to join Ieyasu's army at Sekigahara. If Kobayakawa had not deserted the Toyotomi and thrown in with Ieyasu, the Tokugawa shogun would not exist. Kobayakawa had deserted and changed to Ieyasu's side in the crucial moments of the battle, securing the Tokugawa future.

Whatever the reason, the woman's husband now enjoyed a twenty-thousand koku fiefdom and copious amounts of sake and serving girls. She had not seen him in years and did not expect to ever see him again. While he worked on populating his fiefdom one serving girl at a time, she had been busy raising a future shogun while amassing power by staying close to Ieyasu and the men of power in the Tokugawa government. The old warlord was dead now, and his son Hidetada, the current Tokugawa shogun, never really liked her. However, it did not matter. By the time the old warrior had died, she knew everyone's secrets and was in a position to make or break powerful men. One such sat on a tatami mat at her feet, listening to her make birdcalls.

"I know what your pressing business is Naomasu-san. It involves pressing a young girl in the Yoshiwara into the tatami mat. Such behavior got you into trouble. If I had let the ometsuke continue their investigation a year ago, you would have had to slit your belly in apology. How old was she, Naomasu?

She could not have been older than thirteen. However, look at you now. Instead of being dead, you put your career in my hands and you are no longer a lowly magistrate in the shrines and temples division; you are a member of the Roju."

Naomasu Nagai, the latest member of the Roju, one of six in the land to wear the title of Elder, bowed from his seated position on the tatami floor. "I thank you for the honor you've bestowed upon me and my house."

"There will be more. I have the soba-yonin position in mind for you once my boy is made shogun."

The samurai bowed again and expressed his delight with a guttural, "Hai, to replace Yagyu as the chamberlain is my heart's desire."

"Can you believe that other woman is striving so hard to have that unnatural child as the next shogun? Where would the Tokugawa be if that happened? Does not everyone see that?" she asked.

The slightly gray Naomasu bowed his head as he spoke. "Anyone with any sense, my lady," he said.

"Exactly," she agreed. "Now we have this new Yoshinobu bunch to contend with." The lady stopped talking and froze. "Is that you Hakunnsai?"

A voice from somewhere said, "It is I." The gray-haired samurai jumped at the voice and grabbed for his short sword.

"Calm yourself Naomasu. Even in this castle, your sword would do you little good if Hakunnsai wished you harm," she said. "Now we can begin."

The gray-haired samurai kept looking around, trying to find where the voice was hiding.

"These Yoshinobu trouble me," she said.

"Not as much as they trouble me," the voice said. "I have lost many men to them."

"I guess maybe we sent the wrong ninja to Kyoto," the samurai said.

"I sent thirty good men to Kyoto to handle one boy. Little did we know we were challenging the best swordsman in the country and a ninja master," the voice stated angrily.

"Gentlemen, we must not fight amongst ourselves," she

said. "They intrigue me. They are always doing the unexpected, like accusing us during the meeting of the Roju and Tairo last week. That Nagamasa derailed everything I had planned."

"I broke out in a cold sweat when he accused someone in that room of conspiring with the Fox Gang," the samurai affirmed.

"Yes, but who is the brain? Is it Nagamasa himself? Is it the old one they called Jii? It cannot be the youngster. He is too hotheaded. It is hard to devise a strategy when you know so little about the enemy," she said.

"We know Nagamasa likes women. He has taken up with the Hanzo whelp," the voice said.

"Really? … I wonder how much influence she has and by proxy how much Yagyu exerts?"

"It doesn't matter; kill them all and you get what you want," the voice said.

"Yes, but that has proven difficult to accomplish," the old samurai said.

"My boy will be shogun," the woman vowed. "But what are the Yoshinobu doing? They have less than a month to accomplish the impossible."

"Nagamasa is holding an inspection on the Hatchibori right now," the voice said.

"For what purpose?" asked the old samurai.

"From the tenor of the pre-inspection meeting, to dismantle it," the voice said.

"Tell me about this pre-inspection meeting," the woman demanded.

"The young swordsman visited the Hatchibori with Yagyu Jubei," the voice stated.

"Yagyu Jubei?" the woman asked. "When did he return?"

"We are not sure, but he has aligned his sword with the Yoshinobu," the voice said. "The young swordsman presented a decree from Nagamasa that an inspection was to be conducted, and any crooked police could leave immediately without prosecution."

"I see," the woman said. "Once again, the unexpected."

"We cannot have them dismantle the Hatchobori." The

samurai protested. "There are too many links to me."

The woman looked at the old samurai with a question in her stare. "You have not been there yourself, surely?"

"No my lady, but several of my men have."

"Then you can easily claim you had no knowledge, and that will be the end of that," she said. "Still, these Yoshinobu are troubling." She paced back and forth for a few minutes, then stopped. "We must think of ways to unsettle their plans. Their task is to catch the Fox Gang. Hakunnsai, is he any closer to catching you?"

"I do not see how he could be. As far as we can tell, the Yoshinobu have no intelligence-gathering capability, and only one ninja on their staff," the voice said.

"Then we can assume their efforts with the police have nothing to do with his task of catching and destroying the Fox Gang?" she asked as she paced up and down the center of the tatami floor.

"My lady, if they have identified someone in the government as being tied to the Fox Gang, they could've tied the police to the use of cheap labor in the mines as a source of revenue for political ends. You said yourself they do the unexpected," the old samurai said.

"You may be right, Naomasu. I had not thought of that. We will open ourselves to danger if we underestimate their intelligence again," she said.

"Would shutting down the Hatchobori cripple your efforts?" the voice asked.

"It would hurt us substantially," she replied. "Our forces are large and spread out. We require vast sums of money to keep them employed and hidden."

"Then we should stop them," the voice said.

"Yes, but I want to stop them entirely. Our counter strategy must put us ahead of them, and eventually eliminate them for good."

"Yes, but how?" asked the samurai.

The woman walked to the birdcage and stared at it for a moment. Then she imitated a series of chirps and whistles. When she had finished she turned to the samurai. "Naomasu, we need to embarrass the Yoshinobu in the eyes of the government as well as in their bid to destroy the Hatchobori. I want you to have our trusted contact in the police force arrange to capture the Fox Gang leader."

The old samurai looked surprised. Then he glanced at the ceiling. "Will not Hakunnsai object?"

The woman laughed. "Oh Naomasu, it is such a good thing that you have me to think for you. We will not give them Hakunnsai. But at the same time, we must have the castle officials see that these country samurai are weak," she said.

"That sounds good, but how are we to accomplish such a feat? Everyone thinks they are the embodiment of Bushido."

"What would happen if the Hatchobori were to capture the Fox Gang leader and then the citizens of Edo rise up in a riot in order to get their hands on this leader so they could execute him themselves?" she asked.

The old samurai thought about it. "The officials would see that the magistrate was weak and could not control the city. They would be forced to commit troops from the castle to keep the peace."

"And how would that look for the magistrate?" she asked.

"Very bad, my lady; not only would it look like he had lost control, but there would be many deaths and injuries among the citizens, and he would be blamed for that as well."

"Then don't you think we ought to do all within our power to see that this is exactly what takes place?"

The plan finally dawned on Naomasu. "Very well played my lady; I think I know exactly what to do," he said.

"I hope so," she replied.

"But my lady, even if we embarrass the Yoshinobu and Nagamasa has to admit failure, that is not a final solution to our problem."

"No it is not. But Hakunnsai will take care of that."

The old samurai waited for the voice to say something. When the silence dragged on, the old samurai asked, "My lady, shouldn't you give Hakunnsai his orders?"

The woman moved back to the birdcage and whistled to the bird. This time it responded immediately. "I already have."

Chapter 18: Goro's Knot

Goro was not happy. He was supposed to be wakagashira of the Gumsumgumi. However, he did not feel like the first lieutenant. Life used to be good. The oyabun would give an order, and he would carry it out. Life was simple and had the same clean focus as the sumo ring. As a sumotori, he had found something at which he excelled. He had practiced hard and loved the competition. The rest of the world could be complicated, but sumo was simple. He knew the rules. He knew what everyone expected of him. He practiced until he became good. He had reached the level of yokozuna—grand champion. Even Nichi had not attained that pinnacle. However, when he injured his shoulder and could no longer fight at the high level expected of yokozuna, he was forced to retire. He understood. It was sumo. He knew the rules.

Nevertheless, the adjustment from being yokozuna to being nobody had been difficult. He felt his life was over. He could have opened his own stable, but did not have the money or the head for business. He became so depressed that he thought of taking his life. Then he found Nichi. Or rather, Nichi found him. Goro had been working as a bouncer in a small brothel when Nichi, his old wrestling stablemate, found him and offered him a place in the Gumsumgumi.

Nichi had been persuasive. The townspeople needed protecting, so Nichi had formed a group sworn to protect them. Each member swore a formal allegiance to each other and the organization, and everyone profited when the group profited. Goro saw that Nichi had borrowed the oath and rituals from sumo. Like sumo, you ate, drank, slept, and played

245

with teammates. Like sumo, the entry into the Gumsumgumi began with taking sake and reciting ancient Shinto prayers. Like sumo, you swore allegiance to the group and its advancement. Like sumo, there was a rank structure.

Goro took to it immediately. He had purpose again. It did not take him long to move up from a shatei, or little brother, to a kyodai, or big brother. Then he was shateigashira, or second lieutenant. Within two years, he became wakagashira, or first lieutenant. He liked being number two to Nichi.

The success of the Gumsumgumi had a lot to do with Nichi and his leadership, but it had more to do with the organizational structure he created. The oyabun boss gave the orders and the kobun family carried them out. However, Nichi's genius was borrowing the sumo rank structure and family trappings. As a kobun member attained rank, he had the duty to start his own family of followers and to elevate it to success. The outcasts of society found a place where neither birth nor education nor family ties meant anything. Your ability to help your family and to grow your own family was what mattered. That and your allegiance to the entire Gumsumgumi group could take you a long way in this wide-open city.

As first lieutenant, Goro could stay close to Nichi, and because of all the threats associated with their booming success, Goro had taken responsibility for Nichi's safety. He had really become Nichi's yojimbo. He understood the job, and he was good at being Nichii's bodyguard. Whenever Nichi was threatened, Goro would place himself between Nichi and the threat, and then crush it.

However, his good life changed with the arrival of the young samurai. First, Nichi promoted him to yojimbo. Then, Nichi wanted Goro to take him under his wing and teach him the Gumsumgumi way. It was as if Nichi wanted to make him a member. True, several ronin were now members, but they had given up the two swords and were now involved in business enterprises. No real samurai had ever become a member. Moreover, no samurai would ever be a member if Goro had anything to say about it. That went double for the smart-mouthed young bastard.

First, the young samurai had humiliated Goro by knocking him unconscious in the jail. Then, he had saved Nichi's life twice, making himself a hero in the process. Then, he had engineered their jailbreak, thus becoming a hero to the entire kobun. Now Nichi was spending all of his time with the man, which was not much really, as the samurai was seldom around. He would appear occasionally during evenings and take up a position on a bench in the gambling hall.

Lately he brought a friend. The same tall, one-eyed ronin that he had saved during the jailbreak was now with him constantly. Whenever Goro planned his mental revenge on the samurai, that black-clad, one-eyed demon clouded the picture. Goro was a big man and afraid of almost no one. Nevertheless, the one-eyed ronin frightened him. His appearance and demeanor screamed ferocity. He would kill and think nothing of it.

Even Nichi's attitude toward Goro had changed. All Nichi talked to him about anymore was business. Nichi had him learning all aspects of Gumsumgumi's trade. If that was not bad enough, he had him checking all the books on all the businesses. Nichi expected Goro to know which businesses were profitable and which were not, and why. Goro was never good with numbers, but he was getting much better now.

What concerned Goro was the reason for all this change. Nichi had called him the week after the jailbreak and told him of the role change.

"Goro, you're going to have to become wakagashira in fact and not just in name. You have to learn the entire business. I have too many enemies after me. I may die tomorrow. You have to be ready to step up," he said.

Step up and run the Gumsumgumi? He could not do that. He would not know how. In keeping with all this weirdness, he now had another assignment that he hated just as much. While the Gumsumgumi were in jail, their fiercest rivals, the Yamakai-gumi, had decided to expand their territory. They attacked and captured two taverns and a gambling parlor owned by the Gumsumgumi. Three of his brothers died. It was a slight loss of income and a huge loss of face. Obviously, the Yamakai-gumi had not expected Nichi to survive his stint in jail. Now the Yamakai-gumi must pay. All Nichi had told him was to "fix it." What did that mean? Maybe get the lost enterprises back. If so, how? He hated these general type orders. It was so much easier when he knew what Nichi wanted.

He could ask the young samurai for advice. Knowing the young samurai's willingness to help, he would probably help. He tended to be helpful to everybody. But he could not see himself asking the young samurai. Unlike everyone else, he did not like the samurai. Still, he worried and fretted about what to do.

Myo saw him in the opposite corner of the gambling hall. She was sitting next to Hideki and Nichi. Jubei was beside Nichi.

"Your first lieutenant seems down," Myo observed.

Nichi smiled. "Yes, when he has to learn new things or figure something out, he tends to brood over it."

Jubei glanced at Goro. "He's a little old for brooding, isn't he?"

"Goro is a good man Jubei. He was yokozuna once and has never recaptured the glory he once had. I am training him as my replacement and making him learn everything. If I'm not around, this organization will survive only with someone who has his sense of duty and tradition as headman—like Goro."

"Are you going somewhere Oyabun?" Hideki asked.

"Not planning on it; just being prepared," Nichi replied.

"I think I'll go over and cheer him up," Myo said. So saying, she went through the routine of raising slightly to get her toes curled under her, then rocked back, allowing her kimono-clad knees to come off the floor and twisting slightly, uncoiling into a standing position. It was a graceful motion that Hideki liked watching. Everyone else took such simple things for granted, but he had not grown up around women, so such little things intrigued him. He watched her graceful, swishing motion as she made the toed-in walk of a kimono-clad woman to the other side of the hall.

"That's quite a woman," Nichi said to no one.

Hideki blushed.

"So why do you think she chose you?" asked Nichi.

"I have no idea," said Hideki, "but I'm glad she did."

The woman known as Myo to the Gumsumgumi stopped at Goro's bench and bowed slightly. "What troubles the first lieutenant of Gumsumgumi?" she asked as she took a seat on the bench beside the large man.

Goro flashed a wide smile. "And how are you, lady Myo?"

"I am no lady, Goro. You know that," she teased.

"I'm just happy that I lured you away from the yojimbo. Everyone seems to fall under his spell," he said.

"We'll talk about him later. Let us talk about you. What is troubling you?" she asked.

"I am troubled by many things, lady Myo. The new yojimbo troubles me. That used to be my job, and I was good at it. Now I am figuring interest on loans instead. Nichi used to tell me what he wanted. Now he tells me to "fix it," and I have no idea what he wants. I've got too much new stuff coming my way, and it's hard to think."

"So which is it that troubles you the most?" she asked.

"My immediate problem is fixing the Yamakai-gumi. They took over a couple of taverns and a gambling hall while we were in jail. Now I have to 'fix it.'" he said.

"What will you do?" she asked.

"That is the trouble. I do not know. My initial reaction was to go over and kill them. However, Nichi also said we must keep a lower profile with the new magistrate. So I'm not sure what to do."

"I am only a woman, but I'm a businesswoman, so maybe I could help," she offered.

Goro beamed. "Please, lady. I will listen to anything."

"You are a warrior, Goro," she said.

"I am?"

"Certainly. You have fought more battles than most samurai if you count your time inside the dohyo," she said.

Goro saw the truth in this and grinned. "Yes, I suppose you are correct."

"So look at your task as if it were a sumo challenge."

"I don't understand."

"If you are fighting a smaller opponent in the sumo ring, how would you approach him?" she asked.

He pondered the question and responded carefully. "Well, after the initial tachiai or clash, I would try to immobilize him, probably with a slap to the side of the head to negate his speed. Then move to his side and pick him up or spin him down."

"Well there are your tactics for the Yamakai-gumi," she exclaimed.

"What tactics? What do you mean?" he asked.

"The Gumsumgumi are larger than the Yamakai-gumi. They attacked you because they thought the Gumsumgumi weak with you and Nichi in jail. Now they are preparing for your retaliation. It is as if you are in the sumo ring with a smaller fighter. You have both completed the shiko and leg stomping exercise to drive out evil spirits, and you each are crouching at the shikiri-sen starting line. Any second, both of your fists will touch the ground and you will fly at each other for the tachiai. He is smaller and faster, and you are larger and stronger. If you meet him head-on after the tachiai, he will outflank you and attack you where you are weakest. So you must stun him at the tachiai to stop his momentum and attack his vulnerability."

"I see, lady Myo. You think I should make a show of regaining the lost business, but actually attack somewhere else that will really hurt the Yamakai-gumi?" he asked.

"Exactly, Goro. Now what is the Yamakai-gumi's greatest business asset? What will hurt them the most to lose?"

"That's easy … the warehouses near Nihonbashi. The Yamakai-gumi makes a lot of money transporting, storing, and delivering goods to the merchants," he said.

"Then that should be your real target. If you happen to take back the lost taverns, so much the better. But I would bet that within a day of capturing their moneymaker, they will want to negotiate."

Goro broke out into another big smile. "Thank you Lady Myo. I know what to do now."

"Now, you can do something for me," she said.

"Anything," he said.

"I want you to try to get along with the new yojimbo."

Goro's smile turned into a frown. "For you I will try."

"Thank you Goro," she said as she rose, bowed, and moved toward the exit.

Goro watched her go and then turned to see the new yojimbo staring after her. Not hating him would be very hard.

The Gumsumgumi were going to war. Goro had marshaled his lieutenants and given them the plan. He had waited until the last minute to do so because he did not want any loose talk in a tavern to find its way to the Yamakai-gumi. The lieutenants would brief their troops en route.

The plan was much as he and Myo had discussed. Goro's first lieutenant would lead the diversion. They would attack the Yamakai-gumi directly in an attempt to recover the lost taverns and gambling hall. Goro had sweetened the pot for his first lieutenant by telling him that his family would inherit any winnings and income they recover. It was an opportunity that no one would pass up. The prize insured they would fight hard. Not only would the first lieutenant's family gain money from the enterprises, but the brothels meant his men might find wives. Oh yes, they would fight hard.

Goro would lead the main attack on the Yamakai-gumi warehouses. They were more than warehouses—they were also a small hotel and brothel. It was in the brothel that they would have trouble. A brothel meant a yojimbo. As rough and willing to fight as the Gumsumgumi were, no one was foolish enough to want to fight a samurai. The katana in a trained hand would make mincemeat of four or five Gumsumgumi very quickly. The key to Goro's plan was neutralizing the yojimbo early.

Goro had forty men, and despite the reports of few police about town, he would disperse his men into four ten-man teams to converge on Nihonbashi at the appointed time. Nihonbashi was an old section of Edo with the main bridge over the Sumida River. There were many avenues into and out of it. Goro would use them all to put his men in place without raising attention.

They had all met as one and donned their headbands. It was the universal Japanese sign for hard work ahead. Each man received a sword from the armory, and then they drank sake and toasted each other. Finally, they smashed the delicate cups over the handles of their swords. They were ready for battle.

This was the real difference between the Gumsumgumi and the general population of Edo. This is what separated them. The general population did not fight and die. They worried about the day-to-day strain to stay alive, but they seldom came into direct confrontation with anyone. With the Gumsumgumi, violence was always a close companion. This made them different. Goro had used this difference in his speech to his troops before they had downed their sake. In Goro's mind, it was this difference and their oath to the greater group that set them apart and would make them successful in battle tonight. Goro thought he had done well. It was one part kabuki and two parts sumo.

As Goro was making his way to the docks, his path converged with a large and unruly mob clamoring outside the Hatchobori, chanting, "Kill him!" "Kill him now!" and "No mercy!"

Goro turned to one of his lieutenants. "This is our territory. Find out what is going on. Yohei and I will be at the tea station," he said, pointing to the open-air bench and tea-making kiosk across the street from the Hatchobori.

Goro took a seat on one bench, covering most of it. A middle-aged, somewhat ragged samurai took the adjacent bench. Goro ordered tea for both as a shop woman shuffled out, a small tray in hand. She bowed to the newcomers. When she had retreated with the order, Goro turned to the samurai.

"It has been awhile since you wore the swords, Yohei."

"Yes," Yohei replied. "I was hoping I'd seen the last of them."

"We needed someone familiar with samurai ways. We couldn't have one of us challenge their yojimbo only to have him laugh at us," Goro said. "Besides, if all goes according to plan, you will not have to draw your katana."

"I don't mean to argue Goro-san, but it has been my

experience that these things seldom go as planned."

"Do not worry, Yohei. In a few minutes it will be all over and you can return to your wife and child in that tavern you've managed for us so well."

"I sincerely hope so Goro-san. It is a humble business, but we have been happy."

"And you have enough to eat. More than you can say for your ronin days," Goro said.

"I owe the Gumsumgumi my happiness, Goro. I have taken the oath and drunk the sake. I will not let the group down," Yohei said.

Goro grunted approval.

Goro's man returned and whispered close to Goro's ear.

"The police have captured the Fox Gang's leader. This crowd wants him executed now," Goro said aloud to Yohei as he sipped his tea. Then turning back to his lieutenant, "That makes no sense. When do the chosin worry about a bandit gang who preys on the Tokugawa? Find out more. I want to know who is behind this. We are on a tight schedule, so break some bones if you have to, but find out fast."

The lieutenant bowed and ran back into the crowd.

"Is knowing this information more important than our planned mission?" Yohei asked.

"I don't know yet. However, Nichi pays a lot of money to stay on top of all unusual occurrences; this is an unusual occurrence, and it is in our backyard. We need to get to the bottom of it and still carry out tonight's mission," Goro replied.

The lieutenant returned. This time he did not whisper. "There are two fanning the flames. We have them in an alley. They say they were paid to gather a crowd, and the crowd has free drinks two streets over at the Blue Inn."

Goro carefully considered the news. "The Blue Inn is one of ours, so if trouble is stirred up tonight, blame will be laid at the Gumsumgumi's door."

"Aniki, the men stirring up the crowd are common laborers, but the description of the person that put them up to this fits one of the Yamakai-gumi's local bosses named

Saburo," the lieutenant reported. "He is said to be close to your counterpart in the Yamakai-gumi."

Goro thought a moment as he sipped the last of his tea. "Okay, give this information to one you trust and get it back to Nichi immediately."

"Does this mean we've got more trouble?"

"I don't know, but if the Yamakai are behind this, it will impact us. Send your messenger and let us depart. Yohei has a date with destiny."

At the canal-side warehouse, Goro made sure his men were in place, then gave Yohei the nod. From across the street, hidden in an alley, Goro watched Yohei's demeanor change. He puffed himself up and assumed the arms-crossed posture that so many ronin adopt by placing their hands in the opposite sleeves of their kimonos.

At the entrance to the part of the warehouse that was now a tavern and brothel, Yohei loudly proclaimed his challenge to the yojimbo. After some discussion, a rough-looking samurai appeared at the entrance and sized up Yohei. He did not seem impressed with Yohei and waved him away. Yohei drew his sword, and that stopped the yojimbo. Once a sword is drawn, there was no backing down.

Yohei motioned the yojimbo to the side of the warehouse away from police eyes. A few of the Yamakai-gumi followed their yojimbo, eager for some excitement.

Once in the alley, the yojimbo drew his sword, announced his name and fencing school, and took up a defensive posture. That was as far as he got. A large rope net fell on him from above and four Gumsumgumi attacked. Four Yamakai-gumi and their yojimbo died in the alley.

Then it was a frontal assault on the tavern, brothel, and the warehouse. More Yamakai-gumi died. The surprise was complete. No patrons died and no employees wounded. Goro's team leaders began implementing his takeover. Nothing was to change for any employees. They were to continue as before, but now they reported to Goro. They were now partners with the Gumsumgumi.

On the way back to Nichi's, Goro and his men stopped at

the two taverns and brothel that they had lost to the Yamakai-gumi while in jail. Goro's first lieutenant had retaken both with the loss of three men. Nevertheless, Myo had been wrong. It did not take the Yamakai-gumi a day to negotiate. That evening, Goro's counterpart was at Nichi's headquarters. He was there to speak with Nichi.

When Nichi received this message, he was in his office congratulating Goro and his lieutenants on an amazing night's work. Goro arose from his sitting position to leave, but Nichi waved him back down. "I'm the Oyabun. You are first lieutenant. You meet with your counterpart. I'll abide by whatever arrangements you negotiate," he said, looking into the eyes of a befuddled Goro. Then Nichi arose and departed, leaving Goro and his lieutenants. Goro took the seat of honor at the head of the room and motioned for the Yamakai-gumi representative.

He was a rough-looking man with a full head of hair tied behind his head, accentuating the scars near his mouth that gave him a permanent sneer. He was in a formal black kimono with a black outer jacket tied in front. The mon on each lapel of his haori was the Yamakai-gumi symbol of the umi plum blossom. He stepped to the center of the foot of the room and bowed at the waist. Then he stepped back with his left foot while bending slightly forward and extending his right hand forward with a palm up. This was the kiri cutting ceremony to demonstrate no weapons and no evil intent as well as an introduction.

"I am called Komeya no Toku, wakagashira of the Yamakai-gumi. I have no weapons and come to show my respects to the Gumsumgumi and offer congratulations for their successful retaking of their business and acquisition of our warehouse," he said formally.

Goro nodded his head and pointed to a small desk laden with food and drink. "I know who you are Kome, and I know why you've come. So sit and eat and drink, and we'll discuss the new turn of events."

The evening went as planned, except Kome was too agreeable. Even when Goro squeezed him, Kome kept his composure and agreed. As negotiations concluded, he asked for one concession.

"We want the life of your yojimbo."

Goro controlled his initial desire to yell "Yes" at the top of his lungs. Instead, he responded in the way that Nichi would have wanted him to, simply asking, "Why?"

"I do not know Goro-san. I believe he has upset some of our more favored clients once too often."

Goro grunted. He could understand that. They finally came to an understanding that no other Gumsumgumi would be hurt, and all Goro had to do was get word to Kome where the yojimbo would be during an appointed hour. Kome would take it from there. Two birds with one arrow, Goro thought. Not only had he negotiated tough demands on the Yamakai-gumi, with no retaliation, he had also managed to eliminate a thorn in his side. Nichi might be angry at first, but he would get over it. After all, it was for the betterment of the group. Besides, the yojimbo was not really a member the Gumsumgumi.

Chapter 19: The Trial

There were many places that Naga would rather be. It was the hour of the dog, somewhere between seven o'clock to nine o'clock in the evening. The closer they got to the Hatchobori, the louder the din became. The commander of the Yoshinobu household guards gave a verbal order and the guards formed into a "V" formation, moving the noisy and drunken rioters out of the way. They were not gentle. The guards used bokken. They cracked skulls, broke arms and pushed people out of the way with their wooden practice swords when the noisy mass failed to make way for Naga, Jii, and Yuki. They progressed slowly to the magistrate's offices and the Hatchobori.

Finally they arrived and the commander deployed his squad around the front of the entrance. The crowd continued their loud yelling and calling for the new magistrate to turn the Fox Gang leader over to them, but they kept their distance from the wooden swords wielded by the country samurai.

"I can't believe this. Where are the police?" Jii asked.

"That's what we're here to find out," Naga said.

"If this lasts much longer, the castle will get wind of it and will have to take action. Many will die and you'll be blamed, my lord," Yuki said.

"I know, Yuki. Our enemies in the Roju are up to something. I wish I knew who is financing the drinks for that mob."

As Jii and Naga entered the large day room, Kumogiri Denjiro, the yoriki on duty, was all smiles. He bowed to Naga. "Greetings magistrate; I see you braved our little disturbance."

"I want to know why we had to," Jii said. "Why haven't you put a stop to this?"

"I'd love to Yoshinobu-sama, but I'm understaffed. Ever since your inspection, I've had police turn in their juttes and walk off," Denjiro said.

"How many do you have left Yoriki?" Naga asked.

"I am down to half strength at thirty, and fifteen of those are on patrol. I do not have enough left to control this crowd," Denjiro said.

"You are a miserable whelp. If you had any courage at all you could bring this mob to its knees with five men!" Jii yelled.

"Yoshinobu-sama," Denjiro bowed, "it was not I, but your grandsons, who ran off most of our police force."

"They did not run off enough," Jii said.

"Do not be too hard on Denjiro," Naga said. "I'm sure he has done his best."

"That is my point, Naga. His best is not good enough."

"We will discuss that later." Then Naga turned to Denjiro. "What is the reason for this disturbance?" Naga asked.

"The chosin," Denjiro said, referring to the citizens of Edo by their neighborhood groupings called a cho, "are blowing off steam. We captured the leader of the Fox Gang, and they want us to turn him over for execution," Denjiro explained.

"Without a trial?" Naga asked.

"Without anything," Denjiro replied.

"Unusual," Yuki commented.

"How so, Hanzo-sama?" Denjiro asked.

"The chosin don't usually concern themselves with the legal systems in Edo," she said.

"I guess they have been terrorized enough by the gang and want revenge," Denjiro said.

"I don't know of any incident where the Fox Gang targeted the common people. Their targets have always been Tokugawa families," Yuki said.

"Then you are not well-informed my lady. We have had several robberies that we think the Fox Gang planned and executed," Denjiro said.

"Really?" Yuki replied. "Have you been withholding information from the Ometsuke?"

Too late, Denjiro saw the trap. "Oh no, Hanzo-sama; I mean that we think the Fox Gang was involved. We have no definitive proof."

Jii continued to vent his annoyance. "You cannot control your streets. You make allegations without facts. It is amazing to me you caught anyone in the Fox Gang." Denjiro flinched under the rebuke. Whatever he was thinking did not become words.

"How did you come to arrest the Fox Gang leader, Denjiro?" Naga asked.

"One of his fellow chosin turned him in, Magistrate," Denjiro said.

"Tell me about the arrest," Naga said.

"Not much to tell. One of my doshin received information that the Fox Gang leader was in Nihonbashi. We raided the place and caught the suspect with a fox mask. We brought him in. That was yesterday evening." Denjiro said. "I'm hoping for a speedy trial and execution so we can placate that mob outside. If they get any larger, the castle will send out troops to suppress them. We don't want that."

Naga suspected that was exactly what Denjiro wanted.

"Take me to the prisoner," Naga said.

"You don't want to go back there Magistrate. It is late and he is probably asleep by now," Denjiro said.

Jii could not take it anymore. He grasped his sword and drew it. He took one step towards Denjiro. "By the Buddha, if you question one more order you are given or make one more excuse tonight, I will cleave you in two. Never have I witnessed such impertinence."

Denjiro fell to his knees. "Gomen nasai," he said and then just as quickly he backed up and stood. "Right this way Magistrate."

The walk down the narrow hallway to the main cells assaulted Naga's senses. The closer they got to the cells, the greater the reek of human waste, blood, sweat, and fear. They passed a large cell and moved to the one adjacent to where

Jubei had been housed. A man was hanging from the main beam, suspended by rough hemp rope encasing his shoulders and arms. He was naked except for his fundoshi. The ropes and loincloth hid the only parts of his body that did not appear broken, bruised or bleeding.

"Open the door," Naga ordered.

"Magistrate, you do not want to go in there," Denjiro said. Jii stepped forward and Denjiro jumped to unlock the wooden bars.

Naga stepped into the cell and had to study the dangling man's torso to ensure he was still breathing. "Cut him down, Yoriki, and be gentle about it."

Denjiro paused, saw Jii daring him to falter again, and moved into the cell. He extracted his short sword and cut the rope suspending the prisoner, catching him as he fell. He laid him on his side and began cutting the ropes from around his torso. Once done, he stood up and looked disgustedly at the blood and filth on his clothing.

"Yoriki, send for a doctor. I want this man tended and ready to stand trial tomorrow morning. If he should die, you will take his place," Naga said.

Denjiro's initial pleasure at a speedy trial turned sour at the mention of him replacing the prisoner.

"Yuki, tend him until the doctor arrives, please."

"Hai," she replied and stooped to turn the man on his back. "Yoriki, get four men and move him carefully to the cleanest room available and have two buckets of clean, fresh water and one pot of boiling water brought there. I also want a supply of fresh cloth for bandages."

Denjiro thought to decline but saw Jii move his hand toward his sword.

"Hai," he replied and shuffled away.

When they were alone in the cell, Naga turned to Jii. "He has the wrong man."

"Is it any wonder? That dunce is no more a policeman than I am," Jii said.

"Whoever is pulling the strings in the castle has put me in a box. I have the chosin rioting for an execution, and I have got an innocent man almost beaten to death. If I give in to the crowd and execute the innocent, I will be playing by the corrupt rules that seem to permeate Edo. I will show that I am weak and cannot abide by the Bushido I espouse. On the other hand, if I set the innocent man free, I could still have the rioting and the castle will take the action I am sure they are preparing for, and I look incompetent. Either way, our enemy wins."

Yuki stood beside them. "What will you do?" she asked.

"He will do the unexpected, Yuki-san. He will do the right thing," Jii said.

Naga smiled. "I have the beginning of a plan cooking in my mind, but I'll need help from both of you to flesh it out," he said. "What were the names of those two doshin that Hideki said were young but honest?"

By the hour of the boar, between nine o'clock and eleven o'clock in the evening, the rioters had gone home, the prisoner had been moved to a clean cell, and a doctor and a nurse had been brought in to tend him. Naga had given instructions for them to stay with the prisoner all night and to accompany him to the trial tomorrow. The yoriki's instructions were to gather all of his doshin and to bring writing materials to make flyers announcing the trial of the alleged leader of the Fox Gang tomorrow in the hour of the snake, approximately nine o'clock until eleven o'clock in the morning.

It was to be an open trial and the flyers were invitations to all townspeople. A separate mission sent Hideki's two doshin into the night. Naga left two of his samurai guards with the doctor and nurse with strict instructions that no one was to come into the cell. Then Naga, Jii, and Yuki departed for the Yoshinobu mansion.

By the hour of the dragon, somewhere between seven o'clock and nine o'clock in the morning, Edo was buzzing. Everyone was talking about the trial and preparing to attend. The Yoshinbu had had an early breakfast and arrived with an armed escort early at the Hatchobori. Naga had staged the drama in a manner that would have made a kabuki production manager proud. The Hatchobori had a huge courtyard. It was surrounded on three sides by the building itself. On the fourth side, a large gate opened into the main street.

Like most Japanese buildings, the Hatchobori was built on pilings so the main floor was three steps above the courtyard's grass, sand, and gravel. The hardwood floors of the building extended out to the courtyard with an occasional vertical beam supporting the stories above. The interior rooms' outer walls consisted of sliding paper screens. When left in place, they created a veranda effect along the three sides of the courtyard. In the section at the head of the courtyard, the screens creating the wall were left open so the great room of the Hatchobori would give Naga the backdrop of the huge golden hollyhock mon of the Tokugawa. Those in the courtyard would look up to Naga and see the symbol of the Tokugawa behind him.

On the edge of the veranda Naga would sit on a three-legged camp chair where he could look out upon the entire courtyard. Below and to his left on the courtyard level would be the accused, lying on a stretcher and attended by the doctor and his nurse, both in white coats. Surrounding the accused would be his family and friends. To Naga's right and at courtyard level would be the accusing yoriki, Denjiro, and any witnesses he had present. Behind both them, all the way to the end of the courtyard and gate opening onto the street, would be the citizens of Edo, the chosin, eager to view the proceedings first hand and to judge the new magistrate. Between the accused and the yoriki would be Jii, Musashi, and Jubei. Hideki and Yoshi were to be in the crowd somewhere to warn of any potential trouble.

Naga could hear the commotion in the courtyard as people filed in and took positions on the grass, sand, and gravel.

"How do I look?" Naga asked Yuki.

"Like a most honorable magistrate," she said smiling. Then she frowned. "I hope you know what you're doing."

"So do I," agreed Naga. Tucking his fan into his obi, beside the short sword, he moved through the large room toward the courtyard. Someone announced his arrival and everyone bowed. Naga moved to the backless war stool in the center of the makeshift stage and sat down. He looked into the courtyard and was amazed. He had not thought it could hold so many people. "A cat could not slip through," he thought. There was not an open space available.

"Rise," Naga ordered, and a sea of bodies straightened up with all eyes on him. He looked over the edge of his stage and saw a litter with a bandaged man on it. Beside him were a white-coated doctor and his nurse. Next to them was an old gray-haired woman in a very plain kimono. Beside the old woman were an old man and the two honest doshin who had been sent on the separate mission to retrieve family and friends of the accused. To the right was Denjiro the yoriki, with one doshin at his side. Between the two was Jii's familiar face along with Musashi and Jubei. Naga drew strength from their presence.

Naga took out his fan and pointed at Denjiro. "Yoriki Denjiro, what are the charges?"

Denjiro pointed to the young man on a stretcher. "Magistrate, Yashino the wood carver is accused of being the leader of the Fox Gang, and I request the death penalty."

Naga turned to the doctor. "Can he speak for himself?"

The doctor shook his head in the negative. "No Lord, he speaks in a whisper as the police have bruised his voice box."

"Can anyone speak for him?" Naga asked.

The gray-haired old woman bowed. "Yes Lord, I will speak for my son."

"Very well. What does your son say to these charges?" Naga asked.

The old woman did not confer with her son and spoke instead. "Ridiculous! Yashi has always been a good boy. When my husband died a year ago, Yashi took over the business, and he works night and day to feed my daughter and myself. He has no time for gangs."

"Yes good mother, I'm sure what you say is true. But for the scribes," Naga pointed to two doshin at small tables taking notes, "could you ask your son and give me his response?"

The old mother shook her head at the thought of such

foolishness but moved to her son's head and bent down to his ear. When finished, she raised up and looked at Naga. "He says I'm right!"

There was sporadic laughter in the crowd, which stopped as soon as the yoriki turned to face them.

"For the scribes, Yashino denies the allegations," Naga said.

Naga turned back to the yoriki Denjiro. "What evidence do you have that Yashino is the leader of the Fox Gang?"

The yoriki turned to his doshin, who handed him a rough, wooden Fox mask. "We took this from him the night we arrested him," Denjiro said.

There was a murmur throughout the crowd as Denjiro held up the mask.

"Is that all?" Naga asked.

Denjiro looked a little unsure of himself. "What do you mean Magistrate?" he asked.

"I mean did you find any of the stolen items the Fox Gang is alleged to have taken? Did you find any other gang members? Did you find anything other than this mask to link Yashino to the Fox Gang?" Naga asked.

The murmuring in the crowd stopped as soon as Naga raised his voice to ask the questions.

"No Magistrate, nothing else."

"And what made you suspect Yashino?" Naga asked.

Again, the yoriki looked unsure. "We received information from a reliable source."

"Who was the source?" Naga asked.

"I cannot tell you Magistrate," Denjiro said.

"Why not?"

Denjiro looked very uncomfortable. He could not reveal his source for fear of causing them embarrassment.

Naga enjoyed the yoriki's discomfort. This was going to be a good day.

"I'm waiting Yoriki, as are the citizens of Edo. Who accused Yashino the woodcarver of being the leader of the Fox Gang?" Naga demanded.

"Magistrate, we get much information every day, some

from paid informants and some from passersby. This allegation was from a passerby," Denjiro said.

"So you should have a record of who the accuser was," Naga said.

"No, Lord," Denjiro said.

"How unusual," Naga stated. "Did Yashino confess to being the leader of the Fox Gang?" Naga asked.

"No, Lord," Denjiro said. "You interrupted my interrogation."

"Yes I did Yoriki. I was afraid if I didn't, you might execute the boy yourself, and we both know you do not have that authority," Naga said.

Denjiro was looking at the ground and sweating.

Naga turned back to the accused. "Good mother, has Yashino been away from home for any length of time?" Naga asked.

"Where would he go Lord? He must work from sunup till sundown just to feed us," she said.

"So you have been with him all the time?" Naga asked.

"Every day of his life," the mother said.

"Is there anyone else here who can speak for the boy?" Naga asked.

"Yes, Lord," an old man near the mother, responded. He bowed deeply.

"And who might you be?" Naga asked.

The old man bowed again, "I am Ittobori, Lord, the leader of the woodcarving guild."

"And have you known Yashino long?"

"I have known him since he was born. But I've watched him daily for four years now," Ittobori replied.

"Ever since he joined the guild?" Naga asked.

"Yes, Lord."

"And has he ever disappeared for several days in those four years?" Naga asked.

"Lord, we in the guild live together, work together, eat together, and we share houses in the same cho. It is a true community, and it has to be that way. If one is ill and cannot work, someone else covers for him. If one takes on a project he cannot complete, others help. It is the chosin way," Ittobori said.

There was a murmur of approval from the crowd. Naga let it go.

"So Yashino has not disappeared from the cho for several days at a time?" Naga asked the old man.

"No, Lord. Everyone would have noticed such a skilled carver missing."

Naga turned back to the yoriki Denjiro. "Let me understand this. Someone accuses a citizen of the crime, and you bring him to the Hatchobori for questioning. If he admits his guilt, you turn him over to me for sentencing. If he denies his guilt, you torture him until he confesses or dies at your hand. How is that justice?"

"Magistrate, that is the system," Denjiro said.

"How do you determine if the man who accuses isn't the criminal?" Naga asked.

"We would know," Denjiro protested.

"If I were a robber, all I need to do is commit a robbery and come to you and accuse someone else. You take that someone else into custody. If he confesses, he dies. If he doesn't confess, you torture him until he dies; then I'm free to rob again and blame some other innocent," Naga said.

"No, Lord, we would know," Denjiro insisted.

"Just like you know that this young man is the leader of the Fox Gang?"

"Yes, Lord."

Naga turned his gaze to Jii but he pointed to Musashi. "Samurai-sama, please tell us your name."

Once Musashi knew he was the subject of Naga's question, he bowed slightly and said, "My name is Myamoto Musashi."

Now the murmuring really increased as most in the crowd strained their necks to get a glimpse of the famous swordsman.

"I think we can all attest to your prowess as a skilled swordsman and superior tactician. I understand you've had the opportunity to fight members of the Fox Gang."

Now the murmuring intensified.

"Yes, Lord. In Kyoto, I and a couple of friends were attacked by them," Musashi said.

"And was it your impression that this gang is made up of thieves and cutthroats?"

"No, Lord," Musashi said.

"Why not?" Naga asked. "The yoriki here has sent those reports to the shogun."

"Then the yoriki has fought few battles. Anyone who has engaged the Fox Gang in combat knows that they are not thieves and cutthroats."

"What are they then?"

"They are ninja," Musashi said.

There were loud gasps in the crowd at this revelation.

"And how do you know this, Musashi?" Naga asked.

"The tactics they employed, their weapons, and the way they fought," Musashi said.

"I see." Then Naga stood and addressed the crowd. "Is there anyone here who would dispute the fact that Musashi-sama is an expert with a sword and has superior knowledge in matters of the sword?" No one answered. Naga called into the crowd. "Yagyu Jubei, are you in the crowd?"

The man next to Musashi bowed at the waist and said, "Here, Lord."

There were more gasps from the crowd as many recognized the name of the shogun's former fencing master.

"Jubei, I understand that you are familiar with ninja training," Naga stated.

"Yes, Lord. I have trained with both Iga and Koga."

"How long does it take to become a ninja?" Naga asked.

Jubei looked confused for a moment. "It takes all your life, Lord. Ninja children are born into the ninja clan and are taught from the time that they are two, and the training never stops."

"So you cannot go to a ninja training camp and pick up skills in a short period?"

"No, Lord. Training for a Shinobi no mono, what outsiders call ninjas, is a lifetime commitment," Jubei explained.

"Please look at the youth on the litter and tell me

whether you think he is ninja or not," Naga requested.

Jubei moved to the litter and knelt beside Yashino. "Show me your hands," he demanded.

Yashino had difficulty raising them, so his mother helped. After an examination Jubei rose. "This boy is no ninja."

"And how can you be so sure?" Naga asked.

"His calluses are indicative of a man who works with tools, but not ninja tools," Jubei said.

"I see," Naga said. "Thank you."

Jubei bowed and returned to Musashi's side.

Naga looked directly at the boy on the litter. "Good mother, ask your son why he had the Fox mask?" Naga said.

"He had it because he'd been commissioned to make it," she said.

"What do you mean?" Naga asked.

"Like I said, a man came to our home and commissioned a Fox mask," she said.

"How long ago?" Naga asked.

"Two days ago," she said.

"Do you remember what he looked like?" Naga asked.

"Sure do," she said.

"Could you describe him?" Naga asked.

"Why should I describe him?" she asked.

"So that we can arrest him and get to the bottom of this accusation," Naga said.

"No Lord, I mean why describe him, when he is standing in front of you?" she said.

"What do you mean?" Naga asked.

The old woman then pointed at Denjiro the yoriki. "He is standing next to the yoriki," she said.

"She is out of her mind, Magistrate," Denjiro said.

"Perhaps," Naga answered. "Does your doshin deny the allegation?"

The doshin in a brown kimono answered for himself. "Yes Lord, the old woman is crazy."

Naga addressed the left side of the courtyard. "Did anyone else see the doshin at Yashino's home in the last few days?"

A girl near the old mother bowed deeply. "I did, Lord."

"And who are you?" Naga asked.

"She is my daughter and Yashino's younger sister," the gray-haired mother answered.

"Why are you certain it was this doshin?" Naga asked.

The girl bowed her head as she spoke and stole sideways glances at the police officer. "Because he said foul things to me and said he would enjoy me later."

The leader of the woodcarver's guild spoke again. "I did not see him yesterday, Lord, but Yashi told me of the mask commissioned by a policeman, if that helps," Ittobori said.

"I believe it helps Yashino's story and hurts the Hatchobori's," Naga said.

In the crowd, Hideki was beaming with pride. He knew his brother was smart, but even the slowest in the crowd could see that the new magistrate was dismantling the yoriki's concocted story step by step using his own words against him. The large man next to Hideki elbowed his arm. "Why did you insist I attend the spectacle?" he asked.

"I thought it might be illuminating," Hideki said. "I understand this is the first of its kind."

"If I want to see new and exciting things, I'll go to the kabuki," Nichi said.

"This is better than the kabuki," a man in front of them said over his shoulder. "When did you ever see Myamoto Musashi and Yagyu Jubei together at the kabuki?" "Even stranger than that," his friend said, "when have you ever seen a magistrate with an open court who takes the side of the accused?"

Hideki leaned next to Nichi's ear. "The chosin seem to like it."

"Oh, I'm sure they do, but what's this mean to the Gumsumgumi?"

"I do not know yet," Hideki replied. "But it's better to see things firsthand is it not?"

Nichi just grunted.

On the veranda that was acting as a stage, Naga rose. "Before I pronounce judgment on this case, I need to pass judgment on another." Then taking out his fan he pointed at the yoriki Denjiro. "Denjiro, you are banished from the police

269

force and from Edo. Take your doshin with you. But, before you go, place your jutte on the ground at your feet."

Several people in the crowd gasped. Others started clapping. Naga froze them with a stare.

"You cannot do that. I have a hereditary appointment. You do not have the authority," said Denjiro, the former yoriki.

"Maybe so, maybe not! Therefore, I will broach the subject from a different direction. Yagyu Jubei?" Naga called out.

Yagyu Jubei stepped forward. "Yes, Lord." Jubei answered from the front row.

"I believe you are familiar with Denjiro the former yoriki and his henchman," Naga said.

Jubei eyed both with pure hate.

"Oh yes, Lord."

"And how do you know them?" Naga asked.

"They tricked me into being arrested and then proceeded to beat me within an inch of my life," Jubei replied.

Denjiro and his doshin both involuntarily took a step back under the gaze of the one-eyed samurai.

"Jubei, you have my permission … no, let us be more specific. It is your responsibility as a samurai if you ever see either of these two again in Edo to separate their heads from their bodies," Naga said.

"Excellent!" Jubei replied as he took a step towards the two.

Both men threw down their juttes, turned, and fled back through the crowd.

Laughter started in the front of the crowd and made its way to the back. When it had ceased, Naga turned to Yashino on the litter.

"Yashino, this court can find no wrong in you. You are a victim in this. You are free to go." Then Naga rose and in a loud voice proclaimed, "Ikkin lachaku, one case completed."

A cheer went up in the crowd. The gray-haired mother of Yashino was crying and hugging her daughter. Naga smiled, then turned and moved into the building.

In an adjoining room, Yuki found she had a tear

forming. She wiped it with her sleeve and then felt a presence near. "Hello Yagyu-sama," she said.

"Hello Yuki," Yagyu Muneori said. "Quite a man you have let into your life."

"Yes," she said. "He surprises me each day."

"Well, he surprised your father when he asked for you in marriage," the elder Yagyu said.

"And what was my father's reply," she asked.

"He told Naga he had permission, but that he'd be wise to obtain yours." Yagyu Muneori said.

"He obtained that the evening we met with the Five Families," she said. "Isn't it interesting that I've always been afraid of an arranged marriage that I would hate. Yet here I am marrying the man I love," she said.

"I am happy that you are happy child," the elder said.

"He would make a fine shogun, would he not, Yagyu-sama?" she asked.

"He would make a finer shogun than we deserve," the elder replied. "But I doubt he will get the chance."

"Why Yagyu-sama, surely he is the best choice … ?"

"I have no doubt of that Yuki. After what I witnessed here today, I am even more convinced of his qualities. However, today's actions will send his enemies into panic. They have sold him short until today. You stay close by his side, Yuki. They will move on him and his house soon," Yagyu Muneori said.

Yuki bowed. "Thank you for your wise council, Chamberlain. I will protect him with my life," she said as they rose to join Naga.

Chapter 20: Assassins

"I was proud of you today, Naga," Jii beamed.

"I think all of Edo was proud of you," added Hideki.

"You were magnificent," Yuki said.

"We did what needed to be done," Naga replied. "I thank each of you. I could not have done this without your help."

The Yoshinobu were moving back to their mansion. They were in the part of town known as Nihonbashi. The Yoshinobu had learned the best way for wealthy men to get around in Edo was by boat in the network of canals that cut through the city. They were almost at the point where the dirt road ended at the makeshift docks. There, shallow-draft craft of all sizes awaited their human cargo. Boats could accommodate a single passenger or a squad of samurai. Some had a roof and walls and came equipped with sake, lanterns, pillows, and enterprising courtesans to make the journey as comfortable as possible.

The Yoshinobu entourage was slowing down as they approached the boats. The guard commander sent a samurai forward to negotiate a price as he deployed the remaining nine guards around a larger open area where street met water. The docks were a normally bustling place; this evening, no one was about.

Yoshi looked at Musashi beside him. "We are not alone," he said.

Musashi placed his right hand on his sword hilt. Jubei saw

the motion and did the same. Yuki noticed the men's posture and moved to Naga's side.

"We may be in danger," she said to Naga and Jii. Hideki overheard and started scanning the surroundings but saw no signs of obvious danger. The row houses had given way to large warehouses and mercantile stores which had been closed at the end of the day. The sun was setting in the west. Long shadows cast by the buildings across the street engulfed most of the road. Handcarts and beached shallow-bottomed boats lined the streets. Here, both sides of the road consisted of two-story warehouses. The street at this location ran north and south. On the west side of the road toward the setting sun, the warehouses were storage areas for rice and other dry goods. The buildings were empty. Workers were already on their way home.

On the east side of the street, several warehouses, each two and three stories in height, looked like farmers' barns with all manner of baskets, straw hats, straw raincoats, pulleys, ropes, and boat paraphernalia festooning the rough plank walls. The building closest to the Yoshinobu on the east side had a porch that extended about twelve shaku, about fourteen feet, into the street. The porch, supported by substantial pillars between the overhead and the elevated plank sidewalk, had a ceiling. It looked like a good place to wait out summer downpours.

Hideki glanced at Yoshi for location of the threat. Yoshi retrieved a straight ninja sword from inside his jacket. Hideki unsheathed his sword. Musashi, Jubei, Yuki, Jii and all nine of the Yoshinobu guards followed suit. No one knew the origin of the threat, but the Yoshinobu guards had learned to heed Yoshi's unusual skill in discerning danger.

Three of the nine guards had taken position around a flat-bottomed boat turned upside down on the damp earth just above the waterline by the dock. The head boatman usually occupied this location, taking fares and assigning boats. While they were searching for someone to assign boats, the boat under them exploded. All three Yoshinobu guards flew into the air and toward the street. A single shaved head of one of the guards rolled to a stop at Hideki's feet. Hideki recognized it. It was all that was left of Aoki.

Everyone turned toward the explosion. Everyone turned except Yoshi. As soon as he had seen the flash out of the corner of his eye, he had turned away and scanned the roofs on the opposite side of the street. It was where the next threat would come. Yoshi shifted his sword to his left hand and moved his right hand into his jacket. Two gray clad ninja wearing Fox masks appeared on top of the building across the street. They were holding fully extended bows charged with arrows and seeking targets among the Yoshinobu. One took aim in Naga's direction but an iron-throwing dart penetrated his left eye and fouled his aim. Yoshi did not wait to admire his handy work. He was too busy throwing a second dart at the next bowman. The second ninja saw the dart and deflected it with his bow. He did not deflect the throwing knife Musashi pulled from his scabbard and threw full force into his throat. By this time Jubei had a throwing knife in his hand and Yuki had produced a shuriken from somewhere in her jacket.

In all moments of crisis, eyes turn to the leader. Everyone looked at Jii. Jii felt their eyes upon him and knew the next few minutes would be crucial for the survival of the Yoshinobu. He willed himself out of his inaction and pointed to the boats on the dock. He was about to give the order to embark when Yoshi's voice drowned him out.

"No," Yoshi barked.

Jii froze and looked at Yoshi in exasperation.

"We must do something," Jii shouted.

However, Yoshi was not there anymore. He was racing toward the raised porch on the same side of the street as the explosion. He kicked over baskets, turned over small boats, tore down raincoats and pulled straw hats off the wall.

Satisfied there were no more bombs, he turned to Jii. "Get everyone on the porch, Lord," Yoshi said. "Drag the boats onto the porch to deflect against arrows and firearms. Do it quickly. The arrows will be followed by infantry."

"Do what he says," Jii commanded. "Yuki, get Naga up against the building on the porch."

As the Yoshinobu retreated to the porch, the remaining six guards dragged flat-bottom boats up onto the porch to use as cover. Yoshi picked up several of the large straw hats and tossed them to Musashi, Jubei, and Hideki. "Use them as shields against the arrows."

Hideki nodded his understanding and slipped his left arm through the cloth loops that normally held the wearer's hat to his head. Musashi, Jubei, Hideki, and Yoshi did not move to the porch. They remained at road level in front of the porch. Whatever came would come to them first.

What came was a volley of arrows. The first flight consisted of almost thirty. They peppered the porch sinking into the posts, the upturned boats, and the hasty shields donned by Hideki and his friends. Hideki checked himself and was surprised to find two arrows had penetrated his hakama on either side of his knees, but had not punctured his flesh. Everyone with a makeshift shield had arrows stuck in the straw.

Jubei noticed Hideki's arrow festooned trousers. "Cherry blossoms?" Jubei asked, winking at Yoshi.

"Cherry blossoms!" Yoshi replied.

Hideki was in the center of the four warriors. To his immediate left, Yoshi stood. Musashi stood to Yoshi's left. To Hideki's right stood Jubei. Hideki glanced at each man. Musashi was a rock. No emotion played on his face. Yoshi seemed deeply engrossed in hearing and feeling every movement about him. Jubei was smiling. It was disturbing to see. His eye patch set off his wide grin and gleaming teeth. He looked like a tengu or forest goblin waiting to devour something or someone. Hideki shivered. Jubei was intimidating at the best of times. At this moment, he looked terrifying.

"There will be smoke and darts," Yoshi warned. "Stay behind the boats and protect the Lord."

"Darts?" Musashi questioned. "We haven't seen that before."

"They will be coming for a quick kill. Despite the hour, there may be traffic here. They cannot afford to take too much time with us. They will try their standoff weapons first. Arrows didn't work, so the infantry will come and most likely be hidden in smoke and a hail of darts."

"I hate darts," Jubei said. "I will kill more of the bastards for using darts."

"Is this how you feel before combat?" Naga asked Yuki.

"How do you feel?" She asked.

"It is hard to describe," he said. "I am frightened, yet anxious to see how I shall do."

"I have been in several fights, Naga, but I'm a woman trained as a ninja. I can only tell you what I know. Fear is normal. Anyone who is not afraid in combat is a person to avoid. He is a fool."

"Listen to her Naga," Jii said. "She is correct."

"But look at those four out there. They are like heroes. Even my little brother seems as calm as can be," Naga said.

Yuki smiled "Yes, sweet Hideki has certainly grown up fast. However, he has been in several skirmishes and has trained at the hands of two of the best swordsmen of our age. I would say those four are as deadly a team as you are ever likely to encounter. Besides, they may be calm on the outside, but we have no idea what is going through their minds."

"I don't believe anything is going through their mind, right now," Jii said. "Unless I miss my guess, each is in mushin."

"No mind?" Naga asked.

"Yes. I think Musashi can enter into it any time he wants. Your little brother has learned from him. Jubei may find it more difficult to attain. His desire for revenge may be clouding his ability to focus."

"For what is he seeking revenge?" Naga asked.

"Life itself I imagine. Jubei is estranged from his father for some reason. He may be mad at the world."

"It is not polite to talk behind our backs," Hideki called over his shoulder.

"We apologize, brother," Naga responded. "But you don't often see four champions banded together in a just cause. We were all marveling at your courage."

"Well, do not marvel too long; if this gets scary out here,

I may let them pass and get to you. It would be payback for all the times you bested me in a dojo," Hideki called. "Besides, you stole my first love."

"You can have her back. Ever since I proposed she has been very demanding," Naga called.

His remark earned him an elbow in the ribs. "Oui," he cried.

The guards laughed at his discomfort. Hideki turned to Yoshi. "Where the hell is Myo when you need her?"

"Good question. Probably off looking for the Fox Gang," Yoshi said.

"Yoshi?" Jii called. "Why did we not get into the boats?"

"Half the slips were empty. Either there are many travelers on the canals tonight or we were being driven to the obvious escape by boat. They could have rigged our escape boats with explosives. Or, the other half of the boats are on the water already, waiting in ambush," Yoshi explained. "It is very difficult to flee on the water."

"Smart!" Jii said.

"Besides, the land favors us. Once I was assured there were no explosives on the porch, it afforded us protection from above and behind."

"Excellent," Jii said. There were nods of approval from the samurai behind the boats.

When they came, they came with smoke and explosives. Fox-faced ninja poured around the corners of both the building with the porch and the warehouse across the street. The ninja in front threw gunpowder balls made of papier-mâché mixed with sulfur and mercury. They exploded on contact and blew dirt three stories into the evening air. Hideki had one explode directly in front of him. The concussion blew him off his feet and back into the flat-bottomed boat turned on its side on the porch. He hit with a thud and saw stars as his head smacked against the wooden bottom. His hair tied high behind his head provided some measure of padding so that he did not blackout. By the time he was on his feet again and trying to clear his vision, his three companions in front were fighting on three sides and about to be penetrated in the center.

Smoke followed the explosive balls. A thick fog covered the Yoshinobu defenses. Hideki could just barely make out his three companions. His brain told him he must plug the hole in their ranks that the explosion had created. However, he was having trouble getting his limbs to follow commands. He saw Yoshi reach into his jacket and throw a handful of caltrops in front of the charging ninja just forward of Hideki's old position. The smoke worked against the ninja discovering the barbs until it was too late. Four of the fifteen in the assaulting wave of ninja stepped on the wicked contraptions. They screamed and fell to the ground holding their feet.

The respite allowed Hideki to clear his head and regain his faculties. He stepped forward and assumed his original position with drawn sword.

"Welcome back," Yoshi said.

"What do you call those things?" Hideki asked.

"Tetsu-bishi," Yoshi said. "We usually use them when we're being pursued, but it seemed like a good idea with you abandoning your post."

"It wasn't by choice," Hideki said stepping back online with Yoshi on the left and Jubei on the right.

Hideki noticed that both Jubei and Musashi had angled in to meet the threat coming from the sides of the porched building at their back. They were going to have to fight in two directions. Hideki had little time to think as a second wave moved toward him. This batch was mindful of the caltrops and traveled much more slowly.

The first fox-faced, brown-clad ninja approached Hideki steadily with a shorter straight ninja sword aimed at Hideki's eyes. Hideki's three companions were already engaged in swordplay with at least two brown-clad ninja apiece.

The ninja in front of him lunged at Hideki and let out a loud war cry. Hideki was in the left-front-foot-forward kamai. His blade tip pointed at his opponent's midsection. When the ninja lunged, he thought he was going to take advantage of Hideki's beginner mistake of having the sword tip low. Hideki remembered Musashi's words when he taught him the technique: "The smacking parry is carried out when you are

up against an enemy and you absorbed his attacking cut with
your long sword with the tee-dumb, tee-dumb rhythm, while
slapping at his sword, and cutting him."

Hideki had practiced it so many times with Musashi he
didn't have to think about it. As soon as he had sensed the
lunge, Hideki's sword tip came up and arced outward, smacking
into his opponent's blade just enough to move the attacking
tip away from Hideki's face. Hideki's redirection of his own
blade tip forward was immediate. The ninja's momentum was
already committed and has trajectory had not been blocked but
redirected slightly. He impaled himself on Hideki's sword. He
let out a whimper and tried to bring his sword back into play.
Hideki pulled his sword from the ninja's chest, raised it and
sliced from sky to ground, cutting a large gash from neck to
sternum. The ninja cried out and fell. He attempted to get to
his knees using his sword for support, but crumpled a last time
and bled out into the dirt street.

Hideki did not have time to analyze his kill. There was
another ninja in front of him with a raised sword. As his
enemy brought it down, Hideki lunged forward under the arc,
dragging his katana with him and slicing through the ninja's
diaphragm. Blood and intestines dropped onto the dirt at
Hideki's feet. The instant stench was almost overpowering. The
ninja crumpled in a sickening heap. Hideki had just stepped
back into a neutral stance when he noticed Yoshi defending
against two Fox men.

Hideki lunged to his left slightly and punctured the Fox
man's lungs and heart as he raised his sword for an overhead
strike to Yoshi. Yoshi dispatched his second attacker by
throwing a powder in his face and using a tip of his blade to
slice out the man's throat. This one dropped silently to the
dust and kicked about, unsuccessfully trying to get air into his
severed windpipe. Then he was still.

Hideki glanced toward Musashi. The swordsman was
flicking blood from his two swords. There were five bodies in
various positions of death around him. Then Hideki turned to
his right. Jubei was examining a minor cut to his left wrist. At
his feet were four Fox men, all stilled with major death cuts.

Hideki called back over his shoulder. "Everyone survive?"

"We're fine," Yuki said. "What about the heroes?"

"Jubei has a small cut. Musashi has too many dead at his feet for him to have been hurt, and Yoshi has incapacitated over ten with his ninja dirty tricks," Hideki reported.

There were grunts of approval from the guards behind the upturned boats. Yoshi was rapidly overcoming the normal samurai loathing felt towards ninja. In its place was an appreciation for his fighting skills and his uncanny ability to sniff out danger.

The next wave of assassins came out of the now-dark street from somewhere near the opposite building. These wore the same brown ninja garb to cover their entire body except for the Fox masks. The only difference with these was that their swords were sheathed and on their backs.

"Get your shields up!" Yoshi called.

Hideki had to reach down and pick his straw hat out of the blood-drenched dirt and stinking intestinal ooze at his feet. The attacking wave ran up to Hideki's line just out of sword reach, careful to avoid Yoshi's caltrops. Each stopped and threw five darts directly over Hideki's head.

"Down, Naga!" Hideki called when he understood the tactic.

There was a high-pitched yelp as one of the darts sunk home, but Hideki did not have time to wonder if his relatives were hit. Once the darts started, the third wave charged Hideki's line. This time they formed a "Vee" and attacked directly at Hideki.

Hideki deflected one overhead strike with his katana in his right hand and drew and thrust his wakazashi straight into the attacker's stomach. As he withdrew the wakazashi in his left hand, he sliced down with the katana in his right, cutting through the wrist of a second man in the attacking formation.

Now he was in trouble. Having committed his motion forward and down to his left, his right side was vulnerable. For just a moment, the next ninja would have full access to his flank.

It seemed like an eternity for Hideki to realize his

exposure and correct his instinctive desire to straighten and turn back to the right to meet the attack. Instead of stopping his momentum and straightening back to the front, he continued spinning to the left and rear and took up a position one-step behind his original spot. He had judged correctly. Now he had time to parry the attacker's lunge using an inside parry with the wakazashi as he chopped down with his right into the brown-clad skull with his katana. Hideki's blade sunk into the cloth and bone, and the man dropped instantly, freeing Hideki's blade. He stepped over the fallen body and re-took his position in the line, but there was no fourth wave. It was over.

"Uggh!" A cry of anguish came from the porch. Hideki recognized it as Naga. He ran and leaped onto the porch. The guards made way and allowed Hideki access. When he arrived, he expected to find Jii fallen. Instead, he saw Naga holding Yuki's head in his lap. From her jacket top protruded one of the throwing darts.

"Is she alive?" Hideki asked.

"She is breathing," Naga said. "But not very well."

Hideki heard and then felt Yoshi to his left and Jubei to his right.

"Poison, you think?" Jubei asked Yoshi.

"Almost assuredly," Yoshi said.

Yoshi looked at Naga. "We must get her to the mansion as quickly as possible."

Jii started barking orders, and guards ran to the water gathering boats and oars. Everyone started towards the canal with Naga carrying his fiancée.

Yoshi grabbed Hideki's arm and held him back. "You go with your brother. I'll need Jubei to go with me," he said.

"Where are you going?" Hideki asked.

"He is going to find a witch," Jubei said, stepping up behind them.

"Yes," Yoshi said. "And if you value Yuki's life, do not let a doctor treat her."

Hideki was about to protest when Yoshi and Jubei turned and ran into the darkness of Edo.

Chapter 21: The Review

Naga sat erect. The Tairo and Roju sat directly in front of him. They sat facing Naga, and they did not look happy. Yagyu Muneori, the shogun's chamberlain, was also facing Naga. O'Fuku was once again clothed in her many layered robes and sitting on Yagyu's right. To Yagyu's immediate left there was a vacant cushion. The shogun's wife Oeyo was absent. Naga would miss her as an ally in this hostile group. Nevertheless, it was interesting that she conceded this meeting to her archrival O'Fuku.

Before Yagyu could open the meeting, O'Fuku demanded, "Well, what do you have to say for yourself?"

Jii, sitting on Naga's right, started to respond. Naga's right hand stopped him. It was just he and Jii this trip. Naga had decided to handle this with as few people as possible.

"Concerning what, my lady?" Naga asked.

"Let us start with your inability to capture the Fox Gang," O'Fuku said.

"I would say it is on par with your ability to tell time," Naga said.

"What kind of impertinence is this? We will not be trifled with by a country diamyo!" O'Fuku scolded.

Naga's response came swiftly. "First of all, my lady, I do not answer to you. I thought I made that clear during our first meeting. I take my orders from the men seated in this room. Secondly, they, not you, gave me a month to correct the problems in the magistrate's office and to capture the Fox Gang. That was two weeks ago. By my calculation, I still have two weeks before my deadline," Naga said.

This caused some sharp intakes of breath. No one talked to O'Fuku this way.

"Do you mean to be insulting to this lady?" Naomasu, the newest member of the Roju, asked.

"I have no intention of being insulting. I merely responded to an attack by a person who should have no standing with his body," Naga said.

"Well I have standing in this body, and I am insulted by the way you address O'Fuku," Naomasu said.

"I apologize if you feel insulted, and if that is not enough I stand ready to meet you at any place of your choosing with any weapon you deem to allow you satisfaction," Naga said.

The Roju, and Naomasu in particular, drew back in surprise at this personal challenge.

"I trust that will not be necessary," Yagyu Muneori said.

"It will not," Naomasu replied, bowing to Yagyu as peacemaker.

"You have challenged my position with this body, but it is your incompetence that is on trial today, Yoshinobu. Why did you let the Fox Gang leader go free when the yoriki had captured him for you?" she asked.

There was murmuring from the Roju members at this question.

"I found him not guilty, my lady. He was not a member of the Fox Gang, much less their leader," Naga replied.

"How can you be sure? The yoriki is a professional policeman with years of experience," she persisted.

"Because it was the yoriki's doshin who had contracted for Yashino the wood carver to construct the mask that would be the only proof against the young man," Naga said.

"Is that all?" she asked.

"No, my lady," Naga said, "there were many inconsistencies in the yoriki story, and several people who are expert at such things testified that the young wood carver is no ninja."

"I want to hear no more of this ninja nonsense. No one but you has reported them to be ninja," she said.

"That is probably because all of their targets are now dead," Naga said.

"That proves nothing. It is only your supposition against the police reports," she persisted.

"Well, when the police attempt to condemn an innocent boy to death and then stir up riots among the people, it's time to stop believing the police and get rid of them," Naga said.

"Is that what you have done? Have you gotten rid of the police?" she asked.

"Only the dishonest ones."

"Out of your original contingent of sixty, how many do you have left?" O'Fuku asked.

"I have two," Naga said.

"Two? Are you a lunatic? How can you keep the citizens of Edo safe with two police officers? You overstep your authority. You should be fired in disgrace immediately!" she demanded.

The murmuring from the room heated.

"Calm down, everyone," Yagyu said, "and allow Nagamasa to answer the questions."

Naga bowed his thanks to Yagyu. "I kept two because they were the only ones out of sixty who were not corrupt."

"Ridiculous!" O'Fuku said, her face contorted in angry disbelief.

"No, it is not ridiculous at all. It is the truth. The corruption is so bad that citizens and ronin are convicted of imaginary crimes as a way of obtaining revenue from the gold and silver mines. Any Edo citizen will tell you that Edo's justice is the best money can buy. They laugh at you for it. Things are so bad that gangs of armed men have sprung up to operate as a counterweight to the lawlessness of the police. They call themselves gummi and most recently Eight, Nine, Three. They took this name as it represents the worst hand in oichokabu, the card game that they play in their gambling dens. They see themselves as outside the law and worthless, just like that card hand. The Eight, Nine and Three are pronounced Ya Ku Za. They are proud of the name. These men would get no foothold with the citizens if our own police force were not corrupt."

"You go too far," O'Fuku accused.

"No my lady, I have not gone far enough. Yesterday, the Fox Gang in Nihonbashi attacked my family and me. We lost three loyal retainers and my fiancée lies near the gates of heaven thanks to a poisoned dart. Thieves and bandits do not use poison darts. Anyone with any fighting sense knows this. So do not assume to correct me my lady on the nature of my enemies. They are ninja, and the people who control them are in this room," Naga said.

"Even if what you say were true, Yoshinobu, how much closer are you to catching this leader?" she asked, her voice showing a little more calm.

"We're getting very close," Naga said. "Because I believe the Fox Gang and the corrupt police to be tied to a person or persons in this room, I had the yoriki, Denjiro, followed when he was dismissed from the police force. I am sure he will lead us to bigger prey."

Naomasu, the newest Roju member, dropped his fan onto the tatami. Everyone had been listening to Naga's talk. Now suddenly their attention moved to him. He retrieved the fan quickly.

"Gomen nasai," Naomasu said, trying to recover from the shock of hearing about Denjiro and the subsequent blunder of dropping his fan. "How is your fiancée?"

"She's gravely ill, Naomasu-sama. Thank you for asking."

"An interesting story, but any fool can destroy things. What are your plans to keep the peace in Edo?" O'Fuku demanded.

"I am using my household guards currently, but my brother is working on recruiting and training a new force steeped in adherence to the law."

"I hope for your sake he can do this in two weeks," she said.

"Nagamasa-sama, where do you propose to get fifty-eight samurai to replace the police?" Yagyu asked.

"As I said, Yagyu-sama, Hideki is working on it. He assures me they will be in place and trained by my deadline," Naga said, bowing.

"Very well, I shall report your progress to the shogun,"

Yagyu said. "We are concluded." All turned to the golden hollyhock on the wall beyond and bowed.

On the way out, Jii grab Naga's arm. "I thought I only had one hot-headed grandson."

Naga smiled. "It wasn't anger, Jii. I need to keep them on the defensive. Someone in that room has almost killed my fiancée."

"Yes, I know. I also know that if it were not for Hideki's ability to draw superior friends, we might all be dead," Jii observed.

"Yes. Well, I hope Yoshi returns with the witch, or whatever she is, in time to help. I can't believe I've allowed Hideki to keep the doctor from treating her."

Because they wanted to get back to the Yoshinobu mansion as quickly as possible to be with Yuki, they had brought horses. The return trip was fast. The front gates opened as soon as they approached the mansion walls. Jii and Naga rode to the main house while the guards dismounted at the stables. Attendants took the reins as Naga and Jii dismounted and moved to the raised porch area to take off their sandals. They were still wearing their formal clothing, but did not stop in the changing room. Instead, they moved directly to the inner sleeping rooms.

They came to a larger room with the wives of retainers and women of Yuki's ninja guards coming and going. The men moved the sliding door and entered without announcement. "How is she?" Naga asked when he saw Hideki at Yuki's side.

The doctor dressed in a white frock answered for him. "I have no idea. These idiots will not allow me to examine her."

Naga looked down at his beloved and almost wept. Her normally creamy complexion was almost blue.

"The poison is racing through her system, Lord," the doctor said. "If we don't get that dart out, I will not be responsible."

Naga looked at Hideki. Hideki did not know how to answer his pleading look. "I do not know brother. I just know Yoshi said if I valued her life not to let a doctor treat her."

"Where the hell is Yoshi?" Naga asked.

"I'm right behind you, Lord," Yoshi said.

"Yoshi!" Hideki cried. "I'm so glad to see you." A lovely young woman in peasant garb unceremoniously pushed Yoshi out of the way. A much older gray-haired woman, exuding a graceful beauty despite her tattered clothing, followed her.

"You men talk too much," the old woman said. Then, seeing the doctor, asked, "Have you touched anything?"

"No, this fool samurai would not allow it," the doctor protested.

The old woman looked to Hideki straight in the eyes. "Then he probably saved her life."

"I will not be a party to this," the doctor said standing up.

"Mother, do we have need of him?" Yoshi asked.

The gray-haired woman shook her head in the negative, then as an afterthought, "Tell him to leave the entire ginseng supply he has at the door."

Naga looked nervously at Yoshi. "Can she save Yuki?"

"If anyone can, she can," Yoshi replied.

"Yoshi, get hot water and two buckets of cold," the young woman commanded.

Yoshi started to turn when Jii said, "Ladies, just tell us what you need. We'll see that it is available."

"I would start with the water, Jii," Naga said.

Jii began barking orders and women scurried to comply.

The old woman moved to Yuki's side and listened to her breathing by placing her ear close to Yuki's nose. Then she reached under the sheet and exposed Yuki's hand. He applied pressure to the fingernails and watched the reaction and color. She moved to the foot of the pallet and did the same thing to Yuki's toes. She then turned to the young woman. "Chiyo, I think it is death cap."

The young woman nodded. "I agree, Mother. Rice bran is best for mushrooms, isn't it?" she questioned.

"Yes," the woman said. Then turning to Jii, "We will require rice bran boiled and reduced to a tea. The sooner we get some into her, the sooner we will know if she survives."

Jii gave the orders and people scurried. "Chiyo, get warm compresses ready. We should get the dart out now."

Very quickly, the two women set about pulling the dart from Yuki's flesh and keeping warm compresses on the wound. Upon completion of bandaging, messengers announced the return of men sent to the market for rice bran. Once it was brought into the hall area, women took it to the kitchen for boiling.

When the tea arrived, Chiyo and her mother set about getting cup after cup into Yuki. Because Yuki was unconscious, the old woman used a small hollow reed to transfer the brew from the cup and blow it deep into Yuki's throat. After five cups, the women let Yuki rest.

As the Yoshinobu men paced in the hall outside, servants responded to the orders of the two women with Yuki. The afternoon dragged by slowly.

Jii looked to Yoshi. "I assume the young woman is your wife?"

"Yes, Lord," Yoshi bowed.

"And judging by the resemblance, the older one is your mother-in-law?"

"Yes again, Lord," Yoshi said.

"Why did you not want the doctor to treat Yuki?" "Because without proper diagnosing of the poison, he would've done more harm than good," Yoshi explained.

"Yes, I see. So your mother-in-law has more experience than a doctor in recognizing poisons?"

Yoshi thought about this a moment before responding. "Let me ask you this, Jii-sama. Who is better to recognize all aspects of a sword, the samurai who wields it or the artisan who makes it?"

Jii thought about the question. "I imagine the man who makes the sword would know more about its properties."

"Correct answer, Jii-sama. It is the same with poisons."

Jii looked back into Yuki's room for another look at Yoshi's mother-in-law. "That is scary," he mumbled.

"She scares most ninjas," Yoshi said. "And she is passing her knowledge on to her daughter. Now you know why I'm wary all the time."

Jii shook his head. "You went to retrieve your women, but why did you take Jubei?" Jii asked.

"I knew time was of the essence. Anyone could have delayed me. A policeman, a samurai or even a wealthy merchant, but no one wants to delay Jubei," Yoshi explained.

Jii smiled. "I guess not. Yoshi your ability to see into the unknown is only exceeded by your ability to plan so far ahead."

Hideki was sitting on the tatami just inside the room when Yoshi's wife came to him. "Are you Hideki-sama?" she asked nervously.

"Hai," Hideki said, returning her bow.

"My mother requests that someone bring a raw clove of garlic," she said bowing lower.

"Right away," Hideki said, standing and moving through the door into the hall where the Yoshinobu men, Jubei, and Yoshi were pacing.

"She wants garlic," Hideki said to Jii.

Yoshi smiled at Naga.

"Is that a good sign?" Naga asked hopefully.

"It is a very good sign, Lord. It means the poison has been neutralized and my mother-in-law is now taking precaution against any lingering infection."

Naga started into the room, but Yoshi stopped him. "No, Lord, not yet. Let the women have their time with her. They will summon you when they are ready."

Naga looked confused.

Hideki came to his rescue. "They will wait until she regains full consciousness and is coherent. Then they will clean her up and comb her hair and when she is ready, the women will call for you." he said, adding, "For somebody being considered for shogun, you sure are dense when it comes to women."

Naga blushed. Jii laughed. "It looks like your mother-in-law saved the day. What is her name?"

"Matsu," Yoshi said.

"We owe her our future," Jii said.

"I owe her my happiness," Naga added.

"Please ask Matsu and your wife to stay in our compound," Jii requested.

"I am sure they will stay as long as they are needed. Beyond that, I cannot say," Yoshi said.

"Well, we will speak of it when the time comes. Until then, have them move into your house. You do not use it very often anyway. You certainly have the room. They may as well use it."

"Hai, Lord," Yoshi said, bowing as he moved off to arrange for his new houseguests.

Jii looked after him. "You know, I'm very glad that I didn't hit him with that wakazashi the first time we met."

Naga collapsed into a sitting position on the polished hardwood floor that made up the hallways in the mansion.

"So am I, Grandfather. So am I."

Chapter 22: New Police

"If I didn't know you better, I'd say you intended me harm, Yojimbo," Nichi said.

"Relax, Oyabun; there is someone who wants to meet you," Hideki replied.

The huge leader of the Gumsumgumi turned to the young woman at his side in the brightly colored kimono. "Do you know what this is about Myo?"

"No Nichi, I do not. But if Takezo says it is important, then I'm sure it is," she said, looking into Hideki's eyes and smiling.

"You two are almost indecent in your flirting," Nichi chided.

Hideki blushed. "Trust me Oyabun. I would do nothing to harm you or the Gumsumgumi. The man that wants to meet you is very important."

"But why meet at the Hatchobori? Do you not remember them trying to kill us? Even that outdoor court trial raised the hairs on the back of my neck. I don't like being around police," the leader of the Gumsumgumi said. "Besides, it is a long walk, and I'm too big to walk far."

The closer they got to the center of town and the police headquarters of the Hatchobori, the more crowded the streets became. Myo had to fall back and walk behind Nichi so that his large sumo girth could part the sea of humanity for her. It was the last stage of the hour of the snake, almost eleven o'clock in the morning. The sun was shining, and the summer heat was baking everything not in the shade. Nichi continually wiped his brow with a white cloth and complained with each step that he would rather be back in his hotel.

They finally came to the nexus of several streets. On one corner stood the large two-storied Hatchobori that seemed to take up several city blocks. In front were two guards. Instead of wearing the haori of the police and holding roku shaku bos, these were samurai armed with swords and eight-foot yari or spears.

As they came abreast the guards, Nichi slowed down, expecting some form of identification check. Instead, the two guards bowed low at the waist.

Nichi was shocked that Hideki did not slow down and proceeded into the compound. Nichi hurried to catch up. "Those guards bowed to you?" he said.

"Me? No, they probably were bowing to the leader of the Gumsumgumi," Hideki replied.

Nichi looked wary. "Who would know me here?"

"I think the man who wants to meet you probably does," Hideki said.

"This sounds unhealthy to me, Yojimbo. I have no business at the Hatchobori."

"Humor me one more time, Oyabun. I guarantee the visit will be worth your while and in the best interest of the Gumsumgumi," Hideki insisted.

Nichi did not like it. "I suppose if you are planning me harm, you could've done it the last time we were here."

Hideki bowed slightly and led the way into the large building and onto the main floor. Once they attained the main floor level, they both took off their sandals and moved soundlessly on the highly polished dark wood planks that made up the three-sided veranda of the courtyard. Guards in samurai garb and sporting Yoshinobu mon bowed as they passed. Nichi hastily returned the bows and looked to Hideki for explanation.

"There is no doubt, they recognize you as a leader of the Gumsumgumi," he said.

"Ridiculous. This person you want to meet had better be able keep his mouth shut, Yojimbo," Nichi warned.

"He is good at keeping secrets."

At one of the tatami rooms off the veranda, Hideki
led Nichi into the building. They came to a fusuma, Hideki
pulled the sliding paper door back. Both Nichi and Myo passed
through into an interior corridor of darker polished hardwood
while Hideki closed the sliding door behind them. Hideki then
led them to another room several paces down and to the left.
He placed his hand on the fusuma door and paused. "Gomen
kudasai," Hideki announced. Then he slid the door back,
bowed slightly to the Oyabun, and indicated with an open
hand that Nichi was to enter. Nichi stepped into the room and
saw an old samurai with gray hair seated at the place of honor.
The old gentleman indicated a small mat directly opposite him.
"Dozo."

Nichi bowed slightly and took a cross-legged seat
identical to the old man's posture.

"Let me introduce myself. I am Yoshinobu Masashige,"
Jii said, bowing at the waist slightly.

Nichi was shocked. He quickly bowed his head and
massive body as much as he could. "Nichi desu. Dozo
yoroshuku onagaishimasu," Nichi said by way of introduction.

"Raise your head Nichi," Jii said. "I've asked my
grandson to bring you here because I wanted to see for myself
if what he says is true or if he's been duped."

Nichi turned to his yojimbo. "Grandson?"

"Yes Nichi, I am not really a ronin. I am Yoshinobu
Hideki. This venerable person is my grandfather. He raised my
brother and me. It is my elder brother that you saw the other
day as magistrate. Forgive the subterfuge. When I was arrested
by Denjiro the yoriki I had no idea I would be meeting the
Gumsumgumi."

"So you lied to me," Nichi accused.

"I have never lied to you," Hideki said.

"You mince words, samurai. You let me believe you were
a ronin," said Nichi.

"That is true. But if I had revealed my true identity, what
would've happened?" Hideki asked.

Nichi thought about it for a minute. "We would've
labeled you as a government spy."

"Then you would've killed him?" Jii asked.

"No Yoshinobu-sama. We do not kill people unless they are attacking us. I'm just having a hard time adjusting to the idea that my yojimbo is a brother of the man being considered for shogun."

"Well, you have been around him for several weeks. What do you think of my grandson?" Jii asked.

Nichi rubbed his considerable face. "I could guess that like any grandfather, you're fishing for compliments. Nevertheless, I do not sense that. You are testing me. Therefore, I will give you the truth. Your grandson intrigues me. Granted, saving my life twice has probably clouded my judgment a little. His martial arts skills are superb, and he and that pet ninja of his make a formidable team."

"Yoshi, are you there?" Jii asked toward the door.

The door slid back and Yoshi bowed. "Here, Lord."

"You might as well come in. You're being talked about," Jii said.

Yoshi bowed again, moved to Hideki's side, and sat.

"Go on Nichi," Jii encouraged.

"Well, I'd say he is a terrible employee because he is seldom at work. But then he doesn't take any pay, except for that little room in the hotel he uses for his meetings with Myo."

Hideki reddened.

"I enjoy talking to him. He is educated and has fresh ideas on many subjects. He is extremely bright and also very much naïve to many things," Nichi said.

"Explain please," Jii said.

"Well, he sees good in everyone and has not learned yet to be wary of people."

"I see," said Jii.

"But what draws my men and me to him are his intentions. Takezo, or Hideki, seems to exude a desire to help. His intentions appear pure. He seems to be able to build optimism in others. I believe in a few years, after he experiences life a little more, he will be a man to watch," Nichi said.

"Do you trust him?" Jii asked.

"I would not be sitting in this room now if I did not."

"Well said, Nichi. I must tell you that I had great trepidation about the offer today. I viewed you as most samurai must, as a brigand and worse. My grandson has championed you, however. He believes your motives were born of necessity and good intention. So I wanted to meet you before I brought in my oldest grandson to address an offer."

"What offer?" Nichi asked.

Then in the back of the room, a page announced, "Yoshinobu Nagamasa" and slid back the door. Jii abandoned his spot of honor and Nagamasa along with Yagyu Muneori entered. Nagamasa took Jii's vacated spot and Yagyu moved to Jii's side. Nichi bowed to all and stayed bowed as much as his girth would allow from the seated position.

"Raise your head, Nichi of the Gumsumgumi," Naga said.

Nichi raised his head and met Naga's gaze.

"I am Yoshinobu Nagamasa. I am eldest grandson to Jii-sama, whom you met, and older brother to your yojimbo, Hideki, and I need your sword."

Nichi looked surprised. "Lord, I have no sword."

"It is an expression, Nichi. You are the sword. I want your help," Naga said. "I understand your family was once samurai."

"Yes, Lord, but that was long ago. My father gave up the swords so that we could eat."

"Nichi, why did you form the Gumsumgumi?" Naga asked.

Nichi thought about the question before answering. "Originally, to get even, I suppose," he said, "and later to protect the chosin."

"Money did not drive you?" Jii asked.

"I will admit the money has come. Being outside of society has its monetary advantages. But I don't think I did it for the money."

"You were in the crowd the other day for the trial?" Naga asked.

"Yes, Lord," Nichi said.

"What were your impressions?"

"My first impression was to shout joyfully for your sense of justice and compassion," Nichi said.

"And later?"

"Later I became afraid." Nichi said

At this Naga's eyebrows raised slightly. "What a strange response. Why afraid?"

"I am afraid because you just destroyed the system in one hour that it has taken the Tokugawa twenty-three years to build. I am afraid of what the streets of Edo might look like. The police were evil, but they prevented some crime from happening. Who's going to protect the chosin now?" Nichi asked.

"My question as well," Naga replied. "That is why we are meeting here. I want you to form a police force for Edo."

"Me?" Nichi asked. "Is this a joke?"

"I have never been more serious."

"But I am Gumsumgumi. We are outside of society. The government spies and their ninja have been trying to expose and kill me for years," Nichi protested.

"That is why I have left my fiancée's sick bed and asked Yagyu Muneori, chamberlain to the shogun, here for this meeting. Yagyu-sama controls the ometsuke."

Nichi tried to bow again at Yagyu's name.

"Raise your head, Nichi," Yagyu said. "If you accept this assignment, you will no longer be troubled by the government. You will be supported by it."

Nichi shook his head. It was almost too much to take in.

"Nichi, from 1467 to 1573, this country knew nothing but war. Countless families destroyed, resources wasted and everyone's life restricted. The poor suffered the most," Naga began.

"For over one hundred years, peasants could not take their produce to market. No one traveled from town to town, so there was little trade, and ideas were greatly restricted. But with Hideyoshi Toyotomi and then Tokugawa Ieyasu, peace came to the land.

"The Tokugawa have had twenty-three years to perfect

the peace. With some things, we have been successful. Any citizen with permission can travel the length and breadth of the land.

"Some things, like governing a new city, have not received the attention due them. I was appointed the magistrate so that I could fail. Some in power in the castle want the status quo. I took the job knowing that changes had to be radical if they were to endure. I do not know how much longer I will be the magistrate. However, I know the chosin in the city deserve a police force that is not corrupt. That will be my legacy. I was hoping that I could find a cadre of honest police officers on the force. Out of sixty, we found two.

"I could declare martial law and have my samurai patrol the streets. However, that would disrupt the everyday life of the chosin, and it is not a final solution. So instead I want to form a new police force with men who are comfortable with violence but adhere to a higher code. Hideki thinks you are the man for the job. But I warn you, if you accept this position, you will have to give up your control of the Gumsumgumi."

"You want me to destroy it?" Nichi asked.

"No, Hideki has convinced me it is a necessary organization, as long as it remains true to your standards. But you will have to pass control to another," Naga said. "And there is one more thing dealing with loyalty."

"You want me to be loyal to the shogun," Nichi guessed.

"That would be nice, but I don't require it," Naga said.

"Then you want me to be loyal to you?" Nichi asked.

"That would also be nice, but I want you to be loyal to the right," Naga said.

"The right?" Nichi questioned.

"Yes, the right. I want you and the men you pick to be loyal to doing the right thing in all your dealings."

"It sounds like you want us to be priests."

"Yes, that's it. I want you to be priestly in your efforts to do right," Naga said.

Nichi shook his large head. "This all sounds fine, Lord, but begging the chamberlain's pardon, the castle will fight you on this. Many high-placed samurai will not like what you are doing.

Once I'm in the open, they'll just send someone to kill me."

"I know what I'm asking is not easy, Nichi. You are going to have to give up a very lucrative lifestyle in order to be despised by the samurai and barely tolerated by the chosin. Being an honest police officer is not easy. I will try and take some of the sting out by offering you a 10,000 koku stipend and position of chief yoriki under me," Naga said.

"Just so I am clear, you are offering me the entire Edo police force? How many police do you have?"

"We are down to two," Naga replied.

"So I have to recruit and train my police force?" Nichi asked.

"Yes, and you have a free hand. I demand only two things. I demand honesty and loyalty to the right."

"How do you want me to handle the Gumsumgumi?" Nichi asked.

"Just like any other criminal organization if they break the law," Naga said.

"So, in essence, you're asking me to give up my life for the chance to change the world or my little slice of it?" Nichi asked.

"Yes," Naga said.

Nichi looked at Hideki. "What do you think?"

"This was Hideki's plan," Naga answered.

Then Nichi turned to Yoshi. "What do you think, ninja?"

"I think you are too big and too dumb to handle this, but I'm being overruled," Yoshi said.

"Never ask a ninja," Nichi said. "How many police do I need to raise?"

"The Hatchobori had sixty strong," Naga said.

"That many, huh? Fifty-eight is a lot. When do I have to have them?" Nichi asked.

"Tonight would be nice," Naga said. "But I can keep a lid on Edo for two weeks using my household guards."

"Lord, you have given me an interesting challenge, and with only one way out. Now that everyone knows my face, if I were to refuse, I am sure life would become difficult for me," Nichi observed.

"I would do nothing to jeopardize your group or yourself,

unless you are involved in criminal behavior," Naga said.

Nichi turned to Myo, who sat behind everyone. "What do you think, Lady Myo?"

Myo was surprised. She had not thought her opinion would be sought. "I supposed my relationship with Takezo should cloud my response," she said keeping her eyes down. Then steeling herself, she looked Hideki in the eye. "I think these men's intentions are good. Nevertheless, in case they are not, or if they waver in their duty and abandon the path of righteousness, you have lost nothing. You can always go back into the dark."

Everyone stared at her for a long while. Yoshi spoke. "I think what Myo just said is as close to the truth as you are likely to hear. If you take on this responsibility, only the people in this room will know your sacrifice. The chosin will think you are the fox guarding the hen house and lining your pockets on a grander scale. You must prove otherwise. The other gummi will fear you because you know them and their ways. It is an ugly thing you are being asked to do."

"On the other hand, how many people have the opportunity to change history?" Nichi reasoned. He looked at each person in the room. "Will I have any help in training the new police force?"

"What kind of help do you want?" Naga asked.

"I can pick the kind of men we need. I know who to approach and who to avoid. Most of them will be former samurai who have given up the swords to feed their families. They will jump at a chance to live interesting lives again and to pledge to a calling higher than gold. However, I will need help in training them in everything from how to use a jutte, to arresting techniques, to how to investigate. I will need help in all manner of things," Nichi said.

"Musashi's father was an expert with the jutte. We can get him to teach the new men," Hideki said.

"I will arrange to have the yoriki in charge of the Osaka police to visit the Hatchobori and help with setting up administration and training in detective work," Yagyu said.

"I can help with tracking, trailing, and disguises," Yoshi said.

301

"You will have all the resources at my disposal, Nichi," said Naga.

Nichi nodded at everyone's willingness to help. "Very well, Yoshinobu-sama, I accept your offer. I will run Edo for you." Nichi said.

"Domo arigato, Nichi," Naga said.

All present bowed to Nichi.

Chapter 23: Payback

Yoshi's head popped up. He held up his hand to signal quiet to the gathering of important men. Everyone froze. Then he closed his eyes. "We are not alone."

They were still in the room in the Hatchobori. Nichi had just accepted heading up the new Edo police force. They had sealed the meeting with sake. Nichi had greatly appreciated the sake, but now felt a little uncomfortable in the presence of these high-ranking officials. Despite the light laughter and good wishes the occasion demanded, everyone was immediately serious at Yoshi's announcement.

"Female, I think ... and in the rafters above the ceiling," Yoshi announced.

Everyone's hands went to their sharkskin katana handles.

Myo surprised everyone by speaking. "One day you must teach me that," she said to Yoshi. Then she raised her eyes and then her voice to the ceiling. "Identify yourself," she demanded.

A feminine voice from the rafters responded. "Hai, Midori desu, Oyabun."

Myo directed her gaze back at the gathered men. "It is alright. She is one of mine." Then back to the ceiling, "Enter!"

A ceiling tile dislodged, and a black-clad obviously female figure dropped soundlessly to the tatami just beyond the circle of men. From head to toe, she was covered in black ninja garb. Only a space around her eyes showed. She stayed in a kneeling position with her head bowed. Her ninja sword handle protruded beside her head from its strapped position on her back.

"I have had my suspicions for these last few years," Nichi said. "Your information was always just a little too good to be coming from a courier service."

"Report!" Myo stated conversationally to the ninja known as Midori.

"Hai. We believe we have found some of the Fox Gang," she said.

"Excellent! It is time we hurt them," Naga exclaimed with just a little too much vehemence.

"Easy, Naga," Jii said. "You will not be part of this. You are too valuable to the country."

Hideki looked to Myo. "Where is the location?" he asked.

Myo nodded to the female ninja. "It is a warehouse on the canal between Nihonbashi and Suruga Machi," Midori replied.

"I know the area," Nichi said. "What is the name of the building?"

"Daiwa," was the response.

"I know it," Nichi said. "It is a rice warehouse with a mercantile store on one side and a boatyard on the other."

"How many Foxes?" Hideki asked.

Again, Midori sought permission with a stare at Myo. Myo granted permission with a nod.

"We think ten. There are about fifteen legitimate workers and boatmen and about the same amount of Yamakai-gumi."

Hideki looked at Nichi. "A little fact that slipped your mind?"

"No," said Nichi, "but a fact that may require my expertise."

Naga stood. "I need to get back to Yuki," he said. "Let's reconvene tomorrow with Musashi and Jubei at our mansion and come up with a plan. Hideki, you are in charge. Thank you all." So saying, he turned and departed with Jii and Yagyu on his heels.

"Nichi, do you know the location of the Yoshinobu estate?" Hideki asked.

"No, Lord … but remember, I don't like to walk," the large man replied.

"I will take you, Nichi," Myo volunteered. "You only have to walk to the boat docks."

"Excellent," Nichi said.

"Then we meet tomorrow at our estate at the hour of the snake," Hideki said.

Myo and Nichi arrived at the Kanda landing a little before the hour of the snake. It was a short walk in a southerly direction to the Yoshinobu mansion. Nichi stopped to admire the compound. "It is not as big as my hotel, but it is much grander in its own way," he said.

Myo stopped to look as well. It was a fine samurai villa. It was like many she had infiltrated over the years. They were all massively fortified with samurai guards armed to the teeth. Nevertheless, samurai thought one way and ninja thought another.

While samurai guarded the gates and patrolled streets, she looked for breaks in the wall made by trees, streams, or even the tiled ditches, known as binjo, that carried human waste from latrines to canals and rivers. Where samurai looked for armed intruders attempting to storm their compound, she sought to memorize a natural ebb and flow of the invisible people that came and went during a normal day.

No one notices the old woman allowed entrance into the back gate to sell vegetables to the cook. No one pays much attention to the tinker who comes to mend pots and sells a few new utensils. No one ever goes near the Eta who collects dead bodies and cleans the latrines of the fancy houses and businesses of Edo. There were hundreds of ways to get around sentries, and Myo knew them all. So as much as the eight-foot-high, wooden fence around the compound with its hat-like topping with kiln fired, overlapping blue tile impressed Nichi, she saw it for what it was. It was a source of false security for those inside.

However, stopping to stare with Nichi did allow her to reflect on how unusual it was for her to be going through the front gate, as if she belonged. The compound covered almost three acres, with an eight-foot wall surrounding everything.

At the main gate there were two massive poles sunk deep into the earth, rising above the fence another eight feet. There was a horizontal cross member bolted onto the two vertical posts about twelve shaku, or fourteen feet, off the ground. Between the two large vertical posts were two massive doors that hinged outward from the posts, which in time of siege could be locked from inside with wooden beams. It was through the massive doors that horsemen and merchant carts entered. Just to the left of the two massive doors was a small wooden door built into the surrounding fence. This would remain open during daylight hours and would be the main avenue for foot traffic to and from the mansion.

A raised walkway connected all the eight buildings. The central building sat parallel to the front gate and dominated the view. The large spine of the main building's roof ran from left to right and seemed to fan out as its bluish tile sloped gently down to the top of the outbuildings. Each one of the outbuildings had the same sloping roof but in miniature. It was really quite an impressive array of buildings and a reminder of Hideki's material wealth.

"Could you see yourself being queen of the Yoshinobu mansion?" Nichi asked.

Myo snapped out of her daydream. "Not me. I have no samurai blood."

"Sometimes they might make an exception. These Yoshinobu seem to be strange samurai," Nichi said.

"I am shinobi no mono. No samurai will make that big of an exception." Despite her statement, Myo found herself imagining what it would be like to live with Hideki as man and wife in this big house. "I think it would be fine for a few weeks, and then I would get bored."

"Bored of what?"

"Being queen of the Yoshinobu; do try to keep up, Nichi."

"You mean you could only boss servants around so many times before you would be longing for a good game of oichokabu in the gambling hall?" Nichi asked.

"Something like that," she said. What she really thought was that she would go out of her mind living in the confining world of samurai women. To not be able to travel when she wanted to, or hold her own in arguments with men, or not controlling her own destiny would crush her spirit. No, there were worse things than being ninja.

They did not have to go through the double main gates. They presented themselves to the guard at the smaller door on the left. Their names were on a list. Then they moved across the hard-packed, wide dirt street where the buildings began. From the street, they stepped up onto a wooden walkway that ran throughout the compound and connected the buildings.

Where the sidewalk met an outbuilding, it turned into an enclosed veranda. The floors here were not the rough-hewn planks of the sidewalks. Here the wood was worn smooth, polished, and set together seamlessly. The walkways were about three men wide with the outside edge encased in a knee-high fence of smooth, horizontal poles stained the same dark brown color as every other wooden structure in the compound. Above the knee-high fence were vertical poles reaching to the massive beams supporting the huge blue tile roofs. While on the walkway, one could see directly up into the beams in the latticework of smaller poles and slats that made up the base of the roof above.

The inside wall of the walkway was comprised of fusuma doors and shoji walls. Behind the walls were large rooms at least 15 to 20 tatami. It was into one of these that Nichi and Myo were ushered. Once seated, an attendant brought tea on small, lacquered serving trays.

Jii entered first and nodded to Nichi and Myo. They both bowed to him.

"Early I see. That is a good sign," Jii said.

Then Hideki filed in, followed by Yoshi, Musashi, and Jubei.

"Where is Naga?" Jii asked.

"He is still in with Yuki and her father," Hideki replied.

Jii nodded but was unhappy with the delay.

The next man that stepped into the room was uninvited. "Hanzo-sama," Jii said. "We were not expecting you. How is your daughter progressing?"

"She is getting stronger and stronger each day, thanks to Yoshi's mother-in-law," Hittori Hanzo, the leader of the shogun's ometsuke and hereditary leader of the Iga ninja, nodded to Yoshi as he spoke.

Naga came in behind Hanzo, bowed to all, and took his seat next to Jii.

"I have asked Naga to allow me to witness this gathering of warriors."

He gazed at Jubei. "Jubei-sama I know. Go kudo sama deshita," Hanzo said bowing, thanking Jubei for his hard work. He turned to Musashi. "Musashi-sama; my daughter has told me of your courage at Nihonbashi. Domo." Then he stared at Yoshi. "Yoshi, it was truly fortunate that you did not carry out your original assignment. You have saved many lives since that day."

Yoshi returned his bow.

Then Hanzo noticed the large man in the corner. "I do not believe I know this person."

Nichi was about to respond when Hideki cut him off. "Hanzo-sama, allow me to introduce Nichi, Naga's new chief yoriki."

"Oh yes," Hanzo said smiling. "In your new position, your sumo background may come in handy."

Nichi bowed. "I hope my wit will serve me better, Lord."

"Well said, Yoriki Nichi," Hanzo laughed. "And who is this young woman?" he asked, moving in front of Myo.

Myo bowed. "Myo de gozaimus, Lord," she said, introducing herself in a polite form.

"Myo is a valued member of our staff," Hideki added.

"Raise your face, Myo," Hanzo said.

She raised her head. Hanzo studied her face. "You would be the princess of the Five Families, unless I miss my guess," Hanzo said. Myo remained silent. "You contracted to assassinate a Tokugawa. That is punishable by death."

Myo did not cower. However, she was fearful. This was

the legendary Oni Hanzo. He was the ninja killer everyone called Devil Hanzo. Jii came to her rescue. "Enough Hanzo. Myo has been forgiven past transgressions and is now in our employ."

"Forgive me Yoshinobu-sama, but I do not believe you have the authority to forgive in this case. Her crime is a crime against the shogun." He then pointed a finger at her. "Anyone who is a threat to the shogun must deal with me."

Jii shouted at Hanzo. "Do not make threats against my house, Hanzo! Before you can get to this woman, you must come through me."

Everyone was shocked at Jii's defense of Myo. "She is nothing Yoshinobu-sama. She is a ninja," Hanzo said. "I am to be your son's father-in-law. Would you destroy your son's future over her?"

Jii's response was measured. "She is my ninja, and I have given her my word. Neither you nor the shogun himself can make me break my word once given."

Hanzo smiled and squatted down in front of Myo. "You are truly blessed. These country samurai are hard to understand. They keep everyone on their toes trying to anticipate them. Do not give me reason to hunt for you," Hanzo said as he rose and moved to the door. Once there, he stopped and addressed the room. "Thank you for the work you do this day. I want vengeance for my daughter." Then he turned to Jii. "If I can be of any assistance, send for me." He bowed, turned and moved through the sliding door.

"Perhaps I should go," Myo said to no one in particular.

"No," Hideki said. "You're welcome here."

"You've nothing to fear child," Jii said. "You are part of our household now, and unlike Hittori Hanzo, we are Tokugawa."

Myo felt strange. She was not used to others looking out for her. She was being offered protection by one of the highest-ranking families in the land. The feeling of being wanted, or even needed, was new and intoxicating. "Don't go soft," she told herself. "They need you now." She would be partners with the Yoshinobu while it suited her purposes.

Nevertheless, she was ninja. She only trusted her own, and not too many of them.

"Okay everyone, enough distractions. Let's get to the task at hand," Jii said.

Two adjoining walls of the large room were permanent. The other two walls were made of sliding sections that opened onto the walkway verandas. All of the attendees sat on cushions placed on the tatami floor.

Before each was a portable table with teacups. They sat in a formation like the letter "U." The open end of the letter was toward one of the sliding doors. Jii sat farthest from the door. To his right was Naga, to his left was Hideki. To Hideki's left and down the long side of the "U" sat Jubei. Across from Jubei and down the opposite long side of the "U" sat Musashi. To Musashi's right was Nichi, and to Nichi's right and on the cushion closest to the door sat Myo, with Yoshi on Jubei's left.

Behind Jii was a wall painting of windswept trees along a seacoast. Between Jii and the wall behind him, a samurai's armor complete with fierce helmet and face shield was on display. Along the two permanent walls on the floor were various chests. Two young samurai sat behind Jii and had paper and ink stones on their tables. They would act as scribes, recording the proceedings.

"We will conduct this as we would a council of war. Myo has located a Fox Gang enclave. We are going to do something about it. However, before we decide what that is to be, we had better hear all we know about the situation. So Myo, please tell us what you know," Jii began.

Myo was used to conducting these types of meetings for her father, but she had no idea what the samurai wanted. "There is a large rice warehouse and mercantile store combination in Suruga Machi named Daiwa. It takes up an entire block. Its front is on a city street the locals call Canal Street, and its rear abuts the Nihonbashi canal. The building is actually three smaller buildings combined. The two buildings that are joined side-by-side open onto the street. They are two-story types with traditional roofs like this building. What you do not see from the street is a large warehouse stretching back to the canal.

"Oceangoing vessels transport their goods to Shiba on the bay and offload to smaller lighters. The lighters traverse the Sumida River and onto the Kanda Canal and Nihonbashi. They pull right up to the back of Daiwa where a long beam protruding out of the back of the warehouse is equipped with a pulley system to offload the goods from the lighters and into the warehouse. From there, the goods are loaded onto two-wheel carts or horse caravans and distributed to merchants throughout the city." Myo paused for a breath, allowing her words to be processed before continuing.

"That is how the Yamakai make their money. They started by infiltrating the laborers and did the lifting and delivering. Now they own the warehouses and actually act as middlemen to the merchants—buying from the ships and selling to the distributors."

"They make a great deal of money," Nichi affirmed.

"Why did the Gumsumgumi not think of that?" Hideki asked.

"Probably because I'm not as smart as old Kodama," Nichi said. "He values money over all else, and does not spend time protecting the citizens."

"Let us stay on task. Myo, can you remember anything else?" Jii asked.

The question surprised Myo. She was speechless for a moment, not knowing how to answer. Yoshi came to her aid. "Jii-sama, Myo can remember everything about the building. She has been to it and inside it, and she can remember every detail. While young samurai children are playing with dolls, ninja children learn memory tricks. Whether they eat or not depends on how well they remember."

"He speaks the truth, Yoshinobu-sama," Jubei interjected. "I suggest we save time and give Myo brush and stone and have her draw a detailed a map of the buildings. I would also like to hear why she thinks they chose this building."

Jii motioned to an attendant. He stood and went to one of the many chests along the wall behind Jii. From one he extracted a large scroll of paper and a wooden box. These he took to Myo and sat them in front of her tray. The attendant unrolled the scroll onto the tatami and opened the wooden box. From the box he extracted a short length of bamboo. From the bamboo, he produced a brush. From his belt, he produced a longer tube of bamboo through which he placed water onto the black stone set into the lower half of the wooden box. The brush went into the black mixture at the bottom of the box. The newly inked brush went to Myo.

She began drawing a series of buildings, the street, Nihonbashi canal behind, the fences, the entrances into all three building, the second story with windows, the locations of handcarts, and the various rooms on the second floor, then she identified the buildings on the street and which room the Fox Gang used. When she was finished, Hideki was looking at as good a map as he had ever seen.

"Very impressive Myo," Jii said. "Now to Jubei's question, why the daiwa?"

"I believe the Fox Gang to be using the daiwa and the Yamakai for the same function as the merchants," she said.

"Distribution of supplies?" Naga asked.

"Yes, Lord. I think this is their Edo distribution point for various activities in the Kanto or greater Edo area."

"Ingenious," Hideki exclaimed. "You were right Nichi—the Yamakai are smarter than you."

"Yes, but he has made a mistake this time. He has contracted with an outlawed gang and one that is a threat to the Tokugawa. For this, the Yamakai must perish," Nichi asserted.

"Excellent job, Myo," Jii said. Myo actually felt flush with the praise. She found herself wanting this man's approval.

"How many people are in the buildings night and day?" Naga asked.

"During the day, there are as many as fifteen warehousemen. They quit work before sundown. There are upwards of ten Yamakai men who reside in the corner building facing the street," she said, pointing with the brush. "The Fox Gang resides here," she said, pointing to the other building facing the street. "No one resides on the first floor. There are a series of offices with files in the front. They lead to the warehouse in back."

"And the number of the Fox Gang?" Jii asked.

"The most we've seen is ten. But they come and go constantly. It may be a communication center for them as well," she said.

"Thank you, Myo," Jii said, then he addressed the assembled. "So, on with our planning. What have you learned, and what are your questions for Myo?"

Naga responded first. "I think we should conduct the raid under darkness—to eliminate casualties among the warehousemen."

"Good point, Naga, but only if it does not pose more danger on our forces," Jii said.

"What is our mission, Grandfather?" Hideki asked.

"Now that is an excellent question," Jii said.

"I think arresting the Yamakai should be one objective," Nichi said.

"If it is a distribution point or communication center, capturing it should disrupt their operations," Yoshi added.

"I want to kill as many of the bastards as possible," Naga proclaimed.

"If your intent is to murder, you'll have to count me out," Musashi said.

"And me," Jubei seconded.

Jii stared at Naga. His grandson would have to find a way to rectify this error.

Naga bowed to both. "I am sorry. My distress with Yuki's injury clouded my judgment. I want the Foxes arrested and tried."

"You will learn nothing. They would rather die than speak," Jubei said.

"I want to speak with one of them," Hideki said.

"Jubei just said they will reveal nothing," Naga said.

"I believe they will reveal something to me," Hideki said.

"Do you think yourself such a good interrogator?"

"No, and I don't have time to explain it to you. But I think it is important to your mission as magistrate to let me question a Fox prisoner," Hideki said.

"Take time to explain it to us," Jii said.

"Very well Grandfather, I don't want to interrogate the prisoner. I want to listen to him talk."

"It sounds like the same thing," Jii said.

"The two times we have fought the Foxes, has anyone heard them utter a word?" Hideki asked. Everyone shook his or her head in the negative. Hideki continued. "You have heard them scream when dying, but none of us have heard them utter a command."

"You are correct, Lord," Yoshi said. "I mentioned as much when we met on the Tokaido with Hanzo and Yuki for the first time."

"Why do they not speak?" Hideki asked.

"I don't know," Yoshi said. "I wondered how they communicate."

"Think back to Kyoto. During our fight, did you hear anything strange?" Hideki asked.

"Not really. Only the screams of the dying and those noisy birds," Yoshi said .

"Exactly! I remember thinking we had disturbed the birds of the Temple. I now believe it is the way the Fox ninja communicate," Hideki said.

"Could be that you are correct," Jubei said. "I remember the bird calls in Nihonbashi. But how does this help us?"

Hideki eagerly responded. "They may be using the bird calls to disguise a dialect. I am good at remembering things. If I can listen to one of them, I may be able to determine where they are from. If I can determine what part of the country they are from it may help us know who in the Roju or Tairo is helping them."

"Sounds a little strange to me, but write it down," Jii said to the scribe. "Anything else?"

No one responded.

"Very well, our objective is to seize the building and capture as many as possible for trial," Jii said. "We know the enemy strength. We know the terrain. Now what troops do we have available?"

"We have our sixty retainers," Hideki said.

"We cannot use them for this. Besides, thirty of them

are patrolling the city as police," Naga said.

"Nichi, how many new police do you have?" Jii asked.

"I have thirty. In a brawl with the Yamakai, they will do well. But despite Musashi's constant jutte training, they could not go against ninja."

"They will not have to," Myo said.

"What do you suggest, Myo?" Jii asked.

"I suggest you let your ninja neutralize the Fox Gang."

"Excellent suggestion," Yoshi said. "How many do you think it will take?"

"We have ten rotating on the watch team now. We also have five more trailing their deliveries to try to locate their stronghold. I will need an additional six to neutralize their sentries," she said.

"They have sentries?" Jii asked.

"Not in the manner you are used to, Jii-sama," she said, and then saw the look of surprise on Hideki's face. "I mean Yoshinobu-sama," she corrected.

"That is quite all right, Myo. I am the old man here and in this household, I wear the title with pride. You may call me Jii," he said kindly.

Myo bowed, "Domo Jii-sama."

"Continue with your exceptional planning," Jii said.

"Hai! The sentries are in disguise. A peddler sells children's pinwheels and small dolls. He moves his stall up and down the street during the day. They also have a tinker who sets up a stall to repair pots and kitchen items. At night, a noodle vendor sets up across the street. They also have a boatman taking fares with his water taxi in the evenings. In addition, there is a more traditional sentry on the roof across from the Daiwa at all times.

"If we go in the evening, I will use a three-man infiltration team to eliminate their sentries. The same team will then take a position as a blocking force to preclude reinforcement and stop escape. We will then gain entry with a ten-man team. Three will carry tools to make the entry covertly, and seven will deal with the sleeping Foxes."

"Remember Myo, I need prisoners," Hideki interjected.

"I will attempt to capture some for you, Hideki, but can make no guarantees. Unless we have complete surprise, they may take their own lives," she replied.

"Will there be samurai in the daiwa?" Jii asked.

"We have seen none."

"There is always a possibility of a yojimbo," Nichi said.

Jii began issuing instructions. "Hideki and Jubei will accompany Nichi's group. Musashi, I would prefer if you stayed here with Naga and myself. It never pays to put all your eggs in one basket with these vermin."

"Hai," Musashi said.

"Where do you want me, Jii-sama?" Yoshi asked.

"Myo works for you. You go where you think best," Jii said.

"Excellent."

"Daylight or dark?" Myo asked.

"Naga's point about casualties is appropriate," Jii said, "but I've found it best to leave the details to the men executing the plan, or in this case, the woman. What do you say, Myo?"

"We favor the dark," Myo said.

"Very well. What time?" Jii asked.

"The hour of the Tiger is good." Myo said indicating three o'clock in the morning. "Most are in deep sleep by then," she said.

"Nichi," Myo said, turning to the yoriki, "do not storm the daiwa until we have eliminated the sentries and captured the Fox wing. I would prefer it if you stayed away until I signal you."

"What will the signal be?" Nichi asked.

"I will torch several boats in the adjacent yard. This will cause a distraction. The Yamakai will rise to extinguish the fire as they own the boatyards."

"Excellent work, Myo. That was a masterful plan well-briefed. What do you require from us?" Jii asked.

"Nothing Jii-sama. The Five Families will handle their part. Please inform your men that we will be in black clothing and are allies."

Jii glanced at his scribes before continuing. They

appeared to have caught up. "Hideki, you will take control of the ground element with Nichi. Jubei, you go with Hideki in case they meet samurai. I want our injuries at a minimum."

Roku did not like coming to this compound. They always mistreated him. They would laugh at him. They would spit on him. They would beat him with sticks. They would never touch him. They walked in the world of humans. Roku walked with the animals.

Every day he would start out from his little shack on the canal and push four huge, wooden barrels in his pushcart to the area of Surug-machi, to the wealthy merchant homes and a few warehouses. There he would patiently wait at the back gate. Eventually, he was admitted to the latrines. He would ladle the night soil into small buckets and transfer them into one of the four huge barrels on his cart. The work was tiring and the smell indescribable, but Roku did not mind. He was happy to have the work. His mother and two younger sisters needed the money he earned from hauling the human waste to the night soil barges on the canal. Like most eta, Roku's family went hungry three nights a week. Roku had been hungry for as long as he could remember.

Roku was an eta. He was the lowest of the low. If he even cast a shadow on a samurai, he could die. His whole sixteen years had been one of taunting and ridicule and exclusion. The only learning he would ever get was at the hands of his parents. He had never had any friends except when they briefly lived in an eta colony on Tsuda-shima Island. He could not talk to anyone except another eta, and he had managed a full repertoire of grunts and mumbles to convey understanding in the world of humans.

His father had managed to find a job preparing bodies for burial in the temple. Only an eta could do such a task as only they were lowly enough that the spirits surrounding the dead would not take notice. He only saw his father on Sundays. The family needed two steady jobs. His mother could not take in sewing or washing like other destitute women. What humans would let an eta touch their clothes?

Roku had salvaged an old, abandoned night-soil pushcart

and cleaned and repaired it. Now when his mother and two sisters would get calls to retrieve and bury dead bodies, they had the tools necessary to accomplish the job. The deceased was usually a loner with no family, ronin too slow with his blade, a diseased labor coughing to death, a low-level prostitute or other flotsam and jetsam that Edo coughed up onto the dirt streets. All were his mother's clients.

Innkeepers were the best customers. They had to get the dead body out of their inn before it began to stink and hurt business. Therefore, if the dead person was traveling alone, Roku's mother and sisters were alerted. They would take a single tatami mat from their shack floor and place it on the pushcart. Atop the mat two picks and one shovel rode. Lastly, a former canvas sail, folded and placed atop the tools, would complete their inventory. Then off the three would go.

Roku's mother would never enter the building until she was paid. The going price for removal and burial was two copper coins. The miserly proprietor or innkeeper would always hassle, trying to get the price down, but Roku's mother never budged. She could wait. They had no place to go. The dead body would just get riper with age. Time was on her side.

Eventually the innkeeper, cursing and swearing, would throw two copper coins at her. Once paid, she took the canvas, and tatami mat into the room of the dead. She would wrap the body in the canvas and the girls would place it on the tatami mat. Her daughters would take front and she would lift the back of the tatami. The corpse rode in the pushcart to the cemetery.

Once away from prying eyes, Roku's mother would go over every inch of the corpse's body, looking for money or anything valuable. She knew the innkeeper would have torn the inn's room apart looking for his rent, but they would not check the body as no one would dare defile themselves by touching a corpse. Even staying in the same room without purification by a priest was risky.

Sometimes, a well-meaning passerby in the cemetery would give her money to ensure proper burial and a priest. Roku's mother took their money with a series of appreciative grunts. Then the girls would use the picks and shovels to dig a deep circular hole. Roku's mother would then back the pushcart to the edge of the hole and elevate the handles upward. One of her daughters would hang onto the canvas as the body slid out. If she aimed it correctly, the feet hit in the center of the hole; then the knees would collapse; then the waist and lastly the upper torso and head would lean left or right just short of the rim of the grave. While she and one daughter filled in the grave, the other daughter would steal a small jizo from another grave and leave it as a marker for the fresh one. If anyone asked, a reputable priest chanted the proper prayers. Of course, she pocketed the entire extra for herself and family. She was no fool.

Therefore, when the man met Roku along his route, Roku listened. He talked to Roku as if Roku was a human. Better yet, he offered Roku more than two years wages.

Roku was no fool either. He knew the man planned to do something bad in the compound, but he did not care. The men inside the compound were evil. He hoped that something bad would happen to them. Besides, he needed the job, and he did not want to lose it. The man explained in detail what he needed and how Roku's part would never be known.

What convinced Roku was the man showing him the money. It amounted to a gold ryo, which was a fortune. What amazed Roku was the man's consideration. The money in a leather pouch was in copper bu. The man explained that if Roku received a gold coin he could not buy anything, as someone would take it from him. Etas were not supposed to have gold coins. Someone would accuse him of stealing. But copper coins amounting to a gold coin, if spent sparingly, assured his family need not go hungry.

Then the man had Roku remove his soiled and ragged top while he helped him strap the purse to his waist with leather strips. This way his treasury would always be with him. If he sat it down anywhere, he might lose it to thieves. That was good information, but Roku could not get over the fact that the man actually touched him while tying the leather strips. A human was touching him and talking to him as if he were human himself. His mother would never believe this. However, she would believe the money.

So Roku agreed to the man's proposition, and in an empty warehouse on the canal, the man walked around the night-soil caskets on Roku's pushcart, knocking on the outside of each. When he had found the one that seemed most full, he unslung a black canvas bag and took out a black ninja costume, complete with boots, gloves, pants, a top, and a hood that covered the entire head. These he donned over street clothes. Then the man went back into the black bag and extracted a small wooden bucket. He removed the watertight top and began pouring oil all over his clothing. Within a few moments, his cloths were soaked in heavy whale oil.

Next, the man hopped up onto the pushcart and opened the lid of the full night soil barrel. The stench was overpowering, and Roku saw him turn his head away. Then he stepped into the large barrel and lay down as best he could. A small breathing reed broke the surface of the brown liquid. By prior arrangement, Roku lowered the lid into place.

Roku was not sure he wanted to be human. Humans did some very strange things. Nevertheless, the man was paying for this. All Roku had to do was to complete his route. When they were alone in the compound, Roku would cough. The man would get out, strip off the nasty outer garments, place them inside the barrel again. and Roku would be on his way.

Roku was under no illusion that the money would turn his life around, but it might keep his family a little less hungry the next year. In an eta's life, that was a turnaround.

Roku coughed and Yoshi climbed up out of the stench and clinging ooze. He stripped off his oil-soaked garb, retrieved his sword from the black canvas bag, and placed the filthy ninja garb inside the barrel. Then he retrieved a vile from the black canvas bag his mother-in-law had provided and liberally doused himself. In a few moments, he smelled like a pine tree on a honey-bucket barge.

The boatman poled his narrow barge to the dock. A young woman and her henpecked husband stepped into the prow of his vessel and settled themselves onto one of the seats.

"That will be three bu," the boatman said.

"You pay the man, husband. I'm sure I don't want to traipse around this filthy boat," she said.

"A shrew," the boatman thought. "If I was married to her, I would have to beat her once a day just to remind her of her place."

"Well, go on. We do not have all night. If it were not for your incompetence, we would have been home by now. Pay the man!" She commanded.

The downtrodden husband nodded his head and reached for his pipe and tobacco. She was having none of it. She batted the pipe out of his hand and overboard into the canal. "Do as I tell you. Pay the man!"

The husband watched the sinking pipe for a moment and sighed. Then he turned slowly back to his wife and backhanded her. She let out a loud yelp as her head snapped to the right at the resounding smack and collapsed in the bottom of the boat.

The boatman laughed aloud. "Aieii, by the Buddha, she had that coming."

The husband stood and moved toward the boatman to pay the fare. He reached under his tunic, but instead of the purse, produced a razor sharp tanto and thrust the knife into the ribs of the unsuspecting boatman. Then the husband collected the pole from the dying hands of the boatman and removed the boatman's wide straw hat and top tunic, letting the lifeless body of the dead boatman slipped into the canal's depths. Myo stayed in the bottom of the boat where she reversed her kimono to reveal ninja garb. No words were necessary. One sentry was.

It was the hour of the ox, about three o'clock in the morning. The streets were quiet. Myo had received the signal from the roof across the street as the last guard died. The hard part came next. She had the choice of entry from the roof or through one of the large doors. She had been down these halls and into the sleeping quarters previously, so she knew that there were no nightingale floors.

She sent one man into the overhead anyway, just to

321

cut off that avenue of retreat. Her five two-man teams were stacked in the hallway outside the sleeping quarters of the Foxes. One man held the sliding door still while another poured oil into the grooves at the bottom and along the side. Once liberally lubricated, the man holding the door slid it open enough to allow entry. One by one on padded tabi, black-clad ninja entered the room. They silently placed themselves beside the sleeping figures. Each was carrying the straight, ninja short sword. They simultaneously raised it above the sleeping targets. Standing at the entrance to the room, Myo noticed one of her men had no one to kill. Six Foxes slept here, but one futon was empty. She nodded and five Foxes died, swords plunged into their hearts.

Once completed, Myo signaled the next phase. She and her team moved to the back of the warehouse and two moved to the boat yard to start a fire. Once the fire was blazing, she sent her men back into the shadows. She remained hiding in the overhead, wanting to see how Hideki handled this portion of the plan. If she were honest with herself, she wanted to be close by so she could help him if need be.

This was a new emotion for her. She was supposed to be a professional. She planned the job and she executed the job; she should be long gone. However, something about this boy aroused her. True, the sex was good, but sex was a tool. Was their relationship good for the Five Families? Maybe that is why her father was not prying into the relationship. She was not thinking with her head. Thinking with her heart usually meant doom for a ninja. She started to turn and leave. Then she stopped. She would wait for Hideki.

She knew she would have to face Hideki's disappointment at not having a prisoner. However, once she was in the hall outside the sleeping quarters, she knew capture was too risky. The missing man bothered her. Had he escaped? Was he bringing reinforcements? She needed to wait and be prepared to help Hideki with her own reinforcements. She could not be troubled by prisoners. Five dead Foxes. That should at least please Naga and that old bastard Hanzo, she thought.

Nichi's men came on the run. The ten Yamakai-gumi

were in various stages of undress fighting the blaze. While
there were many dangerous things that lurked in the Edo night,
fire was the most terrifying. The wood and paper construction
combined with live flame (the main source of illumination)
coupled with overpopulation in a small area ensured fires
usually resulted in the loss of many buildings and much life.
That is why in the evening hours each community had a fire
watchman who walked through the streets clacking two blocks,
calling out the hour, and reminding everyone to put out all
flames. To fall asleep with a candle still burning often ended in
tragedy.

Nichi divided his men into two groups. One element
dashed into the boatyard and began arresting the men in the
midst of their firefighting act. The other half broke into the
main door on the canal street and made for the second-story
sleeping quarters. Hideki went with this group; Jubei went
with the group in the boatyard. Hideki did not have to utter
a command. Nichi led flawlessly. It was over in a matter of
minutes with all Yamakai on the ground and tied.

The timing was perfect. The Edo fire brigade that had
responded to the sighting of fire met the boatyard police.
Nichi seized the initiative by yelling to the battalion fire chief
his name and position and the fact that they had just captured
the arsonist. That was enough for the firefighters. The chief
grunted his approval at such swift work and proceeded to put
out the fire. Nichi had the captives marched to jail.

Hideki congratulated Nichi and his men, and Nichi
excused himself and entered the large warehouse to ensure
they had missed no one. Jubei returned and asked if anyone
had ventured into the Fox den in the adjacent building. No one
had, so he and Jubei went up the stairs to see the results of
Myo's work.

"Why did she have to kill them all?" Hideki asked.

"Maybe she had no choice," Jubei replied.

"There is always a choice, Jubei. We needed a prisoner."

"There is one empty bed. Maybe she captured one."

"Let us hope so," Hideki said. "There is too much at
stake here."

As they climbed down to the first floor, they saw Nichi pointing to a chest and giving commands. The chests were loaded onto a pushcart.

"Spoils of war, Nichi?" Hideki asked.

"Yes, Lord. Most of it will go to the Hatchobori as evidence for the magistrate. However, one chest contained money. Each man will receive a share. If they're going to risk their lives, they should be justly paid."

"Take it up with my brother, Nichi. I am not here to tell you how to run the police. Just be sure your men are not setting a dangerous precedent by taking spoils from innocents," Hideki warned.

"There are no innocents here, Lord," Nichi said.

"Has anyone seen Myo?" Hideki asked.

"She must've done her job. I see no Fox Gang, and the fire was set as planned," Nichi said.

Myo stepped from the shadows. "I am here, Lord."

"Myo," Hideki smiled. "I am glad you are not hurt."

"I am fine, Lord," she said, happy that he seemed genuinely concerned.

"Were you able to collect a prisoner for me?" Hideki asked expectantly.

Myo paused before replying. She was searching for words that might lessen his disappointment. She was opening her mouth to speak when a nearly naked man dropped into their midst on a hemp rope. Hideki leaped back and drew his sword. Jubei did not move, but his sword was magically in his hand. Myo knelt and drew a throwing star. As the man dangled inches off the floor of the warehouse, Yoshi slid down the rope and jumped to the ground at Hideki's feet.

"Greetings, Lord," Yoshi said. "I'm delivering the prisoner as Myo directed."

Hideki sheepishly relaxed and returned his sword. Then he looked at Myo. "I knew you would not let us down."

Myo looked at Yoshi. Yoshi winked at her. Then Myo looked at Hideki and smiled. "We aim to please."

Hideki motioned Nichi over. "Take him to the Hatchobori, but keep him separate from everyone. Let him have no food and no drink. I want to question him myself."

"Yes, Lord," Nichi said as he moved off to get more police.

"Yoshi, you stink," Hideki said. Myo and Jubei stepped back from the smell.

"Why is it Lord, that you get cherry blossoms and I get binjo?" Yoshi asked.

Hideki thought a minute, then replied, "Because I am the Prince of the Yoshinobu and you are a lowly ninja. Besides, I am much better looking than you and the Buddha smiles upon me. Go jump in the water and get some of that stench off. We can't have you going back to the mansion smelling like that!"

The next morning at the hour of the snake, about nine o'clock in the morning, Hideki and Jubei entered the Hatchobori. They walked back to the cell of the Fox ninja. He was tied securely to a post in the center of his cell, sitting on the straw with his arms and hands securely bound behind him. Hideki and Jubei pulled their katana swords from their belts with their left hands and ducked down when entering the open cell door.

"Are you hungry or thirsty?" Hideki asked.

"Thirsty," the ninja said.

Hideki signaled to a guard, and a bucket of water with a ladle was brought and set at the prisoner's feet.

"I will not talk," the prisoner said.

"I do not expect you to," Hideki responded.

With that, Hideki ladled water and brought it to the prisoner's lips. The man did not attempt to drink. Hideki looked perplexed by the man's reluctance.

"He thinks it is poison," Jubei said.

"Oh, I see," Hideki reversed the ladle and took a drink from it himself. Then he offered the rest to the prisoner. This time the prisoner drank long.

"I am still not talking," the prisoner said.

"I know," Hideki said.

"You are wasting your time," he repeated.

"I know," Hideki said.

Outside the cell and several feet away, a doshin turned

to Nichi. "What kind of torture is this?"

"The smart kind," Nichi replied.

Back inside the cell, Hideki asked, "Are you hungry?"

"I could eat," the ninja said.

Hideki signaled and a bowl of steaming rice and several smaller bowls of tofu and pickles in lacquered trays appeared. They were placed at the prisoner's feet. Hideki sat down and picked up the rice bowl.

"I will have to feed you. We cannot let you free to eat. You might escape."

"I still will not talk," the ninja said.

"I understand," Hideki said.

Hideki used chopsticks on the tray and took a mouthful of rice for himself as well as a pickle and some tofu from the bowls. He then cleaned off the ohashi with the cloth from inside his robe and started feeding the prisoner.

"Is it to your liking?" Hideki asked.

"Why are you being so kind to me?" the ninja asked after he swallowed.

"We will discuss that later."

"Who are you?" the ninja asked.

"I am Yoshinobu Hideki. Pleased to meet you."

"Even if you are relatives of the Tokugawa, I will tell you nothing."

"As you wish," Hideki said.

"So why am I getting the nice treatment? I expected to be boiled in oil."

"Because I wanted to have a discussion with you."

"Why?"

"So I could listen to your patterns of conversation and see if I could determine from which part of the country you come," Hideki said.

The ninja scoffed. "And has it worked?"

"Oh yes," Hideki replied. "You are definitely speaking with the Shikoku dialect. You are most likely from Shikoku."

"What of it?" the ninja asked. "There are many people from Shikoku."

"You are correct. There are many people from Shikoku.

However, there are very few in Edo Castle from Shikoku. All I must do now is find them, and I have located a traitor within the government."

The ninja clamped his mouth shut so hard, his teeth clicked.

"You do not want to eat anymore?" Hideki asked. "Well, never mind. I must go to Edo Castle. You try to enjoy the rest of your stay here."

Hideki rose out of a cross-legged sitting position. "Let's go, Jubei. We have some grammar to check."

As they passed Nichi, Hideki addressed him. "No visitors and no torture."

"Yes, Lord, it will be as you say."

"Jubei, who do we know in the castle that speaks with a Shikoku bin?" Hideki asked.

"It is said that O'Fuku does," Jubei replied.

"That is what I remember as well. I remember those calculating eyes, birds on her kimono—and a Shikoku dialect," Hideki said.

Chapter 24: Romancing the Nin

Hideki stopped at the sliding wood-and-paper door.

"Moshiagemasu," he said to announce he was reporting.

From inside the room, Jii responded. "Come in, Hideki. Is Jubei with you?"

"Hai," Jubei said.

Both Jubei and Hideki entered the room. Jubei stopped once inside the threshold, turned around, and slid the door closed behind him. Both men held their katanas inside their protective sayas in their left hands. Once in the room, they bowed to Jii and Naga. Already seated, both Musashi and Yoshi bowed to the two new arrivals.

Jubei and Hideki sat cross-legged in front of Naga and Jii, placing their swords to their left, blades away from the old man.

"So what are you reporting?" Naga asked.

"The results of my interrogation of the Fox prisoner," Hideki replied.

"What did you learn?" Jii asked.

"I learned that the ninja is from Shikoku."

"Is that important?" Jii asked.

"I think so," Hideki replied. Then he turned to Musashi. "Do you remember the young boy we saw on the Tokaido with the goblin mask on his back?"

"Vaguely," Musashi said.

"You told me he was going to the Shinto shrine of Kompira on Shikoku Island."

"I may have," Musashi admitted after a slight pause.

"It is a favorite spot for travelers and locals alike."

"Do you remember what pattern was on the young boy's kimono?"

"I am sorry, Hideki. I do not seem to have your eyes for detail," Musashi said.

"It was a tan color with prints of a brown thrush. I remember it because it has a black hood and a red breast. The bird's habitat is almost exclusively on the island of Shikoku," Hideki said.

"All very enlightening, I am sure, but how does any of this help us?" Naga asked.

Hideki was about to speak when a bird chirped and whistled loudly very close by.

Musashi, Jubei, and Yoshi all reached for their swords.

"Relax! It is not a Fox ninja. I brought this bird with me," Hideki said.

Hideki clapped his hands and a young woman slid back the door, placed the birdcage inside the room, followed it, and closed the door. She picked up the cage, brought it to Hideki and then left the way she had come, having met no one's eyes.

"What is the meaning of this?" Jii demanded.

"Jii, did you see how Musashi, Jubei, and Yoshi reacted to this bird's chirps?"

"Yes, it was disturbing. I thought we might be under attack," Jii said.

"As did they; this bird is why they reached for their swords. They are highly trained swordsman. They reacted subconsciously to the noise they heard when last being attacked. They heard the bird chirps and remembered the Kyoto ambush and the Nihonbashi attack." Hideki pointed to the caged bird. "Here is the culprit; the black headed brown thrush."

"Where did you get it?" Yoshi asked.

"Good question, Yoshi. I found this one at the Ikegami Temple here in Edo. A monk there is something of a bird enthusiast. He takes in sick birds brought in by the followers of the Nichiren sect and nurses them to health. He also imports birds and has a very fine collection as well as a large aviary."

"Is there a point to this, Brother?" Naga asked.

"Yes. He raises black-headed brown thrushes."

Naga lean his head back slightly. "So the leader of the Fox Gang is a Nichiren monk?"

Hideki looked at Naga in surprise and then over to Jii. "Maybe I should be shogun, Grandfather. Naga is obviously too dense."

"Maybe I am too," Jii said. "What is the point?"

"His best customer is O'Fuku of Edo Castle." Now Hideki saw recognition in their eyes.

"Not really proof you could take to the shogun," Naga said.

"No," Jii said. "But it is very fine detective work. How did you ever find this monk?"

Yoshi answered for him. "Nichi."

"Yes," Hideki confirmed. "What use is there to having a smuggler as police chief if you don't use him?"

"Does this help us?" Yoshi asked.

"Yes," Jii said. "Now the enemy has a face."

"But if it is O'Fuku, how did she come to command a defunct ninja sect? She is a highborn samurai," Naga said.

"Not necessarily, my lord," Musashi interjected. "Remember what the shogun's wife said of O'Fuku? She inferred O'Fuku to be a person of low birth."

"You are right Musashi. I had forgotten," Hideki said.

"But she need not be low born," Jubei said. "My father has directed the Iga ninja for years, and he is a samurai."

"True, Jubei. My own fiancée was trained as a ninja and she is wellborn," Naga added.

"Well done, Hideki. I believe we now know who the enemy is," Jii said, "but doing something about it will be a different matter entirely."

"Yes, and we better do something about it very soon," Naga said. "I am due back in front of those vultures at the end of this week. We better get some evidence soon."

"Well, either we will have it or we won't," Jii concluded. Then he changed the subject, "How goes the training?"

"Nichi is working his forty-five men very hard," Hideki

replied. "Bringing them to the Yoshinobu compound to practice every day turned out to be a good idea. Not only do they get away from the prying eyes of the city, but the close proximity to Naga has made them feel special, almost as if they were retainers of the Yoshinobu."

"I've noticed they practice with enthusiasm," Naga said.

"Again, you have to congratulate Nichi. He understands men. Have you seen the juttes?" Hideki asked.

"All of Edo has seen the juttes," Jubei said. "They are the talk of the town."

"What is so special about the jutte?" Jii asked. "It is a tool."

"I would've thought so too, Jii-san," Hideki acknowledged. "But Nichi had all of them taken to a swordsmith and each one has been polished and burnished until it gleams in the sunlight like a shimmering lake."

"Well, I suppose it improves a man's self-worth if he has a good shiny weapon," Jii admitted.

"Nichi didn't stop there," Hideki continued. "He paid for a bundle of red silk cord. He then paid the women in the carpet-weaving guild to wrap the handles of each jutte in the special bright-red, silk cord. He told his men he wanted their actions as bold as the red color. He promised them they will be proud to be recognized as members of the 'Red Sticks.'"

"That is interesting, but surely a shiny red jutte isn't going to make a difference," Naga said.

"But it does, Brother. Two weeks ago, these men were ronin; worse, they were Gumsumgumi. They were outside of society. Now they have purpose and a place in the world again. Nichi had the weavers weave tokens into the red silk. A man's rank is reflected in which token he has woven in the silk handle," Hideki explained.

"Does such a little thing make that much of a difference?" Naga asked.

"It does, Lord," Musashi said. "Men set much store by little things. When they are recognized as part of the team, they identify with the team and work harder for it."

"Yoshi also provides a unique brand of motivation," Jubei noticed.

Yoshi looked at Jubei dumbly. "I'm afraid I do not know what you mean, Jubei."

Hideki chuckled and Musashi smiled. Naga and Jii's countenance said they wanted an explanation, which Jubei offered. "Your ninja master was conducting the class on disarming and incapacitating an armed opponent with the jutte. The class did not comprehend the technique. They were not concentrating and generally disinterested. Yoshi was starting to become disgusted when a young, pretty girl, with an arm full of wet laundry and her kimono tucked into her belt, happened through the training yard on the way to the wash stones. Several of the less studious of the doshin made whistles at her and commented on her bare ankles. Yoshi seized a teaching opportunity and called the young girl over. He explained the technique was so simple that he could teach it to this young girl and she would be able to execute it on anyone present."

"Interesting," Jii said.

"Yes, it changed the dynamic of the instruction. Now everyone was interested," Jubei said.

"What happened?" Naga demanded.

"Yoshi taught the pretty girl one technique and then asked for volunteers. Everyone volunteered, hoping to show off in front of the girl and the several female onlookers the spectacle had drawn," Jubei said. "Yoshi chose the largest man to strike the young woman. The large doshin raised his heavy bokken high above his head and charged the girl, screaming a war cry."

"Don't tell me he killed the girl," Jii said.

"No, Lord, he did not. The young woman executed the parry by placing her right hand high, with the handle raised and the blade of the jutte pointed downward, as Yoshi had taught her. As the bokken impacted the jutte, the wooden sword's motion deflected down the length of the jutte, to the right and away from the girl. As the bokken missed her and the attacker was off-balance, she rotated the jutte up and struck the attacker on the top of the head. His violent forward motion provided all the power. He collapsed into the dirt and did not wake up for several moments. Once revived, Yoshi asked if anyone else wanted to try it. No one did. Then Yoshi introduced the laundry maid as his wife. While there were grumblings about being tricked, they quickly understood the lessons of the exercise."

"And those lessons were?" Naga asked.

Jubei turned to Yoshi and allowed him to explain.

"Number one, never disrespect my wife," Yoshi said.

"A very valuable lesson Sensei," Jii concurred.

"Number two, that anyone, no matter their strength, can execute these techniques, and that they do work."

"Another good lesson," Naga agreed.

"And probably the most important lesson of all ... " Yoshi began.

"Never judge a warrior by outward appearances," Hideki, Musashi, and Jubei answered in unison.

Yoshi gave them a disgusted look. "Yes, nothing is as it seems. Be ready for anything. Their number one goal is to return to their families when their patrol is over. They can only do that if they are alert to danger at all times."

Jii laughed. "I would say they are getting the best training available anywhere in the country. They should be ready."

Naga grunted his agreement. "We have to have all sixty ready by my visit at the end of the week."

"They will be ready, Brother," Hideki said. "I shall accompany Nichi to the Gumsumgumi for the last fifteen tonight. They will be here tomorrow afternoon to commence their training."

"How are the rest of the Gumsumgumi taking the defection of their leader to the police?" Naga asked.

"I think there is some grumbling," Hideki said. "But I will know more tonight."

"Very well," Jii said, rising. "Continue the training. I have tea with Yoshi's mother-in-law."

Everyone smiled and bowed as Jii departed.

"You had better be careful, Yoshi. You will have a samurai in the family," Hideki said, barely hiding a smile.

Yoshi shook his head. "Don't even think such a thing. The shame would be unbearable."

Everyone chuckled as they rose and departed.

Hideki enjoyed the twice-daily workout he got with the jutte. He reveled in the instruction from Musashi, Jubei, and Yoshi. He soaked up everything he saw. His youthful speed and unusual coordination allowed him to mimic and internalize all around him.

His instructors took pride in his accomplishments. By the end of the first week, he was the best student. He excelled in disarming and takedown techniques. However, put a jutte in his right hand and anything in his left—a fan, a tanto, or a short sword—and his technique became genius. While everyone marveled at his expertise, Musashi smiled. He knew that Hideki had discovered the fan and jutte combination was just a variation of the countless hours of instruction in his own brand of swordsmanship, Niten Ichi Ryu. In Two Swords, One Mind School, Hideki had discovered the techniques were the same with two swords as with any other two weapons. The two swords were not the basis of the techniques. The key was the man wielding them.

Musashi did not show it, but he was very proud of Hideki. His youthful exuberance and natural athletic skill combined with his ability to internalize something after seeing it only once were an instructor's dream. Now Musashi knew that his style of fighting would survive at least one more generation. He felt his life choices had meaning. He felt vindicated.

The attacker raised a wooden sword skyward. He lunged forward, bringing the hardwood blade down toward the target—Hideki's head. Only Hideki was not there. He pivoted slightly and the arc of the blade barely missed his head. As the attacker's blade passed his body, Hideki used his left hand, the one holding the folded fan, to swat the descending blade to the left. This made the attacker's body travel in that direction and opened up the area between the man's neck and head as a target. The jutte in Hideki's right hand lightly tapped this vulnerable area. The attacker grinned. Had this been real, he would have been unconscious or dead.

Hideki is in his prime, Musashi thought. He will get stronger and more experienced, but he will never be faster than he is now. It would be fulfilling to watch him grow and handle the challenges of manhood. However, Musashi knew his time with the Yoshinobu was at an end. How Hideki handled the challenges of life would measure him as a man. Would he accept the challenges head-on and maintain a straight path, or would he bend from the way that was Bushido?

"I'd love to stay and help him," Musashi thought. "but everyone must tread his own path. I have given him as much as I can."

Musashi looked at Jubei, who was working with Hideki. Jubei would be good for him. He was much closer in age to Hideki, and he seemed dedicated to Hideki's growth. They appeared to get along. Musashi wondered if a man like Jubei had ever had a friend before. "Oh well, not my problem. My time is about up. I must start my journey again," he silently reminded himself.

Hideki looked across the barge at Nichi. Both he and Myo sat on one side of the narrow vessel with Nichi on the opposite side. Even so, the vessel listed toward Nichi's side. Hideki was tired from the day's training and looked forward to food and a hot bath.

"Will the rest of the police be at training tomorrow?" Hideki asked.

"Yes, I will swear in the new men tonight and they will join their brothers tomorrow," Nichi replied.

"How are the Gumsumgumi taking this?"

"About as you would expect. Some think it is a betrayal. Some think it a great honor," Nichi said. "I take it you two will be spending the evening at the inn?"

Hideki looked at Myo and blushed. Myo just smiled.

"Your red face tells me all I need to know. Be careful you two. I think you should find somewhere else for your assignations. Goro is no friend of yours, Hideki, and my stripping the Gumsumgumi of some of their best for the police force has especially soured him of late."

Myo spoke up. "Surely Goro would not harm us."

"I don't want to take any chances," Nichi said.

"That is wise, Nichi," Hideki said. "I will find somewhere else to rest."

Later, they gathered in the great room of the Gumsumgumi hotel. Hideki watched as twenty-five men took the oath as brand-new police officers. "Looks like Naga will be getting ten extra policemen," he observed.

"Nichi thought it better to plan for attrition early," Myo said.

"Nichi keeps surprising me. I must remember that he is very intelligent."

"That would be a wise precaution," Myo affirmed. "Underestimating him has been the downfall of several of his enemies."

"I am not an enemy. Nichi is tied more tightly to the success of my family than am I," Hideki said.

"How can that be?"

"Nichi is the key to Naga's success. If this police experiment works, Naga will be a hero. He will have replaced a corrupt police force with one tied to the people," Hideki explained.

"But it was your idea," she complained.

"Yes, but for the plan to work, Nichi must execute it. Without Nichi, we will all have failed."

Myo nodded her head. "Yes, I see. I am attuned to the vibrations of survival in Edo and on the land, but the politics of the castle confound me."

"You are confounded only because you are not used to them. Given time you would master them as well."

Myo smiled. She liked the compliment. "Would you like a bath?" she asked.

"The last time I bathed here an exotic beauty shared the water with me," he teased.

"If you behave, that could be arranged again," she said.

Hideki looked at her and realized he was happy. He was doing what he was born to do with great friends to help him. Then there was this beautiful, free-spirited, deadly woman in front of him who had introduced him to the joys of the flesh. When he was with her, he was happy. When she was away, he felt a piece of himself missing. Was such a feeling the mysterious "ai" that Jii valued so highly? He did not know. However, he would be careful of how he spoke of it and with whom. He did not want to do anything to jeopardize the feeling.

Hideki and Myo returned from the evening bath wearing the thin yukata kimono. They were both sweating from the liquid heat. Myo was rolling out the futon on the tatami when she tensed and reached under the bedding for a tanto. Hideki saw the motion and grasped his katana from the rack at the head of the futon.

"Gomen," the voice said.

"It is Nichi," Myo whispered to Hideki. "He is alone."

"Hai," Myo said as she moved to the opposite side of the small room.

The door slid back and the impossibly large bulk of Nichi filled the space. He bent down and stepped in.

"My apologies, but things are worse than I feared. Goro is holding a grudge against you, and I do not want you to stay here any longer than necessary. Please gather your things. I will accompany you back to the police station. At least there, I know you'll be safe."

"Nichi, I should be able to protect myself from Goro, even as large as he is," Hideki said.

"What do you mean, Oyabun?" Myo asked, ignoring Hideki's boast.

"I have seen some strange faces around. They dress like Gumsumgumi and even act like Gumsumgumi, but they are not Gumsumgumi," Nichi replied.

"Ninja?" Myo asked.

"I don't know for sure, but I don't want to take any chances."

"What does Goro have to do with ninja?" Hideki asked.

"He should have nothing to do with ninja," Nichi said, "unless he's been drawn into some political intrigue. My guess would be the Yamakai."

"You fear an alliance?" Myo asked as she placed the last

weapons into her kimono and tied an obi in place around her middle.

Hideki thrust both swords into his obi and took a last look around. They were ready to leave. Myo slid back the door and entered the main passageway.

"Goro feels threatened. His world has turned upside down. Instead of seeing the opportunity for the Gumsumgumi, all he sees is a threat. It would not surprise me if he wants to cement a relationship with the world he knows. But his hate for you, Hideki, is almost palpable," Nichi explained.

They clung to the shadows of the dark, dirt streets. However, it is hard to hide a sumotori. "There is someone running back to the hotel," Myo said.

"Probably a spy Goro posted to keep an eye on the exit we used," Nichi guessed.

"Then we should hurry to the boat landing," Hideki suggested.

"You hurry, Hideki. Retired sumo wrestlers don't hurry."

"Then we will hurry with you," Hideki said as he and Myo slowed to match Nichi's lumbering pace.

They had not gone twenty paces when Myo stopped.

"What do you hear Myo?" Nichi asked.

"I hear many people paralleling our path."

Both Hideki and Nichi looked to the left and right at the side-streets and row after row of buildings for as far as the eye could see.

"You will not find them there," she said, and then pointed up.

"They are on the roofs?" Hideki asked.

"Yes, and they are not used to our construction methods. They keep tripping over loose boards and rocks used as weights. As ninja go, they are not very adept."

Hideki looked at Nichi and Myo.

"Nichi, we must separate. It has to be the Fox Gang. They are after me," he said.

"I cannot abandon you," Nichi said.

Hideki raised his voice slightly. "Nichi, you must. The

Yoshinobu future depends on your success with the police force. If you cannot get the police force replaced, trained, and operational, Naga is doomed. Onagai, depart from us," Hideki insisted.

"I don't like it," he said. "But I will obey."

"Myo, you go with him," Hideki said.

"Nonsense, I am entrusted with your protection," she said.

"I cannot bear the thought of you being harmed," he said.

Myo felt her eyes misting slightly. "Nothing will happen to me," she said. Myo turned to Nichi, "Go now, and alert Yoshi to our plight."

Nichi bowed and began his lumbering walk to the boat ramps.

"What is our best tactic?" Hideki asked.

"The ones on the roofs are not adept. But the ones on the ground are," she speculated.

"There are ninjas on the ground?" Hideki asked as he swept streets again.

"Someone has to be trailing us and guiding the roof rats," she said.

"Do we try to hide in a building?"

"I do not believe so. I think we let them think they have caught you unawares in the open in the deserted streets," she said.

"I'm not sure I like that plan," Hideki said.

"Don't be such a baby," she chided. "As you fight them here I will be eliminating the adept ones and thinning the odds."

"You be careful. I like having you around," he said.

"Good," she said and moved to the building face and climbed it, disappearing onto the roof.

Hideki moved to the center of the street and drew both swords. They came at him from two sides. Five came from one side of the street and four from the other. They quickly surrounded him with swords drawn.

"We do not wish to kill you, samurai. Lay down your

swords and come with us. You will not be harmed," a distinct feminine voice said from behind a Fox mask.

"Your past encounter with Tokugawa family members leaves me less trustful of your words than I might be otherwise. I have a better idea," Hideki said. "Why don't you come and get them."

The Fox masks snapped toward the direction of a loud scream in the darkness. They quickly snapped back to refocus on Hideki.

"I guess you are one less," Hideki mused.

The circle around Hideki was just out of his sword range. As the brown-clad Foxes started moving counterclockwise around him, he lowered his right sword hand and let the tip of the katana almost touch the dirt to his front. A Fox behind him let his anxiety get the better of him and lunged with his ninja sword for Hideki's back. Hideki reversed the katana in his right hand and, without looking, struck backwards into the chest of the attacker. He pulled his sword out and reversed the sword back to his front without moving his head. He fought the adrenaline rushing through his body. He must remain relaxed.

"The final state of any discipline is where you forget what you have learned, discard your mind, and accomplish whatever you set out to do without being aware of it yourself. You begin by learning and reach the point where learning does not exist," Hideki mumbled to himself. It sounded like one of Musashi's teachings, but it was not. He had learned this from Jubei. He found comfort in it now. He moved into mushin or "no mind." Nothing existed but himself, the enemy, and his swords.

Hideki's concentration broke as another loud scream came from the dark. The circle slowed, looking for the cause of the screams.

"That is two less," Hideki remarked. Then he charged into the figures directly in front of him by inside strikes with both swords. He cut into flesh and bone and heard cries as he pushed through them and onto the closed entrance of the building. As soon as he was there, he spun and placed his back to the wall. The seven followed him and stopped.

Now they could not surround him. One on his right, a Fox, returned his sword to his saya on his back and reached into his brown jacket. Before he could remove whatever weapon he was attempting to retrieve, he crumpled forward into the area between Hideki and his attackers. Protruding from the base of his skull was a long iron dart with a red tassel hanging from it.

"Three less," Hideki said as he took advantage of their shock and rotating heads to completely decapitate a short Fox that moved too slowly. Hideki had a feeling that he had just killed a woman but could not dwell on it. Three charged him at once.

He used the short sword in his left hand to parry two attackers into the third as he pushed all three to the right then with his katana in his right hand executed a neck-high horizontal strike, attempting to sever the throats of all three just below the mask. He missed the first, but cut the throat of the second and a fine mist of blood showered him. He opened the face of the third at the jawbone sending the Fox mask flying. There were only two left. Hideki moved forward and backed the remaining foxes into the street. Now the open area would favor him.

The two remaining Foxes looked at each other and then at Hideki. They did not like the odds, and they still did not know what was killing their brothers in the darkness beyond.

"You left two for me," Myo said. "How sweet!"

The Foxes spun away from Hideki and toward the voice behind them. No one was there.

They both fled in opposite directions leaving Hideki alone in the street.

Hideki flicked his katana down and to the right to clean off any lingering blood and gore. It was then returned to its saya. He reached into his kimono top and extracted a sheet of white paper. He placed the back of the short sword blade onto the paper and wiped the blood from it. He then discarded the paper into the street. The short sword returned to its scabbard.

"How did you get them to scream? Never mind, I don't want to know," Hideki said.

Myo appeared from a dark corner of the building. "Squeamish?" she asked.

"I just don't want to think of you as being that cruel," he said.

"I am not your normal female, you know that."

"Yes and I am very grateful. This is the third time I have fought the Foxes and each time friends have saved me. This time I owe you my life," Hideki said.

"Good, then your life is mine to do with as I please," she teased.

Hideki smiled. "I suppose so. Just be gentle with me."

Myo was about to reply to that when her impish countenance changed to one of dread.

"What is it?" Hideki asked.

"We are threatened again, but not by beginners this time," she said.

"How do you know?" he asked.

"Because they are upon us and I did not hear them," Myo said, reaching into her sleeve for a shuriken.

Two fox-masked ninjas dropped silently to the street beside him. Hideki drew his sword, parried the strike of one, and darted to his left, dodging the lunge made by the other's sword. From his peripheral vision, he saw Myo fade back into the shadows of the buildings and hoped she would flee.

The two new ninjas were closing on him fast and they were not novices. They struck in unison and without any indication of their movements. He was so busy with these that he did not have any indication that others were approaching him from behind.

He was in mid-swing of his katana when a heavy rope net fell down upon him from behind. It knocked him forward. He stumbled and tried to regain his balance but could not get his weapon up in time. He knew he was going to die in an Edo street. Something hard struck his head, and he saw bright flashes as he fell to his knees. He thought of Myo as all went black.

Chapter 25: Capture

Myo listened from the rafters above the ceiling. The Council of the Yoshinobu was trying to come up with a course of action. They could not agree on what to do because there was little they could do. Myo had already decided what she was going to do. She was hiding in the rafters to determine if any of Hideki's clan and friends was smart enough to arrive at the same course of action. If they did, she would have to act in haste. No matter how well intentioned, they did not have the skill to execute such a plan. Only she had the resources.

Yoshi worried her on two levels. The first was his ability to see in the darkness. He might discover her intentions. Secondly, he might consider himself capable of executing her plan. She had to admit—he was capable. Capturing the Fox during the raid had saved them all. She had not realized how important the prisoner was at the time or how important he was now. But Yoshi also lacked the resources to accomplish her plan.

She listened to the handwringing and anger below. Musashi wanted to kidnap O'Fuku and offer her in exchange for Hideki. Naga explained that such an action would be an attack on the shogun.

Nichi wanted to torture the captured Fox held in the jail at the Hatchobori until he revealed their main hiding place. Jubei injected he would not break, and if he did, there was no guarantee Hideki would be held there anyway.

Jii asked if they must continue under the assumption that

Hideki was lost to them. In the end, they all agreed that they must assume he was dead, and they must proceed accordingly.

Nichi pounded his fat fist on the tatami. "I should have stayed with him."

"No, Hideki was right to order you away," Naga said. "What you can do now is get your police patrolling and hopefully uncover any word of my brother."

"What of Myo?" Jii asked. "Do we assume her demise as well?"

"I think we can assume that Myo is already undertaking a rescue," Yoshi said.

Myo almost fell out of the rafters at Yoshi's comment.

"What do you mean?" Jii asked.

"She is not here. Either she is dead—no one found her body—or she is trailing the Foxes that took Hideki," Yoshi explained.

Myo felt ashamed at Yoshi's comment. Though it had been her intention, the skill of the two Foxes who were sent to delay, detain, and destroy her had been better than she expected. It had taken her vital extra moments to vanquish them. By the time she had returned to the scene of Hideki's fight, only the net and dead Foxes were visible.

Myo moved slowly to a standing position and very carefully retraced her footsteps. She could come and go as she pleased. She was very familiar with the guard's routine. Her only concern lay in Yoshi's unusual skills. His ability to see through the darkness gave her goose bumps. Even with the increased guards and police presence around the Yoshinobu compound, Myo was back in central Edo before the hour turned.

She entered the Abe Courier service building from a secret entrance on the roof. There were several such entrances. This one looked like a barrel of rainwater until you moved a counter weight, disguised as a roofing tile, at the base of the barrel. When shifted, the rain barrel and all its water swung out just enough to let one man or woman pass behind it and into a dark stairway. Once there, Myo stepped down two steps at a time but insured she landed on the middle of the last step. If she got the sequence wrong, spring-loaded crossbows would fire a volley of bolts, peppering the stairs with projectiles. All the secret entrances were equipped with such deterrent devices. A dedicated force might be able to breach their base, but they would pay dearly for it.

She went directly to her room, changed into a lightweight bath kimono, and took a hot bath. After solidifying her plan mentally, she changed into her courier garb and waited outside the main room.

"Shitsurai itashimasu," she said through the closed door, letting the room's inhabitants know that she sought entrance.

"Hai," the old voice said, granting her request.

Myo entered the room and found her father sitting alone with a pipe in his mouth. He appeared to be thinking.

"Oto-san, I need your advice," she said.

The head of the Five Families took the pipe from his mouth and motioned her closer.

Myo moved closer to her father and bowed.

"What can I help you with Daughter?" he asked

"Hideki has been captured by the Fox Gang," she said.

"I have heard," the old man said. "What do the Yoshinobu expect of us?"

"They seem to expect me to be dead or on the trail of the kidnappers."

"It appears neither is the case," he said.

"Yes, Father. I was detained by some very skilled foxes. When I could get away, Hideki was gone."

"Do we know if Hideki lives?" The old one asked.

"We do not. But they used a net, did not retrieve their dead, and there was no blood under the net," she said.

"What advice do you seek?"

"I have a course of action but need your review and consent," she said.

"Are you asking this as the successor to the Five Families or as Hideki's lover?" he asked.

Myo stared directly into her father's eyes. "Both."

"So what is your plan?"

"I want to facilitate the escape of the Fox held captive at

the Hatchobori and follow him with the team to their base and free Hideki," she explained.

"Will the Yoshinobu be privy to your plans?" he asked.

"No," she said. "This will only work if the Fox thinks he has made the escape due to his own skills."

"How many do you need to assist you?" her father asked.

"There are two ways this could be done. The first requires a lot of manpower and time, neither of which are readily available. The plan would be to have bands of our ninja on all the roads leading out of Edo. Besides the manpower and time problem, they would not know what they were looking for.

The second plan requires a special team to deploy at the jail. As soon as the Fox escapes, we track him in teams, passing off the detail as the situation changes and changing costumes as we must. I think five plus myself would be enough," she said.

The old man thought for a while. "I know what I think, but let us see what the family thinks." He clapped his hands.

The wall in the opposite side of the room slid back. "Gomen," several voices said as heads bowed. Five young people filed in, knelt, and bowed again.

"I believe you know these?" The old man asked.

Myo looked into the face of each. She had recognized them when they filed into the room, but now she paid each one a few moments of respect, nodding to each.

"Yes father. I know each of them," Myo said.

"And what is your opinion of each?"

"Each is a promising young shinobi no mono in the family," Myo said. She knew there was more. They were all skilled in the ninja arts, and each was from a high-ranked family in one of the five families. The three women she had known since she was a girl. The two men she had worked with several times.

"And you respect their opinions?" the leader the Five Families asked.

"Yes," she said.

The old man turned to the first young woman. "Ichiko,

you have heard what we discussed. What is your opinion? Should the Five Families undertake such a mission? Or is it the whim of a lover, wanting to protect her mate?"

The small, dark-faced one smiled. Her bright white teeth illuminated her face and offset the dark countenance. "Myo is well respected by all here. She is professional almost to the point of being cold. I do not think she would waste our lives unnecessarily. I would support her," Ichiko said.

The old man nodded to the second female ninja. This one was not smiling. She had a plain face and was considered homely. Her eyes were too close together and she had what the old women called a horse's face. It was too long. "I am Niko. Myo has always been haughty and above us. I was not surprised when I heard she had taken a samurai lover. I am less surprised that he is a Yoshinobu." Then she smiled. "Myo has never done things halfway. If she thinks this is important to the Five Families, it is."

The third female started talking without being asked. "I am Midori. I have known Myo all my life. If she says it is important, I will follow her."

Both male ninja spoke in unison, "to the death."

The old man nodded. "I am in agreement with your team. I think the Yoshinobu are relying on us. If this is the first step in the destruction of their house, we are tied to it. We can only survive if they do. You have my blessing Myo. Execute your plan. This is your team."

Myo bowed to and from her father. She then turned to her team. "Please wait outside for me. We have a lot of work to do."

Myo turned back to her father. "I see what you are doing."

"And what is that?" he asked.

"You have created a team of high-ranked young people, one from each of the five families. If we succeed, we are the saviors of the Five Families. When they go back to their respective families, I will have a stalwart team member willing to support me for succession."

"Is that a good plan?" he asked.

"Yes, there is nothing like combat to forge a team," she acknowledged.

"Then go and make history, Daughter," the old man said.

Myo bowed and departed. She addressed her team in one of the smaller rooms used for planning. "Thank you for your support."

"Have you worked out the freeing of the Fox?" the male ninja with a scar across his left cheek asked. "I think all depends on the Fox thinking he freed himself."

"Sharp as always Chu-san," Myo complimented. "We will use our code names from now on. I will be Kiiro," meaning yellow. She then listed each code name. Ichiko was Aku, or red; Niko was Ao, or blue; Midori was Midori, or green; Chu-san was Cha, or brown; and Koto-san was Kuro, or black.

"I like it," Midori said. "The two men are brown and black, and we women are colorful."

"Read into it what you will," Myo said. "From now on, use only these names. From this moment on, we are people of the grass. Nothing exists for us except this mission."

All five bowed their agreement.

Myo began issuing instructions. "Midori we need you to use your sexy persona to charm the guards at the Hatchobori. The prisoner eats his evening meal at the hour of the rooster. That gives us two hours. They are generally fed the leftovers from the guard's meal, which is prepared by one of the police officer's wives. I have laced her tea with wisteria. She will be sick for the next two days. I recommend you show up as her cousin to prepare the guard's food. They will be too hungry to ask too many questions. You volunteer to take the Fox his meal. If they refuse, use your wiles. You know what to do."

Midori cranked her head, batted her eyes and gave a very sexy smile. "Indeed I do, Kiiro-san. Have no fear."

"Once you are in the cell and feeding him, accidentally drop this hair ornament," Myo said, placing the trinket in Midori's hand. "Like all such shiny trinkets, one side is fairly sharp. If you drop it near him by accident, he will cover it with a portion of his body and use it to cut the ropes."

"What do I do once I serve the meals?" Midori asked.

"Exit and take up location here," Myo said, pointing to a location on the hastily drawn map. "I don't need to tell you to change identities."

"No Kiiro" Midori responded.

"The rest of you will take up locations here, here, and here," Myo said, indicating good observation spots on the map. "I will be here."

Everyone looked at the map and nodded in the affirmative.

"I don't have to tell you that this assignment is important. It is important to me for two reasons. First, the life of a man that I treasure is in the balance. Second, and most important to you, the very life of the Five Families is uncertain. Without the protection of the Yoshinobu, Hittori Hanzo and the Metsuke will hunt us down. I do not know how good this Fox is at going invisible. Some of them are novices, and some of them are as good as we are. Nevertheless, let us enter this mission with the idea that he is very good. I want your best kabuki performances tonight."

To Myo's knowledge, no one had ever actually acted in the kabuki theatre, but the ninja often took roles in lesser places just to keep their acting skills polished.

"I want everyone to have three changes of character ready," Myo said. "We're only six. If he is any good, we will have to be very sharp. Any questions?"

There was no response. "Depart!" Myo said. All stood, bowed, and hustled out.

"Where the hell is that cooking wench?" the chief doshin asked to no one in particular. He was in the cooking area of the Hatchobori. The fire in the sandpit was going strong. He had ordered his guard see to that. Now they were pulling jars of rice from the pantry area. However, that was as far as they could go. They could boil rice. Every foot soldier worth his salt learned that as a youngster. There was a small slab of tofu, green onions, bamboo shoots, a dozen eggs, some spinach, and two long daikon radishes lying on the small cutting table in the corner. They had been since the delivery boy from the grocery around the corner left it as he did each evening.

The doshin had ten guards to feed counting himself—and no one to do the cooking. The regular cook was home ill and her family was tending her. The doshin uttered another curse and reached for the rice. "Don't touch that Mr. Samurai," a feminine voice called. "I bet you haven't washed the rice, the vegetables, or your hands."

The head doshin and six hungry men gawked at the young woman. Their smiles pleased Midori.

"Can you cook?" the doshin asked.

Midori liked the first question. Not, "Who are you?" But, "Can you cook?" These men were hungry. The Buddha was smiling on the Five Families.

"That is what I'm here for," Midori said as she swished her way to the cutting table in her too-tight kimono. "Ooi, samurai just sit back and watch a professional at work." Then she stopped to scan the faces of each and asked, "Is anyone single?"

Several raised their hands. "Don't worry about that, woman. I need to get the guard set, and they need to eat first. How long?" the doshin demanded.

"Is the water boiling yet?" Midori asked.

"Yes," one of the guards said, raising the lid on the black kettle with metal tongs.

"Then if you find me a sharp knife, I will get to work," she complied. "How many men?"

"Ten total," the doshin said.

"Get two to wash their hands and help me wash the rice. They can also help me pour it into the kettle. We will have to wait until it boils down. For ten men, I think thirty minutes will be enough. While the rice is simmering, we will cut the daikon, prepare the miso soup, and drop in the tofu. I will use the eggs and the soy sauce to make a paste to pour over the rice. Then I will add a little seaweed, and we will be eating. Yes, thirty minutes for all," Midori predicted.

For the first time this afternoon, the doshin smiled. "Thank you. I was worried we might be late setting the guard."

"You have nothing to worry about, Mr. Samurai," Midori

said, batting her eyes seductively. "Are you single?"

The doshin dropped his paper roster. "Don't worry about that. Just get us fed. Keep a separate bowl aside," he instructed.

"Oh," Midori said. "Is that your special bowl?"

"No, silly, it is for the prisoner," he said.

"Prisoner," Midori exclaimed. "I have to feed prisoners too? My cousin said I was to feed the guards."

"Don't worry. We only have one prisoner and I counted him in with a ten," the doshin explained.

"Okay," Midori said, appearing unconcerned. "Let's get to work."

As she promised, thirty minutes later, guards slurped miso soup mixed with rice and raw eggs poured over strips of seaweed.

"Woman, this is very good," the doshin exclaimed.

"I have ability," she said, "and did I tell you I was single?"

"You may have mentioned it once or twice," the doshin said. "But you won't be for long when word of your cooking gets out."

Midori blushed on cue and managed a giggle. Now that their bellies were full, the police officers started eyeing her appreciatively. The doshin noticed and decided to nip their attention in the bud.

"Come with me woman. We have to feed the prisoner."

"Oh my! Is he dangerous?"

"Very, he is one of the Fox Gang. But don't worry. He is tied, and I will be there," the doshin said.

"Well, as long as you are there to protect me," she said, "I don't mind." Midori blushed again. Then she retrieved the remaining food, placed it in a bowl along with some tea, and set it all on a lacquered tray. Then she covered the tray to keep it warm. Midori followed the doshin into the bowels of the Hatchobori, her bare feet slapping the hard wood floors.

The doshin stopped at the entrance to the center cell where two guards stood outside the large wooden bars. Midori could see the prisoner in the center of the cell. He was naked except for his loincloth. He was sitting upright with his legs out in front of him. A rope bound his legs together. His arms were tied behind him, and he was lashed to a large post in the center of the cell.

Midori studied the prisoner for a few moments as the doshin asked the guards questions. She was interested in his eyes. They were darting everywhere. She would have to be on her game with this one. He appeared to be a young man. From what she could discern from his appearance, he had not been tortured. She had expected to find him beaten and bleeding. His excellent health could work against their plans. A healthy man was a lot harder to track.

The doshin ordered the guards to report to the kitchen for the evening meal. He and the woman would feed the prisoner. The guards looked approvingly at Midori's face, tight kimono, and bare ankles. They then opted for food instead of exchanging ribald comments about the scullery maid. One passed the keys to the doshin, and then both took off down the dark corridor towards the food.

"Do not get too close to him," he warned.

"Oh Mr. Samurai, surely you tease me. He is all tied up. How is he going to eat if I don't feed him?" she asked.

"Let me check his ropes before you go in," he said. Then opening a small rectangular door and bending over as he entered the cell, the doshin checked the ropes binding the prisoner's hands and feet. Only then did he signal for Midori to enter. Midori bent down and entered the cell, taking offense at the smell with a wrinkled nose. She moved beside the prisoner with her tray, removed the top of the tray, and took out his teacup. Then she placed the lid back on the tray.

"Gomen, Mr. Fox, but I have to feed you because this samurai will not loosen your ropes. Do you wish tea by itself or over your rice?"

The Fox stared into Midori's eyes. "Do you have anything else to go over the rice?" he asked.

Midori broke into a radiant smile. "Yes, I have an egg and soy sauce mixed with some seaweed."

"Then I shall have the tea for later," the prisoner said.

"Excellent Mr. Fox," Midori responded, jerking her head back toward the tray as she did so, which caused her hair ornament fell onto the floor with a slight tinkle.

"Gomen," Midori said, retrieving the ornament and placing it hastily into her hair.

Next, she retrieved the rice, mixed it with soy paste using a clean pair of ohashi eating sticks, and placed a small rectangular section of seaweed onto the mass. Then she closed seaweed around the rice mix with the chopsticks and moved the entire bowl toward the prisoner's lips. She nodded her head to ensure he was ready and lifted the gelatinous mass to his lips. He opened, and took the food, and began to chew.

She chatted away during the whole meal. She talked about nothing and told him he was very good-looking and that she was single. Then she chatted that her cousin was married, but how her mother wanted her to settle down as well, but the prospects were slim. Since she had been at the Hatchobori, she had seen many available men. Maybe her prospects would change. When she had finished holding his tea cup to his lips after the meal, the prisoner looked at the doshin.

"Next time I'll go hungry."

The doshin smiled. "She does get on the nerves, doesn't she?"

As Midori arranged the empty dishes onto her tray, she moved around the prisoner's legs and continued to chatter away as if she had not heard. When the doshin moved toward the small exit, he faced away from the prisoner. She bent and reached for the tray, and her hair ornament fell silently onto the prisoner's legs. He immediately moved his knees apart so that the trinket fell to the floor below his legs and then closed his knees so Midori could not see it had fallen.

Midori rose up and turned toward the prisoner. "Well, it was really nice speaking with you Mr. Fox; I probably won't see you again." She bowed to him and moved to follow the doshin out of the cell. Once in the court, the doshin locked the cell behind her.

"Can you take me back to the kitchen? My cousin would want me to wash these dishes and get everything prepared for breakfast in the morning," she said.

"Follow me," the doshin said.

He and Midori disappeared down the narrow corridor.

An hour later, Midori emerged from the police station and turned down a dark alley. Within moments, she was in the clothing of an Abe Courier and crouched beside Myo. Not a word passed between them; none was needed. The fact that she was there meant all had gone according to plan. Now they must wait for the escape.

Two hours later, a figure clad in the traditional black kimono of a police officer with a red-handled jutte in his obi moved out of the alleyway behind the Hatchobori and onto the street. He looked in all directions before moving. When he did move, he adopted a completely different gate as he sauntered, as any police officer would while making his rounds on familiar ground.

Myo nodded to Midori. The chase was on.

It was late evening, the hour of the dog. Some streets in Edo were barren, and some were bustling. In her Abe Courier clothing, Myo was wearing a blue han-gappa traveling jacket over a light-blue kimono with the hem tucked up into her obi. The coat was loose fitting with wide sleeves and held together by twig-like buttons at the shoulder and waist. The bottom of the coat struck her at mid-thigh. Below the hem of the coat, she wore momohiki underwear tucked into dark blue kyahan cloth gaiters that encased the top of the tabi socks that fit into her waraji straw sandals. A furiwake-nimotsu hung over her shoulder. The cloth covered flat rectangular basket connected by a heavy cloth strap across her back usually containing a straw mat for travelers sleeping in the open. A cloth hachi maki headband wrapped her head. On her forehead, the Abe Courier symbol of a wheel turning advertised on the cloth. In her right hand, she carried the suge-gasa conical straw hat used by travelers to keep out the rain and sun. She was dressed as a traveler. She looked like most everyone traversing the main roads connecting the country.

Myo caught a glimpse of movement to her left. It was Mr. Brown. He knew she was there. However, he made no sign of recognition as he moved along the road that the escaped

Fox Gang member had taken. Mr. Brown was dressed in a kamiko haori, the paper coat favored by commoners.

Myo knew the other members of the team would be on the trail as well. Some would be paralleling the route the Fox was taking, sometimes keeping him in sight and sometimes not, relying on keeping an eye on other team members for course corrections.

Myo realized their target was changing direction often. He was checking his back trail to ensure he had no followers. How wary he was would have a lot to do with how convincing Midori had been as the dizzy, man-hungry, talkative cook. Myo smiled to herself. She marveled at Midori's acting ability. Her trademark character was quite annoying. Her performance must have been good as the Fox quit switching directions and took a western heading.

Now they were moving through the Yoshiwara, the brothel district run by the government. At this time of night, its gates were wide open and the streets bustling. Myo knew that keeping their quarry in sight was going to be difficult. Inside the pleasure quarters, the Fox had the advantage. His police officer costume insured he would not be disturbed in the city, but if he was thinking of changing clothes, the pleasure district would be a good place to do it. All manner of men visited here regularly. Myo signaled Midori to close in and tighten the net.

They tightened it so closely that Myo spotted all five of her team. The Fox disappeared into one of the larger brothels. He did not come up. Midori was closest and wandered over to the fish stall adjacent to the building. Women with painted faces populated the windows and doorways, enticing passersby to come inside. Bouncers hovered around the doorways to keep the peace and to ensure no woman escaped.

Midori had changed her courier garb for that of an Edo housewife. She started to inspect the fish. While she talked to the fish merchant, she inquired of the business. "Not so good today," the young man behind the counter said. He pointed at the fish on the table before him. "It is too bad, because we have sea bream caught fresh today."

Midori conversed with the young man and then with his father. The old man looked worried as he poured fresh water on the fish to keep them from drying out. He also waved a fan over them to keep the flies off. The obviously bored daughter, about Midori's age, eyed every young man as they went by. Midori knew if she lingered any longer, she would draw the interest of the local police. However, she did not want to move as she had the best vantage point to see how and when the Fox emerged.

She knew one of her team would be behind the hotel to ensure he made no exit in that direction. She did not really think that was an option. A high fence surrounded the pleasure district, like many Edo neighborhoods. There was only one gate leading in and out. If the Fox came in here, it was either to contact someone or to change clothes. She was betting on the latter and she needed to remain at the fish stand longer.

"Ogi-san, can I get a discount if I help you sell some of this fish?" Midori asked.

The father winced at being addressed as an old man and was about to answer when Midori moved.

She did not wait for his reply. She tied her hair back and pulled a section of string from the role used to wrap the fish. She put one end of the string between her teeth and the other passed under her left arm over behind her back and under the right arm and then tied the two ends behind her neck. The strain successfully pulled her large kimono sleeves back above her elbows and safely out of the way. Then she grabbed the fish and turned to passersby coming from the brothel next door.

She accosted a merchant as he went by. "Mister, you have enough money to waste on another woman. Why don't you buy this nice fresh fish and take it home to your wife? She will know you've been thinking of her, and it will hide the stench of the whore you were with."

Midori's loud voice stopped passersby. Anything out of the ordinary was worth a second look in the Yoshiwara. "Come big spender, buy a nice fish for your family," she persisted.

The merchant was not pleased with the attention he was

getting. The longer this fishmonger harassed him, the greater the chance someone would recognize him. He reached into his kimono sleeve and produced a cloth purse. He extracted a small silver coin and placed it in Midori's hand. Then he spun to go.

"Mate!" Midori cried. The merchant froze. Midori placed the fish wrapped in brown paper into his arms a little too forcefully. "Make sure you rub some of that on your hair. It is the only way to kill the stink of that cheap perfume."

The onlookers burst into laughter and clapped. The humiliated merchant grabbed his fish and fled.

Midori turned to the old man. "How much is the fish anyway?"

"One copper coin," he replied.

Midori tossed him the silver coin. "Well, I guess I overcharge," she said.

Even the disinterested daughter rushed to her father's side to inspect the coin.

"By the Buddha," the old man exclaimed. "We don't make this much in a week." He was all smiles.

Midori picked up another fish and looked for her next victim. She did not have long to wait. A pilgrim emerged from the brothel and was the same height and weight as the Fox Gang member who entered as a police officer. It was him. Now, in a white traveling jacket and gators, he looked like a religious man on pilgrimage to holy sites and shrines. Midori placed herself in his path. He stopped and eyed her suspiciously.

"Oh religious one, now that you've taken care of your earthly needs in this house of pleasure, why not purchase this fresh fish to offer to the monks so they will forgive you your sins?" she asked loudly.

The traveler looked warily from left to right, checking for danger.

"Do not look away old pious one. Buy this fish and seek redemption among your priests," Midori continued. She hoped for two things. First, that she was making a large enough commotion for one of her team members to notice the man.

Second, she hoped her disguise and voice pitch was different enough so he would not recognize the man-hungry cook who had fed him his supper earlier.

Every time the man tried to slip past her, Midori countered with her fish. "This fish is your salvation. It is a cheap price to pay for your decidedly un-Buddha-like behavior with women of the flesh," she said, pointing to the brothel.

Midori was becoming the center of attention. People were stopping to hear her harass the brothel clients. She was collecting a large following. The Fox Gang member saw the crowd growing and thought about striking this harassing harpy with his large walking stick. In the end, he decided drawing any more attention to himself from the local crowd, and ultimately the police, was not a good idea. Instead, he reached into his sleeve and retrieved a silver coin. He tossed it to her and as she was catching it, he disappeared in the crowd.

"What do you know? Now we are collecting alms from the righteous," she exclaimed.

The crowd broke into cheers and clapping. Midori placed the fish back on the stall table and handed the coin to the old man.

"Thank you old man," she said. "But I don't think I would be good at this." She untied the string behind her head and let the kimono sleeves drop back into place. Then she untied her hair and let it drop back around her face. "Mataai masho," she said, telling no one in particular that she would see them later, and melted into the crowd.

The young man who had been standing behind the fish stall looked to his father. "What just happened?"

The old man looked at the two silver coins in his hand and at the retreating back of Midori. "I think we just saw our future," he said. "Tomorrow we launch our new sales tactics."

The Fox Gang pilgrim did not change direction again. He struck out west of Edo. He did not take the Tokaido as he would need a government pass. Instead, he took the side roads that led from hamlet to hamlet. He traveled at a rapid pace, signifying he had no worry of pursuit. It was much easier for Myo and her team to shadow him. Myo placed three members of her team ahead of him and she, Midori, and Ao stayed behind. Midori was dressed in much the same clothing as the Fox. She was in pilgrim garb. Her two companions were dressed as Abe couriers. Someone always had the Fox in sight. He traveled all night long. Such a thing would be inconceivable to the common person, as bandits preyed on the unwary. A ninja, on the other hand, went where he wanted.

At noon the next day, the team knew the Fox's destination. It was the town of Toi on the west side of the Izu Peninsula. More specifically, he disappeared into a gold mine.

The Toi Gold Mine belonged to the Tokugawa government. Tokugawa Ieyasu, the founder of the Tokugawa shogunate, had a penchant for women. He would satisfy his hunger in many ways. One way was by inviting traveling dance troops to the castle to entertain. On one such occasion after the troop performed, Ieyasu was eating and drinking with them and lamenting the fact that running the country required money. Samurai were not good with money. It meant little to them by training. Unless he could figure out how to obtain it, his shogunate would disappear from history. He said he would give 100 ryu in gold coins to anyone who could solve his money problems.

These types of musings were normally polite dinner conversation preparatory to Ieyasu bedding one or two of the female dancers. A male drum player took the challenge to heart. On the second night immediately following the performance, the drummer decided to seize the opportunity to change his life. He asked if the shogun was serious about the 100 ryu. Ieyasu was mildly amused to be conversing with a drummer, but given the amount of sake, he answered that he was indeed serious.

The drummer indicated he had a way out of the shogunate's money dilemma. When pressed, the drummer stated the shogun should seize all the gold and silver mines in Japan and start mining on a grand scale. Ieyasu loved the idea. He executed it. The largest gold mine was on Sado Island in the Japan Sea up north. The second largest was near the town of Toi on the Izu Peninsula, about a day's travel west of Edo.

Ieyasu not only paid the 100 gold coins, he put the drummer in charge of the Toi mine. The drummer was elevated to official status and began to change the way gold was extracted as well as how it was minted and in what denominations. Ieyasu soon promoted him to minister of gold mines for the whole country. Minister Okubo became a household name. If a merchant became very rich, it was said he had as much gold as Okubo.

The original Okubo was now dead, but his son inherited his post. He had instituted the use of explosives to increase the production of the mines. It did not make him popular with the townsfolk of Toi because the town's men died in the explosions. However, the townsfolk did prosper by the influx of gold poured into the local economy.

Okubo doubled and then tripled the mining process. Now he oversaw three mines instead of just the one his father had run. In the first two mines, the gold veins disappeared. The tunnels were still in place, but there was no active digging. Now the minister's focus was on the current mine and its yield. The escaped Fox Gang member disappeared down the abandoned shaft of the original mine.

It took Myo longer than she wanted to gather her band. They spent the rest of the day watching the comings and goings at the mine's entrance. It became obvious by the traffic that they had found the operations camp of the Fox Gang. People and supplies came and went all day. "We go in after dark. I will take two with me," she said, pointing to Midori and Ao. "I want two lookouts to watch the entrance and be an active reserve if needed. One will commandeer a pushcart. I do not know what condition Hideki will be in physically. We may have to carry him back to Edo."

Once assigned duties, they all took turns sleeping.

Myo and her two companions left their bundles with the lookouts. As soon as it was fully dark, they made their way to the entrance.

Lanterns hung on the wooden beams used to prop up the shaft. They started at the entrance and ran as far as the eye could see. Myo and her team were in full ninja garb to include the head wraps that left only their eyes showing. The air moving down the main corridor moved the paper lanterns, casting shadows in multiple directions. To ninja on high alert, the effect was disturbing.

Myo was amazed. There was no security. This violated basic survival protocol. She and her team inched their way along the dark mineshaft, clinging to the shadowed spaces between the lanterns. The further they went, the darker and colder it became. Water puddled all along the packed-dirt floor.

Myo led and tried to peer into the darkness that slanted down and away from her. Midori was behind her. She and Miss Blue took turns watching their rear. Finally, after what seemed a lifetime, Myo came to the terminus of the shaft. Here the shaft emptied into a large cavernous area with two more shafts running left and right, perpendicular to the entrance shaft. In the large open area, miniature caves looked like huge dark spots in the rock. They were full of crates and barrels.

"The caves must have once housed the gold for shipment," Myo thought. That would explain the thick wooden bars across their front. In the furthest cave on the right, Myo could see torches, lights, and three people. She made hand signals to her team and slipped through the shadows. In the cave opposite the three people, she applied oil to the hinges of the door. She and her team members slipped through the door silently, letting the darkness hide them. They took up positions behind large kegs.

What Myo saw in the cave across the open area disturbed her. In the well-lighted cell across hung a naked man suspended from an overhead beam. He was immobile with arms lashed behind him. Ropes passed around and under his shoulders. His toes swayed in the air as he twisted. Bruises and welts crisscrossed his skin. There were cuts on his face. His hair had come undone and fallen around his shoulders. He appeared unconscious. It was Hideki.

Two others were in the cell with him. One was a woman. She poured water onto Hideki's face to revive him. Hideki shook his head from side to side to clear his thoughts and get his bearings. Once he realized where he was, Myo saw fear in his eyes.

The woman stood in front of Hideki and seemed to be taunting him. The other person in the cell-like cave across from them was in Fox Gang brown, but his face was visible as his Fox mask clung to his back.

The Fox Gang member was a very large man. He looked extremely powerful. Despite the dominating presence of the large ninja, the woman stimulated Myo's curiosity. She was dressed in a multi-layered robe. Myo had never seen one and only heard of them from actors. She looked like the drawings seen on temple byobu, hinged room dividers displaying painted scenes. She was dressed like one of the noble women of the Kyoto court. On her face was a mask. It was not a fox. It looked like a bird's head, complete with long brown beak and brown feathers streaming back onto the sides of her face. It was quite striking. She had an iron fan in her hand, and she struck Hideki on the head and shoulders with it repeatedly. Hideki tried to dodge the blows, but he had nowhere to go.

Myo noticed Hideki's cell was sparse. Near the cell door lay a pile of freshly cut bamboo. Closer to the far wall were two wooden buckets. Myo knew what the bamboo was for when the woman barked a command and the large ninja selected a bamboo shaft from the pile. He sliced the air with it several times, as a swordsman might with a bokken. Myo heard the distinctive swish as it cut the air in its path.

Retrieving a razor sharp tanto from within his jacket, the large ninja placed one end of the bamboo shaft on the cell dirt floor. To the end of the bamboo, now waist high, he placed the cutting edge of his knife. With his free hand he pounded the back of the tanto until the cutting-edge had sliced down to the next joint in the bamboo. He repeated this several times until the long end of the bamboo resembled seven-inch razor-sharp knives. Then he stepped behind Hideki and struck him with full force on the back and the back of the legs.

Hideki screamed with each strike. Myo stifled the urge to lunge from her hiding place and kill her lover's tormentors. During their vigil Myo's team had counted 20 people entering the mine. The ones who had exited were not the ones who had entered. There was no way of telling how many Fox Gang

ninjas were further down the two shafts. If she attacked too
soon, all could die. Her training told her it was best to wait
until they tired of torturing Hideki. Then she could free him.
But would he be alive?

Myo bit her lip each time the bamboo flail struck. She
tasted blood in her mouth. She tried to shut out the screams
of her lover. She could not. For the first time in her life,
Myo felt out of control. She thought she was above caring
for others. She had made decisions before, like the one she
had just made, to wait in order to survive. Now someone
she cared about was in jeopardy because of her decision.
Intellectually, she knew she had made the right choice for
herself and her team. That did not make her lover's screams
any easier to bear.

The air in the dark tunnels tasted stale and thick. She felt
cold. As a child she had learned to shut out pain and noises she
did not want to hear. She tried to shut out Hideki's screams,
but could not. Finally the beating stopped, and Myo breathed
again.

"Well, Lord of the Yoshinobu. You do not appear so
proud now," the bird woman said, looking at the pool of blood
at her feet. "You bleed like everyone else."

Then Myo heard Hideki's strained voice. "Just kill me and
be done with it, witch."

The bird woman laughed. "Why would I kill you? You
have many screams left for me. Nevertheless, you could stop all
this pain. Just sign this letter that I have prepared that tells your
brother to return to Kii, and your life will be spared. Simple."

"Is that so your boy will be shogun?" Hideki asked as he
writhed in pain. The bird woman froze, as did the large ninja.
Hideki saw their reaction through the pain. His back and legs
were throbbing, burning masses. "Oh yes, we know who you
are, O'Fuku. Your perverted son will never be shogun," he
managed in shallow breaths.

The bird woman reached behind Hideki and took the flail
from the large ninja.

"You know, bamboo has many uses. It can be a flask to
capture water. It can be food. It can be a practice sword or a

sword's target. I like the more refined uses for it. Your knife please, Hakunnsai," she commanded.

The large ninja produced the tanto. The bird woman cut large slivers from the side of the bamboo shaft. These she collected carefully and dropped into one of the buckets.

"The buckets contain an extract of coal from China. It burns brighter than our whale oil and with a much more intense heat. The only problem is, it is expensive to import. But I find it admirable for my purposes." She carefully retrieved the three long slivers of oil soaked bamboo. "Let's see, you are right-handed, correct?"

Hideki saw what was coming. He kicked out at the bird woman, but she dodged his blows. The large ninja behind him kicked Hideki between the legs. Hideki screamed again and started to vomit.

"Nasty animal," the bird woman said.

Hakunnsai bound Hideki's legs with a length of rope and ran it through an iron ring in the floor. Now Hideki could twist but he could not kick.

"Get his right hand open and fingers spread," the bird woman commanded. Hakunnsai obeyed.

Myo started up, but Midori placed a gentle hand on her shoulder. Myo stopped. Midori was correct. She could only hope that Hideki would survive this ordeal.

The bird woman shoved a bamboo sliver under the index fingernail of Hideki. Hideki screamed again and tried to twist away from the pain. The large ninja held him fast. Then the bird woman shoved the second sliver under the fingernail of Hideki's middle finger. Again, Hideki screamed and tried to get away. There was just nowhere to go. The last sliver went under the ring fingernail. The screaming stopped as Hideki fainted.

Hakunsai released Hideki's hand as the young samurai slumped against his bonds.

"Oh no, I will have none of that. Revive him Hakunnsai," she commanded.

The large ninja grabbed the second bucket and threw a ladle full of water into Hideki's face. He regained consciousness slowly and moaned softly.

"That is a good samurai," the bird woman said. Then she went to one of the torches lighting the cell and brought it close to Hideki.

"If you think you know pain, you are wrong … but you will." She placed the flames to the three bamboo slivers still protruding under Hideki's fingernails. They burst into flames as Hideki screamed and thrashed and thrashed.

The bird woman laughed and clapped her hands like a young child. "Try to take my boy's castle, will you?"

Hideki passed out again. Hakunnsai brought the bucket up to the still-burning slivers and extinguished the flames. The bird woman replaced the torch on the wall.

"I have to get back to the castle," she said.

"What do we do with him?" Hakunnsai asked.

She smiled. "He doesn't seem to like fire, so burn him alive. I only wish I could stay and see him roast."

The bird woman then bent over, stepped through the small cell door and walked back towards the entrance of the mine.

Hakunnsai stepped out of the cell and out of sight, walking down the corridor to the right. When he returned, he had an armload of wood. This he placed at Hideki's feet. He then gathered some of the loose straw in the back of the cell and placed it over the wood. He went to the wall and retrieved the lit torch. He stood in front of an unconscious Hideki. "This should wake you up."

He bent down to touch the flame to the straw, but he never quite got there. Hakunnsai felt red-hot lightning in his lower back. His face registered pain and surprise. He collapsed forward into the wood at Hideki's feet. Myo turned the large man on his side and bent close to his ear.

"It is a dart in your vertebrae. You are immobilized. You cannot feel much now. But you will in a little while, I promise," Myo said.

Ao and Midori surveyed the damage to Hideki. "I think we had better get him out while he is still unconscious," Midori whispered.

Myo nodded. She took cloth from her jacket and wrapped the three bamboo slivers so they would not cut her hand. She yanked all three out forcefully and straight down. Hideki stirred but remained unconscious. She then went to the bucket of coal oil and smelled it. She brought it to Hideki and submerged his wounded hand in the liquid. Then she bandaged the hand with the cloth. She and Midori cut him down. Myo emptied another ladle of water onto his face. He revived.

"Myo?" he asked.

"Yes, Takezo. We are here to get you out. Can you stand and walk?"

"I can try," he said. Then he tried. Myo and Midori caught him. He tried again. After the third time, he could stand on his own.

Midori got busy stripping Hakunnsai and passing the clothing to Myo. Myo took the contents of the various packets they found in Hakunnsai's jacket. She smelled each, making certain she knew what they were. She kept two and emptied them onto Hideki's back and legs. The cuts from the bamboo were plentiful but not deep. The salve would coagulate the blood and offer a numbing effect. Then Myo helped Hideki cover his nakedness.

Ao stepped into the cell and passed her hand in front of her face several times. The shaft was clear of people. Myo signaled for Midori and Ao to help Hideki to the entrance. She had some work yet to do. She watched as the two female ninja flanking Hideki helped him toward the entrance.

Myo moved back to the team's original hiding place across from Hideki's former cell and picked up a length of rope she had seen there. When she bent over to grab it, she noticed the markings on the wooden kegs she had used as cover and smiled.

Myo returned to Hideki's former cell and tied the large ninja as he had tied Hideki. Then she gagged him with a short length of rope and started the fire at his feet. The large ninja could not feel any pain. Once the fire was going well, Myo reached behind him and yanked out the dart. The large man thrashed and twisted, trying to flee the flames. She had put enough wood on the pile that his legs were already beginning to blister. Myo smiled at his huge, unbelieving eyes and departed. She made one stop. Then she raced to the front entrance.

She caught up with her comrades and Hideki just outside in the daylight. She told them to hurry. When Midori gave a questioning glance, Myo explained. "The cell we were hiding in was loaded with gunpowder. There is about to be an explosion."

The four moved as fast as they could with the burden they carried. They had cleared the entrance and were moving to the compound gate when a tremendous explosion knocked them to the dirt and continued to shake them like dolls. A huge fireball billowed out of the mineshaft and passed over them.

When the rumblings abated in the mine, Myo pushed herself to her hands and knees. She worked her jaws back and forth trying to clear her ears as she rose and knocked the dust from her clothing. The other ninja women rose and checked themselves for missing and broken body parts. Myo looked around and found Hideki still on the ground. There was blood on his forehead where he had struck a large rock.

"By the Buddha, not now," Myo cried.

She raced to him. There was blood oozing through the jacket she had placed on his back and, more importantly, there was blood on a rock.

Two black-clad male ninja appeared with a pushcart. Gently, the troop lifted Hideki onto the cart facedown and covered him with canvas, then they all reversed their clothing. In just a few seconds they were all Abe couriers once again.

Mr. Brown inspected Hideki's wounds, then looked at Myo. "He is in bad shape. I suggest we transport him back to Edo via boat. The road trip would take longer and probably kill him."

Myo agreed immediately and sent Mr. Aka to the port ahead of them to acquire about a vessel. The Abe couriers renting a vessel would not raise eyebrows. However, they needed to get on board quickly as every government official in a ten-mile radius would be at the mines to inspect the accident. Myo thought of finding a doctor and borrowing him for Hideki, but decided against it. She had no idea how many

Foxes she had killed in the mine explosion. It had felt like she had brought down the whole mountain.

Getting to the boat and back to the Yoshinobu compound was her priority. She could treat her lover with her own medicines once on board the ship. Edo was still a very long way away.

Chapter 26: Decisions

"Are the Lord Hideki and Miss Myo lovers?" she asked her son-in-law.

Yoshi's wife looked up from her sewing to hear the answer.

"She was the one who rescued him," Yoshi replied.

"We all know that. When the high and mighty could not do anything, six ninja, four of them women I might add, got the job done," she said. Mother and daughter smiled at each other over the minor slight she had just heaped on her benefactor's head and the male gender in general.

"Yes, Mother. They are sleeping together. Why do you ask?" Yoshi relented.

"She sits in his room at odd hours and checks on him."

"Really? I thought he was to have no visitors." Yoshi said.

"That is the reason for my question. There are many guards posted outside his room as there are throughout the mansion. But how are they going to keep out a ninja in love?"

"Interesting," Yoshi pondered. "What is she doing there?"

This time his wife answered. "She just sits with him. If anyone approaches, she shifts to invisibility." Yoshi knew she meant that Myo hid when anyone came near the room.

"So she believes he is not protected enough?" Yoshi asked.

"That would be my guess son-in-law. Who are you trying to protect him from?" she asked.

"Ninja," he said, seeing her logic. "I will get Jii-sama to
turn security over to me. If she is going to be in there anyway,
she may as well be in charge."

Mother and daughter smiled at each other again.
They had made a good choice. Yoshi was little slow, but he
eventually listened to reason.

Hideki slept for another two days. The first thing he saw each
time he awoke was Myo. He tried to speak but could not. Myo
rushed to him and told him to keep quiet. He had had many
blows on the head and she was worried he might never join the
living again. She summoned the doctors, and they began poking
and prodding him and getting him to drink their herbs. Within
ten hours, Hideki had regained his speech and the movement of
all his limbs. Moving proved painful as his body was crisscrossed
with purple bruises and multiple cuts, but by the third day, he was
almost whole again, except for his right hand.

When the bandages came off, Hideki was shocked at
what he saw. His right hand looked more like a claw than the
appendage he remembered. The fingers were naked without
fingernails. Only his thumb and little finger had escaped the
torture. The backs of his fingers up to the second knuckle
were charred. He could not extend his fingers. He could touch
the end of each finger with his thumb, but only had feeling in
the tip of the thumb and the little finger. There was no feeling
in the other fingers. He was a cripple.

The doctors told him that the loss of sensitivity was a
blessing. They said it would mask the pain from the burns. All
Hideki could think about was the fact that he would never hold
a sword again.

Hideki changed. His usual good nature gave way to
sullenness. He became withdrawn. He did not want to see anyone.
Everyone was banned from his room. Myo continued her vigil
but from the rafters or in an adjacent room. Hideki was not aware
of her presence. He allowed doctors in but grilled them about his
condition, demanding to know if he would ever regain the use of
his hand. No one told him what he wanted to hear.

Neither Naga nor Jii could sweeten his disposition. Their

visits became shorter and shorter. Hideki even refused to see Yuki, who had recovered from her poisoned dart ordeal.

Yoshi's updates on the progression of the police training did little to cheer Hideki. Even the news that Naga's appearance before the Roju and Tairo was postponed did not pick up his spirits.

Then Musashi visited.

"Well Sensei," Hideki said from his futon, "have you come to see how far your star pupil has fallen?"

Musashi ignored the comment.

"I came to say goodbye. I will be returning to my Musha Shugyo tomorrow."

"So, when we need you the most, you depart."

Musashi ignored the rebuke. "There is nothing here for me now."

"There is still the Fox Gang and the Edo castle cabal. There is a new police force that is untried, and there is a big question of what I am going to do with the rest of my life," Hideki countered.

"And why is my presence required for any of that?" Musashi asked.

"I just thought you might like to stick around and see how what you helped create turns out."

"I already know how it is going to turn out," Musashi said

"So you have added prophecy to the list of your accomplishments?"

"No, it does not take a prophet to foretell the Yoshinobu future," Musashi said.

"Then enlightened me," Hideki commanded.

"Gladly. The back of the Fox Gang is broken. Myo's explosion accomplished that. There may be others, but they will never be the threat they were. Naga will marry Yuki and become son-in-law to Hittori Hanzo and surrogate to Yagyu Munenori," Musashi predicted.

"Will he become shogun?" Hideki challenged.

"Unknown. He would be good at it. However, the Yoshinobu have stirred up the government a little too much for the power elite. I would bet he does not become shogun."

"And what does the future hold for me, Sensei? What will become of crippled Hideki?"

"What do you want to become of him?" Musashi asked.

"Well, I wanted to go on a Musha Shugyo and perfect my swordsmanship while helping Naga to rule. But that won't happen now," Hideki said.

"Why not?" Musashi asked.

"Look at this hand," Hideki said, holding his claw-like right hand up. "I cannot hold a sword. How will I ever be able to practice kenjitsu again?"

"How were you able to practice kenjitsu in the first place?" Musashi asked.

"What do you mean? Jii started my training at an early age. I have been practicing with a sword since I was little."

"Then there is your answer," Musashi said.

"No more of your riddles, Sensei. What are you talking about?" Hideki demanded.

"Nothing wondrous. You are facing a crossroads that every returning warrior has had to deal with since the beginning of time. You trained and trained to become good. Then you go off to war. You are injured and come home. Now what do you do? Do you mope and feel sorry for yourself and make life miserable for those around you? Or do you apply yourself to continue to accomplish your goals but with new applications?"

Hideki did not respond, so Musashi continued. "Some do not return at all. They cannot. They are dead. Some return blinded. Some return with a limp. Combat changes everyone. The question is how you allow that change to affect you. Do you embrace the Bushido that brought you this far? Or do you wallow in self-pity and never achieve anything else with your life?"

"You do not know what it is like, Sensei. I cannot do anything anymore," Hideki said.

"Is that why you sent Myo away?"

Hideki nodded. "I still love her, but I am just half a man now. I cannot bear for her to see me like this."

"You idiot. She saw you much worse. Who do you think saved you when the rest of us ran around wringing our hands?" Musashi asked.

"I know. I've heard the stories."

"They are not stories. They are true. You should be proud to have a woman dedicated enough to risk her life and that of her clan to save yours. But if you asked me, the way you've returned her courage means she bet on the wrong man."

Hideki seemed to flinch at the words. "So help me, Sensei."

"I cannot. You have already chosen. You have picked self-pity and making everyone around you miserable," Musashi said.

"What would you have me do, Sensei?" Hideki asked.

"It is not my decision. You have to decide which path you travel."

"What if I wanted to keep my old dream alive with the Musha Shugyo and helping Naga?" Hideki asked.

"Then, were I you, I'd start learning how to be an effective fighter given your current deficiencies."

"But I cannot hold a sword with my right hand," Hideki said.

"Then either learn how to hold one, or learn how to fight left-handed."

"Sensei, will you stay and help me?" Hideki asked.

"If you are serious, I will get you started," Musashi promised.

Hideki smiled for the first time since being crippled. "How do we start?"

"Yoshi," Musashi called.

The paper door slid back. "Hai," Yoshi answered.

"Join us, ninja. We have need of your black magic and the healing arts of Matsu,"

Yoshi bowed. "What you're really saying is that you have need of my mother-in-law now and me afterwards?"

"Exactly," Musashi grunted.

Yoshi bowed and disappeared through the sliding door.

A few moments later, feminine voices were at the door. "Gomen Kudasai."

"Enter," Musashi said.

Yoshi's wife and mother-in-law entered Hideki's room and bowed to both Hideki and Musashi. Then they moved around Hideki's futon, around behind Musashi, and over to Hideki's right. They bowed again.

"Gomen," the old woman said and reached up and took Hideki's scarred and clawed hand. She touched it very carefully. She turned it over and looked at the palm. Then she attempted to straighten out each finger. The fingers would straighten, but would return to the clawed position upon release.

"Does that give you pain, Lord?" Matsu asked.

"No, I do not feel anything at all," Hideki replied.

"I'm going to prick your fingers with some needles. I want to see if you feel anything at all. Is that agreeable to you?" she asked.

"It is not agreeable, but I will endure it."

Matsu turned to her daughter and retrieved a small, cloth packet. From it she extracted several needles. Holding Hideki's fingers one at a time, she began pricking each one and asking if Hideki felt anything. Most of the time there was no reaction. However, on several instances Hideki jumped and said, "Hai."

When she was through, Matsu wrapped the needles in the cloth and returned them to her daughter.

"What is your verdict?" Hideki asked. "Will I ever be able to use my hand again?"

Matsu looked surprised. "Oh, most assuredly," she said. "You may have trouble holding items for a year or so, but you are already gaining feeling in your fingers above the second knuckle. Have not these Chinese-trained doctors told you this?"

Hideki smiled from ear to ear. "No, they have not. Thank you," he managed.

"You may never have all your strength back, but you will be strong enough after a while to do most things."

"Can I wield a sword?" Hideki asked.

"You can do that now with the proper equipment."

"What equipment?" Hideki asked.

"You notice you still have feeling and some strength in your little finger and your thumb. I believe with a specially modified leather glove, I can have you holding a sword in a few days."

Hideki eyes opened a little wider. "Is that the truth?"

"Yes, Lord, it is the truth," she said. Then she turned her attention to her daughter. "Chiyo, please bring me my sewing basket."

"Hai," Chiyo said, rising and shuffling off in her kimono toward the sliding door.

"You are going to sew me?" Hideki asked.

"No Lord. I am going to make a glove for your hand. It will be a special glove. To make it, I must first create a pattern of cloth."

Hideki looked relieved.

Matsu and Chiyo spent the next hour measuring, cutting, and stitching together a cloth glove that fit over Hideki's right-hand. The thumb was exposed from the first knuckle of the thumb to the tip. Cloth encased all the fingers. It looked like a normal glove, with the fingers linked together. They could not be separated.

"You still have movement and feeling in your thumb and little finger. The movement of the little finger will close the remaining fingers around your sword. You will be able to hold it, but you will not have much strength at it for several weeks. In the interim, I would wield a short sword," Matsu advised.

"What about a jutte?" Musashi asked.

"Yes, Musashi-sama. He should be able to wield a jutte," she answered.

"Thank you Matsu. You don't know how much it means to me to have hope," Hideki said.

"I think I had better take over your nursing, young lord. With my oils and compresses, your feeling in the hand will be accelerated. Your hand may permanently stain brown, but that will be better than the red. Your nails will grow back eventually." Then both mother and daughter rose and moved across the room, bowed again, and departed through the sliding door.

"Amazing people," Hideki sighed.

"Yes, the country is full of them," Musashi agreed.

"Ninja?"

"No, amazing people. You just have to stop and listen. Your job starting tomorrow is to start training in earnest to learn to defend yourself and them."

"Yes, but a jutte is not a katana," Hideki said.

"I will have you using a katana tomorrow."

"Sensei, you are a great master and a better teacher, but even you cannot promise to cure this right hand," Hideki challenged.

"I do not have to. The jutte is for your right-hand, or barring that, a short sword. Starting tomorrow you are a left-handed swordsman," Musashi declared.

"A left-handed swordsman? I will be a freak." Hideki feared the ridicule heaped on all things different in the society.

"Well, therein lay your choices. Be a freak and help Naga and people like Matsu and Chiyo by bringing better government—or quit."

Hideki looked at his clawed right hand and then at his left. "I guess I choose freak."

"Good choice, Lord. You have had enough rest and self-pity. We begin at dawn tomorrow." With that pronouncement, Musashi rose and departed.

Hideki tried to will his right fingers to flex. The three inside fingers would not budge. "I will do this and I will make it work, I don't care how hard it is," he vowed. "I will not be a cripple."

From above the ceiling in the rafters, Myo smiled. "Bless you Musashi sensei."

As the sun rose, Hideki made his way to the practice area in the Yoshinobu compound. He was dressed in a plain, brown kimono. His appearance was somewhat disheveled. He would not have passed inspection by Jii. However, Hideki was proud of himself. He had just waged a major campaign and won. He had dressed himself. He was still somewhat independent.

He had used his sageo cord from his scabbard to tie up

his sleeves. To do so was easy for a man with two hands as the sword cord was long, but tying up his sleeves left Hideki exhausted. Just as challenging was tying his cloth hachimaki headband in place. No one would know it, but getting dressed with two swords in his obi this morning had required more courage and determination than the combat he had seen so far. Today was a big day.

Musashi watched him from across the field and nodded with appreciation. Then his eyes dropped to the sword on Hideki's side. The katana was on his left side, as he had carried it all his life. The wakazashi was also in his obi but worn more toward the front as was the tradition. In addition, thrust into his obi next to the short sword was a red-handle jutte.

"What rank did they give you?" Musashi asked.

"I'm told the embedded token means I am a private. I am on the bottom," Hideki said.

"It is appropriate. I see you have your new glove."

"Yes, Matsu and Chiyo must've worked all night. It is a marvel," he said as he raised his hand up for Musashi to see. "It is very light and supple leather, but it is strong and allows me to close my hand. Watch." He grasped the handle of the jutte and drew it out, elevating the tip toward Musashi.

"Can you strike with it?" Musashi asked.

"Yes," Hideki said, raising the weapon and striking down several times.

"Can you parry?"

Hideki blocked inside and outside with the jutte.

Musashi picked up a bokken and prepared to strike. "Can you parry and still hang onto the jutte?" he asked.

Musashi struck to Hideki's left side. Hideki parried the strike to the inside. Musashi reversed and struck to Hideki's right side. Hideki parried to the outside. Then Musashi raised the bokken and struck downward at Hideki's head.

It was a devastating blow and its force frightened Hideki. Even in top form, it was difficult to deflect Musashi's blows. Hideki raised his jutte as high as he could to minimize the downward travel of Musashi's blade. He wanted to negate as much power as possible. The jutte blade met the wooden sword at an angle. The impact struck the jutte with a resounding slap. At the moment of impact, Hideki flicked his wrist to the right, deflecting the blow's downward momentum away from his body. He shuffled forward on his front foot, moving his right side away from the strike and continued his flipping wrist motion to bring the jutte around and up to strike Musashi's head. Musashi jumped to his left at the last minute and missed a blow between the eyes.

"Very good, Hideki. You have not forgotten."

Hideki smiled. He had not thought he could do that. As soon as Musashi had started striking, the copper taste of fear had thrust itself into the back of his mouth. The taste was new to him. He did not like it.

The government was changing. The people were changing. His life was changing. He would have to get used to the new taste and make it work for him. He might never be the same confident young man of old. "Was that okay? No sense wondering. It is what it is. Live with it," he told himself.

Musashi set the wooden sword against the raised portion of the instructor's platform. He removed Hideki's katana and scabbard from his obi. He opened a cloth bundle and extracted a different katana and saya. "Yoshi's womenfolk were not the only ones up late," Musashi said.

The kurigata on the scabbard was on the opposite side of the saya. Now a left-handed man could wear it on his right side. The kurigata is a small circle of Buffalo horn that keeps the sword scabbard or saya from sliding down past the obi.

Musashi stuffed Hideki's katana into the new scabbard. Then he placed the sword on his right side between his hip and the cloth obi. He left the short sword on the left front with the handle towards the right. The jutte with the red silk handle was adjacent to the short sword. Both were within easy reach of his right hand.

"It feels so strange," Hideki complained.

"Do you want to quit?" Musashi asked.

"No, Sensei," Hideki said.

"I once fought a left-handed swordsman. He came close to killing me," Musashi said.

"I had never heard that," Hideki said. "He must've been a fine swordsman."

"He was an average swordsman."

"So how could he come close to killing you?" Hideki demanded.

"All the techniques we practice all our lives are negated. A left-handed swordsman moves differently. You do not know what to expect. It is bizarre and frightening to fight a left-handed swordsman. It is dangerous," Musashi, said shivering as he remembered.

Hideki laughed. "That is what I wish to be—dangerous!"

"Then you must practice to be dangerous. Now draw your sword."

Hideki did so tentatively. His draw was from sky to earth. The katana rests with the blade up inside the saya tucked in the obi. The cutting-edge of the blade points towards the sky. When a samurai draws, it is natural for the edge to cut the sky first as it clears the scabbard and then to cut downward as the ark completes.

"Return it, and try not to lose any fingers," Musashi said.

Hideki slashed down with his left hand, an instinctual move to flick imaginary blood left on the blade. With his right hand he grasped the mouth of the scabbard just below its opening and pulled it up and outward. With his left hand, he brought the back of the katana where the tsuba hilt annexes the blade to meet the mouth of the scabbard. When they met, he used the area formed by his index finger and thumb on the right hand as a groove to guide the tip of the blade into the scabbard opening. Once the tip was safely inside the mouth of the scabbard, the movement reversed, and a razor-sharp blade moved into its hiding place.

"This time, rotate the scabbard upside down to gain an earth-to-sky draw," Musashi ordered.

Hideki grasped the handle of the katana with his left hand and the scabbard with his right. He rotated the scabbard outward and almost upside down and drew the sword. This time the sword came out with the cutting-edge downward, cutting earth first and continued upward to cut sky.

"It is a difficult cut," Hideki said.

"Yes, but not impossible," Musashi said. "Return the sword." Hideki complied.

"Now, this time I want you to rotate the sword with your left hand as you grasp the handle for the draw. You're right hand will have nothing to do," Musashi instructed.

Hideki understood the command. He reached with his left hand, grasped the handle of the katana at rest in the scabbard on his right side, twisted the handle outwardly, and made the earth to sky draw with one hand.

Musashi had him practice the draw 100 times. When he was finished, the sun was high and the compound smoky with the breakfast cooking fires. Hideki felt confident for the first time in weeks.

"Now I want you to execute the earth-to-sky draw as you have been doing, but I want your right hand to grasp the short sword and draw both swords at the same time. Do not cut off an arm!" Musashi said. "Take it slow at first."

Hideki drew slowly. He found he had to let his right hand tarry just long enough to allow the earth-to-sky draw with the left hand to begin. As soon as the katana started its deadly skyward arc, the short sword came out in a horizontal arc, cutting from left to right. Musashi had him practice this repeatedly.

"It is an effective defense against a lunge or any attack except an overhead strike. With the overhead blow you will have to initiate the short sword first to allow a high deflection and then split him from crotch to eyeballs from below," Musashi said as he demonstrated a lightning fast and fluid draw with both swords.

"That is no fair," Hideki said. "You drew from the normal side."

"Yes, young lord. But I am not crippled," Musashi said.

Hideki set himself and managed an almost flawless draw as a left-hander with both swords. "Neither am I," he said.

Chapter 27: End Game

Edo was quiet for a change. The red sticks patrolled and administered the law with an even hand. Any suggestion of a bribe met with a firm refusal and a warning; the second offer of a bribe would land the briber in jail. Gradually, the word got around. There was a new way to do business. The police were not the enemy.

Walking from the Hatchobori, Hideki stopped in front of a noodle stand. "Are you hungry for noodles?" he asked Myo.

"Not really," she responded. "But I'll watch you eat."

As soon as they stepped out of the midday sun into the shade of the noodle shop, they were met with a loud, "Itashaimasine," from the ever-busy Hana as she scurried from bench to bench with noodles and tea. When she recognized Hideki, she exclaimed "Oh, Uesama!" and bowed low.

The small shop was crowded and noisy with slurping sounds, but all motions stopped. All eyes went to the newcomers as everyone wanted to see the man addressed as Uesama—a term reserved for the shogun.

"Mate, you are mistaken. It is only I, Takezo, a lowly ronin come to eat the best noodles in Edo with my lovely companion Myo," Hideki stated.

The old man hurried out front to greet Hideki and Myo. He started bowing three steps away. "Welcome ronin Takezo and courier Myo." He looked around and spied two spaces on the bench nearest the stoves. "Please sit here." Then, turning to his daughter, "Hana, please get them some tea."

Hideki thanked him and the shop went back to the noise of slurping and small talk.

Once seated, Hideki looked into Myo's eyes. "I have not thanked you yet for saving my life," he said with an air of formally.

"There is no need," she replied softly.

Hana brought tea and giggled. "I am to be married," she announced.

"Hana, I am so happy for you," Myo said. "Who is the lucky man?"

"Lord Hideki knows him. He is Kimbei. He is a police officer at the Hatchobori. He carries one of the famous red sticks. He has been elevated to doshin."

"Omedito Hana; you are to be congratulated. I am very happy for you," Hideki said.

The beaming girl turned and departed to wipe down a spot on one of the benches just vacated.

"Do you know the groom?" Myo asked.

"Yes, he arrested Jubei and I the last time we were in here," Hideki revealed.

"Oh dear," Myo said.

"Not to worry, we are friends now. He was one of the few old police who was not corrupt."

Hana brought two bowls of noodles and placed them in front of the couple. She bowed and departed.

"Looks like you get noodles whether you are hungry or not," Hideki said.

Hideki attempted to pick up his eating utensils with his right hand. He could trap the eating sticks with his thumb, but without feeling and strength in his index finger, he could not pick them up. He fumbled with it for a moment and gave up. Eventually he used his left hand.

"Force of habit," he said. "I keep hoping that feeling will return enough for me to do the normal things I used to take for granted."

Myo watched him pick up the eating sticks in his left hand and was impressed with his skill. He could feed himself. "You have become quite good with your left hand."

Hideki blew on the tangle of hot noodles halfway to his mouth. "Of necessity," he said, then opened his mouth and lightly placed the hot white noodles on his tongue, inhaling as he did, to slurp the tasty strings the rest of the way from the hot soup.

After paying for the food above the old man's protests, Hideki and Myo headed back to the Yoshinobu compound. Hideki avoided eye contact with all those that stared at him. Even the little children pointed and laughed.

"Is it always like this?" she asked.

"Yes. We Japanese don't like things that are different." Hideki touched the katana on his right side. "With the blade over here I am left handed and to be despised," he said.

"How does your practice go?"

"Musashi has worked me harder than ever. He is an amazing man."

"Yes, I am so glad your paths crossed," she said.

"I shall miss him greatly," he said.

"Miss him? Where is he going?"

"Where he was always destined to go—back on his quest. I can tell by his intensity with me that it is almost time to go. He wants to give me everything he has before he departs."

"What will you do when he is gone?" she asked.

"I will try and remember what he taught me," Hideki sighed, "and to follow the example he set. But I will still have Jubei and Yoshi to teach me new things."

"Has there been any word of the Fox Gang?" Myo asked

"No, I think you broke their back, Myo."

"Let us hope so."

"I for one am extremely glad you did what you did. But there are some who question whether the explosion of a gold mine might have been a little extreme," he said.

Myo face hardened. "There is no such thing as being too extreme when you are wiping out vermin. They were evil. I only wish I had gotten that bird woman."

"The Yoshinobu are being summoned before the Roju and Tairo in two days' time. This should be the visit that seals our future in Edo," Hideki said.

"I am happy for you, Hideki. Your future is our future now," she said.

"It was a strange summons. We are being asked to bring the red sticks and put on a demonstration of their use."

"I did not think weapons were allowed in the castle," she said.

"Only the castle guards may carry them. You remember Hittori Hanzo?"

"Yes. I remember," Myo replied. "I got the impression he wanted me dead."

"Well, that was then, and this is now. Things change."

"Speaking of change, my Lord Hideki, have you found a new room to lease for your evenings in Edo?" she asked with a tease her voice.

"Yes, I have. I purchased a little bathhouse and hotel in the Nihonbashi area."

"Oh, you want to peek at all the naked women," she challenged.

"Only one."

"Then maybe you better take me there. Now your training must begin in earnest," she said.

Goro looked up in surprise. Four of the famous red sticks piled into his office and struck his companions on the head. They were not playing. The blows were to render unconscious or kill. Four Gumsumgumi dropped to the tatami mat. One required a second blow to ensure he stayed down.

The man sitting to the right of Goro jumped to his feet and pulled a tanto from his kimono. The naked blade glistened in the candlelight. No one moved to intercept him. They had their orders.

"By the gods, what is this?" Goro demanded. "You cannot come in here and strike my men. If this is an arrest, what are the charges?" he demanded.

The large bulk of Nichi entered the room. "You are being charged with being disloyal to the Gumsumgumi," Nichi stated.

Goro laughed. "Look who is talking."

"Oh, I have honored my vows, Goro. I have done nothing to harm the Gumsumgumi. In fact, I have taken measures to elevate it now and in the future."

"Rubbish. You have gone traitor. You joined the government," Goro accused.

"Let us compare crimes, Oyabun Goro. I am now in charge of keeping the peace in Edo. That peace insures commerce. With commerce, everyone wins. The people of Edo win. They can work, live, and prosper. The government wins because when there is peace, things like schools, roads, and houses spring up. Even the Gumsumgumi win. You are free to apply your games of chance, your brothels, and drinking establishments. You make money. If you had accepted the path I put you on, you could have been a great man Goro. Instead, I find you with the likes of the Yamakai villain who is in the pay of the Fox Gang. You disappoint me, Goro," Nichi said.

"You lie. The Yamakai just want to elevate the gumi. They find your sleeping with the Tokugawa as distasteful as I do." Nichi continued. "The Yamakai are in bed with the Fox Gang. We raided their hideout last month and had a prisoner in the Hatchobori. The hideout was the Yamakai boat yard."

"You are making that up," Goro said, but he sounded less sure of himself.

"Goro, have you ever known me to lie?" Nichi asked.

"You lied about being in the Gumsumgumi forever. You broke your oath to us," Goro accused.

"No, I did not. I may not be wearing the mon any longer, but I am still Gumsumgumi at heart."

"I do not see how any of us can trust you," Goro complained.

"Then look at it from a different direction, Goro. I can prove the Yamakai are in league with the Fox Gang. The Fox Gang is killing Tokugawa. If the Yamakai and Foxes get their way, your future is in jeopardy."

"You lie," Goro repeated.

"Have the Yamakai ever shared anything with any other group before?" Nichi asked.

"No," Goro had to admit.

"Then why would they want to start sharing now?"

"I do not know," Goro said, seeing the logic in Nichi's argument but not willing to admit a mistake. "Maybe they need our help."

"Use your head, Goro. The Yamakai-gumi use people and then throw them away. As soon as you have helped, you will die, as will the once-proud Gumsumgumi," Nichi warned.

Komeya no Toku, waving his knife at Nichi, spoke up. "He lies, Goro, just like he changed sides so quickly. He has no honor."

"Think back, Goro. Think back to when your head used to work. What were the Yamakai-gumi known for? Was it for good works? No. Was it for helping the people of Edo in any way? No. Was it for elevating the cause of gumi everywhere? No. What were they famous for?" Nichi asked loudly.

"Making money," Goro mumbled.

"What was that, Oyabun Goro? I couldn't hear you." Nichi almost screamed.

Goro found his voice. "They were good at making money."

"At whose expense?" Nichi asked.

"At everyone's," Goro admitted.

"Yes, everyone except themselves. What did they do the moment they knew we were arrested?" Nichi asked.

"They took over our territory," Goro said, eyeing Kameya no Toku with new suspicion.

"And what did they do the moment you took the territory back?" Nichi asked.

"They made peace," Goro replied.

"Yes, they agreed to all of your demands without argument. Do you think that is because they were afraid of you?" Nichi asked.

"I do not know," Goro said.

"Did you not wonder why they agreed so easily?" Nichi asked.

"Yes, I did wonder."

"Do you not now see, Goro, that they agreed to everything you presented because they knew if the Fox Gang was victorious, you and the Gumsumgumi would be eliminated next?" Nichi asked.

Goro's head was now down. "Yes, now I see."

"And who stirred up the recent riots, trying to execute an innocent wood carver?" Nichi asked. He could see the dawning of recognition and the old fire rising in Goro's eyes.

"The Yamakai," Goro admitted. Now he took a step back from Kameya no Toku.

Nichi pressed his point. "The Yamakai are a blight on society. They do not believe in honor. They do not have a code. Their code is money."

Goro was becoming flustered. "I thought they wanted to bring back the honor," Goro pleaded. "He promised me we'd be great again."

"They were playing on your weakness, Goro. You are too trusting. They convinced you to betray me, the ronin Takezo, and Lady Myo. Would you have hurt Lady Myo if you were in your right mind, Goro?" Nichi asked.

Goro bowed his head. "No. I would never hurt her."

"Well, you almost got her killed, Goro. And you almost got the Gumsumgumi wiped out," Nichi accused.

Goro shook his big head from side to side, his eyes beginning to water. "Never! I would never harm the Gumsumgumi!"

"You let your dislike for the ronin Takezo cloud your judgment. He is really Yoshinobu Hideki, the younger brother of the man now magistrate of Edo, my new boss. My new boss is also being considered for shogun," Nichi said.

Goro's eyes got very round. "Honto? Really?"

"Yes honto, really. If he had been killed, and you had facilitated it while leading the Yamakai and setting him up for the Fox Gang, how much of a future do you think you and the Gumsumgumi would have?"

Goro staggered back another step as Nichi's accusations hammered him.

"Luckily, Hideki does not hold a grudge. But he's got every right to have you hunted and executed along with every last Gumsumgumi," Nichi said.

Goro looked up quickly, grasping at any out. "He does not hold a grudge?"

"Not if I ask him not to. You see, Goro, while you are out to destroy the Gumsumgumi by backing trash like this," pointing to the Yamakai leader holding the knife, "I am creating an alliance with the new government. We red sticks are indispensable to them."

"You are?" Goro asked.

"Certainly. The Yoshinobu had to get rid of all the old corruption in order to restore order and justice. Whom did they turn to? They turned to the Gumsumgumi. I switched from our old life to this new one because I had to. I founded the Gumsumgumi to protect the people. It was never about money. If it had been, we would be as rich as a Yamakai. But you and I, Goro, built the Gumsumgumi around elevating the downtrodden. We swore to protect each other and the citizens of Edo. Yes, we made money. But we also lived by our code. We do not hurt the innocent. We protect the weak. Such is the real strength of the Gumsumgumi. Therefore, when I had the opportunity to tear down the corruption and replace it with the strength of the Gumsumgumi, I took it. It was my destiny. I created the Gumsumgumi to help the people. How much more can I help when I am responsible for the justice in Edo?" Nichi asked.

Kameya no Toku sneered. "I hope you are not believing all these lies, Goro-san." he pointed the naked blade at Nichi. "He is a traitor to the gumi cause. He cannot stand being gumi. He has to be important and keep you down."

"No, Komeya," Goro said, taking a step toward the knife. "Nichi does not lie. But I know for a fact that the Yamakai does."

Komeya no Toku turned the blade in Goro's direction. Goro paid it no mind, continuing the pressure on the now frightened man.

"Foxes? You are working with the Foxes?" Goro asked.

When the Yamakai man did not answer, Nichi answered for him. "Not only was he working with them; they were financing the Foxes and providing supplies to them throughout the land."

The Yamakai man turned the blade toward Nichi again. It was all that Goro needed. With the explosion of the sumo tachiai, Goro launched his incredible bulk at the unfortunate knife wielder. Goro's hands were in front of him. The speed and bulk of the yokozuna were behind the hands. Goro's right hand launched an incredibly destructive thumb and index finger web strike to Komeya no Toku's unprotected throat.

The force of the blow lifted the stocky man off the tatami and launched him backwards into a sliding door. He crashed through it and landed in the adjacent room. His knife was stuck point first in the tatami at the point he left the floor.

Komeya no Toku lay in a heap completely dazed on his back. When his brain got around to sending signals to the rest of his body that no air was coming to his lungs due to his crushed windpipe, his hands grasp his throat as his mouth opened wide and tried to suck in precious oxygen. As he panicked, he thrashed around in the remnants of the wall, spinning in circles trying to find air.

Goro ignored him. He knew the Yamakai man was as good as dead. It was just taking a little longer than he had planned.

Goro knelt on the tatami and picked up the knife. He grabbed the lapels of his kimono and ripped them apart, baring his ample torso. Then he reversed the knife in his right hand and started the motion to plunge the blade into his middle.

"No," shouted Nichi. "I forbid it."

Goro stopped. "But I must make amends for my failure to you and the Gumsumgumi," he said in a calm tone.

"And so you shall Goro. However, killing yourself accomplishes nothing. Why do you think I chose you as my successor? It is your heart that will bring the Gumsumgumi through this."

"My heart?"

"Yes Goro, your heart. The government now relies on me and the red sticks. And I rely on you. Yes. I will keep the red sticks in line. But we are just one police station among many. I cannot patrol the whole city. The Gumsumgumi can.

When there is a corrupt official, I expect you to get me word while you protect the chosin. If one of my new recruits in the future becomes corrupt, I expect you to tell me about it and protect the chosin. And if I turned from the path of righteousness even a little, I expect you to correct me and protect the chosin,"

Goro bowed as low has his bulk in a sitting position would allow. "I accept your trust and vow to honor it. As a token of my atonement, I offer you a part of my body."

Goro placed his left hand on the mat with his little finger extended. Then he drew the razor sharp knife across the finger severing the tip up to the first knuckle. The blood ran red on the straw matting.

Nichi reached into his kimono and extracted a large white cloth. He grasped Goro's wounded left hand and wrapped it with the cloth to help staunch the bleeding. Then he grasped Goro's own cloth towel and retrieved the separated fingertip. He reverently wrapped it in the cloth and bowed and touched it to his forehead. "I accept your apology and we will speak of this no more."

Goro bowed with tears in his eyes. "Arigato."

The red sticks in the room bowed to Goro, amazed at what they had just witnessed.

Chapter 28: Retribution

The days of reckoning were upon the Yoshinobu household. The Roju and Tairo counselors summoned them, several times. Each time they had gotten as far as the castle dressing room. Then they would get the announcement of postponement. No explanation was forthcoming. Yagyu Munenori would meet Jii and simply state that the counselors were not yet ready to receive them. After each postponement, an additional member of the Yoshinobu retinue was added.

Originally, the Yoshinobu contingent consisted of Naga, Jii and Hideki. Musashi was added after the first postponement. Next, Yoshi was added. The most recent to be summoned was Nichi, which bothered Nichi very much. He could think of no good that would come from his appearance before the government. "They will try to kill me," Nichi declared. However, Jii's promises prevailed.

All six men frowned at a bowing Yagyu Munenori. "I am sorry gentlemen. But the counselors now request the presence of the one called Myo at your meeting on the morrow," he said. "It is requested that all who know how to use the famous 'red sticks' should bring one. The counselors would like a demonstration."

"This is too much," Jii said. "Do you think we are playthings to move back and forth as you wish?"

Yagyu raised his head and looked the old man in the eyes. "I do not think that. But I do think it would be wise to heed the council's wishes."

"We have heeded it, all six times." Jii exclaimed.

Naga placed a hand on his grandfather's arm. "We will agree to the council's wishes one more time."

Yagyu Muneyori bowed to Naga. "I appreciate your patience. I think it will be worth your wait."

"What do they want with Myo?" Hideki asked.

"I do not know," Yagyu replied.

"Then who is it that is asking?" Hideki pursued.

"The request comes from the Roju."

"By the Buddha," Jii said. "It is ever the same—grown men playing childish games. They ought to be ashamed."

The next day, the Yoshinobu had their audience. The men were dressed in their best Kamishino with the sleeveless vests of wide-winged shoulders and the long-legged nagabakama of billowing pants that trailed behind as the wearer stepped on the excess length. The movement required a sliding motion to walk.

Yoshi looked like a court jester in his. He took much good-natured abuse as he learned the sliding steps and the lifting of the cloth on the top of the thighs to keep from tripping. He got to where he could move adeptly enough, but not good enough to keep from being the butt of jokes.

Hideki spent several minutes teaching Nichi. Then his attention moved elsewhere.

Myo entered the room, knelt, and bowed to all. She was clothed in a plain, light-blue kimono with a wide, golden obi across her middle and tied in the back. Her hair was up and rolled in the style of the castle. In her shiny, black hair was a simple tortoiseshell comb. She wore no makeup. Her understated beauty left everyone gawking. "Moshiagemasu," she said, letting everyone know that she was reporting as ordered.

"Welcome Myo," Jii said, pointing to a spot beside him. "Come join an old man while we wait for these children to sort out their games."

Myo smiled and nodded to Hideki. Hideki just stood with his mouth open.

"Catching flies, Lord?" Yoshi asked, glad that Myo's entrance had freed him from the taunts of his castle garb and demeanor.

Hideki closed his mouth quickly with a click of teeth.

"Every time I see her, she is a different person."

"Then your life will never be boring," Yoshi said.

"I suppose not," Hideki agreed.

They waited long enough for Jii to mention he was hungry. Then, very quickly, they moved into the grand room that had impressed Hideki during his first visit. They all filed in with Naga once again taking the place of honor facing the huge golden hollyhock mon on the far wall above the raised section of the room. Jii sat on his folded legs to Naga's right and slightly behind. Hideki was in the same position to Naga's left. Musashi, Yoshi, and Nichi formed a second row by dropping to their right knee, sweeping the long-legged nagabakama behind them with a swishing motion of their right hands between their legs, and coming to a seated position with both legs tucked underneath them.

When Myo entered, she was surprised to be motioned to the side of the room where she received a cushion. She knelt upon it with her legs folded beneath her. She had been there just a few moments when one of the few men she feared moved to her left side and knelt on the tatami. He was not wearing the ornate kamishino or the encumbering nagabakama. He was wearing a very expensive black silk kimono with red piping. More startling was the fact that he wore the two swords of the kodachi. Normally, swords were banned in the castle. Upon sitting, he took the long sword from the obi on his left side and placed it away from Myo on the tatami. She wondered if she could get to her tanto in time to save herself. Hittori Hanzo read her mind.

"Relax Princess of the Five Families. I am here to protect you," he said, and smiled.

Myo was not convinced. Oni Hanzo had a fearsome reputation among ninja. It is why "Devil" Hanzo was the nickname given to him by other ninja. However, she could do little now. Her eyes darted around as if dazzled by the grand sites.

Hanzo smiled again. "The tatami are strapped down in this room. There is no escape below. I suppose you might be able to reach the ceiling if you had claws and could jump like a cat. But I would not try it. There are archers waiting to file in and stop you."

Myo bowed to him acknowledging the trap. "Then I will have to be satisfied with killing you," she said.

Hanzo threw his head back and laughed. The laughter seemed forced and incongruous with his menacing features. The whole room stared at him. He seemed not to care.

"Be at ease, Myo. The highest authority in the land has pardoned you. I really am here to ensure no harm comes to you."

Myo stared into his cold eyes. "He means it," she thought. Then she wondered what could possibly happen here in the castle that could be so dangerous as to warrant his protection.

Hideki looked to his left at Myo and Hanzo with some trepidation. Hanzo bowed to him. Hideki returned the bow. To his right, Jii was complaining. "Look at this nonsense. Have you ever seen anything so lavish?" Hideki thought it was hunger as much as any concrete disagreement with the architecture and furnishings, and he was a little worried that someone might overhear Jii's loud whisperings. "Just look at this waste of money. The main level alone must be fifty tatami long and twice as wide. Then the raised tonokoma under that ridiculously large golden hollyhock must be another twenty-five by twenty-five tatami wide. Who needs that kind of space? Are they going to promote everyone in the government at once in this room? There's no reason for this kind of room."

"I guess that's the point, Jii," Naga said. "The gold and the greatness of the room are to awe us country gentry."

"Well it does not awe me," Jii said. "What if they took half of the money they spent on the shoji screens along that right wall and used it to feed the ronin roving around this city? It would probably keep them in rice for a year."

Hideki thought his grandfather had a good point. The wall was beautiful. It consisted of twenty or so sliding funari partitions with beautiful scenes of cherry trees in full blossom beside a gently flowing stream. Highly polished, dark brown wood and lavish gold angles decorated each section of the screen.

Everywhere Hideki looked, he saw wealth. Even the

tatami they now sat upon was not of the style he knew. Instead of the tightly woven straw Hideki had seen all his life, this straw appeared to be a light green in color and even more tightly woven. The effect was the appearance of a newly harvested field of grass.

On the left of the grand hall was another great painting of a battlefield. He knew it to be Sekigahara because Jii had pointed it out to him during the first visit. The ceiling throughout was divided into little squares recessed below the highly polished, dark brown wood with a gold inlay that permeated everything in the room. Inside each square was an intricate design of interlacing golden hollyhock surrounded by floral patterns of a sort that he did not recognize.

"Well, it awes me," Hideki said.

"That is because you are a country bumpkin and not a sophisticate like your older brother," Naga said with a straight face.

Jii rolled his eyes. Hideki smiled and tried to see into the recesses of the raised portion of the floor beyond him and below the huge golden hollyhock that dominated the far wall. It looked as if the hollyhock consisted of two large sliding panels. To the left there was a step up into sliding plain bamboo shoji screens. "Probably the shogun's entrance," Hideki thought. To the right were large, wooden, gold-framed doors that were reinforced with golden hinges. The outside of the door was coated with the same rice paper used for the thick, lacquered funari walls and continued the cherry trees and stream scene up into the shogun's area. Hideki had to admit, it was impressive. However, he could see how it would clash with Jii's sensibilities. Jii was a proponent of Zen. Zen samurai sought the simple life. This room was the antithesis of perfection to Jii.

Jii turned over his left shoulder. "What do you make of this room, Musashi sensei?"

"Ummm!" Musashi grunted.

Jii nodded his head up and down in agreement. "Yes, exactly," Jii said, as if the two agreed.

From the left, the two Tairo counselors shuffled to the

front of the room in the ice-skating motion required of the nagabahama. They stopped at the raised portion and bowed to the golden hollyhock on the far wall. Then they continued the gliding shuffle over to the right wall, turned completely around, and sat on folded legs facing the room.

Next, the same scene repeated with the four members of the Roju. These took their positions on the left, sitting on their legs and facing the room.

Lastly, Yagyu Muneyori entered, followed by Oeyo, the shogun's wife. They moved to the front, bowed to the golden hollyhock, and turned around to sit on folded legs directly opposite the Yoshinobu across from a large open space.

"I ask your indulgence. We are waiting on one other person," Yagyu said, bowing deeply.

Jii had had enough. "Yagyu-sama, you are the personal counselor to the shogun. We have the Roju and the Tairo here and even the lovely Oeyo," who bowed to Jii at the compliment. "Who else could we be waiting for?" Before Yagyu could answer, a commotion in the rear of the room attracted everyone's attention.

"Take your hands off me. I demand to know on whose authority I am being summoned," a distraught feminine voice demanded. All heads swiveled to the rear of the room to see O'Fuku accompanied by six armed castle guards. The guards stopped at the entrance to the room and bowed. O'Fuku waited at the threshold. She attempted to straighten her garments and hair.

Yagyu Muneyori motioned to a spot to his right. "Please join us O'Fuku."

With her head held high, O'Fuku proceeded to Yagyu and stopped. "Oh, it is you, Yagyu. You have really exceeded your authority this time. I do not answer to you," she snapped.

The Roju and Tairo counselors shifted uncomfortably.

"Sit down my lady. You do answer to my master," Yagyu commanded. Heads visibly drew back at the chief counselor's tone of voice. Obviously, something had changed. Even Oeyo , O'Fuku's archrival, felt a little sorry for the other woman.

Naga leaned to Jii and whispered, "Omoshiroi," letting

his grandfather know he thought this was interesting.

O'Fuku obeyed the stern command and plopped herself down amidst her billowing robes. It was obvious that she was not happy. Nevertheless, it did not last for long. As the proceedings began with the announcement of the purpose of the meeting by the attendants of the Roju, O'Fuku remembered herself and put on a warm smile.

"This body has heard much of the red sticks and wishes to see a demonstration of their use," Yagyu announced. "Yoshinobu-sama, are you prepared to show us how they are used?"

Jii bowed. "Yes, Yagyu-sama. Chief Doshin Nichi and my youngest grandson will demonstrate."

Both Nichi and Hideki stood, bowed and moved to the area of the room between Naga and Yagyu. Nichi took on the role of instructor. "The Jutte is an old weapon. It is also the badge of the police officer. In the city, most of the policeman's confrontations are in close quarters and with commoners."

Nichi drew his red stick from his obi around his waist. "If the policeman is threatened with the club," Nichi started as Hideki stepped toward him with a drawn Jutte as if to club him on the top of the head. "Then the police officer can deflect," Nichi said as he parried the downward attack to his head by striking metal to metal, "and then use the Jutte to subdue." Nichi continued Hideki's motion to the right and hooked his right hand around Hideki's neck, bringing the Jutte alongside Hideki's carotid artery. He then applied pressure. Hideki felt himself blacking out and slapped his left hand on his left thigh signaling submission. Nichi released the pressure and added, "as you can see, it can be an aid in submission techniques."

Hideki and Nichi took their original positions. Hideki was about to attack again when he was interrupted by O'Fuku.

"What happened to your hand, young Yoshinobu?"

Hideki turned and bowed to the questioner. "I got a little too close to the flame and burned it, Lady O'Fuku."

"That is an interesting glove. Does it allow you full use?"

"For most things," Hideki responded.

"Can you still wield a sword … or must you go through life as a cripple?" she persisted.

Hideki was about to respond when an unexpected ally intervened. "Only someone of low birth would ask such a question," the shogun's wife, Oeyo said, looking away from O'Fuku.

Hideki smiled and nodded his head towards Lady Oeyo. Then he addressed O'Fuku. "I have learned to adapt."

"It seems our wild city has been cruel to you, young samurai," O'Fuku observed.

"Not the city, just the cowardly vermin that murder the Tokugawa and call themselves Foxes," Hideki said, a broad smile on his face.

"It seems you harbor some hatred for them."

"It did not start that way," Hideki said. "I have learned to hate cruelty and the greedy plotting of the elite who waste the lives of the people on senseless whims."

"Oh my," O'Fuku said raising a fan to cover her mouth, "you are not speaking revolution, are you?" she asked, pleased that Hideki had risen to the bait.

"I think what my grandson meant was … " Jii began.

"I can finish my own thoughts, Jii-sama," Hideki said. "No, O'Fuku, I am not advocating revolution. I am advocating justice, not only for the bloodthirsty killers that execute Kyodai Goroshi, but for the plotters and crafty men and women who use them."

"I am sure we are not interested in your thoughts," O'Fuku said, using her fan to hide her anger. "I want to see a proper demonstration. I am sure you have staged this little act for us to make yourself look good. But I want reality."

"What do you have in mind?" Yagyu Muneyori asked.

O'Fuku rose and walked toward Naga. She looked over the men sitting on their legs in two neat rows. Then she pointed at the little man with the obviously ill-fitting clothes. He appeared very much out of place among the Yoshinobu samurai.

"I want him to show us how to use the famous red sticks."

Hideki was about to open his mouth when Naga waived

him quiet. "He is the newest to our family. He can't possibly give you the demonstration you are looking for," he said.

O'Fuku smelled victory. "No, I want him. You brag that Edo is safe with your new police force. Let us see how safe our citizens are. Let this little monkey defend himself against a real opponent," she challenged.

"And who do you consider a real opponent?" Yagyu Muneyori asked.

O'Fuku gave out a quick bird whistle. From a panel that made up a portion of the Hollyhock emblem on the far wall a large man clad in Brown ninja clothing appeared and ran to O'Fuku and knelt. There was much in taking of breath and a few gasps by the Roju and Tairo. Not only had they not expected to see a masked ninja in the castle, but this one was armed with a ninja sword strapped to his back.

"Do not be alarmed. He is loyal to me," O'Fuku said.

All eyes went from the large ninja to Yoshi. Naga said, "You can do this or not Yoshi. It is up to you."

Yoshi bowed to Jii. "I am fine with it," he said.

Hittori Hanzo was on his feet in a flash and moved to intercept the ninja. "You will die for having a sword in this place!"

O'Fuku waived Hanzo back. "This is my attendant. I have given him permission to be armed. You do not think I am going to allow myself to rush to a meeting I know nothing about without a bodyguard do you? I take full responsibility."

"My lady, you do not have authority to grant permission to bear arms in the castle," Hanzo firmly stated. Then, he glanced to Yagyu Muneyori.

Yagyu nodded his head slightly, granting permission for this spectacle to proceed. Hanzo bowed his head slightly to Yagyu and retreated to Myo's side. Nevertheless, as he sat down he removed his short sword and placed it between himself and Myo. The motion startled Myo. She looked a question at him. "If this goes awry, save the Yoshinobu," he said.

"That was an unnecessary command," she whispered as she moved the short sword closer.

"Ummm," Hanzo grunted his acknowledgement.

Nichi and Hideki resumed their seats as Yoshi stood and shuffled clumsily into the empty area in front of Naga. O'Fuku turned and moved to her seat beside Yagyu Muneyori. The large ninja drew the sword from his back.

"This is a much better test anyway. Our new police force must be able to disarm the many ronin roaming the city," O'Fuku said, nodding approval of her own statement.

Musashi leaned forward so the first row of Yoshinobu could hear him whisper. "The little monkey is such a good actor, I almost feel sorry for the big ninja." All three of the Yoshinobu smiled at his confidence in Yoshi.

They were the only ones smiling. Everyone else in the room, maybe with the exception of Myo and Hanzo, expected the ninja to kill the little clownish man.

The ninja raised his sword and attacked with a horizontal strike that should have separated Yoshi's head from his shoulders. Although the strike had been incredibly fast, all it cut was air. Yoshi was a blur as he timed the blade and deflected it with his Jutte downward into the tatami mat where it lodged. Yoshi then struck the ninja on his exposed wrist causing him to yelp and release the blade and pulled back clutching his damaged hand. The next strike hit the large ninja between the head and shoulders on the right side of his neck. The large man collapsed and lay still. Yoshi turned and faced O'Fuku and bowed slightly. Then he returned to his seat in the second row behind the Yoshinobu.

Yagyu Muneyori clapped his hands. Then Oeyo joined in. Soon everyone in the great room was applauding Yoshi's effortless demonstration. Yoshi smiled slightly and bowed to all.

O'Fuku was furious. She jumped up and ran to the sword stuck in the mat. She wrenched it free with a mighty pull and took two steps towards Naga. She raised her sword skyward to bring it down on Naga's head.

Myo had been moving when O'Fuku took her first step. However, both she and Hanzo knew they were too late. They would never get there in time.

The blow came down in a mighty arc straight toward

Naga's unprotected head. Naga had time to flinch as he saw his death arriving on the edge of a razor sharp sword. The second before it would cleave hair, skin, and brain matter, there was a loud clang of metal on metal as Hideki fired out of his sitting position and launched himself to a stretched-out kneeling position and caught the blade of the sword on his Jutte. The motion of the downward blade hit the Jutte on the shaft. The momentum forced the blade down the shaft, catching it on the single upturned tine.

Hideki kept his upward trajectory going and was on his feet and rotating the Jutte immediately to the left, twisting the sword out of O'Fuku's hand. Then he grasped her right hand with his left and pulled O'Fuku off balance and into a large circle. Her feet tried to catch up with her extended right hand. At just about the time she thought she would fall, Hideki reversed her hand back toward her and over her right shoulder. Her legs came out from under her, and she slammed hard into the tatami mat with a loud smack.

She laid there trying to get air into her lungs. With his thumb firmly on the back of her right hand, Hideki extended her arm and moved around her head, forcing her to roll over on her stomach. He then extended her right arm out perpendicular from her body and knelt down with his left knee deep into her armpit. He passed control of her right hand to his right hand and moved the Jutte to his left hand.

As soon as O'Fuku had pulled the sword from the mat, four more brown-clad ninja emptied into the great room from the Hollyhock emblem door and raced to her aid. They never made it. Hittori Hanzo and Myo intercepted them while they were still on the raised portion of the floor. The four ninja died in a dazzling ballet of steel and silk. By the time Hideki had passed his Jutte to his left hand, Hanzo and Myo were sheathing their blood-soaked swords, bowing to the astonished Roju and Tairo and returning to their seats.

From the back of the room, castle guards filed in and bowed to Hanzo. Hanzo pointed to the bodies and to the unconscious form of Yoshi's opponent and waved them instructions. All the prostrate forms were gathered and taken out the rear exit. Now Hideki and the wildly panting O'Fuku were the focus of everyone's attention.

O'Fuku finally got her breathing under control. "Let me up, you country jester," she screamed. "You dare to touch me. I will have your life pulled from your body an inch at a time."

Then she started calling Hideki and the Yoshinobu all manner of vile names. Hideki was physically shocked. Even in the gambling dens of the Gumsumgumi, he had never heard cursing like this. He could not believe he was hearing such filth out of the mouth of a samurai woman.

Oeyo clapped her hands together in glee. "Finally we see the low birth," she said happily. "I knew I was right."

O'Fuku lay on her stomach with her head turned toward Yagyu and away from Hideki. He was controlling her body with his gloved right hand and his left knee.

"I have been taught by my grandfather to honor women and to protect them just as I was taught to honor and obey the Tokugawa family. However, you, O'Fuku are beyond regular justice. As the wet nurse to the man being considered for shogun, you will be forgiven your killings and barbarism and be free to do it all again. This jutte cannot abide your not receiving some form of physical punishment for your black heart. Therefore, this is for all those you have killed and ruined in your attempt to get your whelp in the seat of power. I want you to remember me as you try to use this right arm just as I remember you tried to consume me with fire."

"You wouldn't dare," O'Fuku screamed. "I am O'Fuku. I have a title. I am protected."

Hideki brought his jutte up in his left hand and crashed it down with amazing power into the exposed right elbow of O'Fuku. There was a sickening crunch as the bone and cartilage turned to mush. O'Fuku screamed and then passed out.

"Now we are both left-handed," Hideki hissed as he rose from her unconscious body.

Jii was too shocked to speak. He looked at Hideki and realized the charming young grandson had changed. Several months ago, he was a carefree young boy who had to be scolded into doing chores. Now, for better or worse, he was charting the course of the nation. Anyone who could cripple an unarmed woman, even one as evil as O'Fuku, had developed a lot of hostility. Jii guessed it was inevitable. Hideki had been exposed to too much violence since leaving Kii. He had seen the ugly side of samurai rule. Jii wondered if his grandson would be courageous enough to pull himself back from the abyss or be consumed by the hatred he was carrying. He hoped for the former. He missed the old cheerful Hideki.

Yagyu Muneyori stood and started to address the Yoshinobu when he dropped to his knees and bowed low. "Uesama!"

Everyone in the great room bowed low on the mat with foreheads touching the tatami. Hidetada, the second Tokugawa shogun, strode into the room in full armor. His personal guards surrounded him and turned outward and knelt. All had hands on swords.

"Raise your heads," he ordered. "I want to look at your faces."

Everyone straightened up. The newly crippled woman at the shogun's feet moaned.

The shogun looked over to his wife. "You were right, Oeyo."

His wife bowed to her husband, acknowledging his praise.

Then the shogun looked at Hideki. "By the Buddha, Hideki, you are hard on castle staff."

Hideki touched the tatami with his forehead. "I have no excuse Uesama. Please punish me. My family had no part in this."

The shogun looked first at Jii, who bowed under his gaze, then to Naga, who did likewise. Then he glanced at Nichi, Yoshi, and Musashi. Lastly, he lingered on Myo. "I see you brought a sword into the castle," he accused.

Myo bowed, holding her breath. She was frightened. None of her training prepared her for being in the presence of the shogun.

"Well, are you going to answer? I would have thought the heir to the Five Families would have more courage. I know you do. I just watched you charge into four armed men. You had plenty of courage then."

Myo stammered. She was not sure what to say.

Hanzo started chuckling, enjoying Myo's discomfort. She looked into his face. If it were not for the sound, you would not know he was laughing. He did not smile. Then she found her courage, raised her head, and looked into the face of the shogun.

"A clumsy man dropped it; I just picked it up."

O'Fuku moaned again. The shogun waved Yagyu forward with the downward motion of his extended hand. The high counselor jumped up, bowed, and signaled attendants to come forward.

"Take her to her quarters and have her physician attend to her," Yagyu instructed.

As they were moving her out of the room, the shogun interjected something. "And tell her when she's conscious again that she is confined to a nunnery." The shogun then looked to his counselor. "We do have a nunnery picked out, do we not?"

"Yes Uesama. We have one picked out and the arrangements have been made."

"Good," the shogun said. Then he turned his attention back to the prostrate Hideki. "Rise, Hideki. You are not in trouble." The shogun then placed his hands on his hips looking at his counselor. "What is next, Yagyu?"

"I believe you wanted to make a clean sweep of things, Uesama," Yagyu said, motioning with his fan toward the Roju on the left side of the great room.

"Ah, yes," he said. "Naomasu Nagai," he called solemnly.

Naomasu froze at the sound of his name. Then he remembered himself and dropped his forehead to the mat in a deep bow. "Yosh," he uttered in as much bass as his tightening throat would allow.

"Your services are no longer required in the Roju. In fact, your services are not needed in Edo. You are banished to your home province of Akita."

Naomasu's forehead touched the tatami floor again. "Hai," was all he could muster.

The shogun turned to his counselor again. "I guess I cannot confine him to the same nunnery with O'Fuku, can I?"

"No Uesama. That would not be prudent. Your original banishment will suffice," Yagyu said.

"Very well," the shogun sighed. Then, sighting Naomasu still in his original position, added, "Well go on. Get out of my sight."

Naomasu stood, bowed, and walked backward out of the shogun's presence and into obscurity.

Laughter shattered the silence in the great hall. All heads spun toward Jii.

Both Yagyu and Hanzo stood and rebuked the elder Yoshinobu, but he kept laughing.

"What is so funny, Yoshinobu?" the shogun asked.

"You are truly the son of that old Fox," Jii said and slapped his thigh.

"Yoshinobu-sama," Yagyu warned. "You go too far."

The shogun waved him silent. "What do you mean, Yoshinobu?"

"You and your chief strategist there," the old man said, pointing to Yagyu, "did not send for us to participate in your succession," he said.

"I didn't?" the shogun asked.

"No, Uesama! You have no intention of stepping down," he accused.

The room went silent at the accusation. The shogun turned to Yagyu with a smile on his face. "You said he was smart."

"I think I understated it," Yagyu said.

The shogun turned back to Jii.

"What were my intentions then?" the shogun asked.

Jii pointed his finger to encompass the Roju and Tairo. "You needed help in cleaning out this nest of vipers," he said.

There was an instant clamor from the maligned counselors but the shogun waved them silent. "Go on," he encouraged.

"You concocted this succession to smoke out O'Fuku and other hostile elements. But you needed a force to assist you that was not tainted by Edo politics or self-interest. That is where we came in. Nine years of samurai rule and your capital city is as corrupt as a gambling house. From the police right up to these men here," he said, pointing to the Roju. "You have men who have allowed themselves to place self-interest above all else and to be blackmailed into truly bad decisions. It was so bad that you had to have a total housecleaning. We Yoshinobu were the broom," Jii said.

Naga saw the logic immediately. He wondered how much of last month was real and how much contrived. His mind went to Yuki.

"Even if your theory were true, do you object?" the shogun asked.

Jii shook his head in the negative. "No Uesama. We serve the Tokugawa."

The shogun nodded in the affirmative. "Good answer." Then the shogun turned back to Hideki. "Hideki, my eldest son Iemitsu may be shogun someday. My father decreed his name would remain in consideration. O'Fuku got him to put it in writing. Iemitsu is very fond of his wet nurse. If that day ever comes, it could go hard on the Yoshinobu."

"I guess it is a good thing that you are not retiring anytime soon then," Jii ventured.

"You are correct, Yoshinobu. It is a good thing," he said.

The shogun turned to his chief counselor. "Yagyu, no more women on the council. Not even as visitors." He then looked at his wife and she nodded her consent. "We have just a few more items of business," the shogun said and signaled to the entrance. Yuki walked into their midst and bowed to the shogun. Naga wanted to call out but he dared not. His worst fears were about to be realized. "Yuki my dear, are you ready to come back to your old master and resume your duties?"

"I believe I am ready for a new master, Uesama."

"I was afraid of that. There is no reasoning with a woman in love." He glanced at Naga. "Very well, go take your place with your new master."

Yuki bowed low, rose, and moved backwards from the shogun. She then turned and moved behind Musashi.

Hideki glanced to the right and thought he saw a tear in his brother's eye. "How strange," he thought.

The shogun turned to his chief counselor again. "Yagyu, it seems we have a vacancy on the Roju. Do you have any suggestions?"

"Nagamasa," Yagyu replied.

"Yes, he would be good, but I was thinking of letting him ripen a little until Edo is made over. He has proven indispensable as a magistrate. I just could not get enough of those stories about the open trial. What a novel idea. No, I was thinking of someone more seasoned with a penchant for speaking his mind. I was thinking of someone whose life is guided by a higher calling, specifically guided by Bushido. I was thinking of the old war horse these people call Jii."

"Wise choice, Uesama," Yagyu said.

"Yes, now that I've found honest men to remake Edo, I am going to look for more to run the country. We must get better at administration or the Tokugawa shogunate will be short-lived," the shogun mused. "So Naga, what do you say to remaining the south magistrate a while longer?"

Naga bowed deeply. "I serve at your pleasure, Uesama."

"Another good answer," the shogun said. Then standing before Jii, the shogun asked, "Well Jii, what about serving in this nest of vipers?"

"I serve at your pleasure, Uesama," Jii said, bowing low.

The shogun looked at his chief counselor. "I like how this family answers questions. Do I have anything else to settle?"

"No Uesama," came the reply. "That settles everything."

"Very well then," the shogun said, placing his hands on his hips and announcing skyward, "Iken Raku Chaku," a phrase meaning "one finished." Then the shogun laughed as he exited toward the hollyhock emblem and his entrance on the side. An attendant was already there kneeling and sliding the door back.

Hideki could hear the shogun talking to himself as he went through the exit. "Yes, I sure get a laugh out of those stories about the trial." No one could see him exit, as all eyes were on the mat as he departed.

Once the shogun left, the room relaxed. Everyone was

abuzz in conversation. Jii and Yagyu put their heads together and then moved to the five Roju counselors.

Naga and Yuki were talking as if no one else were in the room. Musashi approached Hideki.

"I would hate to think that all my training went into a cruel man," he said.

"I do not know what kind of a man I am, Sensei. I hope a kind one. Yet I kept thinking of kyodai goroshi and the deaths of my cousin and his family. Then the site of Aoki's head rolling in the dirt at Nihonbashi Bridge kept stabbing my conscience. And yes, I wanted to hurt her for the way she took my dreams away with fire," he said, holding up his right gloved hand. "But mostly I wanted her to remember that actions have consequences. I wanted her to feel the pain of retribution."

"So was it revenge or justice?" Musashi asked.

"I would like to think justice," Hideki replied.

"Then my teachings were not wasted. Sayonara," Musashi said, as he bowed quickly, spun, and departed.

"How about that," Yoshi said. "He didn't say goodbye to me."

"Musashi's mind is already engaged in his journey. I'm surprised he said goodbye to me," Hideki mused.

Myo moved to Hideki's side. "So what now, Prince of the Yoshinobu?"

Hideki exhaled slowly. "I think everyone's course has been set but mine."

"You will not stay to help Naga?" Yoshi asked.

"I will help him, but not by staying. I think I shall embark on a Musha Shugyo. I need a swordsman's pilgrimage to expand my skills."

"You are going to turn into another Musashi?"

"I could do much worse with my life. I heard what the shogun said today. We have to get good men to run the country. I can help by keeping Jii and Naga informed of what I see across the land."

"Do you want company?" Yoshi asked.

"Not from you, Yoshi. Although I can think of no better companion, both my brother and grandfather will have great need of your skills and advice. But thank you for the offer," Hideki said.

"How are you going to send your information back to your brother and grandfather?" Yoshi asked.

"I have some ideas on that subject," Myo said.

"Oh," Yoshi said. "The Five Families has the infrastructure. Good plan; however, traveling alone can be dangerous. Will your grandfather allow it?"

"He will not be alone," Myo said boldly.

Hideki laughed. "Besides my personal spymaster here, Yagyu Jubei has agreed to accompany me. I want to train and get my right hand back to normal. I think I will be safe enough with Jubei and Myo as companions."

"Probably, but it is a big country and you will not have the police force of Edo to protect you," Yoshi said.

Hideki smiled. "From the time I was a little boy on Jii's knee, my goal was to be the best swordsman in Japan and to help Naga," he said, looking down at his glove-wrapped hand. "Now, my goal is to be the most dangerous swordsman in Japan, help Naga, and make Musashi proud."

About the Author

William Marcus Charles II (Marc) is the author of Simplified Self-defense for Women, published by the Marine Corps Association. He has been published in the Marine Corps Gazette and in Ensign, a global monthly of the LDS Church.

Born in Murfreesboro, Tennessee, Marc spent his formative years in Warren, Michigan. He graduated from boot camp in San Diego at nineteen and for the next twenty-four years wore the Eagle, Globe, and Anchor proudly until retirement as a Lieutenant Colonel of Marines.

He spent much of his military career in Asia where he studied martial arts. He is a Roku-dan (sixth degree black belt) in Okinawan Kenpo Karate and a Roku-dan in Kobudo (the weapons of Okinawa). He has trained in Aikido, Jujitsu, American Kenpo, Shorinryu, Judo and other lesser known styles. He has founded three martial arts schools in the United States.

Marc graduated with honors from Park College with a BS in Management and Finance and has an MBA from National University.

He and his wife Sako currently reside in Encinitas, California.

9780997169560